Jill Mansell lives with her family in Bristol. She used to work in the field of Clinical Neurophysiology but now writes full time. She watches far too much TV and would love to be one of those super-sporty types but basically can't be bothered. Nor can she cook – having once attempted to bake a cake for the hospital's Christmas Fair, she was forced to watch while her co-workers played frisbee with it.

But she's good at Twitter!

By Jill Mansell

Jill Mansell

MIRANDA'S BIG MISTAKE

headline
review

First published in 1999
by HEADLINE PUBLISHING GROUP

First published in paperback in 2000
by HEADLINE PUBLISHING GROUP

This edition published in paperback in 2014
by HEADLINE REVIEW
An imprint of HEADLINE PUBLISHING GROUP

16

Cataloguing in Publication Data is available from the British Library

ISBN 978 0 7553 3257 1

Printed and bound by CPI Group (UK) Ltd, Croydon CR0 4YY

Headline's policy is to use papers that are natural, renewable and
recyclable products and made from wood grown in sustainable forests.
The logging and manufacturing processes are expected to conform
to the environmental regulations of the country of origin.

HEADLINE PUBLISHING GROUP
An Hachette UK Company
338 Euston Road
London NW1 3BH

www.headline.co.uk
www.hachette.co.uk

For Lydia and Cory, with all my love.

For Lydia and Cerys with all my love

Chapter 1

It was the first day of April. Seeing the reception desk temporarily unmanned, Miranda snatched up the ringing phone.

'Fenn Lomax salon, how can I help you?'

'Hello.' It was a male voice. 'I need a complete restyle.'

'We do have a long waiting list,' Miranda warned, uncapping a biro with her teeth. 'Could I have your name, please?'

'Duncan Goodhew.'

Over the phone, she heard gales of background laughter.

'Oh ha ha, well done, very good,' Miranda recited dutifully. 'If only Eddie Izzard was as witty as you.' She rolled her eyes at Bev, the salon's glamorous receptionist, now racing back from the loo.

'Who was that?' said Bev as Miranda hung up.

'A big wally. April Fools' Day, don't you just love it?'

Grabbing her coat and rummaging in the pockets, Miranda dragged out one green woollen glove and one pink leather one. Well, imitation leather.

Bev's manicured blonde eyebrows went up.

'Lunch break already? It's only half past eleven.'

'Dogsbody duty.' Making sure she wasn't being watched,

1

Miranda pulled a face. 'Cigarettes for Alice Tavistock. And a box of herbal tea bags. *And* half a dozen first-class stamps. That woman, honestly, I don't know why she doesn't write out her whole week's shopping list, pack me off to Sainsbury's and be done with it.'

'And when you've finished that,' Bev suggested helpfully, 'you could valet her car.'

'Pop her washing round to the launderette.'

'Mow her lawn.'

'Fill out her tax return.'

'Clean her loos,' Bev blinked innocently, 'with her own toothbrush.'

'Miranda, are you still here?' Fenn Lomax, emerging from the VIP room, shot her a look of disbelief.

'Sorry, Fenn, no, Fenn, I'm gone.' Miranda jammed her gloves on, getting three fingers stuck in one thumb-hole. She grinned at Bev and made a dash for the door. 'Back in ten minutes, okay?'

Fenn called after her, 'Make that five.'

Since Fenn Lomax had landed himself a regular slot on the hugely popular TV show *It's Morning!* his client list had blossomed beyond recognition.

As the show's producer had pointed out, he was a seriously attractive heterosexual hairdresser. How could he fail?

The female producer had been right.

With his streaky-blond shoulder-length hair, thickly fringed hazel eyes and come-to-bed smile, Fenn had a way with women and scissors that had done his business no harm at all. No longer buried in the back streets of Bermondsey (special rates for pensioners on Mondays and Wednesdays), he had been catapulted upmarket to the altogether glossier pavements of Knightsbridge's Brompton Road (special rates, *never*). Celebrities queued up, for months sometimes, for the privilege of shelling out two hundred and fifty pounds and being able to boast to friends, journalists . . . well, anyone who'd listen, basically, that theirs was a Fenn Lomax cut.

Nowadays you could spot his clients a mile off, thought Miranda, teetering on the edge of the kerb as a chauffeur-driven limo pulled up inches from her toes. The snow had all but melted now, leaving only squelchy dregs, but the woman emerging from the back of the limousine was kitted out in enough fur to see her through a hike across the Antarctic. Gingerly, in her fur-lined boots, she picked her way through the slush.

Well, it was an awfully *wide* pavement. All of six feet from the car to the apricot-tinted-glass and brass doors of the salon.

And if you were going to pay a chauffeur to run you around town, it made sense to economise in other areas, Miranda acknowledged, recognising the famous romantic novelist as she removed her dark glasses. That must be why the stingy, face-lifted old hag had only tipped her thirty pence last week.

The stamps and cigarettes weren't a problem, but the Grapefruit Zing herbal tea bags with extra ginseng took longer to track down. By the time she'd bought everything, Miranda was already fifteen minutes late.

He was there, sitting in his usual spot outside the shoe shop. Experiencing a horrid qualm of guilt, Miranda wondered if she could cross the road so he wouldn't catch sight of her, or simply rush past pretending she hadn't seen him.

Then again, perhaps she should just explain that she was in a tearing hurry and didn't have her purse on her right now, but if he hung around for another hour or so, she'd see him later.

Hung around for another hour or so, Miranda thought with a shudder. Crikey, patronising or what?

Poor chap, as if he had anywhere else to go.

Oh, but he looked so cold, so utterly miserable and chilled to the bone.

Too late to try and avoid him now anyway, she realised. He'd spotted her.

'Hi,' said Miranda, feeling rotten already. His blanket was damp, soaked through with slush. 'Look, this isn't my lunch break, I'm just picking up a few things for a client, but I'll definitely be back before two.' Inwardly, she cringed. Oh, help, why did a perfectly good reason have to come out sounding like a feeble excuse? He didn't want one of her sandwiches in two hours' time, he needed something to warm him up *now*.

'Okay.' The man, who was probably in his early thirties, nodded and managed a faint smile. 'Thanks.'

He never begged, never asked for anything. Just sat there, with his greasy black hair falling over his face and his dark eyelashes half shielding his eyes, as he watched the rest of the world march on by.

Miranda had never given him money in case he was a drug addict. The thought of her spare cash being injected into the nearest collapsed vein made her shudder. At least he couldn't fit a prawn sandwich into a syringe.

But today the circumstances were different. And there was a Burger King just across the road, selling hot drinks. What's more, Miranda remembered, Alice Tavistock had given her a ten-pound note to go shopping with . . .

'Here.' Hurriedly she fumbled in her coat pocket for change and thrust seventy pence into his hand. 'Buy yourself a cup of tea. Thaw out a bit.'

'That's very kind.'

Heroin cost more than seventy pence, didn't it?

Worried, needing to check, Miranda said, 'You don't do drugs?'

Another fleeting smile, accompanied this time by a shake of the head.

'No, I don't do drugs.'

Except . . . well, he would say that, wouldn't he?

Miranda gave up; she had to get back. Ugh, this weather, her feet were going numb.

'Okay, see you later.' She flexed her icy toes. 'Ham and tomato or prawn with mayonnaise?'

The man on the pavement shrugged.

'I don't mind. You choose.'

'Sorry I'm late.' Panting, Miranda burst into the VIP room. 'Harrods was packed and the woman in front of me at the counter had a funny turn. Never mind, back now. Here we are, Mrs Tavistock.'

Fenn was putting the finishing touches to Alice Tavistock's French pleat. Not believing the funny turn story for a minute, he watched Miranda empty her pockets of stamps, cigarettes and change.

'Take the towels out of the tumble dryer,' he said, 'and give Corinne a hand with Lady Trent's highlights.'

Miranda wondered if Alice Tavistock might say thank

you, but getting a cigarette out of its packet and into her heavily lipsticked mouth was evidently more important. She watched the expensive silver lighter go click and the tendons of Alice Tavistock's skinny neck stick out like trapeze wires as she sucked in the first lungful of—

'Miranda. Towels.'

Five minutes later, Miranda was dutifully passing rectangles of silver foil to Corinne when Fenn and Alice Tavistock emerged from the VIP room into the main area of the salon.

As Fenn beckoned her over, Miranda clearly saw coins glinting in Alice Tavistock's hand.

Hooray, tip time!

Then again, maybe not. The expression on her freshly powdered face wasn't exactly brimming over with gratitude.

'I gave you a ten-pound note,' Alice Tavistock announced without preamble, thrusting her outstretched palm under Miranda's nose. 'And this is how much you handed back. Do you think I'm incapable of adding up?' she demanded stroppily. 'You've short-changed me.'

'God, sorry, I forgot!' Miranda clapped her hand to her forehead. 'I meant to give it back, make up the difference, then Fenn told me to sort out the towels and I—'

'And you thought you could get away with it.' Alice Tavistock always spoke with a plum in her mouth. Now she sounded as if she were spitting out the stones. 'Swindler. Thief.'

'I am not a thief!'

Fenn closed his eyes.

'Miranda, what did you do with Mrs Tavistock's money?'

'Gave it to someone.'

Frowning, Fenn said, 'What? Stop mumbling, talk properly.'

Miranda lifted her head. Oh Lord, he wasn't looking happy.

'I gave it to a homeless person so he could buy himself a cup of tea.'

'My money!' squawked Alice Tavistock. 'You're telling me you gave my sixty pence to a filthy scrounging beggar? For crying out loud, girl, are you mad?'

So much for boasting about her ability to add up, Miranda thought mutinously.

'He isn't a beggar.' She couldn't let it pass, somebody had to defend him. 'He never begs! And it wasn't sixty pence either,' she concluded, 'it was seventy.'

Miranda loved hairdressing, despite the abysmal rates of pay for trainees. She was happy working in Fenn's salon, she adored cutting hair – on the rare occasions when she got the chance – and she really enjoyed the contact with clients.

Well, most clients.

The big drawback was having to carry on being nice to them when they were being horrible to you.

'I'm not a thief,' she told Fenn when he had reimbursed his outraged client from the till, apologised profusely and shown her out of the salon.

'I know that. But you aren't exactly Mensa material either,' Fenn pointed out, 'are you?'

'She's a hag! That woman spends her life boasting

7

about all the charity committees she's on. How can she be so *mean*?'

'Hardly the point. Alice Tavistock is our client.'

'She's a stingy old battleaxe,' Miranda muttered.

'Stop it. Now listen to me.' Fenn consulted his watch. 'Bev has to see her dentist at one o'clock. I'll need you to take over at the desk for a couple of hours.'

'You mean . . . work through my lunch break?'

Horrors! Miranda's dark eyes widened in dismay. She was already ravenous.

What's more, she remembered guiltily, I'm not the only one.

But it was no good. Fenn was giving her one of his serious, I'm-the-boss looks.

'I think that's fair, under the circumstances. Don't you?'

Chloe watched the checkout girl pick up each item in turn, pass it over the scanner and send it on its way along the conveyor belt. Like the prizes on *The Generation Game*, minus the cuddly toy.

Packet of chicken breasts.

One lemon.

Pint of milk, semi-skimmed.

Shrink-wrapped bouquet of broccoli.

Small carton of hugely expensive new potatoes.

Pregnancy testing kit.

The Generation Game. Very apt.

Chloe held her breath, wondering if the girl would glance at her in a secret, knowing way, but when she looked up all she said in a bored voice was, 'That'll be fifteen pounds seventy. Got your Clubcard?'

It clearly took more, these days, than a few chicken breasts and a pregnancy testing kit to arouse a checkout operator's interest.

Back at Special Occasions – perfect gifts for *every* occasion – Chloe hung the Tesco carrier on her coat hook and locked herself in the tiny downstairs loo.

Her fingers shook as she tore the cellophane wrapping off the testing kit. The words on the accompanying leaflet danced in front of her eyes.

Oh, help, this is it, this is serious.

Right, can't afford any mistakes, thought Chloe, feeling sick already. Treat it like an exam, read the instructions slowly and carefully. Concentrate, concentrate, and for goodness' sake stop this stupid *shaking*.

The sudden hammering on the door almost catapulted her off the loo seat.

'Chloe? That you in there?'

Well, who else was it likely to be? thought Chloe resignedly.

'Um . . . yes.'

At least she hadn't been in the middle of some tricky form of gymnastics involving pipettes and mid-stream flow.

'Okay.' Bruce, her boss, sounded impatient. He had never understood why any woman needed to spend longer than thirty seconds in the loo. 'Keep an eye on the shop, would you? I need to make a phone call.'

'Two minutes,' Chloe called out in desperation.

'What?'

She couldn't not find out now, the suspense was killing her almost as much as the need to pee.

'Just give me two minutes, okay?'

Outside the door, Bruce shook his head in bewilderment. Women and their inner workings, it was all a mystery to him.

'Okay.'

Out in the shop, the bell above the door went ding, heralding the arrival of a customer. Relieved, Chloe heard the sound of her boss's retreating footsteps. She couldn't possibly pee on to a stick with Bruce lurking just inches away on the other side of the toilet door.

The crucial stream of urine was duly passed. Chloe closed her eyes and began to count.

When she opened her eyes again, the end of the stick was blue.

'Oh, good grief,' Chloe whispered, the words almost drowned out by the thundering of her heart. Pulling open the neck of her angora sweater and peering down at her stomach, she said in an unsteady voice, 'Hello.'

Out in the shop, Bruce was wrapping up his customer's purchase, a wildly expensive yellow and white Italian vase. When Chloe eventually reappeared, looking pale, he said, 'Chloe, before I forget. Bit of a do on at the golf club this evening. Verity and I were hoping to get along for an hour or two, but the blasted babysitter's let us down. Any chance of you riding to the rescue?'

Having ridden to the rescue before, Chloe wasn't fooled for an instant by his jovial tone. Like cat years, Bruce's idea of an hour or two generally meant seven or eight.

'Bruce, I'm sorry. I can't.'

Taken aback wasn't the word for it.

'But you said you didn't have anything on tonight.' His tone was accusing.

Be brave, stand your ground, don't let him bully you into it.

'That was this morning.' Chloe spoke as firmly as she dared. 'I do now.'

Chapter 2

Florence Curtis had led an action-packed life; she had always lived for the day and crammed as much as was humanly possible into each and every one of them. Married at twenty, a mother at twenty-five, divorced by twenty-seven, married again, widowed, married for the third time at thirty-three . . . good Lord, it made her dizzy nowadays just to remember those hectic years when, juggling homes, staff and the needs of her much-loved but incredibly demanding son, she had followed her various husbands all over the world.

Then her beloved Ray, number three, had died of a heart attack on the steps of the casino at Monte Carlo and Florence had decided to call it a day on the husband front. Twice widowed was enough; the pain was almost too much to bear. From now on she would stick to lovers. Apart from anything else, she glibly informed her friends – because sympathy was anathema to Florence – she was tired of endlessly changing her surname on chequebooks.

The next twenty years had been spent in the relentless pursuit of fun, with Florence adoring every last minute. Her motto had always been 'You're a long time dead', and until the first signs of stiffness had begun to seep into her joints, it had never occurred to her that perhaps it should have been 'You're a long time crippled with arthritis'.

It was hard, adapting to life in a wheelchair when your brain sometimes fooled you into thinking you were still as active as you'd always been. Every now and again Florence dreamt that she had been dancing all night at the Café Royal. When she woke up, exhilarated and in the mood to carry on, she would think, That's what I'll do today, go somewhere a bit swish and *dance* . . .

Until she tried to turn over in bed, only to groan aloud with the pain. These days she was lucky if she could make it as far as the kitchen before collapsing in a heap.

Last year Florence's well-meaning GP had suggested wheelchair ballroom dancing. Every Thursday night, apparently, busloads of disabled pensioners descended on nearby St Augustine's church hall and had a high old time of it, spinning and twirling their partners around the floor.

'What, in their wheelchairs?' Florence had roared with laughter. 'Sorry, darling, not my scene. Sounds like two teenagers with clonking great braces on their teeth trying to have a snog.'

If she sometimes felt a bit down in the dumps, Florence made sure she kept it to herself. What good would it do, after all, to drone on about how depressed you were and how narrow your life had become? That was a surefire way to end up a Nellie No-friends.

Instead, she concentrated on presenting her cheerful, fun-loving face to the world. She also made sure she counted her blessings regularly. She had her home, and no money worries. She had Miranda. And her legs might be useless, but at least she still had the use of her hands, which meant she could hold a champagne glass, play a mean game of poker and put on her own make-up. Not always brilliantly, as Florence was the first to admit. But hell, there were worse things in life than a bit of wonkily applied eyeliner.

As the clock on the mantelpiece chimed six thirty, Florence wheeled herself over to the sitting-room window. She liked to watch out for her lodger. As soon as she saw Miranda coming up the street – usually searching in her pockets for her front door key – she would fetch a bottle of lager from the fridge and pour herself a decent measure of dry sherry.

That was another great thing about wheelchairs. If the first drink of the day went straight to your knees – well, so what?

Florence was still tussling with the ice cube tray when the front door slammed shut and Miranda yelled, 'I'm home.'

'You're frozen. Go and sit by the fire,' Florence protested when she came through to the kitchen to help. 'I can manage.'

Miranda bashed the tray against the top of the fridge, scattering ice cubes in all directions.

'My hands are numb already.' She clattered ice cubes into Florence's sherry glass. 'There, done. Now we can both sit by the fire.' She pulled a face. 'And I can tell you about my wonderful day.'

Sleety rain dripped down Miranda's neck as she tipped her head back to drink the lager straight from the bottle. Her short black hair, urchin-cut and currently streaked with dark blue and green low-lights, gleamed like a magpie's wing.

'. . . so I missed my lunch break and by the time I left the salon he'd gone,' she concluded, unaware of the rim of froth on her upper lip. 'Poor chap, I feel terrible letting him down like that.'

'You know your trouble,' Florence said comfortably, 'you're a soft touch.'

'I just worry about him. What kind of life does he have? I mean, imagine not having anywhere to *live*.'

Florence snorted into her sherry. 'Ha, feeling sorry for him's one thing. Just so long as you don't bring him back here and expect me to feel sorry for him too.'

She wouldn't put it past Miranda to give it a go, to try and persuade her to allow some smelly old tramp to move in with them.

'You're heartless,' said Miranda.

'I'm not a pushover, that's all. Anyway,' Florence grew serious, 'there's something I have to tell you. Not good news, I'm afraid.'

'What?' Miranda's dark eyes widened in alarm. 'Are you ill?'

'I'm not, but my bank account's feeling pretty sick. You heard about that stock market crash last week?'

Miranda hadn't, but she nodded anyway. Matters of high finance tended to pass her by.

'Well, my accountant phoned me this afternoon. My shares have gone down the toilet. Basically I'm skint.' Florence paused and looked embarrassed. 'The thing is, I'm afraid I'm going to have to put your rent up.'

Miranda swallowed. She began to feel queasy.

'Oh. Okay. Um . . . by how much?'

'Well, double it?'

Good grief.

The look on Miranda's face was a picture. Florence roared with laughter and clapped her hands.

'Ha, April Fool!'

Miranda's mouth dropped open.

'You mean . . . my rent's not going up?'

'Of course it isn't!'

'You aren't broke?'

'There hasn't been a stock market crash. You should try reading the paper occasionally,' Florence cackled, 'then you'd know.'

Miranda breathed again.

'It's after midday,' she protested. 'April Fools don't count after midday.'

'I didn't get a chance earlier. Anyway,' Florence's grin was unrepentant, 'still worked, didn't it?'

'That's cheating,' grumbled Miranda.

With an air of complacency, Florence said, 'Ah well, I'm allowed to cheat, I'm a batty old woman in a wheelchair. That means I can do what I want.'

Greg wasn't due home from work until eight. Feeling that an extra-special dinner was called for, Chloe marinaded the chicken breasts and mushrooms in garlic and olive oil, tossed the tiny new potatoes in butter and made sure there was enough blackcurrant sorbet in the freezer before running her bath.

She fastened her hair up with the diamanté clips Greg had bought her last Christmas and took out the red satin dress he had given her for her birthday. Since his favourite scent was Obsession – though she wasn't wild about it herself –

she squished it on with abandon. She even dug out her old suspender belt and the sheer black stockings Greg was so keen on, determinedly ignoring the scratchiness of the lace around her waist.

Every little helped.

She hoped.

And let's face it, thought Chloe as she began – albeit shakily – on her make-up, tonight I'm going to need all the help I can get.

Twenty-five past eight.

Still no sign of Greg.

God, the one time I desperately need a drink, and I can't have one.

By eight thirty Chloe's nerves were in bits. When she heard the click of Greg's key in the front door, she catapulated out of her chair as if she'd been zapped with a cattle prod.

Appearing in the living room, loosening his tie, Greg let out a low whistle.

'I say, what's all this in aid of? Not our anniversary, is it?'

Chloe began to tremble. She'd overdone it. Now he was going to want to know right away why she'd made such an effort.

'I just felt like dressing up.'

She managed a bright smile. Telling Greg was going to be so much easier once he had a good meal and the best part of a bottle of wine inside him.

'Suspenders too.' He tilted his head, observing the telltale bumps beneath the tight red satin. 'This is the kind of dressing up I like.'

Hmm, maybe dinner followed by sex, *then* tell him. That might be better.

That is, if Greg didn't fall asleep and start snoring like a rhino within six seconds of rolling off her.

It had been known to happen in the past.

'Is that garlic?' Greg sniffed the cooking smells wafting through from the kitchen. 'I'd better give that a miss. Big meeting first thing tomorrow – don't want to knock the clients senseless.'

'Oh.' Chloe's face fell. She'd put garlic in everything. That meant dinner now consisted of blackcurrant sorbet.

'Is everything okay?' Sensing her anxiety, he moved towards her. 'Sweetheart, you're shaking. Is something up?'

'I'd better turn the oven off.' Chloe heard her own voice echoing in her ears. It was like listening to someone else talking. She hadn't wanted to launch right in and say it, she needed time to gear herself up, run a few more practice lines through her head.

Then again, was that really going to make it any easier?

'Chloe?' Greg's hands were on her bare shoulders, gently massaging them. 'What is it?'

'Oh Greg, we're going to have a baby.'

There, she'd done it.

Blurted it out.

Like Bambi's legs collapsing on the ice – whoomph – Greg's hands slid off her shoulders.

'What?'

Another deep breath.

'A baby. We – we're going to have one.'

He took a step backwards.

'You mean you're pregnant?'

With an effort, Chloe stopped her smile from wobbling, though her knees carried on regardless.

'Well, we didn't win one in a competition.'

'Is this a joke?'

'No! I wouldn't joke about something like this!'

Greg gave her an odd look. A not very encouraging one.

'How long have you known?'

Her heart was flapping around in her chest. It felt as if it was trying to get out.

'Seven hours.'

'Chloe. This can't happen. You know it can't.'

'But it *has* happened,' Chloe protested, dry-mouthed.

'We agreed. No babies. We don't need them. I don't want them. I don't even like them.'

'I know, I know,' she pleaded, 'but it's happened. It was an accident but now it's happened—'

'Sure about that?' said Greg coldly. 'Are you sure it was an accident?'

'I swear to you!' Oh God, this was awful. 'I'd never do anything like that. It was just as much of a shock to me—'

'Good. So all we have to do is sort it out.'

Chloe stared at him, unable to speak.

'Don't look at me like that.' Steadily, Greg held her gaze. 'What did you seriously expect me to say? Chloe, you are *not* going to have a baby. We'll get this taken care of. It's no big deal, sweetheart, it won't even hurt.'

Fear was replaced by fury. Chloe felt her fingernails digging into her palms.

'We aren't talking about a . . . a *wisdom* tooth . . .'

19

'It's smaller than a wisdom tooth.'

'It's a human being!' Why couldn't he understand how she felt? She fought back the urge to scream at the top of her voice. If he truly loved her, why couldn't he understand how she felt? How could he just reject the idea out of hand?

'I'm not being brutal,' said Greg, 'just realistic.'

'But it doesn't have to be the end of the world!'

'No, just the end of our marriage.'

Chloe reeled back as if he'd hit her. She felt physically winded.

'So that's why you made all this effort,' Greg drawled, gesturing at her dress. 'Oh, I get it now. Slap on a bit of make-up, dig a suspender belt out of the back of your knicker drawer and that'll do the trick. One flash of stocking-top and you'll have me at your mercy, gibbering, "Darling, how wonderful, you've made me the happiest man in the world, of *course* I want a baby."'

Chloe looked away.

Well, yes.

Basically it was what she had hoped would happen.

'Sorry, Chloe. I can't do it. I told you before we got married how I felt about children, and I'm not about to start changing my mind now. See?' Greg waved an arm in the direction of the window. 'No flying pigs.'

No, thought Chloe, just one two-legged one right here in the living room.

'I can't get rid of it,' she whispered, 'I just couldn't.' Hating herself for being so feeble, knowing it was a waste of time even saying the words, she begged.

'You might change your mind.'

'No.' Greg picked up his car keys, his grey eyes cold. 'No, no, no. By the way,' he added dismissively as he made for the front door, 'don't worry about saving my dinner for me. I'll eat out.'

Chapter 3

'Look, I'm really sorry about yesterday,' said Miranda. 'I got into all kinds of bother with a customer and ended up having to work through my lunch break, otherwise I'd have—'

'It's okay, doesn't matter. You don't need to apologise.'

Miranda blinked icy rain out of her eyes and rummaged through her bag. If her fingers were frozen she couldn't imagine how his must feel.

'Ham and tomato today, is that all right? And I thought these might come in handy.' Digging deeper, she unearthed a pair of tan leather gloves and a black knitted scarf.

'They're great. Thanks very much.' He smiled up at her. 'Did you knit this?'

She rolled her eyes.

'God, no, picked it up in Oxfam. I couldn't knit to save my life.'

'Well, thanks anyway. Very warm.'

He had a nice voice. Miranda watched him wrap the scarf around his neck and slide his fingers into the gloves. She ruffled her own hair, unexpectedly embarrassed. All of a sudden she felt like a bossy maiden aunt forcing her nephew to try on his least favourite Christmas present.

And be suitably grateful.

Damn, she wished she hadn't given him the stupid things now.

'Better get back.' Hurriedly, she consulted her watch. 'Don't want to get into any more trouble.'

'These are expensive gloves.' He was peeling one back at the wrist, reading the label. 'Harvey Nichols, it says here.'

'I didn't buy them,' said Miranda, anxious to get away. When his dark eyebrows went up, she added, 'Don't worry, I didn't steal them either.'

The phone rang in the salon an hour later. Miranda, busy sweeping up hair, dimly heard Bev, at the desk, exclaim happily, 'Oh hi, yes we *do* have them, we wondered who they belonged to!'

Another two minutes elapsed before Bev tapped her on the shoulder.

'Miranda, that was a client on the phone. Any idea what's happened to those gloves that were left in the cloakroom? He's dropping by this afternoon to pick them up and I can't find them anywhere. D'you know if Fenn put them in his office?'

'Oh hell.' Miranda straightened up and let out a groan. For three and a half weeks the gloves had lain unclaimed on a shelf in the cloakroom, and now . . . well, sometimes life was just too unfair.

'What does that mean?' Bev was instantly suspicious. 'Oh hell what?'

'They went to a deserving cause.'

'Don't tell me, you gave them to that tame tramp of yours.' Bev guessed at once from the look on Miranda's

23

face. 'Oh, you are hopeless. What on earth am I going to say to the client when he turns up?'

'Um . . .'

'And Fenn is going to kill you.'

'He won't.' Miranda spoke with more conviction than she felt. 'I asked if I could have them. He said it was okay.'

Well, he had. Kind of. The only niggling drawback was, Fenn had been pretty busy at the time. And although *technically* he had said yes, Miranda couldn't help feeling that maybe he'd meant yes, she could have the gloves if nobody turned up to claim them within, say, the next six months.

Rather than the next six seconds.

She bit her lip.

'Well, if Fenn told you it was okay,' said Bev, 'that's fine. He can make the grovelling apologies when the client gets here. Maybe he'd even like to pop along to Harvey Nichols and buy him another pair.'

Miranda winced.

'After all,' Bev continued remorselessly, 'those gloves cost about two hundred quid.'

They were great friends. She was extremely fond of Miranda, who was dippy and good-hearted. The trouble was, Miranda was always getting herself into . . . well, trouble. She had a habit of making mistakes.

'Well?' said Bev.

'Okay, okay,' Miranda groaned, thrusting the broom into her hands. 'Just cover for me. If Fenn asks where I am, tell him I'm in the loo. I'll be back in *two minutes.*'

As she raced to the door, Bev called after her, 'Honestly,

the muddles you get yourself into.' She broke into a broad grin. 'I'm glad I'm not you.'

Me too, thought Miranda as she pelted hell for leather up the Brompton Road, I wish I wasn't me either.

Oh God, this was definitely going to be awkward.

He was still there, thank goodness. When he spotted her running towards him, he nodded and raised one hand briefly in greeting, waggling his fingers to show her he was still wearing the nice warm gloves.

'This,' said Miranda, 'is *so* embarrassing.'

'What's wrong?'

Her teeth began to chatter with cold and shame. It was still raining and she'd dashed out without her coat.

'The gloves. They . . . er, belong to someone. And . . . um, well, now they want them back.'

Dear God, what must he think of me? Playing Lady Bountiful one minute, and all but stripping him naked the next.

He didn't even blink.

'Okay.'

'Sorry,' said Miranda with an air of desperation. 'I feel terrible.'

'And I keep telling you, no need to apologise.' He peeled off the gloves and held them out to her, smiling faintly as he did so. 'They weren't really me, anyway.'

'Thanks.'

Feeling a complete heel, she took them from him.

'Do you need the scarf back as well?'

'No! *Stop*,' she almost yelled in alarm as he began to unwind it from around his neck, 'you can definitely keep the scarf!'

'That's okay then.' Relieved, he patted it back into place. 'Actually, I prefer the scarf.' His dark eyes registered self-deprecating amusement. 'It's much more my style.'

As she burst through the tinted glass door to the salon, Miranda heard a male voice saying, '. . . at least now I don't have to buy a new pair.' In the nick of time she shoved the gloves under her T-shirt.

Bev, who had been stalling the man and simultaneously doing her best to impress him with (a) her chest and (b) her dazzling repartee, visibly exhaled with relief when she saw Miranda and the odd-shaped bump protruding beneath her own, considerably smaller, breasts.

'Mission accomplished,' Miranda murmured when they met up seconds later in the cloakroom. Producing the gloves with a flourish, she waggled them in front of Bev, like cow's udders.

'This is known as a skin-of-your-teeth experience. He's in a rush.' Bev grabbed the gloves, wafting them suspiciously under her nose. 'God, if he knew where they'd *been*.'

Miranda looked offended. 'I had a shower this morning.'

'Not you, you idiot. Homeless Herbert. It's probably weeks since he saw a bar of soap.'

Miranda followed her out of the cloakroom.

'Great, thanks.' The man took the gloves, then frowned. 'They're warm.'

He looked at Bev. Bev, stumped, gazed back at him.

'It's cold outside,' Miranda chimed in helpfully. 'As soon as you rang, Bev put them on the radiator to warm up.'

Relieved, Bev nodded vigorously.

'That was nice of you.' He grinned at her.

'Bev's a thoughtful girl,' said Miranda. 'Single, too,' she went on, barely wincing as beneath the desk a stiletto heel jabbed into her foot. 'She'd make someone a wonderful wife.'

When the client had left, Fenn beckoned Miranda over to him.

'So the gloves have been claimed?'

'Mmm. Lucky he came back before I ran off with them.'

'Very lucky.'

Fenn kept a straight face as he returned his attention to the hair he was cutting. Did Miranda think he was blind *and* stupid?

'What's that smell?' Miranda wrinkled her nose as she burst into Florence's living room. 'It's all in the hallway . . . crikey, it's even stronger in here. Ah, you've had a visitor.'

'I have been visited,' Florence solemnly agreed, as Miranda eyed the teapot and two cups and saucers on the table. 'By Elizabeth.'

'Poor you. What was it this time,' Miranda shrugged off her coat, 'more raffle tickets?'

Elizabeth Turnbull, their next-door neighbour, was a divorcee in her mid-forties who devoted half her life to charity fund-raising and the other half to squirting on perfume. She was a nice enough woman, if a bit on the bossy side. Overpowering in every sense of the word.

'Worse.' As she spoke, Florence pushed a couple of stiff white invitations across the table. 'Tickets to a cocktail party, if you please. Twenty quid a head, but they've rustled up a few celebrities,' she raised her asymmetrically pencilled eyebrows, 'so apparently it's a bargain. You get a free glass of champagne and the chance to hob-nob with the rich and famous. And, of course, it's all in a *tremendously* good cause.'

'I'm sure it'll be *tremendous* fun, too.' Miranda, in turn, mimicked Elizabeth's strident tones. She glanced at the gilt-edged invitations, each one admitting two guests. 'Actually, it might be fun. You could do with a night out.'

'Oh, I'm not going.'

'Why on earth not?'

'The party's being held in a third-floor flat. No elevators in the building.' Drily Florence added, 'No Stannah Stairlift either. The only way I'd get in is if a helicopter dropped me through the roof.'

'So you paid eighty pounds for tickets and you aren't even going to turn up?' Miranda shook her head, bemused. 'Honestly, and you call me a soft touch.'

Florence shrugged. She had her caustic-old-battleaxe image to think of.

'It was the only way to get rid of Elizabeth before the stench of that godawful scent of hers started dissolving the carpet. Anyway, I'll give one of the tickets to Verity and Bruce. The do's being held on their wedding anniversary – those kind of meet-the-celebrity functions are right up their street.'

Chapter 4

It didn't help that Bruce kept shaking his head and telling her she looked terrible. Every time he said it, Chloe longed to blurt out that maybe if he was pregnant and his wife wanted him to have an abortion, he might look terrible too.

But she couldn't.

She didn't dare.

As long as nobody else was aware of the situation, Chloe felt superstitiously, there was a chance it could somehow sort itself out, be magically resolved.

It didn't seem likely, she had to admit. But you never knew, miracles did happen.

The other reason she was reluctant to tell Bruce was . . . well, her job.

He was her employer, and if Greg did leave her, she was going to need, rather badly, to stay employed.

Chloe couldn't help wondering how a man who disapproved of women spending more than thirty seconds in the loo was likely to react to the idea of time off for antenatal appointments, visits to the doctor, maybe a whole day off to actually give birth . . .

No, no, safer all round to keep this kind of news from him, Chloe thought with a shudder.

For the time being, at least.

She felt doubly guilty on Friday morning when Bruce came into the shop carrying a box from the patisserie around the corner.

'You're not eating properly,' he told her, dumping the box on the counter. 'This dieting business doesn't suit you. Here, I picked us up a couple of coffee éclairs.'

Even a fortnight ago, the prospect of a coffee éclair at nine o'clock in the morning would have made her feel sick. Now, gazing lovingly at them, Chloe realised that she was so ravenous she could eat not only both éclairs but the box as well.

'That's really kind.'

Does he seriously think I'm looking terrible because I'm on a diet?

'Got something else for you too.' Digging in his inside pocket, Bruce pulled out a gilt-edged invitation. 'My mother sent it to us. Some charity bash in Belgravia. Sounds pretty good, but we've made other arrangements for that night – it's our wedding anniversary – so I thought you and Greg could give it a try. Might perk you up a bit.'

'Lovely.' Dutifully, Chloe studied the invitation. Right now the only thing capable of perking her up would be a husband with a brain transplant.

'Lots of famous people going.' In case she'd forgotten how to read, Bruce leaned over and pointed to the list of names. 'Wayne Peterson, the footballer. Caroline Newman, she's the one who does that holiday programme. And Daisy Schofield . . .' He hesitated. The name was familiar but he couldn't place it.

'Australian model, sings a bit. And she's acted in a couple of films,' said Chloe. Greg had something of a crush on Daisy Schofield, so she was in a position to know.

'Well, should be fun.' Bruce gave her an encouraging wink. 'No getting yourself chatted up by Wayne Peterson, mind. He's a good-looking chap.'

Oh yes, highly likely, thought Chloe. The moment Wayne Peterson claps eyes on me, that'll be it, no question.

Bowled over.

Literally, she decided with a rueful smile, if I carry on eating at this rate.

Greg waited until Chloe had left for work the next morning before hauling the suitcases out from under the stairs.

Doing it this way might seem unkind, but he didn't mean to be. It would just be far more upsetting for Chloe, he knew, to be there watching him pack.

Easier all round to clear his things out while she was out.

Was that so cruel?

It didn't take him long to fill four suitcases; he wasn't making off with the household appliances, only clothes and a few CDs.

Forty minutes later, Greg took a last tour around the living room. Not the happiest day of his life, but he'd survive.

None of this is my fault, he told himself, imagining Chloe's reaction when she came home at five thirty and found his note. It really *isn't* my fault, though. Chloe knew the rules and she broke them. How can I be to blame when she forced me into this?

He looked at the clock on the mantelpiece. It had been

a wedding present from his grandmother, but he wouldn't take it with him. He wasn't a bastard, for one thing. This might be the end of the road for himself and Chloe but that didn't mean they had to turn into the kind of couple who fought over the last curtain hook.

Anyway, what use would he have for a clock like that? He was moving in with his old mate Adrian, whose own wife had run off last year with a stockbroker. The last thing he needed was the chiming brass monstrosity his grandmother had ordered through her catalogue.

Much as he loved her, there was no getting away from the fact, Greg decided; it was one seriously naff clock.

The gilt-edged invitation was propped up next to it on the mantelpiece. With time on his hands, Greg picked it up and idly read through it again. Last night, Chloe had produced the invitation from her bag and said: 'Why don't we go to this? Look, Daisy Schofield's going to be there. You'd like to meet her, wouldn't you?'

It had been, he guessed, her way of trying to pretend nothing had happened.

'Chloe, what's the point?' He had been gentle with her, but firm. 'I've already told you, I'm moving out. If you want to go to the party, you go.'

'I couldn't.' Chloe's blue eyes had filled with tears. 'Not on my own.'

That had been it. Greg had shrugged, indicating that this was hardly his fault, and Chloe had flung the invitation to the floor before rushing from the room. Greg had been the one to bend down, retrieve it from beneath the coffee table and put it safely on the mantelpiece.

Daisy Schofield.

God, she was gorgeous.

That *body* . . .

Oh, what the hell, Greg thought as he slid the invitation into the back pocket of his jeans. It wasn't as if Chloe was going to be using it, was she?

Let's face it, some opportunities are simply too good to miss.

It was a cold, bright Sunday. For what seemed like the first time in months, the sky was blue and the sun was out.

Florence was sitting gazing out of her window when she heard Miranda clatter down the stairs.

'It's me, I'm going shopping.' She poked her head around Florence's door. 'Anything I can get you?'

'Absolutely. A bottle of Montrachet, please.'

Miranda's expressive eyebrows slanted at right angles.

'Sounds like a sneeze. What is it, some kind of cough medicine?'

'Wine. Better than medicine.' Florence wheeled herself across to where her handbag lay. 'Here, let me get you the money.'

'It's all right, I'll pick it up in Tesco. Pay me later.'

Florence waggled a fifty-pound note at her.

'We aren't talking plonk here, this should just about cover it. And you'll have to go to the wine merchants in Kendal Street.'

'Blimey. Special occasion?' Privately Miranda thought Florence must be mad. Tesco did some great special offers. If she was in the mood to push the boat out she could get a really nice Australian Chardonnay for £3.99.

'It's April the tenth. Ray's birthday. We always drank Montrachet on his birthday.' Briskly Florence snapped her purse shut, determined not to sound like a sentimental old fool. 'I've kind of kept up the ritual. Well, we always said we would. It was Ray's favourite wine. Flashy bugger,' she glanced fondly at his photograph, on the table next to her, 'he reckoned he was worth it.'

When Miranda arrived back with the wine an hour later, she found Florence waiting for her by the door.

'Why are you wearing a hat?'

'It's cold outside.' Florence adjusted the tilt of her jaunty red fedora. 'You've been ages. The cab will be here any minute.' She took the tissue-wrapped bottle as carefully as if it were a newborn baby. 'Was the fifty enough?'

'Three pounds change. Where are you going?'

'Hampstead Heath. Parliament Hill.' Florence grinned at the expression on Miranda's face. 'The sun's shining. I could do with the fresh air. Anyway, it's where Ray and I first met.'

'People will stare at you.'

'Oh well, I'm used to that.'

'You're going to sit on Parliament Hill drinking a forty-seven-pound bottle of wine?' Miranda said in disbelief. 'Have you got a corkscrew?'

'I'm in a wheelchair.' Comfortably, Florence patted her bag. 'I'm not senile.'

The bag, when she'd patted it, had made a clinking noise. As a minicab pulled up outside, Miranda said cautiously, 'Two glasses. One for you and one for . . . ?'

If Florence said, 'Ray,' she would have to stop her. There was such a thing as too weird.

'You, of course.' Florence opened the door and began to wheel herself through it. 'Who else d'you think's going to push me up that bloody hill?'

Chapter 5

The view over Hampstead was breathtaking. White clouds scudded across a duck-egg-blue sky and the kite flyers were out in force. Miranda, feeling the cold, dug her woolly orange beret out of her jacket pocket and pulled it on, Benny Hill style, over her tingling ears.

Florence held the glasses on her lap and Miranda wrestled the cork out of the bottle. When the wine was poured, they toasted Ray and clinked glasses. Reverently taking her first sip, Miranda tried hard – and failed utterly – to appreciate the finer points of £47-a-bottle wine.

'Mm, yum,' she lied.

'Ha, and I'm the Queen of Spain. Doesn't matter if you don't like it,' Florence said cheerfully, polishing off her first glassful and smacking her lips. 'I'll manage the rest.'

To steer the subject away from her own shameful ignorance, Miranda huffed on her frozen hands and said, 'So how did you and Ray meet?'

'Haven't I told you before? Oh, it's a great story.' Florence held her glass out for a refill. 'I was up here early one Sunday morning with Bruce. He had a new bike and I wouldn't let him out on the roads. So of course he set out to prove he could ride the thing – he was eight, you know what they're like at that age – and the next minute he was hurtling out of control down that path there.' She nodded in the direction of the narrow path curving to the left below them. 'Poor little sod ended up going slap into a tree.'

'You've never told me this!' Enthralled, Miranda leaned closer, cross-legged on the grass. It wasn't difficult to imagine Bruce as a stubborn eight-year-old. 'What happened next?'

'Blood and teeth everywhere. One wrecked bike, one sprained knee. Bruce was screaming blue murder and there was me without so much as a tissue to mop up the blood.'

'Poor Bruce.'

'Poor me! I was in a complete flap. Bruce wasn't the only one in tears, I can tell you.'

'Hang on, I can guess the rest,' Miranda said excitedly. 'Then – trumpets, trumpets! – over the hill came Ray riding to the rescue on his motorbike' – she had heard all about Ray's devotion to his Norton 500 – 'with a first-aid kit slung over one shoulder and a big bag of false teeth on the other.'

Florence chuckled.

'Not quite. Over the hill came Ray, on foot and hungover, making his way back to Highgate after an all-night party. But he came to the rescue, bless his heart, and he had a clean handkerchief, which was more than I did. He cleaned up Bruce's mouth, managed to stop him screaming and insisted on giving him a piggy-back home. He even carried the smashed-up bike,' Florence remembered fondly. 'It's a wonder he didn't have a heart attack there and then. Well, that was it as far as I was concerned. Love at first sight. There was Ray with his Clark Gable hair – that was when he still had hair, of course – and me trotting along carrying his dinner jacket. Bruce was dripping blood all over his white evening shirt and he wasn't even bothered. He made us both laugh. And he wasn't even doing it to impress me, because as far as he was concerned I was just a young housewife in need of a hand. When we got back to the house he said, "Your husband's going to have his work cut out getting that bike fixed."'

'This is *so* romantic,' Miranda sighed. 'And . . . ?'

'I said, "He certainly is, seeing as he died three years ago."'

Miranda wrapped her arms around her knees in delight. 'Then what?'

'Well, he just stood there for a minute, grinning at me. Then he said, "In that case, I'd love an aspirin and a cup of tea."'

'Oh! Did he mend the bike as well?'

'I suggested it.' Florence snorted with laughter. 'He told me he wasn't the fixing kind. When things got broken, he bought new ones.'

'And did he buy Bruce another bike?'

'Certainly did, four days later.' Florence waggled her left hand at Miranda. 'And so I wouldn't feel left out, an engagement ring for me.'

Having disposed of the rest of the bottle, Florence contentedly closed her eyes and said, 'Okay for five minutes while I have a little snooze?'

Miranda sat back, stretching out her legs and propping herself up on her elbows. In this position she could enjoy the faint warmth of the sun on her face and view the kites performing their colourful acrobatics in the sky.

Squinting in the sunlight, she surveyed the panoramic view spread out before her. There in the distance was St Paul's Cathedral, pointing up into the sky like a silicone-stuffed Hollywood breast. And there was Big Ben. To the east stood Canary Wharf, and the old Caledonian market clock tower. To the west, the chimneys of Battersea power station and the Trellick Tower. Heavens, it made you realise how vast – and how eclectically beautiful – London really was.

But the unaccustomed brightness of the sun soon made her eyes water. To give them a rest, Miranda turned her attention instead to a battered green BMW being driven slowly along the road below her. Idly she followed its progress until it braked and reversed into a parking space. Seconds later the passenger door was flung open and a boy aged around five or six jumped out on to the grass verge.

Miranda watched the driver emerge from the other side, open the car's boot and take out a yellow and white kite. From this angle his face wasn't visible, but at a guess he was around thirty, dark-haired like his son and wearing a white rugby shirt and faded jeans.

Another Sunday father, thought Miranda, bringing his child out for a spot of kite-flying then whisking him off for a burger at McDonald's before depositing him back with his mother at the designated time.

Hampstead Heath was full of them.

The spiralling divorce rate had done the fast-food business no harm at all.

As Florence dozed peacefully beside her, Miranda watched the boy yell out instructions to his dad. Dad was evidently no expert; as they edged their way up the hill he unravelled the nylon line and made two or three unsuccessful attempts to get the kite airborne.

Miranda smirked as he threw it up again, this time narrowly avoiding decapitation. She heard his son yell out in disgust, 'You're useless! Come on, let *me* have a go.'

They were closer now, moving towards her. The man said, 'Charming manners, Eddie, you take after your mother.'

'She says you've always been a hopeless case. You can't even put a shelf up straight.'

'Maybe I don't want to. Anyway, your mother's not so clever herself,' he retorted. 'Ask her how many times she's pranged the car trying to reverse it into the garage.'

Miranda watched the boy impatiently seize control of the kite. Playing one adult off against the other, she thought, feeling sorry for him. Poor little lad, caught in the middle between two warring parents.

It couldn't be much fun.

Except . . . wasn't there something oddly familiar about the father's voice? A familiarity that for some reason didn't quite fit with the visual image of the man twenty yards in front of her, now struggling to untangle a section of line which had somehow managed to knot itself around both legs?

Miranda sat up, hugging her knees and pushing her beret to the top of her forehead in order to get a better look. She was sure he wasn't a visitor to the salon.

Damn, where have I heard that voice before? she thought with mounting frustration. And why do I keep feeling something isn't right?

The kite, miraculously, made it up into the air. The boy let out a whoop of delight and galloped a few yards further up the grassy slope.

'You did it, you did it!'

'Now who's useless?' his father demanded with a triumphant grin.

'Don't let it crash!'

'It's okay, I've got the hang of this now. A genius, that's what I am, and you can tell your mother that when we get back.'

The wind was taking control, carrying the kite towards the top of the hill. Following his son, the man moved closer to Miranda. Next to her, Florence snored peacefully in her wheelchair. Glancing across at them, he smiled.

The moment his dark eyes locked with Miranda's, she knew.

Oh no, *it couldn't be*.

But it was.

It was him.

The beggar from the Brompton Road.

Her whole body stiffened in disbelief. Incredibly, he was still grinning at her.

He hasn't recognised me, thought Miranda. He spends his life sitting on his bum watching the world go by. For God's sake, how can *he* not recognise *me*?

Outraged, she shoved a stray strand of hair out of her eyes. The orange beret, already tipped to the back of her head, promptly slid off.

At last, with her spiky blue-and green-tipped hair revealed, the penny dropped. His broad smile faltered and faded. The kite was momentarily forgotten.

The kite, taking advantage of this lapse in concentration, swallow-dived to the ground.

'You let it crash!' wailed the boy, racing after it. 'You're supposed to keep the line tight. Come on, pay attention, make it fly again!'

Florence woke up from her doze with a start. Next to her, using the arm rest of the wheelchair for leverage, Miranda was scrambling to her feet. Florence heard her say in a low voice trembling with fury, 'You cheat, you bloody despicable liar, how can you *live* with yourself?'

Florence brightened at once. Well, well, this was a turn-up for the books. She'd never heard Miranda have a go at anyone before.

Peering around Miranda's quivering form, Florence eyed with interest the object of her rage. Tall, dark-haired and rather good-looking – if currently a bit shell-shocked – hmm, not bad at all. In excellent shape, too, from what she could see.

One of Miranda's hapless ex-boyfriends, Florence guessed. Presumably one who'd done the dirty on her. Well, no wonder she was upset.

'Look, I can explain—' he began, but Miranda held up both hands to stop him.

'Oh, please don't, we already know what a great actor you are.' She spat the words out with contempt. 'Tell me, is that why you and your wife split up? Did she find out how you were spending your days and kick you out? Does your son know he has a con-artist for a father?' She longed to yell the accusations at the top of her voice but the boy was only yards away. For his sake, Miranda managed to control herself.

The man, looking startled, followed the direction of her

gaze. Turning back to Miranda, he said with a placatory half-smile, 'I promise you, I really can explain. For a start, I'm not married. And Eddie isn't my son, he's—'

'Daddy, come and *help* me!' howled the boy, now firmly entangled in the kite's line. 'You're wasting time – Mum said we had to be home by four.'

'You're damn right you can explain,' Miranda hissed, kicking the brakes off Florence's chair and yanking her in the direction of the path. 'You can explain why you take my money and eat my prawn sandwiches when you clearly earn more than I do.' She was flinging the words over her shoulder as she jolted the wheelchair over the uneven ground. 'And you can explain why you drive a BMW,' she bellowed. 'Because you make me *sick*!'

'Wait,' he called after her, but further up the hill his son was yelling for him and Miranda was by this time scooting downhill with the wheelchair at a rate of knots.

Relieved to reach the bottom in one piece, Florence said sympathetically, 'The best-looking ones are always the biggest bastards.'

She patted Miranda's thin arm, sensing it was best not to mention the two rather good Waterford crystal wine glasses they had left at the top of the hill. 'What happened, he forgot to mention he was married?'

Poor, impulsive Miranda, she deserved better than that. Still, if she wanted to impress a man, she really should learn to cook, Florence privately felt. When you invited someone round for dinner, you couldn't expect them to be too bowled over by a prawn sandwich.

Chapter 6

Chloe, flicking without much enthusiasm through a magazine in the doctor's waiting room at ten to nine on Monday morning, came across an article detailing the break-up of some minor celebrity's marriage.

In the accompanying photograph the woman – an actress in her late thirties – was looking suitably devastated in full make-up and a short clinging dress that showed off . . . well, practically everything.

The article was headlined: EVERY NIGHT I CRY MYSELF TO SLEEP.

Lucky you, thought Chloe, her shoulders sagging with exhaustion. I cry every night but I still can't sleep.

How much could she seriously be expected to sympathise, anyway, with a woman who clearly didn't cry much at all? She was wearing mascara, wasn't she? Her eyes weren't permanently swollen like a frog's. Furthermore, she had a teeny-weeny waist.

Hating her, Chloe threw the magazine back on to the pile. She shifted on her uncomfortable moulded plastic chair – moulded for someone with a far smaller bottom than hers, by feel of it – and eased a finger under the safety pin strain-hold together the waistband of her loosest skirt.

There was a poster blu-tacked up on the wall opposite her. It said: *Postnatal Depression?*

I've got pre-natal depression, thought Chloe. Ha, beat that.

'Chloe Malone,' the tinny voice of the doctor announced over the intercom, 'to room six.'

In the space of the next five minutes, everything became astonishingly real. Armed with the date of Chloe's last period, the doctor twiddled a circular chart contraption, consulted a calendar, then pronounced, 'Your baby is due to arrive on Tuesday the third of December.'

Chloe gazed at him. He spoke with such absolute certainty.

Heavens. Move over, Mystic Meg.

'Call it an early Christmas present.' The doctor smiled at her stunned expression. 'So, everything okay? Husband happy about it?'

Uh oh, here we go.

'He left me five days ago,' said Chloe, and waited to burst into tears.

The doctor looked as if he were waiting for her to burst into tears too.

Chloe wondered why it wasn't happening.

Instead, the doctor's words, *Your baby is due to arrive on Tuesday the third of December*, kept dancing through her mind.

Somehow, miraculously, they seemed more important than the brutal ones Greg had flung at her last week.

'He's never wanted children,' Chloe told the doctor, marvelling at the steadiness of her own voice. 'But it's okay, I'll cope.'

Well, cope might be putting it a bit strongly. Somehow muddle through was probably nearer the mark.

'In that case, let's pop you on the scales,' said the doctor.

Oh dear, how dainty. That was what you did in the supermarket with a bag of seedless grapes.

'I'm only seven weeks and I've put on loads of weight already.' Chloe kicked off her shoes, embarrassed, and shuffled over to the scales. 'I can't stop eating, I just feel so hungry all the time.'

'Don't worry about it. Just try and eat healthily.'

How healthy was pecan toffee ice cream? And bags of liquorice allsorts? Not to mention strawberry Angel Delight.

'Morning sickness, that's what I need.' Chloe sounded rueful. 'I keep waiting for it to happen and it just won't.'

Amused, the doctor tut-tutted.

'My wife's pregnant. If she could hear you now, she'd hit you round the head with her sick bag. You stay as you are,' he advised Chloe good-naturedly. 'You're a lucky girl.'

Was he a real doctor?

Or, Chloe wondered, an escaped lunatic masquerading as one?

Me, a *lucky girl*?

'You're late,' said Fenn.

'I know, I'm sorry.' As she swung round to face him, Miranda caught a glimpse of her frazzled reflection in one of the salon mirrors. Well, was it any wonder she was looking frazzled? 'Oh, but Fenn, you'll never believe what happened!'

Excuses? Fenn had heard them all.

'Don't tell me. You were seized by a gang of kidnappers and held hostage,' he guessed, 'until they found out nobody was going to pay to get you back, so they let you go.'

'Oh ha ha.' Miranda was clearly miffed. 'I'm being serious.'

'The tube was held up. Body on the line.'

Always a trusty stand-by. It was a wonder London still had a population, the number of times Fenn had heard this one.

He got glared at.

'No.'

'Okay, a puppy ran out into the road and you had to rescue it.'

Fenn was grinning. Miranda could have hit him. The puppy excuse was a standing joke in the salon. The really frustrating thing was, it had once actually happened. It was one of her few genuine excuses and nobody – *nobody* – had ever believed her.

'If you must know, I've been looking for that beggar,' she announced. Fenn might be a pig, but she was bursting to tell someone. 'You know, the one who sits outside the shoe shop?'

'You mean the beggar you gave Alice Tavistock's money to?' Entertained, Fenn raised an eyebrow. 'The one you keep insisting isn't a beggar because he never begs?'

'Okay, okay, don't rub it in.' Impatiently Miranda waved the interruption aside. 'Anyway, it turns out he isn't a real beggar at all. He's not hungry and he isn't homeless – he's a total *fake*. I saw him yesterday on Hampstead Heath wearing normal clothes. He was with his son, flying a kite. And you'll never guess what kind of car he drives.' Her dark eyes flashed with renewed outrage as the words tumbled out. 'Only a BMW.'

Fenn tried not to smile. Poor Miranda, she was positively fizzing with indignation. All her illusions, so brutally shattered.

'Well, it happens.' His tone was mild.

'I gave him a scarf and that pair of gl—' in the nick of time she stopped herself, 'er . . . glasses, an old pair of sunglasses.'

Nodding slowly, Fenn said, 'I see, sunglasses. Always useful.'

'I can't believe I was so stupid. The whole time he must have been laughing at me. Can you believe it?' Miranda seethed. 'A bloody BMW.'

'So did you say anything to him yesterday?'

'Well, a bit, but his little boy was there. Anyway, I've thought of a whole *load* more things to yell at him today.' In fact she had lain awake half the night coming up with bigger and better insults. In the end there were so many she'd had to write them down. 'Look, here's my list.'

It was a big list. Fenn could just imagine her standing over the poor fellow in the street, bawling, 'Wait, wait, I haven't *nearly* finished yet!'

'Well, good,' he told Miranda mildly. 'But I'd prefer it if you confronted him in your own time, not mine.'

He wasn't there at lunchtime.

'Look on the bright side,' said Bev, whom Miranda had dragged along for moral – and physical – support. 'At least you won't have to share your lunch any more.'

This didn't console Miranda. There was a nasty feeling growing in the pit of her stomach. She was beginning to suspect she'd blown the whole operation.

'I bet he's moved to another pitch.' Gloomily she shoved her hands into her pockets. 'Damn, I should have kept my mouth shut yesterday.'

There again, keeping quiet had never been her forte.

Bev was just relieved that she'd be getting back to the salon with her expensive false nails intact. She wrapped a consoling arm around Miranda's shoulders.

'Hey, cheer up. Maybe you've frightened him into going straight.'

By ten to six the last client had left. Miranda was in the back room unloading the tumble dryer and folding a mountain of parma-violet towels – the Fenn Lomax signature colour – into neat piles.

Well, neatish.

When Bev put her head around the door there was an odd expression on her face.

'Someone's here to see you.'

Miranda looked at her. It was actually a really weird expression; Bev seemed half enthralled, half perplexed.

'Who?'

'He didn't say. And he doesn't know your name either, he just asked to speak to the girl with the magpie hair.'

Hastily, because Fenn would only give her grief if she didn't, Miranda semi-folded the last of the towels before bundling them up on to the shelf. She hadn't mentioned it to Fenn – well, you don't, do you? – but one of his clients this morning had come into the salon with her son, who had

49

shown definite signs of interest in her. He'd been good fun. Good-looking, too. And – Miranda had discovered – he was a policeman!

She'd always had a bit of a weakness for men in uniform.

And now he's off duty, she thought with a rush of excitement, he's come to find me again.

Whisked away from your workplace, hmm, very *Officer and a Gentleman*, daydreamed Miranda. And how apt, seeing as he actually *was* a police officer!

Although maybe not a terribly bright one, if he hadn't even remembered her name.

Hup, the last of the towels flew through the air, landing – more or less – on the top shelf.

'It's okay, I think I know who it is.' Eyes shining, Miranda pushed her magpie hair behind her ears and presented herself to Bev for inspection. 'Do I look all right?'

'Fine,' Bev was still bemused, 'but—'

'Don't be surprised if he picks me up and carries me out of here,' Miranda fantasised happily. 'You can all clap and cheer if you like. Oh, but don't say: Is that a truncheon in your pocket or are you just pleased to see her? because it might be a truncheon and that would be really embarr—'

'Will you stop wittering on and get out there?' Exasperated, Bev gave her a hefty shove in the direction of the door. 'He can't wait for ever, he's parked outside on double yellows.'

Hang on, something not quite right here, thought Miranda.

Policemen were honest, law-abiding citizens, weren't they?

Surely they wouldn't park on yellow lines?

Chapter 7

'Here she is,' said Fenn, who was pulling on his jacket and preparing to lock up. 'What happened, Miranda? We were beginning to think you'd fallen into the tumble dryer.'

Miranda didn't even hear him. She was too busy looking at Hungry and Homeless.

With his shiny clean hair.

And his red crewneck sweater worn over a dark green shirt.

And his black trousers and highly polished black shoes.

Slowly, very slowly, she breathed in.

And his Christian Dior *aftershave* . . .

'Time for that explanation now?' His dark eyebrows lifted slightly as he spoke. 'I could take you out to dinner if you're hungry. Or if you'd prefer, just a drink.'

Miranda had a small but interested audience. Bev, Corinne and Lucy, all with their coats on, were loitering at the desk, clearly dying to know what she'd been getting up to in her spare time.

He's spent the last month sitting outside the shoe shop up the road, she marvelled. Between them, they must have walked past him at least fifty times.

And none of them had the slightest idea who he was.

51

'Why would I want to have dinner with you?' Miranda squealed, outraged by his colossal nerve. 'I mean, seriously, how gullible do you think I am?'

'So,' he grinned at her, 'just a drink then.'

'*No.*' Miranda backed away as he reached into his back pocket. 'No dinner, no drink, no nothing. How do I know you're not a raving psychopath?'

Having pulled his wallet out of his pocket, he said in a reassuring voice, 'Actually, that's a good sign. If you really thought I was a psychopath, you'd keep it to yourself, you wouldn't accuse me of being one. I'm not, anyway,' he went on, sliding a card out of the wallet and holding it towards Miranda. 'I'm a journalist.'

Miranda looked at the NUJ card. It belonged to someone called Daniel Delancey.

There wasn't a photograph on it. 'All this tells me is that you mugged a journalist and stole his wallet.'

Her expression truculent, she shrugged and passed the card back.

Fenn intercepted it.

'Miranda, come on, lighten up. The guy's a journalist. He was researching a piece about how it feels to be out on the streets. You blew his cover and called him some terrible names, but *still* he's forgiven you.' Fenn reached for the door; it was time to lock up and go home. 'For heaven's sake, let him buy you dinner.'

Miranda hesitated. Behind Fenn, Bev was saucer-eyed and nodding so fast her eyelashes were in danger of flying off.

Nothing about Bev was real.

'Just something simple, a pizza maybe.' Daniel Delancey

– *if* that was his name – gave her a nod of encouragement.

Sod that, Miranda thought indignantly, he owes me more than a lousy pizza.

If he's taking me out to dinner, we're going to go somewhere expensive.

They went to Langan's Brasserie, on Stratton Street. It wasn't a restaurant Miranda had ever been to before, but she'd heard enough about the place from clients at the salon to know it probably cost a bomb.

Well, good.

As far as Miranda was concerned, the bigger the bomb the better.

And she was going to order the priciest things on the menu.

'I'm glad you changed your mind about coming out,' said Daniel Delancey, when the waiter had taken their order.

'I didn't have a lot of choice.'

Miranda fiddled with her cutlery. She still had a terrible urge to punch him. He had humiliated her and she couldn't forgive him just like that.

'I've got your wine glasses in the car, by the way. You left them behind yesterday.'

His eyes were friendly. He was willing her to smile back at him.

'Look, what do you expect me to do?' Miranda demanded stroppily. 'Say thank you and apologise for yelling at you? Because I don't see why I should. You made a fool of me, you let me give you sandwiches . . . and chocolate . . . and a crappy old scarf . . . Do you have any idea how *stupid* that makes me feel?'

'Okay, let me explain.' His voice was soothing, as if he were dealing with a toddler on the verge of a tantrum. 'I couldn't give your food to a genuine homeless person but I made a donation to the Salvation Army, so someone else could have a meal on your behalf. And any money I was given went to them too. You don't have to worry,' he assured her, 'nobody missed out.'

Except me, thought Miranda, all the times I shared my lunch with you when I could have eaten the whole lot myself.

Depriving oneself of chocolate wasn't the easiest thing to do. Heavens, it was practically an unnatural act.

Miranda sighed, silently mourning the loss of all those Mars bars.

'So how long d'you have to keep this up?' Curiosity finally overcame belligerence. 'Seems like a lot of work for one article.'

'I've finished. Friday was my last day.' His dark eyes registered amusement. 'You can have your scarf back as well, if you like.'

Their first course arrived. Miranda dived greedily into her scallops.

'Bet you were glad to be able to wash your hair.'

'I washed it every night,' said Daniel Delancey. With a shrug he added, 'And rubbed Mazola into it every morning.'

Ugh, imagine.

'Still seems like a lot of work for one magazine article.'

He laid down his fork and smiled slightly at Miranda.

'What?' She wondered why he was looking at her like that. 'Do I have cream on my chin?'

'No. This wasn't for a magazine article. It's for TV.'

'Don't be daft,' Miranda scoffed, 'you need cameras for TV. You need lights, and those clapperboard things, and directors with megaphones shouting *Action*.'

'For *Lethal Weapon*, maybe,' said Daniel Delancey, 'but not for a documentary. Not this kind, anyway.'

'You still need a camera.'

He nodded.

'I know that.'

'And you definitely didn't have one.'

'Actually, we did. In the shoe shop.'

Oh, good grief. Miranda almost choked on a scallop. If the camera had been strategically positioned behind him, that meant . . .

'Are you telling me I'm going to be *in* this documentary?'

'Oh yes. The producer's crazy about you. If he has his way,' Daniel Delancey looked as if he were enjoying himself, 'you'll end up a star.'

Miranda was appalled. Terrible mental images spiralled through her brain, of all the times she had raced up the road to see him in her scruffy black jacket with the wind and the rain splattering her hair in all directions. And in next to no make-up.

Oh God, and when it was cold her nose always went bright red, like a Comic Relief one.

'That is *so* unfair,' she blurted out, loudly enough to startle the couple at the next table. 'Why couldn't you have warned me? What am I going to *look* like?'

Amused, Daniel Delancey said, 'According to Tony, everyone's going to fall in love with you.'

'Oh yes, and by this time next year I'll be a supermodel, all five foot two of me.' It wasn't funny. Miranda quailed, imagining the hideous footage they must have of her on their beastly hidden camera. 'Couldn't you just do some of the filming again?' she pleaded desperately. 'Give me a chance to comb my hair and put on a bit of make-up?'

Not to mention a Wonderbra.

'You shared your lunch with me. How you look isn't important.'

Ha, thought Miranda, only a total *man* could think that.

'You could blur me out,' she had a brainwave, 'have one of those splodgy things covering my face, like they do with criminals who aren't allowed to be identified.'

'Look, if you're really against this,' said Daniel Delancey, 'you can always say no.'

She gazed at him, startled.

'I can?'

'Obviously we need your permission to use you. If it bothers you that much,' he said simply, 'refuse to give it.'

'Oh!'

Miranda was taken aback. She hadn't expected him to say this.

She wasn't completely anti the thought of being on television. In fact, secretly, she was quite taken with the idea.

If only she could appear on it looking . . . well, a bit *better*.

More of a human being, basically. And less of a dog.

Yuck, dilemma.

Daniel Delancey had finished his first course. 'You're

dithering. Maybe you should just say no.' Nodding at her plate, he added, 'I won't get stroppy and march you out of here, if that's what you're worried about. You can finish your meal. Although . . .'

Miranda hurriedly forked the last scallop into her mouth before he could change his mind.

'Although what?'

'No, I was just thinking it could be nice publicity for the salon.' He shrugged, indicating the Fenn Lomax logo on the front of her parma-violet T-shirt. 'But that wouldn't benefit you, would it? Only your boss.'

Only her boss?

Miranda's brain leapt to attention. Daniel Delancey might have dismissed the idea already, but that was because he didn't know her.

It was actually a powerful incentive.

The prospect of massive Brownie points wasn't to be sneezed at. Particularly by a humble employee who couldn't help feeling sometimes that she was only hanging on to her job by the skin of her teeth.

For instance, thought Miranda, someone like me.

Actually, quite a lot like me.

'Publicity for the salon would be good,' she agreed cautiously as their next course arrived. 'I'd be happy with that.' Her lamb cutlets glistened in the candlelight, weakening her resolve. 'Oh, I don't know . . . it's just the thought of all those people seeing me on TV and yelling, "God, look at the state of her, what a *loser*." They'd probably think I fancied you.' She winced at the idea. 'That I'm so sad, ugly and desperate that chatting up beggars and bribing them with sandwiches is my only hope.'

It would have been nice if, at this point, Daniel Delancey could have protested, 'Oh now, come along, you're not ugly!'

But he didn't. Chivalry clearly wasn't his thing. He just smiled that irritating half-smile of his again and said, 'Okay, they might think that.'

Thanks a lot, thought Miranda, deeply miffed.

'Then again, when they see you being interviewed in the second half of the programme . . . well, that's when they'll realise they were wrong, won't they?'

Interviewed?

Miranda's glass of wine was halfway to her mouth. It stopped dead.

'Hang on, what interview?'

'It's a fifty-minute programme. In the first half,' Daniel Delancey explained, 'we use the hidden camera footage. The viewers get the chance to make up their own minds about the people they see. People like you, who try to help, as well as the other kind,' he said evenly, 'the ones who yelled at me to get a job. Not to mention the bunch of kids who stole my money and gave me a kicking.'

Miranda's eyes widened in horror.

'They didn't! Were you hurt?'

'Pretty bruised.' Briefly he pushed up the sleeve of his sweater, revealing a boot-shaped mark on his forearm. 'I won't show you the rest.'

'Bastards!'

Miranda had forgotten all about dinner. The lamb cutlets were growing cold on her plate.

'Goes with the territory.' With a shrug, Daniel rolled his sleeve down again. 'Anyway, so that's the first half. In the second, we run a series of interviews with the people our audience have come to know. Most of them good, some bad. You'd be one of the good guys, of course.' He paused for a second. 'That is, if you agreed to appear.'

Oh well, this changed *everything*.

'Where would I be interviewed?'

Miranda was by this time quite breathless with excitement.

'That's up to you. The plan is to interweave different strands. Walking along the street . . . at work . . . in your own home, if you'd be happy with that. You're a young girl, a salon junior,' he explained with enthusiasm, 'without much money yourself. If the viewers see you living in a crappy bedsitter, they'll warm to you even more.'

Crappy bedsitter?

'If my landlady heard you saying that,' Miranda told him, 'she'd run you over with her wheelchair.'

'That was your landlady, was it? I thought she must be your grandmother.'

'Oh dear, now she's going to run over you twice.'

Daniel shook his head.

'I'm sorry, I'm a journalist, I can't help asking questions. What were you doing out with your landlady yesterday, drinking wine on Parliament Hill?'

'She has arthritis. I look after her a bit, do stuff for her, in exchange for paying not much rent.' Forking up asparagus, Miranda moved swiftly on to more interesting matters. 'So in these interviews I'd be able to wear nice clothes?'

'Of course.'

'And tons of make-up?'

'Well, ounces maybe. No need to go too mad.'

Was he laughing at her?

'And I could have my hair looking nice?'

Solemnly Daniel Delancey nodded.

'So they'd definitely know I wasn't ugly and desperate.' Miranda heaved a sigh of relief. 'That's fine then, I'll do it.'

'Great.'

Belatedly, a horrid thought struck her.

'Oh! Except there's one bit you mustn't show.'

'Don't tell me,' Daniel Delancey intercepted her with a grin, 'the stolen gloves.'

Miranda was indignant. 'How did you know?'

'Tony and I ran through a few of the tapes this morning. That was his favourite bit.'

'Well, he can't use it,' Miranda said firmly.

'I did warn him.' Another broad grin. 'I had a feeling you might say that.'

The bill for the meal was astronomical. Miranda determinedly didn't feel guilty; if Daniel Delancey was involved in making TV programmes, he must be rolling in it.

Anyway, there was the small matter of the other lie he had told her. A totally unnecessary lie, Miranda thought, considering that when he'd said it, his cover had already been blown.

'You still haven't told me why you and your landlady were out on the heath yesterday, drinking wine out of Waterford crystal glasses.'

He was driving her home in his scruffy BMW. Miranda, sitting next to him nursing the two glasses on her lap, cast a sidelong glance at his profile.

'And you haven't told me yet why you said you weren't married.'

The traffic lights ahead turned red. He braked and turned to look at her.

'Because I'm not.'

He sounded genuinely surprised. Fine, Miranda accepted that. You didn't have to be married to have a child.

'Okay,' she persisted, 'but you were with your son yesterday. Why did you say you weren't his father?'

'Eddie, you mean? I'm *not* his father.'

Men, honestly. You couldn't trust them further than you could kick them.

'I heard him,' Miranda said pointedly. 'He called you Daddy.'

Daniel Delancey's mouth was twitching. The lights turned green and he let out the clutch.

'Eddie's my sister's son. I'm his uncle. He was calling me Danny.'

Chapter 8

'Verity and I are throwing a small party this evening.' Bruce popped his head around the door of the back room, where Chloe was on her knees unpacking stained-glass lampshades. 'Nothing elaborate, just a spur-of-the-moment thing—'

'You'd like me to look after Jason for a couple of hours?' Chloe looked up from her sea of bubble-wrap.

'No, no, Jason's staying overnight at a friend's house,' Bruce assured her. 'That isn't why I mentioned it. Actually, we wondered if you and Greg would like to come along. Seven until ten, drinks and canapés. Nothing elaborate, just a friendly gesture,' he explained, 'to welcome our new neighbours.'

Since discovering last night that their new neighbours were a bank manager and his accountant wife, Bruce had decided a welcome party was definitely in order. It never did any harm to be on excellent terms, socially, with a bank manager.

'Well?' he prompted, wondering why Chloe wasn't saying anything. 'Is that a yes?' To encourage her, he added, 'We haven't seen Greg for a while.'

You're not the only one, thought Chloe, breaking into a light sweat.

Still, maybe this was the opener she needed. Bruce had to know sooner or later, and she'd been having palpitations wondering how to announce it.

Oh, by the way, Bruce, I've been dumped.

Chloe licked her lips. He was still peering down at her.

'Bruce, the thing is, Greg and I aren't together any more. We've . . . um, separated.'

There, done.

Oh bugger, thought Chloe, as her eyes filled with tears.

'Good grief.' Bruce took a step backwards. Tears weren't his thing at all. 'Why?'

'Oh, you know,' Chloe mumbled. 'Things just weren't working out.'

'Well, I'm sorry to hear that. Can't . . . er, be easy.'

It was Bruce's turn to nervously lick his lips. We must look like a couple of cannibals, Chloe thought.

'I'll be okay.'

He shifted from one foot to the other.

'Do you . . . um, want to talk about it?'

Alarmed, she shook her head.

'No, no, really, it's fine.'

Bruce was hugely relieved. Female emotions were a minefield best steered well clear of.

At least he'd offered, he told himself. When Verity pressed him for the gory details tonight, wanting to know who'd left who and if Greg had run off with another woman, he'd be able to say, 'She didn't want to talk about it.'

'So.' His tone was hearty; he rubbed his hands together in a let's-change-the-subject way. 'How about this little get-together tonight then? You'll still come, won't you? You and Verity could have a good old chat—'

'Thanks,' Chloe blurted out, 'but I'm not really up to it at the moment. I wouldn't be much fun. Another time, maybe.'

Bruce put on his understanding face. At least he knew now why Chloe – certainly no slouch in the looks department – had been looking so pallid and puffy-eyed of late.

'Of course,' he assured her. 'Don't worry about it.'

'But . . . um, if you ever need a babysitter I'd be happy to do it.' Chloe knew she was gabbling; still, now seemed as good a time as any. 'As much babysitting as you like, actually.' May as well be upfront about it. 'The thing is, I could do with the money. Oh, I'm not asking for a pay rise,' she went on hurriedly, intercepting the look of horror on Bruce's pudgy face. 'It's just, paying the rent on the flat is going to be a bit of a tight squeeze. So any extra work I can do . . . well, it'll come in handy.'

'Right, I see.'

Bruce's tone was guarded.

'I'm not looking for another *proper* job,' Chloe rushed to reassure him. 'I love working here.'

True. Well, fairly true.

Anyway, changing jobs now would mean she wouldn't be entitled to any maternity benefits.

Bruce visibly relaxed.

'Okay, I'll let Verity know. I'm sure we can work something out. And you get on well with Jason,' he added encouragingly. 'That's a plus.'

It was more than that, it was a downright miracle. According to Greg, if Bruce and Verity wanted to earn themselves a quick buck they should cart their beloved son along to the headquarters of the nearest condom manufacturers. Feature

Jason in a series of adverts for their product, Greg had declared – often – and condom sales would go through the ozone layer.

'If you don't get one of these,' he had intoned, dangling an imaginary condom from his fingers then affecting a look of horror, 'you'll get one of *these.*'

And I laughed, Chloe remembered.

Well, it had seemed funny at the time.

The trouble was, it wasn't actually funny at all.

Bruce left the back room and Chloe went back to unpacking lampshades.

Bundling a mountain of bubble-wrap into an empty box, she forced herself not to think about Greg.

Two minutes later she lurched back on her heels in shock.

God, how could I have been so stupid? How could I have offered to babysit for Verity and Bruce?

Bruce was all right, he was only a man. Men never noticed anything.

But stick-thin, eagle-eyed Verity was another matter altogether, Chloe realised with a sinking heart.

One look at my stomach and she'll be on to me like a shot.

Oh help, I need to sign up for Creative Bluffing classes, she thought helplessly. I'll have to tell Verity I've joined Overeaters Anonymous.

Chapter 9

'This is the right building,' said Miranda, pushing her way through the revolving door. 'I can feel it in my nose.'

'Sometimes I worry about you.' Bev ran an anxious hand over her hair, checking her sleek chignon was still secure after its encounter with the howling gale outside. 'God, what a night. You'd better not have dragged me here under false pretences,' she warned. 'If there aren't any decent men here, I'm going straight home.'

Miranda crossed her fingers as they followed the trail of Elizabeth Turnbull's perfume up three flights of stairs. Her extravagant promise to Bev that there would be sackfuls – if not wagonloads – of gorgeous spare men at this evening's party was gnawing slightly at her conscience.

But if she hadn't said it, Bev wouldn't have come.

And since Florence had insisted that she take the spare ticket-for-two, Miranda had been desperate. The prospect of bowling up at a cocktail party on your own where the only people you knew were Bruce and Verity Kent – aargh – and Elizabeth Turnbull – double aargh – was too terrible for words.

She'd had to bring someone along for moral support. And

basically, with her social life currently in such a dismal state, Bev needed all the help she could get.

Poor Bev, thought Miranda, it must be awful to be so helplessly at the mercy of your hormones.

It wasn't as if Bev wasn't pretty, because she was. And she took immaculate care of herself.

It wasn't as if she was old, because she wasn't. Well, maybe oldish, but not ancient. Only thirty.

It wasn't even as if she had a horrible personality, or knock-you-dead halitosis. Or acres of cellulite.

No, the only problem with Bev was something so easily remedied it could make you cry.

Sadly, it was this very flaw that sent horrified men scurrying backwards out of rooms the moment she clapped eyes on them.

The trouble with Bev was that she was Desperate.

Her biological clock was clanging like the 'Oh-dear-we're-in-trouble' bell on the *Titanic*. It had been for the last three years.

And she didn't just want a baby, she wanted a husband too, preferably one as keen on the idea of settling down to a lifetime of domestic bliss as she was.

Although failing that, well, pretty much anyone would do.

Just so long as Bev could GET MARRIED and HAVE A BABY.

It was something of a standing joke in the salon.

'Oh well, there must be one around somewhere,' Miranda had consoled her only yesterday when Bev had been wailing over the failure of the latest fling in her life to ring her. 'In a zoo, maybe. With a little sign fixed to the front of his cage saying: "Commitment Man. Possibly the only surviving member of this species. Likes to eat home-made steak and kidney pies and wear hand-knitted tank-tops. Spends his weekends carrying out helpful little DIY jobs around the cage. Seeks ideal mate, can't wait to start a family."'

'I can't think why I'm your friend,' Bev had replied loftily. 'I hate you.'

'I know, but you'll come to the party with me tomorrow night, won't you?' Miranda had wheedled. 'I promise there'll be oodles of men.'

It was no good explaining to Bev she scared men witless. She knew that already. She couldn't help it, that was her trouble. The light of matrimony was in her eyes and she couldn't switch it off.

And if one more well-meaning person tried to tell her that the reason she wasn't getting anywhere was because she was trying too hard – that if she stopped looking for a man she'd find one before you could say three-tiered cake . . . well, Miranda didn't give much for their chances.

They were likely to get more than their head bitten off.

'Miranda, how lovely to see you,' gushed Elizabeth Turnbull, leaning towards her and going mwah, mwah several inches away from each cheek.

She was wearing Poison. The air around her was as thick as pea soup. Miranda, her lips clamped together, could still taste it seeping down the back of her throat.

Frantically, over Elizabeth's plump shoulder, she scanned the room for men, any men, who might do for Bev. Honestly, it was like scavenging for scraps to feed a ravenous baby starling. Wayne Peterson, the footballer, was over by the window. Looking quite sober, for him. But since Bev wasn't a Malibu-swilling bosom-flashing page-three girl, he probably wouldn't be interested.

Oh dear, thought Miranda, still searching. Every other man she'd clapped eyes on so far was either diabolically ugly, older than the Tower of London, or clearly married.

Behind her, like telepathic acupuncture, she could feel Bev plunging imaginary pins into her back.

'No sign of Florence's son and his wife yet,' Elizabeth announced, assuming that this was who Miranda was so eager to locate. 'What's her name? Valerie?'

'Verity.' A waiter approached, bearing a tray. Hurriedly relieving him of a couple of glasses, Miranda said, 'I'm sure they'll be here soon. Don't worry about us, we'll just mingle.'

'Do, do! Caroline Newman's over there, by the way.' Elizabeth gestured grandly towards the fireplace. 'The travel presenter, you must recognise her. Charming lady, so easy to talk to, she and I have been getting on like a house on fire.' She preened visibly, like a cockatoo.

'I can't see Daisy Schofield,' said Miranda. 'Wasn't she supposed to be here as well?'

Next to her, Bev knocked back her drink in three seconds flat.

Their hostess pursed her bright orange lips.

'I'm afraid we've been badly let down by *Ms* Schofield. Some of these so-called celebrities, they just don't take their duties seriously.'

'So what happened?' said Miranda. 'She just didn't turn up?'

'Pretty much.' Elizabeth's mouth narrowed further still, as if some internal vacuum cleaner was trying to suck her lips down her throat. 'The party began at eight. No word from Daisy Schofield. I mean, you almost expect it from alcoholic footballers . . .' she gestured carelessly in the direction of poor Wayne Peterson, 'but if even *he* could manage to get here on time, I don't see why I should be made to look a fool by a third-rate *Australian* model-cum-actress.'

'Maybe she's on her way,' Miranda suggested. As someone not famous for getting to places on time herself, she felt obliged to leap to the other girl's defence. 'She could have been held up in traffic.'

Her nasal passages were by this time becoming accustomed to the scent cloud. Either that, Miranda decided, or they'd gone into self-preservation mode and given themselves a general anaesthetic.

'Hmmph,' Elizabeth snorted, 'that's what I was hoping, until the phone call ten minutes ago. Man's voice, wouldn't give his name, ringing to tell me Daisy was unwell. Said she was in bed with a viral illness and that she wouldn't be able to make it tonight.'

'But you don't believe him?' said Miranda.

'He wasn't exactly going out of his way to sound believable. He treated the whole thing as a joke: "She's in bed with a virile – oops, sorry, viral illness." And she was there, I could *hear* her, giggling away in the background like a silly teenager playing truant from school.'

'Daisy Schofield's nineteen.' Miranda remembered reading this in one of the salon's glossy magazines. Feeling incredibly ancient – at twenty-three – she said, 'She *is* a silly teenager.'

'People have come here tonight expecting to meet her,'

Elizabeth replied frostily, 'and she's let us down. That girl needs to get a grip.'

Frankly, if Daisy was in bed with a virile male, Miranda thought, getting a grip was probably what she *was* doing right now.

By nine o'clock Greg Malone was beginning to wish he hadn't dragged Adrian along to this party. When Ade got it into his head to be argumentative there was no stopping him. God, it wasn't as if either of them was even interested in meeting some bleached-blonde clapped-out travel show presenter.

'It's breach of promise though, isn't it?' Adrian was enjoying the organiser's discomfort. 'We paid good money for these tickets' – big lie – 'and you haven't delivered. No Carol Newman—'

'Caroline,' Greg murmured.

'She *was* here,' the organiser insisted. 'She had to leave early.'

'And no Daisy Schofield. I mean, how fair is that?' Adrian tilted his head accusingly. 'We came along to meet celebrities and instead here you are, palming us off with a roomful of . . . nobodies.'

Stung, the woman said, 'We've got Wayne Peterson.'

'Oh big deal,' Adrian drawled. 'He's *sober*.'

This was true. Having been given the mother of all talking-tos by – well, his own mother, Wayne Peterson was here tonight on his very best behaviour. Miserably clutching his seventh glass of Perrier – and trying hard not to burp – he was currently doing his best to appear interested in some old bore's blow-by-blow account of the 1966 World Cup.

Sadly, Wayne was only fun when he had fourteen pints of Newcastle Brown inside him. Without the aid of alcohol, he was a personality-free zone.

Even Elizabeth had been sorely tempted to spike his water with vodka.

'Look, I'm sorry if you're disappointed.' She struggled to appease her two difficult guests. 'Let me get you another drink—'

'Never mind another drink,' said Adrian. 'How about a refund?'

'He doesn't mean that,' Greg put in hurriedly. God, Adrian could be a pain sometimes. 'Of course we don't want a refund. And yes, another drink would be great.'

Typically, there wasn't a circulating waiter in sight. In her rush to reach the sanctuary of the kitchen, Elizabeth knocked into Miranda, jolting her arm. A sesame prawn canapé flew out of Miranda's hand and landed with a plop in a bowl of floating candles.

'Oh God, oh God.' Elizabeth pulled a handkerchief out of her sleeve and mopped her perspiring forehead.

'Are you all right?' Miranda peered at her. 'You look a bit, um . . .'

Flappy, was the word that sprang to mind.

'. . . hot and bothered.'

'Troublemakers.' Elizabeth inclined her head stiffly in the direction of the door. 'Those two, just arrived. Kicking up a fuss because Daisy Schofield isn't here.' Shuddering because her whole reputation was at stake, she wailed, 'Why can't people simply relax and enjoy themselves? I'm not Tommy Cooper, I can't click my fingers and produce a hatful of celebrities out of thin air.'

'Neither could Tommy Cooper,' said Miranda. 'He'd have clicked his fingers and produced a hatful of sausages.'

'It's not my fault.' Elizabeth was by this time close to tears. 'One of them threatened to sue me for breach of promise.'

'Which one?' Miranda demanded, indignant on her behalf.

'Blue shirt. Oh Lord, look at the state of me. And I'm supposed to be g-getting them another d-drink.'

Dyed-in-the-wool battleaxes weren't supposed to cry.

Swivelling around to glare at the offending pair, Miranda discovered they were already gazing at her.

The one in the blue shirt smirked and murmured something to his friend.

Prat, thought Miranda.

'Come on, put your shoulders back,' she instructed Bev, 'and stick your chest out.'

'Are we going to talk to Wayne Peterson?' Bev looked worried. She wasn't at all sure she wanted to marry an alcoholic shaven-headed footballer. Then again – the thought flashed unstoppably through her one-track mind – maybe she could be the one to tame him. They could live together happily ever after in a mock-Tudor mansion in Middlesbrough, buy each other matching diamond-encrusted identity bracelets and have lots of boisterous, shaven-headed mini-footballers—

'Wayne Peterson? No way.' Briskly interrupting this fantasy, Miranda seized the two glasses Elizabeth had returned with from the kitchen. 'Right, just pay attention,' she told Bev, 'and follow me.'

73

Chapter 10

Having eased herself into bed and arranged the duvet to her satisfaction, Florence shook out last night's *Evening Standard* and began to read.

Politics, politics, boring, boring. Impatiently she skipped over the first couple of pages.

BUNGEE-JUMPING GREAT-GRANNY, trumpeted the headline on page four, above a photograph of a wizened old woman in a crash helmet. Game-for-anything Alma Trotter, Florence read, jumped for joy when she found out what her family had planned as a surprise for her eighty-seventh birthday.

Ha, thought Florence, with family like that, who needs enemies? Bumping her off, that was what they'd been planning. Except it hadn't worked, had it? No wonder the old bird was looking so smug.

But it was ten minutes later that an article on page twenty-three really made Florence sit up and take notice.

THAI BRIDE ODDS-ON FAVOURITE FOR COLONEL TOM.

'You old devil,' Florence exclaimed, peering at the photograph below of a grinning man in his seventies sitting with one arm around the slender waist of a pretty Oriental girl. 'Tom Barrett, what are you up to now?'

Florence and Ray had first met Tom Barrett and his wife Louisa back in the early seventies, and following Ray's death Florence had remained friendly with them. The last time she had seen Tom was at Louisa's funeral three years ago, following which he had disappeared to Spain in order to spend some time with his daughter and her family and come to terms with the loss of his adored wife.

Hmm, thought Florence, studying the photograph once more and noting with approval the twinkle in her old friend's eye, it looked like he'd done that, all right. And he'd brought his young bride-to-be back to Hampstead, had he? She wondered idly if he was still living in the same house, in which case . . .

On an impulse, Florence rifled through her bedside drawer until she found her old flip-up phone directory. Within seconds she was dialling Tom's number.

'I don't believe it,' Tom exclaimed, 'a call from the Dancing Queen herself! I swear, the phone hasn't stopped ringing today. Do you have any idea how many long-lost friends have come crawling out of the woodwork since that piece appeared in the paper? Not that you'd ever crawl, my darling,' he went on with habitual gallantry. 'You'd shimmy.'

Florence laughed.

'My shimmying years are over. These days, I'm afraid, I definitely crawl.'

'Arthritis still playing up?' Tom sounded sympathetic.

'Oh, you know, the odd twinge.'

'And am I delighted to hear from you?' Florence heard the note of caution in his voice. 'Or have you rung to tell me I'm off my rocker?'

'Is that what everyone else has been doing?'

'Come on. What d'you think?'

Florence glanced at the article spread across her lap.

'You saw her in a mail-order catalogue and met her how long ago?'

'Three months.'

'She's from Thailand,' said Florence. 'Are you sure she isn't a boy?'

Much gravelly laughter at the other end of the phone.

Finally Tom managed to say, 'Oh yes.'

'That's a start. Do you love her?'

'I do,' Tom replied.

'Does she love you?'

'I think so.'

'Are you ridiculously happy?'

'So happy it would make you sick.'

'Oh well,' said Florence, 'in that case you're absolutely barking mad and I couldn't be happier for you. Go for it, prove those miserable doubters wrong, have a ball. And don't forget to invite me to the wedding.'

'You can be a bridesmaid if you want.' Tom's relief was audible. 'Dear Florence. So you don't think I'm making the biggest mistake of my life?'

'If you're having fun, how can it be a mistake? The last thing I ordered from a mail-order catalogue was a non-stick saucepan,' Florence told him, 'and after a week the bloody handle dropped off.'

'Christ, I hope mine doesn't.'

She had to ask.

'How does Jennifer feel about all this?'

Jennifer was Tom's daughter. And Tom was a wealthy man. It was bound to concern her.

'Oh, Jennifer's a diamond. She's fine about it, behind me all the way. Says if I'm happy, she's happy. Look,' Tom spoke with enthusiasm, 'we must get together again, it's been too long. Come to dinner next week, Flo. I want you to meet Maria.'

Hanging up the phone some minutes later, Florence sank back against the pillows and flipped through a few more pages of the paper. For want of anything better to do, she read her horoscope:

Oh dear, you've got yourself into a rut, haven't you? Time to do something about it. A bored person is a boring person . . .

'Blah blah blah,' said Florence, chucking the paper on to the floor. Honestly, talk about cheering you up. It was a good job she didn't believe in horoscopes.

Except there was no getting away from the fact that – whether she believed in them or not – this one was depressingly true.

Lucky Tom, she thought. Okay, so what he was doing might not work out, but at least he was giving it a go.

And even luckier Tom, Florence idly mused, to have a daughter who backed him all the way. Jennifer, after all, was the one who stood to lose out financially if the marriage went horribly wrong.

'Can't imagine you being so generous,' she said aloud, addressing the framed photograph of Bruce on her bedside table. 'You wouldn't be so keen, would you, my sweet, if

77

you thought there was a chance of my money not going your way?'

'. . . and in June we start shooting the new Madhur Jaffrey film in Norfolk, starring Helena Bonham-Carter and Stephen Fry. My role isn't huge,' Miranda said modestly, 'but it'll be great for the CV. Madhur and Jaffrey are so well thought of, that's the thing. If you've worked with them, people sit up and take notice. It proves you aren't just some bimbo,' she explained, 'and that you really can act.'

And by jingo I *can*, Miranda thought happily. Was this a performance of a lifetime or what? Adrian – yeurgh, dumb name – was lapping it up.

'Have you worked with Sylvester Stallone?' he asked eagerly.

'No.' Miranda looked regretful; it wouldn't do to show off too much. 'I auditioned once, but didn't get the part.'

'So what was Pierce Brosnan like to work with?'

'Oh, he was *great*. You must go and see the film when it comes out. The bit where he rescues me from the river just as the crocodiles are about to drag me down was the scariest thing I've ever had to do—'

Adrian's eyes were practically out on stalks.

'Were they real crocodiles?'

Um . . .

'Well, no, not *real* crocodiles.'

He frowned.

'So why was it scary?'

'Because Pierce is such a fantastic actor he made me *think* they were real.' Miranda shook her head in admiration. 'Plus, it was real water. And I can't swim.'

'Ahem,' said Greg, when Bev had disappeared to the loo and Adrian had gone in search of more drinks. 'It's Merchant Ivory.'

Miranda turned to look at him. Until now she had been concentrating solely on Adrian, the one in the blue shirt. He was her project and Greg was Bev's.

'Merchant Ivory, not Madhur Jaffrey. Their names are Ismail Merchant,' he explained patiently, 'and James Ivory.'

'Oh my God,' said Miranda, 'no wonder they kept giving me funny looks on set. How embarrassing.' She clapped a hand to her forehead. 'I've always been hopeless with names.'

'And dates.' Leaning closer, Greg whispered in her ear, 'Unless he's Superman, I don't know how Pierce Brosnan has managed to spend the last six weeks in California *and* find the time to make a film at Pinewood Studios with you.'

Miranda went pink.

'Concorde.'

'Bullshit.'

Indignantly she said, 'What makes you think he's been in California?'

'I know for a fact that he has.'

'How?'

'He's my uncle.'

'Oh *hell*. Really?'

'No.' Greg looked amused. 'That was bullshit too.'

Rumbled, thought Miranda. Damn.

'Did Bev . . . ?'

'Oh no, she did very well, considering. I've heard all

79

about her record contract and the time she and Jarvis Cocker got lost on the way to the *Top of the Pops* studios, not to mention the time she went to a party and her trousers split and she ended up having to wear one of Boy George's dresses.'

Miranda's eyes darted around the room. Maybe it was time to leg it, just get out before he had a chance to make an embarrassing scene. But there was no sign of Bev either.

'Adrian's going to be back any second,' she muttered.

'In that case,' Greg seized her clammy fingers in his cool ones, 'we'd better hide.'

He led her out on to the balcony, shielded from the room by a heavy curtain. Below them, the wet streets glittered in the reflected lamplight. Much to Miranda's relief, it had stopped raining and the wind had dropped.

'What about Bev?' she protested. 'She'll wonder where we are.'

'I've spent the last thirty minutes talking to Bev. I've done my duty,' said Greg. 'Now I want to swap.'

Miranda watched a man on the pavement across the street, taking a furtive pee up against a pillar-box. In Belgravia, imagine.

'Is that fair?'

'I think it's fair.' Greg turned her sideways to look at him. 'I didn't just get the *Top of the Pops* and Boy George stories; I've had the "aren't-babies-wonderful" spiel as well.'

Honestly, thought Miranda, how many times have I told her not to *do* that?

'And I don't happen to think they are,' he went on, his smile crooked. 'Anyway, I'd much rather talk to you.'

He had dark-blond hair – natural, she noted automatically

– and laughing grey eyes and a really nice mouth. Feeling her stomach go a bit squirmy, Miranda realised how attractive he actually was.

'I'm not really an actress,' she said.

'I gathered that.'

'I only said I was because—'

'It's okay, I know why you did it.'

'Elizabeth Turnbull's my next-door neighbour. You made her cry.'

'Now I feel terrible. I'm sorry, I know we didn't behave very well. But it was more Adrian than me.'

'He's going to be wondering what happened to you.'

'Adrian can talk babies with Bev. Serve him right for upsetting your neighbour. So who are you really?'

'Nobody.' Miranda was unrepentant. 'A trainee hairdresser.'

'That explains the hair.' Reaching up, he touched the feathery dark-blue tendrils at the nape of her neck. 'I like it.'

Miranda shivered. She liked it too. Things were beginning to hot up here.

'How about you, what do you do?' It wasn't exactly sparkling repartee, but time was short and she wanted to know.

'Something extremely boring. Insurance. You have my permission to yawn.'

'Are you single?'

'Oh yes.' Greg smiled. 'Are you?'

That smile. Those teeth. Plus, a thrillingly fit-looking body. Barely able to stop her knees knocking with excitement, Miranda nodded.

'In that case,' he took a pen out of his inside pocket, swiftly uncapping it, 'why don't you give me your phone number?'

God, I love a fast worker, thought Miranda.

She took the pen and waited.

'Paper?'

Greg shook his head.

'Haven't got any on me. Here, write on my hand. No, better make that my arm.' He began to fumble with a cuff link. 'We don't want to upset Adrian.'

Miranda, experiencing a brief pang of guilt, said, 'Or Bev.'

The next moment they both jumped at the sound of an aggrieved voice on the other side of the curtain.

'They can't have gone, they must be around here somewhere.'

Miranda froze. She heard Bev say, plaintively, 'But I've already looked in the bathroom.'

'Okay, ask that chap if he's seen your friend. Tell him you're looking for the girl with the blue hair.'

In the darkness, Greg was still struggling to unfasten his cuff link.

Too slow, too *slow*, Miranda thought frantically.

Grabbing the front of his shirt, she wrenched it open and began scrawling her phone number across his chest.

Chapter 11

Thank goodness it wasn't a hairy chest.

'Ouch,' whispered Greg, wincing as the sharp nib of the fountain pen dug into his skin.

'Sorry.' There, done. Hurriedly refastening the buttons, Miranda murmured, 'Next time, carry a magic marker.'

'I can take the pain.' He grinned at her. 'You're worth it.'

The curtain was abruptly whisked aside. Miranda sagged against the balcony railings.

'Oh, for heaven's sake, *there* you are.'

Bev sounded like a teacher berating a lost child on a school trip.

Adrian, peering suspiciously over her shoulder, said, 'What are you two doing out here?'

'Felt faint.' Sagging a little further, Miranda waved an apologetic arm in the direction of the party. 'Sorry, it was too hot in that room. I had to get some air. Oooh,' she clutched her stomach, 'I still feel a bit sick.'

'She needs to get home,' Greg told them. 'She's really not well.'

'If you throw up, you'll feel better in no time,' Adrian urged.

Miranda rolled her eyes.

'I don't think I will.'

'At least give it a try.' He looked dismayed. 'Oh, come on, you can't go home now, it's only ten o'clock! I was going to take you to Stringfellows.'

'Good grief,' said Bev, astonished. 'Stringfellows! Why?'

'She's famous, isn't she?' Adrian gave Bev a 'God-you're-stupid' look. 'And she knows Peter Stringfellow.'

'Not in the biblical sense,' Miranda put in hurriedly.

'Okay, but we won't have to pay to get in, will we?'

'No,' Bev muttered, 'you just have to pay to get out.'

Adrian thought it was a brilliant idea. He'd never been to Stringfellows. Furthermore, it was his lifetime ambition to be snapped by the paparazzi.

Generously he told Bev, 'You and Greg can come along too. I'm sure Peter won't mind.'

Oh dear, time to leave.

'I really do feel ill,' gasped Miranda.

'You pulled then,' said Bev in the cab on the way home.

'Mm. First prize in the Pillock of the Year contest.'

Having smeared baby lotion all over her face, Miranda was now wiping it off with a tissue. It was the only way; she never felt like removing her make-up once she got home.

'Adrian really fancied you.'

'Fancied the fact that I was an actress, you mean.'

'He'll definitely phone you.'

'No he won't,' said Miranda. 'I made that number up.'

Bev sighed.

'At least he asked for it.'

Oh help, more guilt.

And I shouldn't even feel guilty, Miranda thought frustratedly. All Greg had done was talk to Bev for half an hour. It wasn't as if he was her boyfriend, for heaven's sake.

'Greg didn't ask for yours?' To cover her shame, she slapped on another handful of baby lotion and began vigorously scrubbing away with the already shredded tissue.

'No.' Bev fiddled for a moment with one of her bracelets. 'Well, I gave it to him.'

'Oh.'

'Just to be on the safe side.' Bev sounded defensive. 'He might have meant to ask, but forgotten. Or he could have been too shy.'

'Right.'

'The thing is, I really liked him.' Miserably, Bev began picking at a snag on one of her stockings. Within seconds the snag had become a hole. 'I know Adrian was a prize pillock, but Greg was really nice.'

'Well, he might phone. You never know,' Miranda said feebly. The harder she tried not to think about scribbling her own number across Greg's naked chest, the more ashamed of herself she felt.

'He won't, he won't.' Bev shook her head, waving her hand in a 'give-me-that-tissue' kind of way. 'Who am I trying to kid? I've blown it, I'm never going to hear from him again.'

Over his shoulder, the taxi driver said, 'Come on, love, cheer up. Chances are he's not worth it anyway. He's probably married with five kids.'

Oh golly, thought Miranda, I hope not.

'He isn't married.' Bev blew her nose with an unromantic trumpeting noise like a mating elephant. 'I checked.'

'You mean you frisked him for peck-marks?' The taxi driver chuckled at his own wit.

But Bev was no longer listening. Instead she was gazing with revulsion at the tissue in her hands.

'When I asked you to pass me a tissue,' she told Miranda disgustedly, 'I meant a dry one.'

Gluey white baby lotion was sliding down both cheeks and dripping off her chin. The taxi driver, pulling up at traffic lights, swivelled round and said, 'Blimey, I saw a Hammer Horror film once just like that.'

'Sorry,' said Miranda, who had squirted a Mr Whippy-sized dollop out of the bottle, 'I thought you wanted to take your make-up off too.'

'Swampwoman,' cackled the driver, 'that's who you look like.'

'Taxi driver without a tip, that's what *you* look like,' Bev muttered. Honestly, were there *any* men left on the planet who weren't complete pigs?

Miranda knew as soon as the phone rang in her flat two days later that it was Greg. She felt her heart do a quick exultant tarantella at the sound of his voice on the other end of the line.

Which, at seven thirty in the morning, was no mean feat.

'The reason I didn't ring yesterday,' Greg announced, 'was because I was playing it cool.'

'Me too,' Miranda said joyfully. 'So it's just as well you didn't, because I wouldn't have answered the phone.'

He was smiling, she could tell.

'That's got that out of the way, then. We've done the being-cool bit. Now we're allowed to move on to stage two.' Greg paused. 'So, how are you?'

'Great. How's your chest?'

'Still covered in your phone number.' He sounded rueful. 'That was indelible ink, you know. I had four showers yesterday.'

'What you need is a Brillo pad,' said Miranda. 'That'll do the trick. Or you could use one of those sanding discs,' she added brightly. 'You just fit them on the end of your Black and Decker and off you go . . .'

Whoops, unintentional double-entendre. Miranda held her breath, praying Greg wouldn't let her down. If he said anything remotely building-sitey, she'd go off him in a flash.

Just because she'd ripped open his shirt and scribbled across his bare chest didn't mean he was allowed to be crude.

She almost jumped up and down and cheered when Greg passed the unspoken test.

'I may have to do that.' He sounded amused. 'Adrian's already wondering why I've taken to wearing a dressing gown around the house.'

'Tell him you're a born-again virgin and that nudity is a sin,' said Miranda. 'Has he tried ringing me yet?'

'Yesterday. He got through to a Mrs Finkelstein.'

'Was he okay about it?'

'Put it this way,' said Greg, 'he was on the phone for twenty minutes, begging at first, then getting madder and madder. When she finally hung up on him he yelled, "Can you believe it? Miranda's mother won't even let me speak to her, just because I'm not Jewish."'

Miranda, who had plucked the number out of thin air, sent a mental apology to poor, shouted-at Mrs Finkelstein.

'Anyway,' he went on, 'that's enough about Adrian. When can I see you?'

Double-checking, Miranda said, 'Have we definitely stopped playing it cool?'

'Definitely stopped.'

'Oh well, in that case,' she said happily, 'how about tonight?'

Crammed on to the tube forty minutes later, Miranda was strap-hanging and swaying in unison with everyone else in the carriage when she saw a face she recognised.

She ducked her head and peered more closely at the copy of the *Daily Mail* being held up by the woman against whom she was currently squashed hip-to-hip. The paper was open at the Dempster page and the girl she had spotted in the main photograph was Daisy Schofield.

The woman to whom the paper belonged was reading the other page. Annoyingly, she was obscuring with her fingers the bit Miranda most wanted to see. But Daisy Schofield was certainly looking happy enough, with her thin arms draped around the shoulders of some man or other – oh, come on, move your fingers – and although the accompanying text was partially hidden, Miranda was clearly able to make out the words 'in fine form', 'sizzling romance' and 'Wednesday night'.

So much for being laid up with a virus, thought Miranda. Elizabeth Turnbull had been right.

'Lying bitch,' she muttered under her breath.

When the woman flinched and glanced sideways in alarm, Miranda realised the words hadn't been as far under her breath as she'd thought. Oh well, never mind, maybe if she apologised and explained, the woman would move her fingers and let her read the rest of the piece.

But the owner of the newspaper was too fast for Miranda. Before she even had a chance to open her mouth, the train screeched to a halt at South Ken. The doors scissored open and the woman, still clutching her paper to her chest, jumped off.

Now I'll have to buy one myself, Miranda thought indignantly, peering after her. Honestly, some people were so *selfish*.

Chapter 12

'Yap yap,' said Miranda when Fenn arrived at the salon an hour later.

'I knew it.' Fenn raised his eyebrows at Bev. 'She's finally gone barking.'

'God, you're slow,' Miranda protested. 'It's Friday, isn't it? Tabitha day. You said I could be your guard dog.'

Tabitha Lester, known in the salon as Try-it-on Tabitha, had been a hugely successful actress back in the seventies. Now past her sell-by date but steadfastly refusing to admit it, she spent her days having face lifts and fat hoovered out of her thighs, and her nights tottering along to film premières on the arms of embarrassingly young men.

She also had a massive crush on Fenn, who had once gone to her house alone and had barely escaped with his leather trousers intact. Since then, his regular trips to Tabitha's home in St John's Wood were strictly chaperoned, much to her disgust and his relief.

Miranda loved going too. If Tabitha Lester was willing to pay silly money for a house call, she didn't mind at all. The house was vast and decorated in wonderfully over-the-top Hollywood style. They were always plied with Hollywood-type food, and Tabitha – in an attempt to weaken

Fenn's defences – was forever opening bottles of pink champagne.

'I don't know why you don't sleep with her,' said Miranda, feeling quite Hollywoody herself in the passenger seat of Fenn's gleaming black Lotus. 'Just make a hash of it, be completely useless. Then she won't pester you any more.'

'Is that your bright idea for the day?'

'It's a brilliant suggestion!'

'Right.' Fenn nodded. 'We're talking about the queen of the tabloids here. That'll do my reputation the world of good, won't it? I can just see the headline: "My Quickie with Crimper Fenn – a Wizard with Scissors, Crap in the Sack."'

'Yes, but no one would believe it,' Miranda protested. Fenn's girlfriends tended to be supermodels and he was generally regarded as one of London's most eligible bachelors.

When you were a gorgeous heterosexual hairdresser – and a very successful one, at that – well, you could do no wrong. You were officially a great catch.

'I'd rather not take that chance,' Fenn remarked, 'if it's all the same to you.'

'Fenn, you're looking wonderful as usual,' Tabitha exclaimed, greeting them on the doorstep. Drawing him inside, she confided, 'Do you know, I had the most amazing dream about you last night. Quite, quite naughty.' As she spoke, she winked at Miranda and jerked her head in the direction of the kitchen. 'Darling, it's Cook's day off. There's a Charentais melon in the fridge, and a mountain of Parma ham. Why don't you help yourself while Fenn and I head on upstairs?'

'Later,' Fenn said firmly, meaning in half an hour when

Tabitha's head was shrouded in foil and she couldn't pounce on him. 'I need Miranda to help me get started.'

'Yap yap,' Miranda murmured as the three of them trailed up the staircase, Tabitha clutching an unopened bottle of champagne in one hand and the hem of her sea-green négligé in the other.

For someone with five walk-in wardrobes stuffed with clothes, Tabitha appeared to spend an awful lot of her time wafting about in see-through nighties.

The master bedroom had been redecorated since Miranda's last visit, the ankle-deep turquoise shag pile having been replaced by ankle-deep ivory shag pile. The wallpaper, ivory and gold, matched the damask hangings artfully draped around the four-poster bed.

'This is nice.' Glancing inadvertently upwards, Miranda saw that the mirror was still there on the ceiling.

'I know.' Tabitha smiled meaningfully across at Fenn. 'I've got great taste. Oh, sorry, darling,' she went on as Miranda pulled out a chair and something metallic half buried in the carpet went clunk. 'Just pop them in that drawer, will you? Good girl.'

As she dropped the slim but efficient-looking gold handcuffs into the drawer, Miranda didn't dare look at Fenn. If she did, she knew she would burst out laughing. Biting her lip and gazing out of the window instead, she watched a bronzed figure in black shorts dive into the swimming pool below.

Although he was some distance away, she couldn't help thinking he looked familiar.

'Miranda, put some towels down around the chair,' Fenn instructed. 'We don't want bleach on the carpet.'

A second splash heralded the arrival in the pool of another figure, paler and fleshier than the first, and wearing multicoloured trunks. By the look of things, Tabitha had found herself a couple of toyboys.

'Miranda. Towels.'

'For heaven's sake, Fenn, give the girl a break,' Tabitha chided good-naturedly. 'She's just admiring my young friends.'

'Sorry, Fenn.' Miranda tore herself away. She was sure she'd seen the one in the black shorts somewhere before.

'Relax. Don't let him bully you.' Tabitha settled herself comfortably on to the chair.

Fenn, laying out the contents of his case, raised an eyebrow in disbelief.

'You're kidding. Miranda bullies me.'

'Oh, I love a man who knows his place,' Tabitha said with a smirk. The kind of smirk that signified, *especially when he's handcuffed to a four-poster*.

'Foil, please, Miranda.' Fenn was beginning to sound slightly desperate.

'Come on, let's open this first.' Patting his arm in a soothing manner, Tabitha handed him the bottle, managing to brush her wrist against his thigh en route. 'You do the honours. Popping the cork is a man's job.' She winked again, saucily, at Miranda. 'Poor Fenn, all on edge this morning. He looks as if he could do with a drink.'

Retouching Tabitha's bombshell-blonde highlights took three-quarters of an hour. By the time the last few greying roots had been painstakingly painted and wrapped in foil, the furious growls emanating from Miranda's empty stomach had reached bear-like proportions.

'Go on, run downstairs and get some food inside you.' Waving her empty glass at Fenn, Tabitha indicated that she was in need of a refill.

Miranda glanced at Fenn, who nodded. For the next twenty minutes he was safe; even Try-it-on Tabitha wouldn't risk dislodging the dozens of little foil packets and wrecking her hair.

Besides, if Miranda didn't eat soon they were going to need earplugs.

The kitchen door, leading out on to the sun terrace, was open. As Miranda crouched in front of the fridge, drooling at the sight of Parma ham, marinated mushrooms and punnets of strawberries, she could hear the sounds of shouts and splashing outside in the pool.

She was carrying a ciabatta loaf and the Charentais melon over to the table when a wolf-whistle behind her made her jump. Twisting around, she lost her grip on the melon, which slid out of her hand and went bowling across the floor.

'Hey, great idea!' It was the paler of the two men she had seen from the window earlier. Scooping it up, he grinned at her. 'Water polo!'

'You can't take that melon,' Miranda protested. 'Tabitha just asked me to cut it up—'

'I am a representative of the Melon Liberation Front,' the intruder declaimed, spinning it basketball-style on the tip of his index finger. 'This melon' – dripping water all over the tiled floor, he began to back away – 'shall Be Free!'

He was out of the door in a flash. Miranda, who had spent the last hour daydreaming about melon, skidded across the wet floor after him.

Racing on to the terrace, she was just in time to see the

melon sailing through the air. It landed with a splash in the pool and was promptly leapt on by the other man. Shaking his blond hair out of his eyes, he held the melon triumphantly aloft.

'Don't let her have it,' yelled his friend. 'She's a murderer.'

'Look,' Miranda tried to sound reasonable, 'you can't play water polo with a melon.'

'We aren't playing water polo,' said the blond one, 'we're playing watermelon.'

Grinning broadly, he lobbed it over Miranda's head, where it was neatly caught by his friend. Miranda, beginning to feel stupid, moved towards him.

The melon flew over her head once more.

'Look, you can play too if you like,' the blond one offered. 'You can be on my team.'

He was by far the better-looking of Tabitha's two toyboys. What was more, he was still tantalisingly familiar. If his hair wasn't plastered to his head and he had clothes on, Miranda thought, she was sure she'd recognise him.

'Do I know you?'

'Of course you do. I'm the other half of your watermelon team. Come on,' he said persuasively, 'jump in. The water's fantastic.'

'Look, I'd love to play watermelon with you' – she was still trying to humour him – 'but I just can't.'

Big mistake.

'No such thing as can't!' The one in the multicoloured trunks, having loomed up behind her, lobbed the melon back into the water. Grabbing Miranda around the waist, he lifted her into his arms and raced to the edge of the pool.

Right up to the last second, she was convinced he'd stop.

He didn't.

With a monumental splash, they landed together in the deep end. Miranda shuddered as the icy water caused every cell in her body to contract with shock.

By the time she had swum back to the surface, the better-looking toyboy was treading water next to her.

'Well, that's a relief. For a minute there I thought you couldn't swim.' His green eyes were alight with laughter, his tone conversational. 'Thought I was going to have to rescue you.'

He was still clutching the melon. Miranda made a grab for it.

'Oh dear, I can see I need to explain the rules of watermelon to you.' Effortlessly, he whisked it out of her reach. 'You see, we're on the same side. You're meant to tackle the opposition, not me.'

Miranda's teeth began to chatter. Keeping afloat fully clothed was no picnic either.

'This p-pool isn't heated. You l-lied to me.'

'I didn't.' He grinned, his teeth Persil-white against his tanned face. 'I told you the water was fantastic, I didn't say anything about it being warm.'

'I am going to get into so much trouble for this.' Miranda glanced fearfully up at Tabitha's bedroom window. No sign of Fenn's outraged face, thank goodness.

'Oh, come on, you're in now.' Her team-mate held the melon towards her in enticing fashion. 'Just one game.'

'I've got my shoes on.'

'Take them off.'

'I'm still wearing all my clothes!'

He didn't say anything, just grinned at her. His eyes were extraordinary, Miranda realised now that she was close enough to tell, an intense greeny-blue with yellow flecks.

'Hey, you two! Are we playing watermelon or not?'

The one in the multicoloured trunks had by this time clambered out of the pool. 'Over here!' he bellowed, pointing to his forehead.

'Don't!' Miranda clapped both hands over her eyes as her teammate took aim. 'You'll knock him unconscious.'

'Nothing knocks Johnnie unconscious.'

He was right. The melon came off worse. The force of the impact split it in half, and seeds and juice exploded in all directions like shrapnel.

'Ouch,' said Johnnie, scooping a lump of orange melon flesh off his shoulder and popping it into his mouth.

'You killed it,' Miranda said sorrowfully. 'I'm reporting you to the MLF.'

'Too late,' murmured her playing partner as Fenn appeared on the terrace. 'Looks like they're already here.'

Chapter 13

Miranda sat huddled on one of the kitchen chairs with a towel around her shoulders and a spreading puddle of chlorinated water at her feet. Her teeth chattered dramatically against the rim of her coffee cup. Her hair, which had been subjected to a cruelly brisk towel-dry by Fenn, stood out in spikes.

'I can't take you anywhere.'

'It wasn't my fault,' Miranda protested. 'Blame melonhead. He was the one who threw me in.'

'But why does it always have to happen to you?' Mystified, Fenn shook his head.

'I don't know. Stuff just does.' Even as a child, Miranda gloomily remembered, her despairing mother had called her incident-prone.

'Those naughty boys,' said Tabitha, appearing in the doorway with an armful of dry clothes. 'I'm going to give them a good talking-to. Here you are, darling, pop upstairs to my room and get yourself out of those wet things.'

In Tabitha's bedroom, Miranda peeled off her sodden clothes, dried herself and changed into a white sweatshirt and leggings. Sitting on the edge of the bed to pull on a pair of pink angora socks, she felt something crackle behind her and pulled out a copy of the *Daily Mail* from under the rumpled bedspread.

Tabitha had even left it lying open at the Dempster page, which was handy. One sock on and one sock off, Miranda leaned over to find out exactly what Daisy Schofield had been up to on Wednesday night.

There was a knock on the door.

'Are you decent?'

'As I'll ever be.'

The bedroom door swung open. Her team-mate, now fully dressed and with his blond hair slicked back from his face, said, 'Is your boss furious with you?'

'No, but I'm not too thrilled with you.' Miranda recognised him at once with his clothes on. She pointed an accusing finger at the photograph in the paper. 'What were you doing on Wednesday night with Daisy Schofield?'

He grinned.

'Are you sure you want to know?'

No wonder he had looked familiar. Miles Harper, Formula One racing driver, had burst on to the motor-racing scene less than a year ago, but the publicity he attracted was unrelenting. With his extravagant good looks, undoubted talent and laid-back personality, he was being touted as the new James Hunt.

'I'm not interested in gory details. I meant, *why* was she with you?'

'Probably because she fancies me.' Miles Harper winked. 'Oh dear, don't tell me you're jealous.'

'Daisy Schofield was meant to be at a cocktail party. She cancelled, said she was ill. Or rather you did,' Miranda pointedly remarked, realising that the mystery man who had spoken to Elizabeth Turnbull on the phone must have been him. She frowned. 'You lied. Wasn't that a bit of a mean thing to do?'

'You went to the party, I take it?'

'Yes.'

'Was it dull?'

Miranda hesitated. She'd been okay, she'd met Greg. But if she hadn't, it would have been crashingly dull.

'There you are then.' When she didn't immediately reply, Miles Harper shrugged, unconcerned. 'That's why she didn't go.'

'But she was a celebrity guest.' Miranda wanted to make him understand. 'You wouldn't like it if you organised a charity event and nobody else bothered to turn up.'

'Oh.' He had the grace – at last – to look ashamed. 'I didn't know it was for charity.'

Miranda wasn't sure whether or not she believed him.

'Anyway, what are you doing here?' Changing the subject, she wriggled the angora sock on to her foot. 'When I saw the two of you in the pool, I thought you were Tabitha's latest toyboys.'

Miles laughed.

'Johnnie dragged me along, that's all. He's an old mate of mine and Tabitha's his godmother. Five minutes after meeting her,' he went on, 'I realised the middle of the swimming pool was the safest place to be. I'm telling you, that woman has seriously wandering hands.'

'Weren't you scared she might jump in after you?'

'She told us her hairdresser was on his way over, so

she mustn't get her hair wet. That,' he told Miranda with a crooked smile, 'was when I dived in.'

'If you can handle a Formula One racing car, I'd have thought you could cope with a middle-aged nymphomaniac.'

Miles considered this for a second.

'The difference is, Tabitha doesn't have brakes.'

Downstairs once more, with her soggy clothes bundled into a Fortnum and Mason carrier bag, she was formally introduced to Johnnie, Tabitha's godson. He dutifully apologised for giving her a ducking. Miranda in turn admired the splendid bump on his forehead, inflicted by the melon. Then it was time to roll up the sleeves of her borrowed white sweatshirt and help Fenn with the defoiling of Tabitha.

'Aunt Tab, we're off.' Johnnie poked his dark head around the bathroom door as Miranda massaged conditioner into Tabitha's scalp.

'Have fun, you two. Don't do anything I wouldn't do.' Tabitha's head was bent over the basin. 'And where's Miles? I haven't had my goodbye kiss yet.'

'His manager called. He's outside, on the phone.' Johnnie's wink indicated that Miles had legged it to the sanctuary of his car. 'By the way,' he addressed Miranda, 'we're off to a party at the Unicorn Club tonight. Miles wondered if you'd like to come along.'

Astonished, Miranda stopped massaging. She felt her cheeks go pink with pleasure.

Miles Harper was actually inviting her to a party?

Well, maybe not asking her himself, but getting his friend to invite her.

Golly, was that exciting or what?

She had been beaming idiotically at Johnnie for a couple

of seconds before her brain clicked in, reminding her why she'd been in such a good mood this morning and why she was already looking forward to tonight.

Talk about rotten timing.

'I'd love to.' Miranda's insides crumpled with regret. 'I mean, I would have loved to. But I can't, not this evening. I've already . . . er, got something on.'

'Okay.' Johnnie sounded unperturbed. It clearly didn't bother him either way.

But it bothers *me*, Miranda thought frustratedly.

'What a shame, it would have been great.' She plastered a bright smile on to her face. 'Maybe another night? I mean, I'm usually free. In fact, *any* other evening and I'd definitely be able to make it.'

She clamped her runaway lips together. Oh dear, how desperate could a single girl get? Now she sounded like Bev.

Johnnie, nodding, checked his watch and backed out of the bathroom door.

'Okay, right, see you around.'

'You blew it,' Tabitha said flatly when he had gone. 'Darling, you must be mad. With people like Miles Harper, you don't get a second chance.'

Miranda poured an extra dollop of conditioner into her hand and gloomily resumed the scalp massage. Typical. Six whole months since her last boyfriend, and now this had to happen. Maybe it was God's way of punishing her for pinching Greg from Bev.

'So what is it you're doing tonight?' Tabitha persisted with annoying cheerfulness. 'Flying over to LA for the première of the new Tarantino movie? A cosy dinner for two at the Ritz with Leonardo DiCaprio?'

'I met this chap on Wednesday night,' Miranda mumbled. 'It's our first date.' She couldn't bring herself to say they'd probably go for a couple of lukewarm beers and a limp pizza.

'Would I have heard of him?'

'No. He works in insurance.'

'Good grief.' Tabitha burst out laughing. 'And you turned down Miles Harper for that!' Rather heartlessly, in Miranda's view, she went on, 'I only hope he's worth it.'

Remembering suddenly how unreliable men were and how often she had been let down in the past, Miranda wondered if Greg would even turn up tonight.

Feeling distinctly uneasy, she murmured, 'So do I.'

Chapter 14

Chloe had known she was making a big mistake when she phoned her mother the night before. But some things – no matter how much you didn't want to do them – had to be done.

'What do you mean, he's left you?' Pamela Greening had barked when she had finally managed to stammer out the words. 'Chloe, don't be ridiculous, is this your idea of a joke? Why on earth would Greg want to leave you?'

Quailing in the face of her mother's wrath, Chloe had promptly chickened out of telling her about the baby. Instead she had mumbled something feeble about not getting on and things not really working out.

'My God, that boy has a nerve! You just wait until I get my hands on him, I'll make him realise—'

'Mum, please, there's nothing you can do,' Chloe had begged. 'He's gone. It's not the end of the world. Marriages break up all the time.'

'Not in our family they don't,' her mother had grimly replied. 'Never before in our family.'

'Well, one has now.'

'You give up too easily, my girl. You always have.'

'Oh, for heaven's sake,' Chloe had yelled, exasperated,

'what was I supposed to do, tie him up and lock him in the broom cupboard?'

'Now you're just being stupid. There are ways and means, Chloe. If you want to keep your husband there are *always* ways and means.'

Her mother had sounded almost crosser with her than she was with Greg.

That had been last night. And now it was about to get worse.

As she rounded the corner, Chloe saw the familiar outline of her mother standing on the pavement outside her flat.

'Mum, you didn't have to do this. Truly, I'm fine.'

'You've put on weight.'

No kiss, no reassuring hug, thought Chloe. No words of comfort either.

Oh well, no change there.

'A bit.' She sucked in as much of her stomach as she could.

'Come on then, where's your key? Three hours on the coach, this trip's taken. You can make me a cup of tea before we get down to business.'

'What business?' Fumbling, Chloe fitted the key in the lock. The flat wasn't hideously untidy, but her mother wouldn't be impressed when she spotted last night's saucepans still lounging in the sink.

'Greg, of course.'

'But—'

'Don't even try and talk me out of it, Chloe. That lad stood up in church and made public vows. Marriage is for life,' she wagged a terrifying finger at her daughter, 'not for as long as it suits him. He needs to be reminded of that,' she announced ominously. 'And if you won't do it, I will.'

After a long day at work, Chloe was exhausted. To give herself a bit of breathing space, she went on ahead into the kitchen.

'I'll make that pot of tea. If you're staying the night, you can have my bed and I'll sleep on the sofa.' Since her mother was carrying a small suitcase, she guessed this was the plan. 'But you aren't going to be able to lecture Greg about his wedding vows,' she called over her shoulder – quite bravely for her – 'because he isn't here.'

'We aren't all as useless as you,' her mother retorted. 'I'm going to pay him a visit, aren't I?'

Startled, Chloe looked around. Her mother was standing in the kitchen doorway like Wyatt Earp in a crimplene shift, brandishing a notebook in one hand and a biro in the other.

'You can't do that!'

'Just give me his address.'

'I don't have it.'

'Don't be ridiculous.'

'I'm not,' Chloe lied, her palms beginning to sweat. 'I don't know where he is.'

She did. Word had filtered through on the local grapevine that Greg had moved in with Adrian, but she'd had enough pride not to contact him.

Largely because there was no point.

And if there was anything more publicly humiliating, thought Chloe, than turning up on the doorstep of the husband who'd dumped you, begging him to change his mind and come back . . . well, it was having your mother do it for you.

'I can always tell when you're lying,' said Pamela Greening. 'Of course you know where he is.'

Chloe's hands shook as she poured boiling water into the sugar bowl. Oh God, how much more of this could she take?

'Mum, Greg's gone. He didn't tell me where. I haven't seen or spoken to him for weeks. Now why don't you stop interrogating me, put your pen away and just go and unpack?'

For a woman who wore Hush Puppies, Pamela Greening could certainly stomp her feet. Taking a deep breath, Chloe managed this time to fill the teapot. She was emptying the sugar bowl down the sink when the stomping grew louder. The floor began to quiver.

Oh, for heaven's sake, thought Chloe wearily, what now? It was like something out of *Jurassic Park*.

The split second before she turned round, she guessed.

But since there was no chance of escape – not even through the tiny kitchen window, which would never accommodate her hips – she turned anyway.

Her mother was doing that Wyatt Earp thing again. Only this time she was clutching a copy of the paperback Chloe had been reading last night in bed.

Miriam Stoppard's *Book of Pregnancy and Birth*.

At that moment Chloe quite envied Greg. She wished she'd never given her mother this address.

'Oh yes.' Bracing herself, she mumbled, 'I forgot to mention it. I'm expecting a baby.'

Pamela Greening's face went purple, then white, then purple again.

Finally she thundered, '*Whose?*'

*　　*　　*

107

It took Pamela no time at all to find out where her runaway son-in-law was now living.

Thirty seconds to look up the number of his insurance company in Chloe's Yellow Pages.

Another thirty seconds to learn that Greg had left the office early.

Forty-five seconds to inform his startled secretary that it was imperative – yes, *imperative* – she be given his new address. 'I don't care what your company policy is. My name is Dr Blake and I'm calling from St Thomas's Hospital. I need to speak to Gregory Malone regarding a matter of extreme urgency.'

At the other end of the sitting room, cringing on the sofa, it occurred to Chloe that her mother had been watching too many episodes of *Hetty Wainthropp Investigates*.

When it came to intimidation, Patricia Routledge had nothing on her.

'There.' Pamela hung up the phone and stuck the address under her daughter's nose. 'You could have done that.'

Chloe watched her grimly shove her arms back into her sensible navy mac.

'Oh no, you can't do this.'

'Watch me.'

'It'll just make things worse!'

The look her mother gave her was loaded with contempt.

'You're pregnant. He's abandoned you. How much worse can it get?'

'He's not here.' Warily Adrian clutched the towel around his hips. He dimly remembered Chloe's ferocious mother from the wedding, when she had told him in no uncertain terms to stop dancing on the tables.

'You mean he's hiding upstairs, too frightened to face me? Tell Gregory his mother-in-law is here to see him and I'm not moving from this spot until I do.'

'But he isn't, I swear! You just missed him,' Adrian insisted. 'He left five minutes ago. You can search the house if you like.'

Pamela Greening eyed the stranger before her with distaste. If Gregory wasn't there, she wasn't about to put herself at risk by entering a house with a naked man in it.

'What time will he be back?'

This, Adrian thought fleetingly, rather depended on whether or not Greg got lucky with whoever he was seeing tonight. But since Chloe's battleaxe of a mother wasn't likely to appreciate this information, he said, 'I don't know. Probably not too late.'

Just as well he was going out himself. He didn't envy Greg one bit.

Before leaving the house an hour later, Adrian wrote a note on the back of a gas bill and propped it up in full view on the kitchen table.

Poor Greg, the least he could do was warn him that his mother-in-law was in town and on the loose.

At the end of the road, not taking any chances, Pamela Greening lurked behind a postbox. She watched Gregory's friend let himself out of the house and head up the road in the opposite direction.

No sign of Gregory.

She rang the doorbell again, to check. Still no reply.

Never mind, she was in no hurry.

Grimly Pamela thought, I can wait.

It wasn't a terrible anticlimax. Miranda had been petrified it would be, but it wasn't. When she saw Greg climb out of his car outside the house – looking even more handsome than she'd remembered – she found herself leaning so far out of her bedroom window that she almost toppled out.

Grinning and waving like some besotted groupie, she yelled, 'I'm coming down. You're *early*.'

Not very cool, maybe, but who cared?

Certainly not Greg, who grinned and waved back, and shouted up, 'I couldn't wait.'

He took her to Le Vin Rose, an unpretentious candle-lit wine bar in Bayswater packed with couples holding hands.

'How's your chest?' said Miranda, and he undid the middle button on his shirt, revealing the scrawl of faded black numbers.

'They won't go. I'm tattooed for life.'

'God, I'm sorry.'

'I'm not.' Smiling, Greg buttoned himself back up. 'Some people are worth getting tattooed for. Did you tell Bev who you were seeing tonight?'

'I couldn't. She's still suicidal because you didn't ring her. How about you?'

'Oh, I'm not suicidal.'

'Berk. I meant, have you told Adrian yet?'

'No.'

'Every time Bev mentions your name,' Miranda blurted out, 'I blush. Honestly, it's mad. I feel so guilty, as if I'm sneaking around with somebody who's *married*.'

110

'You poor thing.' Greg took her hand, curling his fingers protectively over hers. 'So you've had a terrible day?'

The physical contact sent quivers of pleasure zooming up Miranda's arm and down her spine. Heavens, it was ages since she'd felt like this.

'Actually, it wasn't that bad. I went for a swim with Miles Harper in Tabitha Lester's swimming pool. He invited me to a party tonight but I had to turn him down because I was seeing you. Still, he was okay about it.' She shrugged, flicking her blue-tipped fringe out of her eyes. 'He took it pretty well, in fact.'

'Same here,' Greg confided. 'I had Madonna in the office this morning, pestering me to take her out to dinner tonight. Had to call security in the end to get rid of her. *No*, Madonna, I kept telling her, I can't see you this evening, I've already arranged to meet Miranda.'

Having opened her mouth to say yes, but he was joking and she wasn't, Miranda promptly shut it again. Boasting wasn't an attractive quality in a girl. Besides, what if Miles Harper did contact her? Much as she liked Greg, it was very early days. Being brutally honest here, if Miles rang the salon and invited her out again – and this time she happened to be free – well, she'd be there like a shot.

Instead, she said gravely, 'Thank you. I'm glad you chose me.'

'So am I. Glad you chose me, I mean. You wouldn't want to get involved with Miles Harper anyway,' Greg assured her. 'You can't trust blokes like that, they'd mess you around no end.'

'Oh, I know.'

'He's seeing Daisy Schofield,' he went on. 'There was a picture of them together in the paper this morning.'

Miranda took a gulp of wine. She nodded sagely over the rim of her glass.

'I saw it too.'

An hour later, Miranda's stomach began to rumble noisily. Too nervous to eat earlier, she was now starving.

'I've booked a table at L'Etoile,' said Greg, 'for nine thirty.'

'You always say just the right thing.' She could have kissed him. This was a definite step up from warm beer and soggy pizza.

Not that she was mercenary, but it showed he cared, Miranda thought hastily, hugging herself as she watched Greg make his way over to the bar to settle their bill. In fact the evening was going so well, she wouldn't care if pizza was all she ate.

I've met someone I really like, she thought joyfully, and he really likes me too.

'Damn.' Greg was back, frowning. 'My credit card's expired.'

'Oh!' Miranda reached for her bag and began hunting for her purse. 'I've got some money here somewhere . . .'

'It's okay, I had enough cash on me to pay the bill.' He motioned her to put her purse away. 'It just means a bit of a detour. The new card's at home. I need to pick it up before we head for the restaurant.'

Chapter 15

Not keen to be arrested for loitering, Pamela Greening had spent the last two and a half hours pacing the length of Milligan Road, planning in detail what she would say to her abysmal son-in-law when she finally got her hands on him.

She was at the far end of the street, three hundred yards from the house, when she spotted a familiar car approaching from the pillar-box end.

Oh yes, that was definitely his white Rover pulling up under the streetlamp outside number forty-two.

Pulling her navy mac more tightly around her waist, Pamela marched purposefully towards the car.

'Two seconds,' Greg assured Miranda as he climbed out. 'I know exactly where it is.'

'Don't worry, I'm not going anywhere.' Waving him off, Miranda turned up the volume on the stereo as U2 launched into 'Sunday Bloody Sunday'. This was blissful, they even shared the same taste in music. Imagine how horrible it would be, meeting someone as perfect as Greg, the two of you getting on like a house on fire, and then discovering that while you were a U2 girl, he was a . . . well, a Des O'Connor man.

With her eyes closed and the music blasting out, Miranda neither saw nor heard the middle-aged woman in the tightly belted mac hiss the word 'Whore!' at her through the car's closed window before storming up the front path.

In the kitchen, Greg stared in disbelief at the scrawled note Adrian had left propped up against a dirty coffee cup.

Warning! Your mother-in-law was here looking for you and she's *coming back later*. If you want to hang on to your ging-gangs, hide the bread knife!
    Cheers, Ade.

PS If you murder her and need to dispose of the body, use the black binliners under the sink.

It was all right for Adrian to joke about it, Greg thought, she wasn't his mother-in-law. Then he went hot and cold; if they hadn't been late for the restaurant and Miranda had come in with him, she would have seen the damning note.

Crushing the gas bill into a ball, he threw it into the bin.

He liked Miranda a lot, too much to want to blow it on their first date. He certainly wasn't about to tell her he was married, with a pregnant wife. Not that that was his fault, Greg thought with renewed irritation, but some girls could be funny about things like that.

So much for tidying his bedroom earlier and changing the sheets. No way now was he going to risk inviting Miranda back later for a nightcap.

The sudden shrill of the doorbell made him jump. Jesus, who was *that*?

Miranda?

Or the mother-in-law from hell?

Feeling sick, Greg realised that either way, he couldn't not answer it.

Praying it was Miranda, he pulled open the front door.

His head jerked back as Pamela Greening slapped him hard across the face.

'So that's why you left, is it?' Furiously she indicated the car behind her with Miranda inside. 'That's why you abandoned my daughter? Well, let me tell you, I won't stand for it! You're going to face up to your responsibilities, my lad. Chloe needs her husband, that baby needs a father and you have a *duty* to—'

'Pamela, not now.'

Greg froze as over his mother-in-law's shoulder he saw Miranda, in the passenger seat, observing the goings-on. This was a nightmare. He had to get out of here fast.

'Oh no you don't,' Pamela Greening yelled as he slammed the front door shut behind him and tried to move past her. 'I came here to talk to you!'

'I don't need this.' Gritting his teeth, he forcibly removed her clawing hand from his arm. 'I do *not need* this.'

In the car, Miranda stared open-mouthed at the bizarre scene. Until a few seconds ago she had been oblivious to everything, drumming her heels and singing along with Bono. Only when the last stirring chords of the song had faded away had she opened her eyes and seen Greg remonstrating with a middle-aged woman on his doorstep.

Now she watched him push past her and head back to the car. As he yanked open the driver's door, she heard the woman – hot on his heels – shout furiously, 'You're not going to get away with this!'

'My God, what's going on?' squealed Miranda.

'Just ignore her.'

'You *won't* ignore me! I'll make you sorry you ever—'

As the engine roared into life, Greg managed to wrench the door shut. The woman, her hands still scrabbling at the handle, leapt away as he stuck his foot down and screeched off down the road.

'Sorry about that.'

'Greg, who *was* she?' Miranda swivelled round in her seat, peering back at the woman on the pavement. Then she turned and stared at Greg. 'What the hell was that about?'

He shook his head and braked as they took the corner.

'Client with a grudge. It happens, I'm afraid. She and her husband took out massive life insurance. Then he killed himself. The policy didn't cover suicide but she won't accept that.' Greg breathed out slowly. They were safe now; his hands had stopped shaking. 'Poor woman, I think she's lost her mind. I've told her a hundred times the insurance isn't valid and that the company aren't going to pay out. But it just doesn't sink in. She thinks I'm cheating her out of three hundred grand.'

'You're kidding!' Miranda's eyes were like saucers. 'That's *terrible*.'

Greg nodded.

'She's been harassing me at the office. Now, clearly, she's found out where I live. I mean, I feel sorry for her, but what can I do?'

'Tell the police, for a start.' Urgently, Miranda clutched his arm. 'She could be dangerous!'

Bloody dangerous, thought Greg.

'We've already spoken to the police. It's not worth it.

116

They can't arrest her until she actually does something illegal. But they're aware of the situation,' he added. 'If my windows get smashed or the house burns to the ground, they'll have a good idea who to blame.'

'If your *house* burns to the ground?' Miranda echoed the words, aghast.

'Don't worry,' Greg smiled at her, 'I'm fully insured.'

Was that meant to be reassuring? Miranda wasn't the least bit reassured. It was, she thought indignantly, an outrageous state of affairs.

'But what about breach of the peace, can't they get her for that? Or . . . or, those stalking laws,' she exclaimed. 'I mean, that's what this madwoman's doing, isn't it? Stalking you?'

Any minute now, Greg sensed, Miranda was liable to make a dash for the nearest phone box and start dialling 999.

'She's an old lady,' he told her, 'who's just lost her husband. She's out of her mind with grief. Would a spell in Holloway really do any good? And besides,' he went on gently, 'imagine how I'd feel, knowing I'd helped to put her there. I wouldn't be able to live with myself.'

'Stop the car,' said Miranda.

'What?'

'I said, stop the car.'

'Why?'

Nervously, Greg looked around for a phone box. He couldn't see one, but dare he risk it?

'Because you are the nicest, kindest, most generous man I have ever met.' Her voice catching with emotion, Miranda reached for him. 'And I'm sorry, but I just have to give you a massive, *massive* kiss.'

'Okay, moment-of-truth time,' Greg murmured several highly satisfactory minutes later. 'You may be about to change your mind about me.'

Miranda, wondering if she'd ever been happier in her life, kissed his earlobe before snuggling her head further into the curve of his shoulder.

'Why?'

'I have a confession to make.'

'About what?'

'The bit about me being generous.'

'Why?'

'My credit card. I forgot to pick it up.'

'Oh. Well, I've got eight pounds in my purse.'

'I've got about eight pounds fifty.' Greg's smile was rueful.

Miranda turned his watch towards her and peered at the hands in the dim amber glow of the overhead streetlight.

'We've missed our table now anyway. That's all right.'

'Why is it all right?' said Greg.

Between kisses, Miranda whispered, 'Because sometimes I actually prefer pizza.'

Chapter 16

Saturday was always the busiest day in the shop. By five o'clock Chloe was looking forward to getting home and putting her aching feet up. Or she would have been, if only she knew her mother wasn't going to be there, ready to launch into round three of her tirade against Greg.

'Hell,' Bruce said suddenly, 'I haven't done the present yet.'

'What present?'

'Mother's. It's her birthday, that's why we're all trooping round there tonight.'

By the way he rolled his eyes, Chloe guessed he wasn't enthralled by the prospect of a duty visit to Florence.

'What are you getting her?'

'God knows.' Faster than a lizard's tongue, Bruce's gaze flickered over the stock on display. 'Something around the hundred-pound mark. That fruit bowl, maybe. No, she had one of those for Christmas. Ah, candlesticks, that'll do. Those two over there.' As he nodded towards a pair of enamelled silver candlesticks, he picked up the phone and began punching out a number. 'Gift-wrap them for me, would you, Chloe? There's a good girl. And pick out a card.' With his free hand he gestured towards the carousel.

119

'I don't know what kind of card your mother would like.' Chloe was indignant, hurt on Florence's behalf.

'She's sixty-two years old.' Bruce hunched his shoulders impatiently. 'What more d'you need to know? Just grab something with flowers on.'

As she listened to him arranging a game of golf for tomorrow morning, Chloe wondered if he expected her to sign the card as well, maybe pp it on his behalf. She had never met Bruce's mother but they had chatted briefly on the phone several times when Florence had rung the shop to speak to him.

She'd sounded brilliant, Chloe thought rebelliously. Far nicer than her mean old son.

'Use the gold paper,' Bruce called over his shoulder.

'You mean the three-pounds-a-sheet stuff?' Behind his back Chloe pulled a scandalised face.

'What the hell.' He flapped a pudgy, indulgent hand in the air. 'It's her birthday. She likes a bit of gold.'

'I'm sorry, we're about to close,' Bruce informed the customer pushing the door open at five thirty.

'I know that, I'm Chloe's mother.' More than a match for Bruce, Pamela Greening swept past him. 'He still isn't at home,' she told Chloe, who was lugging a box of china Dalmatians out of the stockroom. 'That's four times I've been round there today and no one's in. Out with his floozy, I'll be bound. Scared to face me. Should you be lifting that?' She fixed her daughter with a disapproving eye.

Too late, Chloe realised that there were one or two facts she should have warned her mother not to mention in front of Bruce.

'Mum, I don't care if Greg's out with his floozy.' It was a lie, but Bruce's attention had to be diverted somehow. 'I don't care if he has a whole harem of floozies. Mum went to see him last night,' she told Bruce, pink-cheeked, 'and he was with a girl.'

'So that's why he walked out on you. He's found someone else.' Bruce nodded; he had suspected as much all along. Then he frowned. 'But—'

'Okay if I leave these until Monday,' Chloe blurted out, 'now that Mum's here? And you've got Florence's birthday do to get to . . . oh, mustn't forget the present . . .' She thrust the gift-wrapped box, trailing spirals of gold ribbon, into Bruce's unsuspecting arms. He stared down at it, then with bewilderment back at her.

'Why shouldn't you be lifting anything heavy?'

'Bad back. Nothing to worry about,' Chloe assured him. 'Just a touch of psoriasis.'

'Psoriasis?'

'Not psoriasis. Sciatica.' Was that right? She felt herself break into a light sweat. 'Or lumbago.' That was definitely a back-achey kind of thing. 'Maybe lumbago,' she amended, 'the doctor wasn't sure.'

'You didn't tell me you had lumbago.' Pamela Greening's tone was accusing.

'It's not serious, just the occasional twinge. Come on, Mum, let's go.'

'All right, all right, but you watch yourself,' her mother warned. 'You shouldn't be lugging heavy boxes around anyway.' For good measure she wagged a finger at Chloe. 'It's no good for the baby.'

*   *   *

121

'Stay,' Florence urged when the doorbell rang. 'Just for a bit.' She gulped down her tumbler of whisky. 'I can't face them sober. Lord, this is worse than a visit from Social Services.'

Miranda got up to answer the door.

'I'll stay on one condition. If Jason kicks me, I'm allowed to lock him in the microwave.'

'Happy birthday, Mother.' Dutifully Bruce pecked Florence's powdered cheek.

'Many happy returns,' Verity echoed, nudging Jason forwards. 'Go on, darling, give Granny a kiss.'

'You smell of whisky,' Jason told Florence.

'Thank heavens for that, I'd hate to think I'd been drinking cold tea. And speaking of drinks.' She turned to Miranda, who was gazing with longing in the direction of the microwave. 'Could you be an angel and do the honours?'

The birthday gift was unwrapped and duly admired. Elegant though the candlesticks were, they weren't to Florence's taste.

'Beautiful, Bruce. Really beautiful. Wherever did you find them?'

This was purely for Florence's own amusement; did he seriously think she didn't know?

'Spotted them in a little shop down in Covent Garden.' Bruce looked pleased with himself.

'You should track down their supplier. This kind of thing would sell well in your shop. How's business, by the way?'

'Oh, pretty good. Pretty good.'

'And Chloe?'

Bruce's expression changed. He shook his head.

'Ah well, bad news there. She's pregnant.'

'Oh dear. Chloe's husband left her only a few weeks ago,' Florence briefly explained to Miranda. 'My word, what a muddle. Poor Chloe.'

'Never mind poor Chloe,' spluttered Bruce. 'Poor *me*, more like.'

Florence kept a straight face.

'Oh Bruce, what *have* you been up to? Don't tell me the baby's yours.'

Now it was Verity's turn to splutter.

'Florence, of course it isn't his!'

'Joke,' said Florence.

'It's not a joking matter,' Verity declared vehemently. 'How can Chloe *do* this to Bruce? She'll be wanting maternity pay, for heaven's sake! Months and months off work, money for doing absolutely nothing—'

'She won't be getting it, of course,' Bruce interrupted. 'I'll have to sack her. But it's not going to be pleasant . . . and as for the inconvenience it's going to—'

'Oof!' gasped Miranda as Jason kicked her.

'Darling,' Verity cooed, 'how many times have I asked you not to do that? People don't like to be kicked.'

'You can't sack Chloe just because she's pregnant,' Florence protested. 'That's awful. Anyway, aren't there laws against that kind of thing?'

'I can see up your skirt,' Jason told Miranda.

Miranda beckoned him towards her.

'And I can see right through your head.' Peering through one ear, she said, 'In here and out through the other side.'

'You can't.' Jason was outraged.

'Oh, I definitely can. Hang on, give me that drinking straw. If I slide it in, it'll go all the way through—'

'Miranda's teasing you.' Verity's tone was stiff with disapproval. 'Come over here, darling, and sit by me.'

'I won't be sacking her because she's pregnant,' Bruce was explaining with exaggerated patience. 'I'll come up with something else.'

Florence thought how much she disliked his habit of treating her like a seven-year-old.

'But I thought Chloe was a model employee.'

'She was. But now she's pregnant, she'll have to go.' He shrugged. 'Money's money. We're a small business, not a charity.'

Bruce had it all planned. Since he may as well get maximum use out of her, he would allow Chloe to work right up to the birth, but keep a diary recording anything that could count as a black mark against her. When the baby arrived, the chances were she'd change her mind about coming back to work anyway, Bruce privately thought. But if she didn't – well, he'd have enough ammunition by then to prove to any tribunal that he was within his rights to sack her.

Jason was practising violent karate chops on the edge of the coffee table. Glancing across at Miranda, Florence caught the reproachful look in her eye. You lied, the look told Florence, you promised I could put him in the microwave if he kicked me.

'Darling, aren't you in a hurry to leave?'

The moment she said it, Miranda perked up. As she bent to give Florence a hug, she whispered, 'Cheer up, soon be over.'

Verity pointedly looked away as Miranda's abbreviated pink and white polka-dotted skirt rode up her smooth brown thighs.

'I can see your pants,' Jason crowed.

'Have a good time.' Fondly, Florence patted her arm. 'Miranda's found herself a nice young man,' she explained to Verity and Bruce when the door had closed behind her.

Verity, who disapproved mightily of Miranda's indecently short skirts and iridescent highlights, said coolly, 'Has she indeed? And what colour is his hair . . . *mauve*?'

Chloe hated it when her mother was right and she was wrong, but this time there was no getting away from it.

No matter how hard she tried to juggle the figures, they simply wouldn't balance.

'You see, that's you all over,' Pamela Greening declared, 'living in cloud-cuckoo land. If this is how much you bring in,' she tapped the sheet of paper with her biro, 'and this is how much you have to shell out' – another triumphant tap – 'well, let's face it, you're sunk.'

Chloe rubbed her aching temples. She didn't know which was worse, struggling to add up or having to listen to her mother's incessant outpourings.

'Set about getting that husband of yours back, that's what you've got to do.' Pamela nodded briskly

Oh God.

'Mother, I know Greg. He's not going to change his mind. I'm on my own now.'

'Ah, but you're not on your own, are you? You've got a baby on the way. You can't live on fresh air, my girl. Not that you could call London air fresh.' This last remark was accompanied by a snort of contempt.

'I'll give up this flat. Find somewhere cheaper,' Chloe said wearily.

'Oh yes, that'll do the baby a power of good, growing up in some filthy tenement with muggers and drug addicts lurking on every corner. No no *no*,' Pamela Greening went on, her expression firm. 'Have another talk with Greg. I'm sure he'll help out. After all, that's what husbands are for.'

Chapter 17

'You see, the thing is, Mother,' said Bruce, 'if we go through the bank, the amount of interest they'd charge would be extortionate. Then it occurred to me that you've got all that money sloshing around in your accounts . . . and it's not as if you're *using* it for anything . . .'

Verity had taken Jason through to the kitchen in search of Coca-Cola. As soon as Bruce had pulled his chair closer to hers and assumed an earnest expression, Florence had known what to expect.

Her heart had sunk.

It's my birthday and what do I get? A brief duty visit from my family and a request for money.

A request for *more* money, Florence amended. Whatever had happened to the last ten thousand . . . and the twenty before that?

'How do you know I'm not using it? I may have plans,' she said calmly.

Bruce shot her a look of disbelief.

'Plans to do what? You don't have a business to keep running. You never do anything, go anywhere . . .'

'I know.' Florence shrugged, indicating with a wiggle of her empty glass that a refill wouldn't go amiss. 'So maybe it's about time I started. Doing things and going places,' she mused, enjoying the expression on her son's face. 'Jolly expensive things and frighteningly expensive places.'

'Okay, fine, but surely you can spare *some* cash.'

Bruce's neck had reddened, signalling his discomfort. Normally, Florence remembered, she said yes straight away and scribbled out a cheque on the spot.

Oh Bruce, I'm your mother, not a gourmet meal-ticket for life.

Aloud she said, 'Darling, pour me another drink, would you? Plenty of ice this time.'

In the kitchen a lot of furious whispering ensued.

'I don't know why she has to be so difficult,' Florence heard Verity hiss. 'You'll get everything when she dies anyway.'

'Is Granny going to die?' Jason sounded enthralled. 'When, *soon*?'

If this were a P.D. James thriller, Florence thought, I'd be lucky to see out the night.

Wheeling herself over to the kitchen doorway, she announced, 'I'm sixty-two, Verity, not a hundred and two.'

'Sorry, Florence, you weren't meant to hear that.' Tight-lipped, Verity braced herself against the fridge. 'But it's true, isn't it? Bruce is your son. It's practically his money, and I don't think you're being terribly sensitive here. Can't you understand how humiliating it is for him having to ask you for something that's rightfully his anyway?'

Since nobody appeared to be getting her that drink, Florence manoeuvred past them and did it herself.

'How much do you need?'

Bruce's stubby fingers fiddled with the knot of his topaz Armani tie.

'Fifteen.'

'Fifteen pounds or fifteen thousand?'

Not in the mood for jokes, Bruce flicked her a glance and helped himself to a good inch of gin.

'I'll give you five thousand,' said Florence.

Verity, looking as if a couple of hundred volts had just shot up her bottom, yelped, 'Oh, come *on*, that's not—'

'If it isn't enough,' Florence went on, 'I suggest you sell that shiny new Mercedes.'

Heavens, this was so liberating! Like wriggling out of the world's tightest corset, Florence thought delightedly. I should have done this *years* ago.

'You mean you want us to live like paupers, Mother? Is that it?'

'I just think it would be nice to see you learning to support yourself,' Florence said pleasantly. 'Living within your own means instead of relying on endless hand-outs from me.'

'Okay, if that's how you feel.' Draining his glass, Bruce pointedly examined his watch. 'Anyway, we'd better be off. Don't worry about us, Mother. The shop will probably go under, we'll sell the house, Jason will have to go to some godforsaken state school, but don't let that bother you for a second—'

'Bruce, do you love me?' Florence interrupted him in mid-rant.

'What?'

'Do you love me?' Reaching for her cigarettes, she lit one, chiefly to annoy Verity. 'Do you care about me, do you want me to be happy?'

'That's a ridiculous question.' Still flushed with anger, Bruce shook his head. 'Of course I do.' He put his arm around Verity's thin shoulders for emphasis. 'We both do.'

'It's just, you've been here for over an hour.' Florence gazed steadily at the pair of them. 'And all we've done so far is talk about you. You haven't even asked me yet how I am.'

She saw Verity give him a meaningful jab in the ribs.

'Mother, I'm sorry.' Like a small boy prodded into politeness, Bruce recited dutifully, 'How are you?'

'Extremely well, thank you. Feeling quite – what's the word – rejuvenated.' Florence beamed. 'That's the amazing thing about ruts, isn't it? You don't realise quite how much of one you've been stuck in, until someone comes along and hauls you out.'

Bewildered, Bruce said, 'You've lost me, Mother.' Surely this wasn't something to do with religion?

'I have met someone,' Florence announced, 'who makes me very happy.'

'Good grief.' Bruce's double chins quivered, signalling his amazement.

'A gentleman friend,' said Verity. 'Florence, how nice. I'm so pleased for you.'

'We want to enjoy ourselves. Have fun,' said Florence. 'Travel the world, *in style*.'

'So he's retired.' Bruce nodded with approval. Fellow must be loaded if he could afford holidays like that. 'What line of work was he in?'

'Ooh, this and that.' Florence gave her son and daughter-in-law a bright smile. 'But he's not retired.'

'If he isn't retired,' said Verity, 'how's he going to manage to travel the world with you?' Although with computers these days, she supposed, anything was possible.

'Easy.' The extravagant rings on Florence's fingers flashed as she waved her hand. 'He's between jobs right now.'

'So how can he afford to whisk you off—'

'He's not whisking me,' Florence announced, 'I'm whisking him.'

'Mother, are you *mad*?'

'He takes care of me. He makes me laugh. When I'm with him I feel *alive* again, for the first time in years.' Calmly Florence blew a perfect smoke ring. 'And I don't care if people think I'm a silly old fool, because they don't know what he's really like. We're happy, and that's what counts.'

Bruce didn't like the sound of this at all. Suspicion wrinkled his forehead.

'Why would people think you're a silly old fool?'

With a careless shrug, Florence said, 'He's what you might call a younger man, that's all.'

Oh, terrific.

'How much younger?'

'Look, it's my life. If it doesn't matter to us, why should anyone else be bothered?'

'Mother. How much younger?'

'Quite a bit younger than me. Oh, all right, all right,' she admitted with a sigh. 'If you must know, younger than you too.'

'Look at you, all sparkly-eyed,' Florence said fondly, when

Miranda returned just before midnight. 'No need to ask if you had a good evening.'

'I did, I did.' Kicking her shoes off, Miranda pirouetted around the sitting room.

'So where is he?'

'I'm playing it cool, keeping him keen.' Dizzy from spinning, Miranda threw herself down on the velvet sofa. 'Don't want him thinking I'm a pushover. I mean, you know I am and I know I am, but he doesn't have to find that out just yet.'

'Tactics,' said Florence. 'I'm impressed.'

'Me too.' Miranda grinned. 'So how was your evening?'

'Remarkably similar, as a matter of fact. I refused to give Bruce what he wanted. Except in his case, of course, it was money.' Florence's mouth began to twitch. 'Actually, I did a bit of a naughty thing tonight.'

Sitting up, Miranda hugged her knees.

'Don't tell me, you ate all the vanilla truffles. No, better than that, Jason kicked you too. You went berserk and dangled him by his ankles out of the window until he squealed for mercy.'

If Jason had tried to kick her, Florence thought, she would certainly have been tempted to go in for a spot of ankle-dangling.

'I told Bruce and Verity I couldn't give them the money they wanted because I needed it for myself. I said I'd got myself a toyboy and that we were going to take off together on a round-the-world cruise and spend spend spend until every last penny was gone.'

'You didn't!' Miranda squealed and clapped her hands.

'Oh yes. You should have seen their faces. Sheer bliss,'

sighed Florence. 'When I assured Bruce that if we married he wouldn't have to call Orlando Dad, he almost had a panic attack on the spot.'

'They really believed you?'

Miranda was by this time crying with laughter. She wiped her eyes with the front of her black lacy top; being black, it was handy for soaking up mascara.

'They believed every word.'

'But . . . Orlando!'

'Seemed like the kind of name a gigolo would have.' Florence looked pleased with herself. 'I didn't plan any of this in advance, you know. All spur-of-the-moment stuff. I just made it up as I went along. It was brilliant, I was *so* impressed with myself . . . heavens, I could become the next Barbara Cartland.'

'One's enough,' said Miranda. 'Anyway, there isn't enough pink lipstick in the world for the two of you. A fortune-hunting gigolo,' she went on, reaching for the box of vanilla truffles and generously offering one to Florence. 'What gave you that idea?'

'Tom Barrett and his mail-order bride, the girl he brought over from Thailand. I told you about him, remember?'

Miranda nodded.

'You told me it wouldn't last.'

'He knows that. Tom isn't stupid. But he's having fun, doing what he wants to do,' said Florence. 'And his daughter isn't giving him grief about it. As long as Tom's happy, she's happy. She isn't having a nervous breakdown at the thought of all the money she won't be inheriting.'

'So how long are you going to keep this up?' Miranda spoke through a mouthful of truffle.

'Ooh, a couple of months, I thought.'

'A couple of months! Isn't Bruce going to want to meet this no-good lover of yours?'

'Probably.' Florence shrugged. 'But he won't be able to, will he?' She took a jaunty swig of Scotch. 'I'll tell him Orlando's fussy about who he meets and that, basically, Bruce just isn't rich enough.'

Chapter 18

For Chloe, the next two weeks were a nightmare. Every day, during her lunch hour and after work, she trudged from hideous flat to even more hideous flat, desperately searching for anything remotely habitable.

Every evening, when her mother phoned from Manchester, Chloe lied brightly to her, insisting she was fine and giving the impression that the only reason she hadn't found somewhere else to live yet was because there were so many gorgeous properties to choose from.

And then there was work itself, more of a minefield nowadays than a shop, with Bruce feigning concern for her well-being when all the time – Chloe just *knew* – he was desperately plotting how he was going to sack her. His mood hadn't been improved, either, by the news that his mother had taken up with some unscrupulous toyboy and was evidently planning to squander all her money on him instead of giving it to Bruce.

'She's gone barmy, completely barmy. I could get her sectioned for this,' he raged. 'As for the business,' he muttered ominously, 'I don't know how I'm going to keep it together, I really don't.'

The atmosphere in the shop wasn't a happy one. And,

sod's law, the harder Chloe tried to be the perfect employee, the more things went wrong. Having never been late back from lunch before, she promptly earned herself two black marks in a week.

'I'm so sorry, the bus broke down and I had to run the last half a mile,' she gabbled, bursting into the shop at ten past two. The flat she had rushed out to view had gone before she'd got there; another one pound forty wasted on bus fares.

'I need you to be here on time,' Bruce told her, even though the shop was empty. As he noted Chloe's lateness in his diary with secret satisfaction he announced ominously, 'This isn't good enough.'

As she was leaving that evening, Chloe saw a car she recognised parked on double yellows outside the shop.

Greg's friend, Adrian, beckoned her over.

'Chloe, it's about your mother. These phone calls, they've got to stop.'

'I've already told her that.'

Chloe reddened; every evening her mother delighted in recounting the details of her latest torrent of abuse. It was so humiliating. Not to mention pointless.

'We have to keep the answering machine on all the time now,' said Adrian. 'It's a real pain.'

'I'm sorry. I don't want her doing it any more than you do.' Chloe fiddled agitatedly with the newspaper in her hands. She had three more flats to see and was desperate not to be late.

'Anyway, Greg's moving out next week, so after that she'll be wasting her breath.' Adrian took a last drag of his cigarette and flicked it into the gutter. 'Maybe you could pass the message on.'

Chloe's hands went clammy.

'Greg's moving out? Where?'

Adrian gave her a measured look.

'Since your mother's the reason he's going, I don't think he'd be too happy if I gave you the address.'

Be brave, be brave.

'Is he . . . um, moving in with his girlfriend?'

'I really can't say. Chloe, don't ask me any more questions, okay? I'm just the go-between here.'

At least he had the grace to look embarrassed. Chloe thought of all the meals she had cooked for Adrian during the first weeks after his own wife had left him. Then, he had been shocked to the core, frequently drunk and desperate for company. She had listened to his endless self-pitying ramblings, fed and watered him, even ironed his shirts when he'd told her Lisa had run off with their only iron.

How many times during those weeks had Adrian shaken his head and told her how grateful he was? 'True friends, that's what you and Greg are,' he had burbled in maudlin fashion after his ninth or tenth can of Stella. 'I mean it, I don't know what I'd do without the two of you.'

That had been then, of course, and this was now.

A whole year later.

Adrian was over Lisa. And he was sober.

'I'm looking for a flat as well,' said Chloe. 'Actually I'm late for an appointment. I don't suppose you could give me a lift to Finsbury Park?'

'I would,' Adrian lied, 'but I'm in a bit of a hurry myself.'

'I've seen forty-three flats in the last fortnight. They've all been terrible.' She gave it one last try. 'Please.'

But it was no good. He wasn't her friend any more, he was Greg's.

'Sorry, Chloe. I just can't. You'd be better off taking the tube anyway.'

Better off jumping in front of it at this rate, thought Chloe as she watched the car pull away.

Two of the flats were awful but the third – in Clerkenwell – was okay. Chloe told the landlord she was very, very interested.

By the time she got home, there was a message on the machine from the landlord telling her that he had let the flat go to someone else.

Chloe reheated the remains of last night's pasta and drank a pint of her latest craving, strawberry milkshake. Then she ate two Chelsea buns and a tin of rice pudding, before running herself a bath.

While she could still afford hot water.

Afterwards, she surveyed herself in the bedroom mirror, peeling off her dressing gown as cautiously as a plastic surgery patient having the last bandages removed.

No wonder nobody wants to rent me a flat, Chloe thought, I'm so fat and hideous-looking I don't deserve one.

Covering herself back up – well, it wasn't fair on the mirror – she made her way through to the kitchen and unwrapped a packet of custard creams.

It was either eat or cry, and she was running short of tissues.

Not to mention time, Chloe realised with a stab of anxiety. In just over a fortnight she had to be out of here. If she didn't find herself somewhere else to live – and fast – she would be homeless.

Or, worse still, back in Manchester with her mother.

A bit of Dutch courage would have come in handy. Since she wasn't allowed to down a bottle of wine, Chloe psyched herself up with another biscuit instead.

Swallowing her pride along with her custard cream, she punched out Adrian's number.

Predictably, the answering machine picked up the call.

'Greg, it's me. Chloe. I need to speak to you urgently.' Her voice began to quaver. 'Please ring me back.'

Dropping the receiver on to the hook, she gazed at the phone.

Less than two minutes later, it rang.

'What's happened?' Greg spoke without preamble. 'Is something wrong?'

Was something *wrong*?

Oh no, everything's fine, thought Chloe, I'm pregnant and my husband's walked out on me and I'm probably about to lose my job and I don't have anywhere to live and if I don't stop eating I'm going to end up the size of the Millennium Dome—

'Chloe? Are you there?'

It was weird, hearing his voice again. She gripped the receiver in both hands.

'I've spoken to my mother. There won't be any more phone calls.'

'Well, good. Not that it makes any difference to me,' said Greg. 'As Ade told you, I'll be out of here by next week.'

Right, here goes, thought Chloe. She took a deep steadying breath.

'Greg, I can't cope. Financially, I mean. I'm looking for a cheaper flat, but it's still going to be almost impossible to manage on my wages.'

Long pause.

'You should have thought of that before you got pregnant,' he replied coldly. 'So? What does this have to do with me?'

How had it come to this? We were so happy once, thought Chloe. Nobody could have been more charming than Greg when they'd first met.

But she thought she knew, now, what it was. The thrill, for Greg, was all in the chase. Once the novelty of marriage had worn off, he had begun to lose interest.

Basically, he had a short affection-span, Chloe reminded herself. Oh yes, and when it came to money, he'd always been a bit mean.

'I thought . . . I thought maybe you could help me out.' The empty custard creams wrapper crackled as she curled her fingers helplessly around it.

'Impossible, I'm afraid. I'm moving too, aren't I? This new flat's costing me a bomb.'

This new love-nest, you mean, thought Chloe.

'The thing is, I was talking to Bruce about it. He told me I was legally entitled to maintenance. If I go to a solicitor, he'd be able to serve you with—'

'No chance, Chloe. I'd fight it all the way. You chose to have this baby, I didn't. God,' he sounded disgusted, 'you're a bitch, aren't you? First you wreck our marriage and now you have the nerve to expect *me* to support you. If you're in a mess, that's your fault, not mine. I'm the innocent party here and I'm damned if you're going to bleed me dry.'

'I don't want to bleed you dry.' Chloe was instantly consumed with guilt; he had always been able to argue a case with terrifying efficiency. 'But I'm desperate, Greg. I have *no* money, and as the law stands, you have to—'

'Don't threaten me with the law! I'm changing my address, I can change jobs too. So the law's going to have its work cut out, making me do anything.' He spoke with an air of finality. 'Because they'll have to catch me first.'

Chloe was alone in the shop the next morning, disentangling bubble-wrap from a boxful of alarmingly delicate porcelain figurines.

When the phone rang, her shattered nerves reacted as if a bomb had gone off. Chloe's fingers jerked and an especially fragile porcelain daffodil, clutched to the bosom of a pallid-faced young country girl, caught on a corner of bubble-wrap and snapped off in her hand.

The figurines weren't wildly expensive, but that was beside the point. This miniature daffodil, Chloe thought, was in effect her P45.

She pictured herself, bags packed, climbing on to a coach about to head up the M1.

Home to Mother.

Truly a fate worse than death.

'Hello,' she sighed into the phone.

'Oh my word, that won't do at all. No no *no*,' a familiar voice scolded her good-naturedly. 'You're supposed to say "Good morning, Special Occasions, how may I help you?" in a *sickeningly* cheerful manner. I'm sorry, Chloe, you don't sound nearly enough like a lobotomised air hostess. Instant dismissal for you.'

Against all the odds, Chloe felt her spirits lift a little. Just a notch.

'Too late. I think I've just instantly dismissed myself. Hello, Mrs Curtis. How are you?'

'In a very good mood. Is Bruce glaring at you?' Florence chuckled. 'Don't worry. Put him on, I'll tell him not to sack you.'

'Bruce isn't here, I'm afraid.' (This was a lie; she wasn't afraid, she was glad.) 'He's at a trade fair in Birmingham. Shall I ask him to phone you when he gets back?'

'Don't worry, it's not important. I'll give him a ring this evening. So,' said Florence, 'how are *you*?'

'Oh, fine.' Another lie.

'Any customers in the shop?'

Puzzled, Chloe said, 'No.'

'Good. In that case, stop being polite and tell me how you are really.'

A lump sprang into Chloe's throat. These were the first words of genuine kindness she had heard in weeks. And they were coming from Bruce's mother, a woman about whom she may have heard a great deal – not all of it good – but whom she had never even met.

'How am I really?' She felt hot tears prickling at the back of her eyes. 'Not great.'

'I shouldn't imagine you are. Bruce told me the situation,' Florence said in her brisk, kindly way. 'Tricky to say the least. For other people too,' she went on. 'I mean, they must wonder which they're supposed to do when they see you, congratulate or commiserate.'

'I know.' Chloe sighed. 'I've got myself into a bit of a muddle.'

'So what's all this about instantly dismissing yourself?'

Florence didn't miss a trick, thought Chloe.

'I've just broken a china ornament.'

'Was it hideous?'

The pallid-faced country girl, minus her daffodil, gazed balefully up at her.

'Pretty hideous.'

'Probably a blessing then. Tell Bruce one of the customers did it.'

The lump in Chloe's throat threatened to expand.

'I don't think he'd believe me.'

'Is he trying to sack you?'

'I think so.' Chloe's voice began to wobble. 'Well, I can't really b-blame him.'

'How about the flat-hunting? Any joy yet?'

Joy, thought Chloe. When did I last have any joy?

Her nose began to run with the effort of holding back a torrent of tears. Scrabbling in her pocket for a tissue, she mumbled, 'No . . . sorry, I've got a bit of a cold . . .'

Clamping her hand over the receiver just in time, Chloe let out a sob – an inelegant great honking sound like a grief-stricken goose. Tears slid down her face and dripped on to the bubble-wrap on the counter.

'Chloe, are you still there?'

'A customer's just come in, I'll have to g-go.' Chloe stumbled over the words and hung up.

Twenty minutes later the phone rang again.

'Find yourself a pen, write this down,' Florence instructed her. 'Twenty-four Tredegar Gardens, Notting Hill.'

Chloe wondered what it was. The address of the nearest Samaritans, probably.

'Got that?' Florence said briskly. 'Good. Come and see me after work.'

Chloe began to understand why Bruce called his mother a domineering old witch and a law unto herself.

'Um . . . actually, I've made appointments to view a couple of flats . . .'

'Come and see me after work,' Florence repeated. 'I'll expect you at six o'clock.'

Chapter 19

Wheeling herself to the front door, Florence pulled it open. The girl on the doorstep was coatless, shivering and soaked to the skin. With her long blonde hair plastered to her head, stuck-together eyelashes and ankle-length blue cotton dress clinging to every curve, she looked like a voluptuous mermaid unceremoniously plucked from the sea.

'Mrs Curtis? Sorry I'm wet, it was sunny this morning so I didn't bother with a coat, I didn't think it was going to rain—'

'Even the weather's against you.' Reversing the chair, Florence waved her through. 'Come in, Chloe. And call me Florence, for goodness' sake.'

Florence set great store by first impressions. It never took her longer than a few moments to decide whether or not she liked someone. She had done it with each of her husbands, and with Miranda too, when the arthritis had worsened last year and she had been forced to advertise for a lodger-cum-helper.

Twenty-three uninspiring applicants later – when Florence had been on the verge of giving up hope – Miranda had arrived. Apologising profusely for being late because she'd been so busy eavesdropping on the tube that she'd sailed straight past her stop, she had promptly launched into the risqué joke she'd overheard.

They had taken to each other instantly. Florence, her life at the time something of a joke-free zone, had offered her the flat practically on the spot. And Miranda, with no family of her own – her parents having died in a car crash three years earlier – had been entranced by Florence's bawdy, irreverent attitude to, well, pretty much everyone and everything. She had moved in the next day, thrilled to be there and amazingly eager to please, and had been making Florence laugh – not always intentionally – ever since.

A cup of tea and twenty minutes in front of the fire, meanwhile, had done wonders for Chloe. Her rippling blonde hair was almost dry and the colour had returned to her cheeks.

She didn't look as though she was about to reel off a string of jokes, but given the circumstances, that was understandable.

'So you phoned your husband last night,' Florence prompted when Chloe paused halfway through the story.

'Humiliating, I know. But I was desperate.' Chloe's shoulders rose and fell. 'Not that it got me anywhere. Even if I did manage to drag him through the courts . . . well, that could take years.' Sadly she shook her head. 'Anyway, I'm not the dragging-through-the-courts type.'

This, Florence decided, was more than likely what Bruce was banking on too.

Intercepting her thoughtful gaze, Chloe straightened her back and swept her hair away from her face.

'I know it seems unlikely, looking at me now, but I do actually have some pride. If my husband's that desperate

146

not to have any contact with us' – her hand touched her stomach in an unconsciously protective gesture – 'well, then I don't want his money. I'd rather do without it, manage by myself.'

The cobalt-blue eyes were clear, the set of her chin determined. If she had been crying earlier – and Florence was pretty certain she had been – there was no sign of tears now.

Down but not out, Florence noted with approval. The spark had been well hidden, but it was still there.

'You've worked for my son for over three years and he's sung your praises more times than I can remember. Don't worry about your job,' she told Chloe. 'I'll make sure he doesn't give you the sack.'

Chloe breathed out slowly. 'That's really kind. You don't know what a relief that is.' Sensing that the meeting was at an end, she glanced at her watch. Six thirty-five. She'd missed the first appointment, but if she hurried she could just make the second.

'Where are you going?' Florence raised her eyebrows.

Reaching for her bag and levering herself to her feet, Chloe said apologetically, 'Florence, I'm so grateful. But I hope you don't mind if I rush off. You see, I have to—'

'That isn't why I asked you to come here. I could have told you that on the phone. Oh well, you're up now,' Florence sighed, 'you may as well take a look at it before you go.'

Chloe was confused.

'Take a look at what?'

'You'll have to go up on your own.' Florence indicated her wheelchair. 'Top of the stairs, third door on the left.'

What was in there, Chloe wondered, Bruce's old cot?

'Okay. Um, what am I looking for?'

If it was a cot, she hoped Florence wasn't expecting her to take it away with her now – to tuck it under her arm, perhaps, and lug it home on the bus.

'I'm asking you to look at the room, child.' Florence's tone was suddenly brusque. 'It's empty. If you want it, it's yours.'

'Honestly, it's terrifying, like being a double-agent!' Miranda had to shout to make herself heard above the roar of the vacuum cleaner as she belted around Florence's sitting room hoovering up biscuit crumbs at a rate of knots. 'I keep telling myself I'll wait until Bev hasn't mentioned Greg's name for a whole day. Then, when that happens, it'll mean she's over him and I'll be able to confess. But I'm beginning to wonder if it's ever going to happen. She talks about him practically nonstop. The only time she stops talking about Greg is when she asks me how things are going with my new boyfriend. I'm telling you, it's fraught. One slip of the tongue and I'm dead.'

She was kneeling on the floor now, bottom in the air, energetically hoovering under the sofa. Florence, from the safety of her chair, said, 'So what do you call him?'

'Nothing!' Leaning back on her heels and pushing her spiky fringe out of her eyes, Miranda reached across and switched off the vacuum cleaner. 'Just "my boyfriend", or "my chap". Of course, Bev's convinced the reason I won't tell her his name is because he's called something awful, like Horace or Percy. Or Engelbert.'

'Wouldn't it be easier to *call* him Engelbert?'

Miranda gave her a measured look.

'No, it would not.'

It was seven thirty and Greg – the boyfriend with no name – was due over at eight. Miranda kept glancing compulsively at the clock on the mantelpiece.

'Go on, run upstairs and get ready.' Florence shooed her towards the door.

'What's this?' Bending down, Miranda dug a pink ruffled hairband out from between the sofa cushions.

'I had a visitor this afternoon.' The hairband must have fallen out of Chloe's bag, Florence realised. 'I'll tell you about it later. You go and have your bath.'

The doorbell rang at seven forty-five. Mr Keen, thought Florence with amusement as she wheeled herself through to the hall. From upstairs came the sound of Miranda still splashing away happily in the bath.

'He's here,' Florence yelled up the staircase. 'Don't worry, I'll be gentle with him!'

Pulling open the front door, she came face to face with Miranda's new boyfriend. Black hair and dark-brown eyes, Florence noted with approval; she had always gone for men with dark eyes herself. The clothes – old jeans and a faded black polo shirt – were something of a disappointment, a bit casual for a hot date in Florence's view, but that was young people today. Anyway, the body beneath the shabby clothes more than made up for it.

'Hello, come on in, lovely to meet you at last.' He reminded her of someone; an actor, she guessed, from the telly. 'I've heard so much about you from Miranda. She's in the bath, by the way, so I'll look after you until she's finished tarting herself up.'

'Oh, right.' He looked surprised but pleased. 'Fine by me. It's nice to meet you too.'

'Through here.' Reversing, Florence expertly guided him past her into the sitting room.

'You aren't going to run me over with your wheel-chair, are you?' he said with a grin. 'Miranda warned me you might.'

'Why would I want to run you over? Now, tell me what you'd like to drink. I've got a bottle of white wine open, but there's beer in the fridge if you'd prefer.'

'Wine would be great. We'll try not to lose your glasses this time.'

'My glasses?' Florence wondered why he sounded so amused. She hadn't the faintest idea where her glasses were – buried at the back of a drawer somewhere, probably. 'To be honest, I never wear them. Too vain.'

When she turned around, Miranda's boyfriend was giving her a slightly odd look.

'I meant the wine glasses you left behind on Parliament Hill.'

'Oh, those! Miranda told you about that, did she?' Florence laughed, remembering their abrupt departure. 'Ha, that was a funny old day.'

'Actually—'

'So where are you taking her tonight?'

'Um, I think we've got a few wires crossed here.'

Click click, went Florence's brain. She put down the bottle she was in the process of pouring and gazed steadily across at her visitor.

There was definitely something about those dark-brown eyes.

Click click click . . .

'Oh dear,' she exclaimed at last, 'you must think I'm completely dotty. You aren't Greg, are you?'

He smiled.

'No, I'm not Greg.'

Now Florence knew why he had seemed so familiar. He didn't resemble a television actor at all; he was someone she had seen before in the flesh.

Only fleetingly, mind you. And from a fair distance. Not to mention minus the spectacles she never wore but should perhaps start thinking about wearing . . .

'You're Hungry and Homeless,' said Florence.

'Well, kind of. But you can call me Danny,' he replied with a grin.

He might not be who she'd thought he was, but Florence had already made up her mind. She liked him.

'So you aren't Miranda's new boyfriend,' she announced, holding his glass of wine out to him. 'Pity. Never mind, you can still have a drink.'

When Miranda had heard the shrill ring of the doorbell earlier, her immediate instinct had been to leap out of the bath and race downstairs. Well, maybe throw on a few clothes first.

But Greg was early, she hadn't even washed her hair yet and she'd been looking forward to this bath all day. Besides, Florence was there to entertain him.

Maybe I shouldn't rush down, Miranda thought, sinking lazily back into the steaming, scented water. Let them have some time alone together; that way, they can get to know each other in peace.

'Here she is,' Florence announced twenty minutes later. 'Oh my word, and she's actually wearing a dress! Darling, you look a treat.'

Having been encouraged by the explosions of laughter filtering up the stairs – Florence and Greg were clearly getting on like a house on fire – Miranda had taken her time getting ready. Now, completely thrown by the sight of the wrong two people getting along like a house on fire – well, right woman, wrong man – she ground to a halt in the doorway.

Was Jeremy Beadle responsible for this?

Chapter 20

'Hello.' Miranda looked at Danny Delancey, then at her watch, then at Florence. 'Where's Greg?'

'Sshh.' Florence raised her eyebrows in alarm. 'Careless talk costs lives. Forget you heard that,' she instructed Danny. 'Miranda's boyfriend is officially The Man With No Name. Honestly, darling,' she returned her attention to Miranda, 'if you're going to be a secret agent, you'll have to do better than that.'

Miranda took in at a glance the almost empty bottle of wine on the table, the relaxed way Danny Delancey's arm was draped across the back of the sofa, the barely suppressed grins on both their faces. Almost as if they were in league with each other.

'Where is he?'

Florence looked innocent.

'Who?'

'Greg.'

'Sshh!'

'It'll never work.' Danny was shaking his head. 'You'll have to call him something else. How about Percy?'

They were definitely making fun of her. Miranda sighed. And it was ten past eight, so where *was* Greg?

'We mustn't tease. Poor darling, she's only just met the boy,' said Florence. 'It's a traumatic business, this falling in love. No sign of him yet.' Airily she waved Miranda over to the sofa. 'But don't worry, I'm sure he'll be here soon.'

Being ganged up on was bad enough. When it was coupled with the first niggling oh-God-don't-say-I'm-about-to-be-stood-up ripples of anxiety, the effect was horrible.

'What are you doing here anyway?' Miranda knew she sounded irritated but she didn't care. Greg had never been late before. He wouldn't stand her up, surely?

Daniel Delancey patted the space next to him on the sofa.

'I was passing; just dropped by on the off-chance. We need to fix up a couple of dates for filming. This week, if you could manage it.'

Pointedly, Miranda perched on the arm of the sofa, as far away from him as possible.

'I'm busy this week. I can't take any time off work.'

'Okay, but we could interview you here. Thursday evening would be good for us.' He consulted his battered Filofax, then looked up. 'Actually, any chance of seeing your room now?'

Not a chance in the world, Miranda thought with a shudder. Her room was currently awash with all the clothes she had tried on, discarded and flung to the floor.

'No. And I'm busy on Thursday evening too,' she added for good measure. Honestly, talk about impertinent. Did she look like someone with no social life at all?

'Seeing your boyfriend, you mean?' Danny glanced at his watch, his eyebrows registering dismay. 'Oh dear, twenty past.'

Miranda gritted her teeth until her jaw hurt.

'Danny, your glass is empty,' Florence protested. 'Come on now, have another drink.'

The doorbell went before he could reply. Miranda flew to answer it.

'You're here! You're late!'

'Accident on the Bayswater Road.'

'Oh *no* . . .'

'Not me,' said Greg. 'A bus and a Fiat Uno. The fire brigade are still trying to cut the driver out of the Fiat.'

'That's all right then.' Miranda threw her arms around him. 'So long as you're okay.'

Smiling, Greg said, 'Maybe I should be late more often, if this is the kind of welcome I get.'

'Don't you dare. I thought you'd stood me up.' She covered his face with kisses, breathless with relief. 'Come on, I want to introduce you to Florence.'

'Well? What d'you think?' said Miranda eagerly ten minutes later. Danny Delancey had made his excuses and left, and before they followed suit, Greg was paying a quick visit to the bathroom.

'I think you should ring Danny and say Thursday evening's fine. Playing the prima donna only works if you're Elizabeth Taylor,' Florence pointed out, 'and you haven't won any Oscars yet. They can always make this documentary without you, you know.'

'I meant, what do you think of Greg?' Miranda waved an impatient arm in the direction of the door. 'Do you really like him?'

'Oh. Well, yes, of course I like him. He seems very

155

nice, quite . . . charming.' 'Quite' was a useful word. It could mean perfectly charming, or it could mean slightly charming. You could take your pick.

Oh dear. Florence struggled to be fair. Greg did seem nice and he did seem charming; she just hadn't automatically clicked with him as she had with the other one, Danny. Out of the two of them, she knew which one she preferred.

But that was beside the point; Greg was the one Miranda wanted her to like, and how could she fault him? He was good-looking, smartly turned out, polite . . . and clearly as taken with Miranda as she was with him.

And if the charm seemed a bit forced, a touch excessive . . . well, Florence conceded, he probably couldn't help that. It was undoubtedly an unfortunate side-effect of having worked for years selling insurance.

'He seems very nice,' she repeated, reaching for her cigarettes and swiftly changing the subject. 'Anyway, before you go, let me tell you about my visitor this afternoon.'

Miranda hid her disappointment. She didn't want to hear about some boring visitor, she wanted Florence to sing Greg's praises – with delirious enthusiasm, preferably – and tell her over and over again how *perfect* he was. So far, all she'd got was *very nice*, pronounced in the kind of voice adults reserved for five-year-olds when they were handed a painting – Is it a tractor? Is it an aeroplane? – to admire.

Swallowing her impatience, Miranda forced herself to sound interested. She jiggled the loose shoe dangling from her foot and said, 'Visitor. Okay, fire away.'

'I asked Chloe to come round. Pregnant Chloe who works for Bruce,' Florence prompted when Miranda looked blank.

'Oh, right.'

'She's had to give up her flat. The husband refuses to help out financially. She's a lovely girl.'

Just not very bright, thought Miranda, if that was the kind of man she'd chosen to marry in the first place.

At a guess, Florence had slipped the girl some money.

'I told her she can move in with us.'

'What!'

'Not for ever,' Florence explained. 'Just until she sorts herself out.'

'But that could take years! She hasn't even had the baby yet.' Miranda was alarmed. 'You mean you've offered her the room next to mine?'

Oh great, thanks a lot.

'She's desperate,' Florence said calmly.

'Honestly, and you call me a soft touch! All I did was share my sandwiches with a down-and-out,' Miranda protested. Well, a bogus down-and-out. 'Here's you sharing your whole *house*.'

'It's big enough. Anyway,' said Florence, 'I get bored here on my own. I'll enjoy the company.'

'The company of a screaming baby?' Agitated, Miranda jiggled the shoe right off her foot. 'It won't know how to play poker, if that's what you're after. And what about all the sleepless nights? You definitely won't enjoy those.'

'I'm sure Chloe will have found herself somewhere else to live by then. Like I said, this is only temporary.'

'Well, I still think you're mad.'

'Not mad, just bored. And look on the bright side,' Florence said cheerfully. 'It'll annoy Bruce and Verity no end.'

Bruce and Verity weren't the only ones. Miranda was relieved to hear Greg's footsteps on the stairs.

'You aren't thrilled,' said Florence as Greg appeared in the doorway. 'I'm sorry, darling. Maybe I should have asked you first.'

She sounded disappointed. Miranda chewed her lip as guilt kicked in. It really wasn't like her to be so uncharitable.

Oh, all right, so selfish and stroppy and mean.

This was Florence's house, after all. She could fill it with whoever she liked.

'Don't worry, it's fine by me.' Miranda turned to Greg. 'Florence is collecting waifs and strays,' she explained. 'We're going to have a homeless pregnant girl moving in.'

'Rather you than me,' said Greg. He jangled his car keys, impatient to leave; pregnant women weren't his favourite topic of conversation.

'The thing is, the room's going to need redecorating.' Florence looked at Miranda. 'I wondered if you wouldn't mind giving it a coat of paint before she moves in.'

'No problem.' Miranda nodded vigorously, eager to make up for her grumpiness earlier. She touched Greg's sleeve. 'We could do it on Sunday, couldn't we? Make it look really nice.'

'I'd love to,' Greg lied, 'but I'll be pretty busy myself this weekend. I'm moving too, remember.' Clasping Miranda's hand, he pulled her to her feet. 'Right, we'd better be off. Nice meeting you,' he added, flicking back his fair hair and smiling broadly over his shoulder at Florence.

'Oh, and you.'

'I feel a bit rotten,' Miranda murmured, out in the hall.

'I wasn't very nice when Florence first told me about this girl moving in.'

'I'm not surprised.'

'Still.' She paused, half in and half out of her jacket. 'It might be fun. Babies can be cute, can't they?'

'Do you mind if we change the subject?' said Greg, opening the front door. 'You're beginning to sound like Bev.'

'Chloe's doing what?' Bruce pressed the phone to his ear and gestured furiously at his son to lower the volume on his Play Station. 'Mother, hang on – I can't hear a word. Jason, for crying out loud, turn it *down*. Now, Chloe's doing what?'

'Moving in with me,' Florence repeated with maddening cheerfulness. 'Isn't it the most marvellous idea? Killing two birds with one stone!'

I should be so lucky, thought Bruce. Anger began to well up in his chest. Oh, this was too much.

'I don't see what's so marvellous about it.' His voice was cold. 'I don't see why you have to interfere with matters that have absolutely nothing to do with you. For heaven's sake, Mother, you don't even know Chloe!'

'I do now. She came to see me last night.'

'She came to *see* you?' Bruce spluttered. 'You mean she—?'

'Don't get your knickers in a twist,' Florence interrupted. 'I asked her to. Chloe needs somewhere to live and I have room to spare. I don't understand why you're shouting at me, Bruce. I thought you'd be pleased.'

Bruce's mind was in such turmoil that for a couple of seconds he couldn't remember why he wasn't. Then it came to him: he was planning to sack Chloe.

Soon.

He exhaled heavily. Once you'd sacked an employee, it was easier all round if you never had to clap eyes on them again. If Chloe was going to be living with his mother, that wasn't going to happen.

It would, in fact, be bloody awkward.

Knowing Florence, Bruce thought darkly, that was more than likely why she'd done it.

For this reason alone, he forced himself to calm down.

'Okay, I can see why it helps Chloe out. But what's in it for you?'

'I'll be getting myself a house-sitter,' Florence replied chirpily. 'Now that Miranda's found herself a young man, she's not going to be around so often. All the hanky-panky, I imagine, will be taking place over at his flat. And I'm going to be away a fair bit myself, of course . . . did I tell you that Orlando and I are thinking of Vegas? . . . so it makes sense to have someone here, taking care of the house.'

Las Vegas.

Bruce shuddered.

Twenty-four-hours-a-day gambling *and* a gigolo on your arm.

This was truly a nightmare. Florence had lost her marbles and now she was planning – *gleefully*, dammit – to lose all her money too.

'Mother, I'm not sure Vegas is a good idea.'

'Why not, too many wedding chapels?' Florence teased. 'Don't worry, darling, Orlando's already asked me and I turned him down.'

Thank Christ for that, thought Bruce. His hands were slippery with sweat.

'I have no desire to be married by a crooning Elvis lookalike in a white crimplene jumpsuit,' Florence went on consolingly. 'I told Orlando straight. If we decide to get married, we'll do it in England, with a real vicar and in a proper church.'

Chapter 21

Greg's new flat, in Maida Vale, was situated on the third floor of a modern apartment block set in landscaped gardens. The flat itself was small but adequate, and had been recently redecorated in shades of creams and greens that were only faintly reminiscent of municipal toilets.

'This is great, I *love* it,' Miranda enthused as she was given the full guided tour. It wasn't strictly true, she much preferred old buildings to new ones, but what else could you say when someone was proudly showing you around their new home?

And this was Greg's new home, so she would grow to love it.

'Really?' He put his arms around her. 'I know it's not huge, but it has its advantages. No Adrian, for a start.'

Miranda kissed him. Adrian meant well, but privacy – or rather the lack of it – had been an increasing problem recently. The other evening, back at Adrian's house, things had been progressing nicely in a bedroom direction when he had arrived home unexpectedly with a crowd of friends from the pub. Discovering Greg and Miranda sitting bolt upright on the sofa, taking in at a glance Miranda's pink cheeks, lack of bra and wrongly done-up blouse, he had waved a four-pack of lagers and yelled, 'Oops, coitus interruptus! Hey, don't mind us, feel free to carry on. We were going to watch the football but we can always watch you two instead.'

Miranda blushed again just thinking about it. How embarrassing had that been? Almost as embarrassing as the moment thirty seconds later when she and Greg were making their escape through the front door and a roar had gone up in the living room as one of Adrian's friends, chucking a sofa cushion to one side, had triumphantly unearthed her bra.

Honestly, it was bad enough *being* a 34A without having it announced to a roomful of half-cut football fanatics who immediately launched into a raucous chant to that effect.

Oh yes, the prospect of total privacy had a lot going for it.

'No Adrian,' Miranda agreed happily, 'just us.' She kissed him again, sliding her hands longingly under his rugby shirt. 'I don't think you've shown me the bedroom yet.'

Greg stroked her hair.

'We're going to do this properly. There's no rush, we've got all the time in the world. Look, it's only seven o'clock,' he showed her his watch, 'and you've been at work all day. You must be starving. I thought we'd go out and get something to eat first. Then, when we come back . . . well, you can see the bedroom.' He grinned. 'It's Sunday tomorrow, no need to get up. If we want to, we can spend the whole day in bed. And I think I should warn you now, I'll definitely want to.'

'Except I promised Florence I'd decorate that room,' groaned Miranda.

'Put it off.'

'I can't. She had the paint delivered today.'

'I thought you said the girl wasn't moving in for another week.'

'She isn't, but Florence really wants the room done tomorrow. Otherwise the smell of paint will still—'

'Don't let her boss you around,' Greg interrupted impatiently. 'She can't *make* you do it. What is she, some kind of slave-driver? Just tell her tomorrow isn't convenient.'

'Florence isn't a slave-driver, she just wants the job finished. And I promised I'd do it. I don't want to let her down.'

Greg was frowning, not bothering to conceal his irritation.

'I wanted us to spend the day together.'

'But we can!'

'In bed,' he said pointedly. 'Not painting bloody walls.'

There was a horrible silence.

'Oh God,' Miranda wailed suddenly. 'We're having our first argument. Today of all days!'

Greg's expression softened at once.

'No we aren't.'

'I'm sorry!'

'Don't be.' He didn't want to argue either. 'I'm disappointed, that's all. I wanted our first day in the flat to be special.' Taking Miranda's face between his hands, he slowly kissed her. 'You don't know how much I've been looking forward to this.'

'I'm not hungry,' Miranda murmured against his warm mouth. 'I don't want to go out to dinner.'

Greg, who was starving, said, 'We can order something later.'

'Do you hate me?'

'No.' His lips brushed her neck. 'I love you.'

It was true. He hadn't planned to meet someone so soon after Chloe, but it had happened. He had found Miranda and he didn't want to lose her.

He felt her shudder in his arms.

'You do?'

'I do.'

Miranda closed her eyes. This had definitely been worth waiting for. And to think that she had tried to wriggle out of Elizabeth Turnbull's hideous fund-raising party. She had only gone in the end because Florence had insisted and she'd thought it might turn up a marriage-minded man, with I-love-Mothercare signs in his eyes, for Bev.

'We don't have to wait until later, do we?' Her embarrassingly out-of-practice fingers fumbled with the top button of his jeans. 'I think I'd like to see the bedroom now.'

'We've waited this long,' Greg teased. 'Are you sure you wouldn't rather leave it until next weekend?'

Miranda unfastened a couple more buttons. They were in the hallway now, and she was easing him in the direction of the closed door that hadn't yet been opened.

'Oh, I'm sure.'

Her hand landed on the door handle. The door opened and she began to reel him inside.

Oops.

A lot of clattering ensued.

'Junk cupboard,' Greg murmured, pulling her out again. 'Wrong door.'

'I bet Mata Hari never had problems like this.'

'I don't suppose Mata Hari wore a 34A bra.'

'She didn't have Adrian and his friends to deal with.' Miranda unfastened the final button on his jeans. She leaned on the handle of the last door, nudging it open with her hip. 'They aren't in here, are they?'

'Better not be,' said Greg.

Reeling home at eight o'clock the next morning, light-headed from lack of sleep, Miranda only hoped she didn't look as bow-legged as she felt.

Oh, what a blissful night.

'No need to ask if you enjoyed yourself,' said Florence with her customary lack of discretion. Her eyes bright with laughter, she handed Miranda a mug of strong coffee. 'Go anywhere nice?'

Miranda tried hard to look demure.

'Just a quiet evening in.'

'Not too quiet, I hope. That's the trouble with these modern flats, the walls are so thin you can't unscrew a bottle of aspirin without the neighbours asking if your headache's better.'

Demure clearly wasn't working. Miranda slurped her coffee and grinned.

'I didn't have a headache last night.'

'You had a couple of phone calls.' Expertly reversing her chair, Florence reached for the message pad. 'Your friend Bev rang, wondering what you were up to today. Said she might pop over later and give you a hand.'

Miranda didn't get her hopes up; Bev's hands were too perfectly manicured to be of any practical use. Sunday was traditionally her day to be at a bit of a loose end, that was all. Bev's idea of being helpful would be lounging about gossiping and every so often pointing up at a hard-to-reach corner and saying knowledgeably, 'Missed a bit.'

'Okay. Who else rang?'

'Danny Delancey.' Florence held the pad at arm's length in an attempt to bring the scribbled message into some kind of focus. 'He has to fly to New York tomorrow, so he wondered if you could do the interview this afternoon.'

'Dangling from a step-ladder, with a paint brush clenched between my teeth? Oh yes, lovely.' About to roll her eyes, Miranda shot her a suspicious look. 'I hope you said no.'

'I did not, I said it would be fine.' Florence was unrepent-ant. 'Today's the only time they can manage it, and you've put them off twice already. Anyway, I told them to come over at five, so you should be finished by then.'

'*Five?* But I've arranged to meet Greg at six!' Honestly, this was so unfair. Was it Danny Delancey's mission in life to spoil all her fun?

'Absence makes the heart grow fonder.' Florence shrugged with irritating lack of concern. 'Ring him, tell him you'll see him at eight.'

'Missed a bit,' said Bev, too busy flipping through one of the Sunday supplements to even point an acrylic false nail in the appropriate direction. Instead, she wriggled her eyebrows and nodded at a remote section of wall high above the door frame. 'See? It's gone blotchy.'

'It's all going blotchy,' Miranda grumbled. She leaned back on her ladder, rubbing her aching spine. 'I'm going to have to do two coats.'

'There's a piece in here about the best places to go to meet men.' Bev sat up on the dust-sheet-covered bed, sending half

167

a dozen *Sunday Times* sections slithering to the floor. 'It says health farms are good.' She looked up, interested. 'I've never been to a health farm.'

'The only men you'd meet there would be overweight, stressed-out businessmen who've been warned by their doctors that if they don't lose six stone they'll be dead by Christmas.' Miranda blinked as a spray of crocus-yellow emulsion ricocheted off the roller into her eyes. 'And they'd all be going cold turkey because they'd had their mobile phones and laptops confiscated.'

'True,' sighed Bev. 'I can't bear men who twitch.' She read on down the list. 'How about evening classes in car maintenance?'

'Full of women desperate to meet men,' Miranda said briskly. 'And no real men would ever go because it would be too unmacho for words.'

'Kite flying!' Bev exclaimed, jabbing the page. 'That's how you met Thingy! Well, it certainly worked for you.'

Miranda tried to imagine Bev, in her high heels, teetering up Parliament Hill, struggling to keep her hair in place with one hand and clinging for dear life to the handle of a somersaulting kite with the other.

Still, Thingy was a good name for Daniel Delancey.

'I didn't so much meet him,' Miranda protested, 'as hurl abuse at him.'

'I could hurl abuse.' Bev looked indignant. 'I'm great at that. I haven't always worked at Fenn's place, you know. I was once a doctor's receptionist.'

Splat, a dollop of paint slid off the end of Miranda's roller and landed on top of her head. This was worse than being dive-bombed by pigeons in Trafalgar Square.

Only yellower.

'My legs ache, my arms ache, my back aches.'

'Oh, stop being so neurotic. Take a couple of painkillers and stop moaning. You can't see the doctor until a week on Tuesday and that's final.'

Amazed, Miranda swung round.

'What?'

'That's me being a doctor's receptionist.' Bev was smug. 'Told you I was good.'

'But I *do* ache.'

'I don't see why. You've only done half a ceiling and one wall.'

And spent most of the night having rampant, muscle-wrenching nonstop sex, thought Miranda semi-guiltily. Still, better not mention that.

'I thought you came here to help me.' She tried a spot of wheedling.

'I am helping you, I'm keeping you company.'

Great.

'You could keep me company up this ladder.'

'I get dizzy on ladders. And I'm allergic to paint.' Cosily, Bev snuggled up with the *News of the World*. 'If I got any on me I'd go as blotchy as your wall.'

'I wouldn't mind.'

'I would. Anyway, I'm doing my bit later, aren't I? Making you look presentable for the TV cameras.'

As soon as Bev had heard that Danny Delancey was coming round, she had excitedly volunteered to do Miranda's make-up.

'Nothing outrageous,' Miranda warned her now, a terrifying vision of Zandra Rhodes looming into her mind. 'A bit of eyeshadow, a bit of lipstick, that's all. Not too much foundation.'

Especially the last; Bev had a tendency to get carried away when it came to foundation.

'Don't panic, you'll look great.' Leaning over, Bev smugly patted her handbag, bulging with every cosmetic known to Harrods Beauty Hall.

'Okay, but easy on the foundation.'

'Believe me,' Bev's tone was soothing, 'right now you need all the help you can get.'

'You're not my friend.'

'I am your friend, I'm just being honest.'

'If you were really my friend,' Miranda said sorrowfully, 'you'd get off your big lazy bum and make me a chocolate spread sandwich and a banana milkshake.'

Miranda was jabbing paint into a corner of plaster coving when the door swung open behind her. She heard the satisfying clunk of china against glass.

'I take it all back, Bev, you don't have a big lazy bum, and you're definitely my friend.'

'That's really kind,' said an unfamiliar voice, 'but actually, I'm not Bev.'

Miranda let out a snort of laughter and swung round. Blonde, pretty, curvy, loose shirt over stretchy trousers . . .

'Chloe, right?'

'Right.' Chloe grinned and held up a plate. 'Chocolate spread sandwich, right?'

'Hooray. Coming right down.' Miranda dropped the brush messily into the pot of paint and leapt off the ladder. 'I'm Miranda, by the way.'

'I guessed.'

'I'd shake hands, but I'm all painty.'

'I spoke to Florence on the phone earlier,' Chloe explained. 'She told me what you were doing. I've come to help.'

'Oh no, I couldn't let you do that!' Miranda gestured vaguely in the direction of her stomach.

'I'm pregnant, not paralysed from the chest down. This is a great colour.' Having briefly admired the repainted wall, Chloe began to climb the ladder. 'Go on, have a rest. Eat your sandwich and drink your milkshake.'

Enchanted by this order and all in favour of a spot of cosseting, Miranda grinned at her.

'You sound like a mother already.'

Chapter 22

By one o'clock the second wall and the rest of the ceiling were finished and Bev had read aloud an entire two-thousand-word article in the *Sunday Express* speculating on the likelihood of Miles Harper and Daisy Schofield marrying before Christmas.

'She's dead set on it and he's fending her off.' Bev held up the colour supplement so they could see the accompanying photograph. 'Miranda met him a few weeks ago,' she explained slyly to Chloe. 'Miles asked her out, Miranda turned him down and she's regretted it from that day to this.'

'Oh, no.' Chloe was sympathetic.

'Ignore her,' Miranda said loftily. 'I haven't regretted it for one minute. I'm perfectly happy with the way things turned out.'

'Just as well,' Bev picked up her crossword pen and gave Daisy Schofield a handlebar moustache, 'seeing as you haven't heard from Miles Harper since.' She studied the photograph with a critical eye. 'I don't think she's that stunning, you know. Is it just me, or does she have a lopsided face?'

'Only because you gave her a lopsided moustache,' Miranda pointed out.

'My husband . . . well, ex-husband, whatever . . .' stammered Chloe, 'thought she was pretty stunning.'

Miranda, thinking of Greg, drawled, 'Show me a man who doesn't.'

'So how long ago did he leave you?' asked Bev, for whom no situation was too delicate.

'The day I told him I was pregnant, pretty much. It was April Fools' Day.' Chloe's tone was dry.

'Can you believe that? What a bastard!' Bev made vigorous poke-his-eyes-out gestures with her fingers. 'And what's he doing now?'

'Don't know, don't care,' Chloe replied not altogether truthfully. Trawling her roller through the paint tray, she turned her attention to the third wall.

'But up until the minute you told him about the baby,' Bev persisted, 'you were happily married?'

Chloe nodded.

'Yes.'

'Is he likely to change his mind and come back?'

'No.'

'Has he found someone else?'

'Bev, shut up.' This was more than even Miranda could stand.

'Why? It's interesting!'

'Chloe might not want to talk about it. She might find it upsetting. You could be about to make her cry.'

'Okay,' Chloe said equably. 'I think he does have a new girlfriend. But you're right, I would rather not talk about him any more.'

'See?' Delighted with herself for being so sensitive, Miranda flicked her brush at Bev.

'Not because it would upset me,' Chloe explained. 'I just don't want to be bothered with thinking about him. If he doesn't want to know, that's his loss. But *this*' – she gestured around the half-painted room – 'is going to be my new home, and *I*' – she pointed to her stomach – 'am going to have a baby. And right now,' she announced firmly, 'that is all I care about.'

Heavens, so strong and brave, thought Bev, just like one of those Danielle Steel heroines you secretly longed to punch in the teeth. She gazed at Chloe, impressed.

Miranda, who had never read a Danielle Steel book and was altogether less gullible, said, 'So how much of that was bullshit? Seventy-five, eighty per cent?'

'Pretty much,' Chloe admitted with a grin of relief. 'Still, getting better. A fortnight ago it was ninety.'

Miranda spent the next hour washing and blow-drying her hair into a less spiky and altogether more grown-up style, and getting her make-up done.

'I'm sorry, we've come to the wrong house,' Danny Delancey apologised when she pulled open the front door.

'Oh, ha ha.' Why did he always have to make fun of her? 'Bev did my face for me. It's okay, isn't it?'

'The face is fine.' Danny took a step back in order to admire Miranda's outfit, top to toe. 'It's the rest of you that's taken me by surprise. I'm just trying to think who you remind me of.'

Somebody nice, I hope, thought Miranda.

'Got it!'

Some gorgeous, bright-eyed perky young actress, preferably. The kind everybody fancied.

'Margaret Thatcher,' Danny announced, pleased with himself. He turned to the man behind him. 'Don't you think?'

'Minus about sixty years.' His companion stepped forward, holding his hand out for Miranda to shake. 'Hi, anyway. Tony Vale. I'll be pointing the camera at you this afternoon.'

'This time I've definitely got it! She looks like a teenager going to a fancy-dress party *as* Margaret Thatcher.' Danny grinned at her. 'Is that your going-for-an-interview suit?'

Miranda ran her hands protectively over the navy-blue knee-length gaberdine skirt. However had he guessed?

'Um . . .'

'Have to take it off, I'm afraid.'

She bit her lip.

'You mean, actually while you're filming?'

'That's entirely up to you.' Cheerfully Danny lugged a heavy tripod past her into the hall. 'We wouldn't force you.'

'We're in here.' Miranda led the way through to Florence's living room. 'I'm not sure about this nude stuff, though.' She sounded doubtful. 'I mean, is it absolutely essential to the script?'

'Nude stuff! What the hell's going on here?' Bev leapt up, outraged.

'This is Bev,' said Miranda, as Florence and Chloe started to laugh. 'Told you she was gullible.'

The filming, once Miranda had changed out of the terrifying navy suit and into her favourite cropped top and white jeans, took less than an hour. Danny's interviewing style was informal, which helped a lot, and Tony Vale organised the lighting and camera positions and generally made himself as unobtrusive as possible in the unnaturally tidy bedroom. Before Miranda knew it, Danny was saying, 'That's great, now let's shift this stuff downstairs,' and Tony was scurrying out through her bedroom door with the light reflectors tucked under one arm and the camera cases swinging from the other.

'Er . . . why?' said Miranda.

'Your landlady. Great character,' Tony called over his shoulder.

'Ten minutes, if that,' Danny explained. 'She's just going to say a few nice things about you. Well, that's the general idea, but I suppose with Florence you never know.'

'She'd better say nice things.' Miranda held the door open so he could manoeuvre the tripod through. 'Or I'll twist her arms off.'

'Florence, you're a natural,' said Danny when it was over.

'A disgrace, you mean.' Miranda shot her an accusing look. 'She was flirting with the camera.'

Florence's grey eyes sparkled. Thanks to the attentions of Bev, her make-up was immaculate and, for once, symmetrical.

'Why not? You never know who might be watching.' She spread her gnarled fingers, palms upturned. 'Just think, there could be some lonely Texan billionaire out there, desperate to find someone to keep him company in his rich old age . . . then he switches on the TV one day and *boom*, one look at me and he's smitten—'

'I think that's being a bit greedy,' said Miranda. 'You've already got Orlando.'

Danny looked interested.

'Who's Orlando?'

'Clear the table,' Chloe shouted, emerging from the kitchen with two massive plates of sandwiches. Bev, behind her, staggered in with the wine.

'We're having a wrap party to celebrate the end of filming.' Florence eyed with amusement the front of Bev's flimsy white top, transparent where the condensation from the chilled bottles had sunk in. 'Or we could make it a wet T-shirt contest, if you'd prefer.'

The phone rang just as Miranda was shovelling an asparagus sandwich into her mouth.

'Shall I get it?' offered Chloe, who was nearest.

'Don't worry.' Florence reversed like Damon Hill through the gap between the coffee table and the sofa and snatched it up. 'Probably Bruce, ringing to make sure I haven't eloped.'

She listened for a moment, then waggled the phone at Miranda, who still had her mouth full.

Chew chew, swallow swallow.

'Who is it?'

Florence smirked, relishing the moment.

'He didn't give his name.'

'What's going on?' said Greg when Miranda had seized control of the receiver. 'Sounds like you're having a party.'

'Oh, hi.' Miranda couldn't help it; she felt herself going bright pink.

'Who is it, your new chap? Brilliant! Tell him to come on over!' Bev turned excitedly to Florence. 'She's been keeping this one under wraps, it's all *deeply* mysterious. I haven't even been allowed to meet him yet!'

'I thought you were decorating some bedroom,' Greg protested as Danny pushed a glass into Miranda's hand. As he filled it, the neck of the bottle went clunk against the rim.

'I was! I mean, I have! Florence's new lodger turned up and helped me finish it in double-quick time. Then Danny and Tony arrived, we've just done a bit of filming—'

'Shall I come over?' Greg wasn't at all sure he trusted Danny Delancey.

'Tell him to get himself over here this *minute*,' Bev bellowed across the room.

Miranda jumped, then hesitated. Should she? It had to happen sooner or later . . .

'Did you hear that?' she said lightly into the phone. 'My friend Bev's here as well. Why don't you come on over? She's dying to meet you.'

'Jesus, no thanks.' Greg sounded horrified. 'You haven't told her, have you?'

Miranda knew exactly what he was thinking: a potential bunny-boiler on his case, that was all he needed.

'Not yet, but—'

'Just say I'm busy.' She could almost hear Greg shudder. 'And you, watch yourself with that Danny character. Better still, fix him up with Bev,' he declared with satisfaction. 'That should do the trick; those two deserve each other.'

Now there was an idea. Miranda gave it some thought as she hung up. Then, still lit up with happiness just from hearing Greg's voice, she grinned inanely across the room at Danny.

Making his way over, he studied her mouth with apparent concern.

'Why the dopey smirk?'

'It isn't a smirk. I never smirk. I'm not dopey either. I just wondered, do you have a girlfriend?'

Danny topped up her glass.

'Why, are you offering? All applications for the post in writing, please. Just send a copy of your CV and a brief letter outlining why you feel you'd be the best woman for the job. If you make the short list, you'll be invited to attend for an interview—'

'So is that a yes or a no?' interrupted Miranda. Behind him, Bev was chatting to Tony Vale, but in a half-hearted fashion. Probably because he was in his forties, on the scrawny side, and had already told her all about his wonderful wife.

'It's a no.' Danny's mouth twitched. 'And if you don't mind me saying so, I think it's very brave of you to take the initiative like this.' He consulted his watch. 'Look, I have to be at Heathrow by six tomorrow morning so I can't stay out too late, but we could have dinner somewhere if you like. I'm afraid I don't sleep with girls on a first date, but I'll only be away for a few days, so play your cards right—'

'Honestly, are you ever serious? I was thinking of Bev!'

'Excuse me,' said Danny, 'are *you* being serious? Is this baby-making, desperate-for-a-man Bev we're talking about?'

Bugger, thought Miranda, who had forgotten she'd told him about that. It was like trying to sell someone pleurisy.

'What?' Bev demanded, popping up behind Danny right on cue. 'Who mentioned babies?'

Miranda sighed. Honestly, she did herself no favours.

179

'Jelly babies,' Danny told Bev. 'I was just saying, the green ones are my favourite.'

'Mine's orange. So, is he coming over?'

'Who?' said Miranda.

'Your chap!'

'He can't make it. He has . . . stuff to do.'

'Oh well, never mind. Time I was making a move anyway.' Sunday night was leg-waxing night for Bev. She beamed at Danny. 'Still, it's been fun, hasn't it?'

Florence wheeled herself over to them.

'I've been looking at this one here.' As she addressed Miranda, she patted Danny's arm. 'Imagine him with his hair slicked back. Wouldn't he make a marvellous Orlando?'

'What is going on here?' Danny's dark eyes narrowed. 'That's the second time I've heard the name. Who *is* this Orlando?'

'Hi, it's me again,' said Miranda, grinning at Chloe as Greg picked up the phone. 'The coast's clear. Bev's just left. It's safe to come over.'

Across the room, Chloe rolled her eyes like a mad woman and said teasingly, 'Well, relatively safe.'

'I'll be there in twenty minutes,' said Greg.

Chapter 23

'You'll really do it?' Florence was delighted. 'You'll be Orlando for an evening?'

'Why not? I've always wanted to be a gigolo.'

Danny grinned; the idea appealed to his journalistic instincts. Human reactions were what interested him more than anything. Particularly the meaner ones.

'You won't be able to wear those clothes,' Miranda pointed out.

'Look, who's the master of disguise here,' said Danny, 'you or me?'

'Couple of gold chains around your neck,' Florence prompted.

'Shiny shirt,' said Chloe.

'Skin-tight trousers, pointy patent-leather shoes. With heels,' Miranda added with relish.

'This isn't *Saturday Night Fever*,' said Danny.

'He's right, he mustn't be cheap and slimy,' Chloe told Miranda. 'Bruce and Verity wouldn't fall for it. They know Florence would never go for someone like that.'

'Okay, good clothes.' Reluctantly, because cheap and slimy would have been more fun, Miranda began ticking each item off on her fingers. 'You'll have to borrow an Armani suit or something.'

'Thanks.' Danny exchanged a look with Florence.

'One gold chain,' said Chloe. 'One's enough.'

'Bit of fake tan,' said Miranda. 'Ooh, and a diamond ring on your little finger! You can tell them it was a gift from your last lady friend.'

'Go on then,' Danny gave her an encouraging nod, 'lend us twenty grand.'

'Cubic zirconium,' Chloe said promptly. 'Argos catalogue. Let me know your size,' she told Danny, 'and I'll pick one up.'

Miranda wrinkled her nose.

'They still cost money.'

'You take it back to the shop and get a refund,' Chloe explained. She was loving every minute of this. 'When are you going to do it?'

'Next weekend?' Florence looked at Danny. 'Is that okay with you?'

'Fine. You sort out the details and I'll speak to you when I get back from the States.' Danny stood up. 'And now, I'd better make a move.'

When Tony Vale had left earlier, he had shaken hands – somewhat sweatily – with each of them in turn. Now, Miranda watched Danny bend and give Florence a kiss on the cheek, before moving around the table and doing the same to Chloe. Having mentally prepared herself – after all, she was next in line – she was miffed when he left it at that. All she received was a wink and a broad smile.

Miranda's toes clenched with irritation. What had the wink been, some kind of consolation prize? Even more embarrassing, she'd been tilting her head at an about-to-be-kissed angle, and now she had to pretend she'd simply been stretching her neck.

Men! Honestly, how pathetic were they? Danny Delancey was happy enough to bestow meaningless kisses on wrinkled old women – sorry, Florence – and ones who were pregnant, but when it came to real girls, girls like herself, he couldn't bring himself to do it. He was intimidated by the fact that she had a boyfriend. Scared, probably, that Greg – who was due to arrive at any minute – might burst through the door and challenge him to a duel.

'Is your neck okay?' said Danny.

Wimp.

'Just pulled a muscle.' Miranda carried on massaging vigorously, to prove that she hadn't been expecting any kind of kiss in the first place.

As he hoisted the camera case over his shoulder, Danny turned back to Chloe.

'I can give you a lift home if you like.'

'Are you sure? Oh no,' Chloe protested, 'I'm miles out of your way.'

'No problem.' Danny glanced with amusement in Miranda's direction. 'I don't have a girlfriend, you see. So, plenty of free time.'

He was making fun of her *again*, Miranda realised, and bloody annoying it was too. Anyway, why was he offering Chloe a lift home? He didn't fancy her, did he? Okay, so she was a pretty girl, you couldn't argue with that, but oh dear, a pretty girl who was three months pregnant . . . ?

*   *   *

'I enjoyed that,' said Florence, watching from the window as Danny held open the passenger door of the green BMW.

With an odd sense of unease, Miranda saw him say something that made Chloe laugh. She tried to remember whether Danny had held the passenger door open like a gentleman when he had given her a lift home that time from the salon, or if he had simply jumped into the driver's seat and shouted, 'It's open.' Which, let's face it, was pretty much par for the course these days in her experience. When men clapped eyes on her, Miranda realised sadly, their initial reaction wasn't to come over all exquisitely mannered, start tipping their hats and bowing and calling her ma'am.

She was no Scarlett O'Hara.

Maybe it was something to do with having blue hair.

I could dye it, thought Miranda, and stop being accident-prone, and learn to do flirtatious things with parasols—

'They get on well together,' Florence declared with satisfaction as the car pulled away.

Chloe had swivelled round to wave up at them. Automatically Miranda waved back. Then she turned and frowned at Florence.

'Yes, but it's hardly ideal, is it?'

'What?'

'You, matchmaking! Why would Danny want to be lumbered with someone else's baby?' Miranda began to hyperventilate; she flapped her hand indignantly out of the window. 'And why would Chloe want to get involved with anyone *at all*? It's not fair on either of them, in fact it's—'

She stopped abruptly. Florence was spluttering with laughter.

'Come on! Did I just offer to pay for their honeymoon? They get on well together, that's all I said. Where's the matchmaking in that?'

Oh dear, she'd overreacted. Biting her lip, Miranda paid elaborate attention to the BMW as it disappeared from view.

'It was more the look in your eye,' she said defensively. 'I know what you're like when you hit on an idea.'

'Hit on a great one this evening, didn't I?' Florence gave her a nudge. 'Asking Danny to go gigolo for a night. Roll on next weekend,' she chuckled. 'I can't wait.'

Miranda's spirits lifted at the sight of Greg's car drawing up outside. As Danny and Chloe had been disappearing around one corner, Greg had been making his approach from the other end of the street. Like a relay race, Miranda thought, only without a baton.

Or synchronised swimming minus the nose-clips.

'I'll just get my stuff,' she told Florence, jumping down from the window seat.

'Staying over at his place tonight?'

'Is that okay?' Miranda hesitated. 'If there's anything you want me to do before I go . . .'

Florence looked at her, so eager to get away. It was stupid, she knew, but she felt like a mother bird watching her chick prepare to launch itself from the nest. In the year she and Miranda had lived together they had grown so close, it was hard to come to terms with the possibility that, for Miranda, the time had now come to move on.

I should be thrilled for her, thought Florence. She's falling in love, maybe for the first time in her life. I should be happier than this.

Oh, but if only Miranda could have chosen someone else to fall in love with.

'I'll be fine,' she announced robustly. This was ridiculous, a severe case of empty-nest syndrome and she wasn't even the girl's mother.

I'm not going to have an empty nest either, Florence reminded herself. Miranda hasn't left yet. And when she does, I'll still have Chloe.

'Party over?' asked Greg when Miranda greeted him at the front door with her overnight bag – otherwise known as an Asda carrier – clutched to her chest.

'I thought we'd have another one, back at your place.'

'Was that Danny Delancey's car I saw leaving just now? Are you sure he isn't a bit keen on you?'

'If he's keen on anyone, it's Florence's new lodger.' Miranda wondered why the idea still rankled. Determinedly she pushed the thought to the back of her mind.

'I thought she wasn't moving in for another week or so.'

Reaching up on her toes, Miranda kissed Greg full on the mouth. The last people she felt like talking about right now were Danny Delancey and pretty blonde pregnant Chloe.

'She isn't.'

'So why was she here today?'

Greg didn't really want to know, he was just being polite.

'Came to lend a hand with the painting, that's all. Now, can I ask you something personal?'

They reached the car. Greg leaned her backwards across the still-warm bonnet and ran his fingers across her exposed midriff.

'How personal?'

'Extremely, deeply and outrageously personal.'

Greg hesitated for a fraction of a second.

'Go on then.'

'Do you ache as much as I do after last night?'

Up close, with the last of the evening sunlight on her face, he could see the tiny, barely visible freckles scattered over Miranda's nose. Her dark eyes sparkled, her mouth curved up at the corners and her complexion was flawless.

Most people looked better from a distance, thought Greg. Miranda was even more gorgeous close up.

'You're beautiful.' He couldn't help himself, he had to say it.

'And you're a salesman.' She raised a sceptical eyebrow. 'Anyway, you haven't answered my question.'

'I love you,' said Greg.

'You're still a salesman.'

Outwardly, Miranda was still joking, but inwardly he knew she believed him. Which was just as well, Greg thought. Because it was true.

'You want me to be totally honest with you?' He was smiling as he spoke, his mouth inches away from hers. 'Okay, I do, I ache just as much as you do. I ache like mad. And you know something else?'

'What?' Miranda wondered if all the neighbours were watching. Spreadeagled across the bonnet of a car in broad daylight in the middle of dear old Notting Hill . . . well, it was hardly discreet.

'I don't care that I ache,' said Greg. 'It's not going to stop me. So if you want a good night's sleep, you'd better turn around now and head back into that house.'

As if she could, Miranda thought joyfully. She flung her arms around him. So what if she couldn't walk tomorrow, or push a broom, or wash hair. Who cared?

Apart from Fenn, of course, her stroppy employer, who could get quite funny about salon juniors who staggered into work incapable of carrying out the simplest tasks.

Then again, what did Fenn know about love? All he ever went out with were spaghetti-thin supermodels with minds as blank as their faces and Press Here buttons in their backs for when you wanted them to speak. And they never lasted longer than a few weeks; with his low boredom threshold, Fenn freely admitted that he didn't know why he bothered.

It was, all in all, a bit of a sad existence, Miranda felt. As if being photographed and appearing in as many magazines as possible was more important than being with someone you actually liked. Poor Fenn, he didn't know what he was missing.

'If it takes you this long to make up your mind,' said Greg, 'I must be losing my touch. Maybe I'd better just go home after all.'

He was doing his best to sound offended. Miranda ran her fingernails down his back.

'I was thinking about my boss.'

'Oh, great. Don't think about your boss, think about me!'

'Okay, let's go.' Blissfully, she breathed in the scent of his aftershave. 'Who needs sleep anyway?'

'I love you.'

Miranda knew why he was saying it again. It was her turn now; he was waiting for her to return the favour. She shivered with happiness.

'I love you too.'

Above them, Florence's living room window was flung open.

'Any more of that malarkey in a public parking bay,' Florence yelled down at them, 'and you'll get clamped.'

Chapter 24

Chloe had an appointment at the hospital for an ultrasound scan on Friday afternoon. She was wondering how to break this unhappy news to Bruce – unhappy for Bruce, that is, not for her – when he burst into the shop on Wednesday morning with news of his own.

'Well, we're finally being allowed to meet him.'

His chins wobbled with disapproval, his chest was puffed out like a penguin's. Time to get down to Argos and pick up one of their is-it-or-isn't-it? diamond rings, thought Chloe.

Aloud, she said, 'Meet who?'

'The gigolo, who else? On Friday.'

'You mean Orlando?' Her eyes lit up with pleasure. 'Oh, you'll like him, he's great!'

Bruce swivelled round en route to his office, his mouth clamped in a tight line.

'You what? You mean you've met him already?'

'He was there on Sunday.'

'You didn't tell me any of this.' Bruce shook his head in disbelief.

'You didn't ask.' Chloe put on a bewildered look. 'I'm sorry, was I supposed to tell you?'

'For crying out loud, he's a con man,' Bruce bellowed.

'As soon as he's finished bleeding my mother dry – of *my* inheritance – he'll move on to the next wealthy widow . . . of *course* I want you to tell me about him!'

'Well, I thought he was really nice,' said Chloe. 'Charming, friendly . . . and he and Florence get on tremendously well together.'

'Hah, I'll bet they do.'

'He does seem to be very fond of her.'

Bruce shot Chloe a dark look.

'He's a gigolo, for Christ's sake. It's his job to seem fond of her.'

'But the thing is,' Chloe protested, 'he was lovely to me too. And it's not as if I've got money coming out of my ears, is it? I'm hardly likely to buy him a Porsche—' She broke off in mid-sentence and looked away.

'A Porsche,' Bruce exploded, 'a bloody *Porsche*, is that what my stupid senile mother has gone and bought him?'

'Not yet.' Chloe flapped her hands apologetically. 'She's only thinking about it.'

'Right. I'll have a few words with her about that.'

'But you might be mistaken about him. Like I said just now, he seems to really like Florence, and he was *so* nice to me.'

'He probably fancied you.' Bruce sounded irritated. 'My mother's business, you were pleasure.' Abruptly a thought struck him. 'Hey now, there's an idea! This could be just what we need. You can lure him away from Florence—'

'Me! Oh, fine, easy, no problem,' Chloe spluttered. 'I'll just be upfront about it, shall I? Ask him why he's wasting his time jetting around the world with some millionairess when he could be buggering off to Bognor instead with

191

a penniless shop assistant who can't even spell Porsche and who, by the way, just happens to be three months pregnant.'

'I'm not saying you have to run off with him into the sunset.' Bruce dismissed this suggestion with the scorn it deserved. 'Up to the bedroom will do the trick. We just need to catch him out,' he went on, warming to his theme. 'Show my mother what he's really like. And you could do that, no problem. You're moving in next weekend, he's already showing a bit of interest . . . what could be simpler? That'll bring Florence to her senses in no time. She might be stupid but she still has her pride. As soon as she finds out he's been cheating on her, she'll kick him out,' Bruce concluded triumphantly. 'End of problem. Fantastic.'

Chloe inwardly marvelled at his smugness.

'I couldn't do that to Florence, I just couldn't.'

'Cruel to be kind,' said Bruce, rubbing his hands.

'But I'm pregnant. Don't you think that might . . . um, bother him?'

'For pity's sake, the man's a gigolo! He wouldn't know a scruple if it jumped up and head-butted him! You're a pretty girl, Chloe. That's all men like him care about.'

'Florence might blame me. She might kick *me* out,' Chloe protested.

Bruce considered this. Finally he spoke.

'Look, if you manage to get rid of this . . . this Orlando,' his lip curled as he pronounced the ludicrous name, 'I'll give you two thousand pounds.'

'What?'

'All right, three.'

192

'Hang on a second,' began Chloe.

'Okay, okay, five thousand.'

Bruce heaved a sigh. It was a lot of money, but what the hell, it would be worth it. And five grand was a small price to pay if it meant saving his inheritance.

'I'm not sleeping with him,' Chloe said flatly.

Bruce looked resigned; somehow he had known she wouldn't.

'Okay, just so long as you do enough to make my mother realise he's a waste of space.'

'If he is,' Chloe reminded him. 'He may not be.'

'That's your trouble, you're too trusting.' What Bruce actually meant was gullible. Jesus, was it any wonder her husband had run off?

'You shouldn't judge people until you've met them,' Chloe persisted. 'You might like Orlando.'

'Hmm.'

Maybe it was the pregnancy, thought Bruce, doing bizarre things to her brain.

'Well, we'll find out on Friday,' she went on brightly. 'That's when I'm moving in.'

Bruce perked up. This could be interesting.

'I'll be able to see how he behaves towards you.'

'Oh, that would have been brilliant. But I'll still be upstairs, ploughing through all my unpacking. Unless . . .' Chloe glanced hopefully across at him, 'you could let me have the afternoon off?'

'You look lovely.' Miranda was full of admiration. 'Nice and sleazy.'

'But subtle sleaze,' said Danny, standing back from

Miranda's bedroom mirror and letting her blast away with the hairspray.

'There, done.'

She bounced on to the bed, admiring her own handiwork.

They had settled on slicked-back hair and fake tan for that Latin-lover look, teamed with a navy blazer over a white polo shirt and precision-ironed jeans. The overall effect, together with the jewellery and aftershave, was just right.

'Smile at me,' Miranda ordered.

Danny smiled, gigolo-style, oozing charm and sincerity and playful flirtation.

Somewhere in the depths of her ribcage, something went zinnggg. She shook her head, marvelling at the effect.

'Damn, you're good.'

'I know. Scary, isn't it?' Reaching for her hand, he pressed a warm, lingering kiss on the tips of her fingers.

'Oh dear,' Miranda murmured. 'You could live to regret that.'

'Why? Oh God—!'

Danny pulled a face as the terrible taste belatedly reached his tongue.

'What did I just plaster all over your head?' Gleefully Miranda waved her hands at him, Al Jolson-style. 'Hair gel.'

Danny watched her run a comb through her own gel-free hair. It was almost eight o'clock – Bruce and Verity would be here at any minute.

'Not seeing the boyfriend this evening?'

The boyfriend. Honestly, how derogatory was that?

'He's away.' Miranda vigorously rubbed a bit of blusher

into her cheeks, hoping she sounded like a girl who could take separations in her stride. Since Greg had left for Birmingham on Wednesday she had missed him dreadfully, had practically been reduced to counting the minutes, but tonight was the last night. By lunchtime tomorrow he would be back, hooray!

'He's at an important sales conference,' she explained airily over her shoulder. 'In Birmingham.'

Danny sounded amused.

'You hope.'

'What are you talking about? Of course he's at a sales conference.' Miranda swung round and glared at him.

'How do you know? He could have another girlfriend tucked away somewhere.' Danny shrugged. 'I'm not saying he *has*. It's possible, that's all.'

'Why are you always doing this?' she demanded. 'Does it give you some kind of thrill?'

He feigned innocence.

'Not at all. I was just thinking of a piece I did in one of the Sundays last year, about bigamists. It just amazed me the way the wives had absolutely no idea what was going on.'

Miranda almost felt sorry for him. It couldn't be much fun having a nasty suspicious mind.

'Look, just because you're a journalist you don't always have to think the worst of people,' she told him patiently. 'Not everyone's a liar and a cheat, you know. I'm not, Florence isn't . . . and Greg isn't, either. He's honest and trustworthy and when he tells me he has to go to a sales conference in Birmingham, I believe him. So just shut up about it, okay?'

'Okay. I'm sorry.' Danny flashed her an apologetic –

well, *fairly* apologetic – smile. 'I must not cast aspersions on Miranda's perfect boyfriend, I must not cast aspersions on Miranda's—'

'Stop it!' Miranda howled, blushing and hurling the comb at him.

'Must be true love.' He eyed her pink cheeks with enjoyment. 'Bet you wish you hadn't put all that blusher on now.'

'It's eight o'clock.' Miranda pushed him towards the door. 'We'd better get a move on. Bruce and Verity aren't going to be wildly impressed if they arrive to find you locked away upstairs with me.'

Chapter 25

Bruce wasn't wildly impressed with Orlando anyway. Miranda, keeping herself busy pouring drinks and passing around trays of M&S hors d'oeuvres, could only watch and admire Danny's performance. He might be a pig, but when it came to playing the part of the *almost* totally devoted younger man, he was perfect.

Florence was good too, as the besotted older woman.

Even Chloe was doing her bit, exchanging meaningful looks with Danny whenever Florence's attention was diverted.

If Bruce looked as if he was chewing a lemon, thought Miranda, Verity looked as if she was chewing a lemon with a maggot in it.

'So we thought a few weeks in Las Vegas first,' Danny was busy explaining to them, 'then maybe fly on down to Miami.'

'If we've got any money left by then,' Florence put in cheerfully.

Danny gave her hand a squeeze.

'Don't worry, we will. I told you, we're going to bring each other luck.' His smile as he turned back to Bruce was warm. 'And I'm on a winning streak at the moment, wouldn't you say? Meeting Flo has been the best thing that's happened to me in years.'

I'll bet it is, Bruce thought savagely, suppressing the urge to take a wild swing at him.

He cleared his throat. 'So where did you two meet?'

'The Grosvenor Casino. You know Flo, fond of a flutter.' Danny draped his arm casually around Florence's shoulder. 'I've always been attracted to the kind of woman who isn't afraid to take risks. This is a fantastic colour on you, by the way.' He paused to admire the crimson brocade of Florence's dress. 'You're looking stunning tonight.'

Patting his hand, Florence leaned forward and stage-whispered to Verity, 'Isn't he a dream? Can you imagine how wonderful it feels, after years of . . . nothing, to be showered with compliments?'

Verity couldn't, actually. The only times Bruce remarked on her appearance were when he pointed out that her nail polish was chipped or her bra straps were on show.

'But doesn't she *deserve* compliments?' Danny protested. 'I mean, forget she's your mother-in-law, just look at her! She's a beautiful woman, a fabulous, original human being. She has a mind of her own—'

'Not to mention a fair amount of money,' Bruce blurted out before he could stop himself.

Florence glared at him.

'Bruce!'

'What?' Defiantly, he glared back. 'I'm stating a fact. Aren't I allowed to mention that?'

Danny nodded understandingly.

'It's all right, I'm not interested in Florence's money,' he assured Bruce.

'So what's this I hear about a Porsche?'

Danny looked hurt.

'I didn't ask Flo to buy me a Porsche. She offered.'

'That's absolutely right. Anyway, we haven't bought it yet.' Florence rushed to his defence. 'There's a waiting list.'

For the first time in his life, Bruce was grateful for a waiting list.

'What kind of work do you do?' he demanded.

'Oh, this and that.' Danny shrugged, unembarrassed. 'I'm not really your nine-to-five type.'

As he smoothed back his hair, the fake diamond glittered in the light. Miranda saw Verity and Bruce look at it, then at each other.

'I love that ring you're wearing,' she told Danny. 'Where did you get it?'

'This?' Danny raised his eyebrows and waggled his little finger. 'A gift, from a dear friend of mine. Heavens, is that the time already? We should be ordering a cab.'

'Where are you going?' said Bruce, startled.

'Darling, the casino,' Florence exclaimed. 'Didn't I mention it? We go every Friday!'

'To celebrate our anniversary,' Danny chimed in. 'That's when we met, you see, on a Friday night.'

'It's great fun,' Florence told Verity and Bruce. 'You'll come along, won't you? We'll have the most wonderful time, the four of us together.'

'Why would we want to watch you throw your money away?' snapped Bruce. 'More to the point, why would *you* want to throw it away?'

'Because it's fun.' Calmly, Florence opened her bag and

199

took out a lipstick. Pursing her lips, she dashed on a layer of glossy crimson to match her dress.

'*Fun . . .*'

'Bruce, lighten up. According to you,' Florence patiently reminded him, 'playing golf is fun. And membership of that fancy club of yours doesn't come cheap, I'm sure. To each his own, darling. You hit little white balls into sandpits, I happen to prefer blackjack and roulette. Besides,' she went on as she squirted scent on to her wrists and throat, 'we need to practise. We're in training for Vegas.'

'Good God,' Bruce spluttered under his breath. He tipped back his head and drained his glass of Scotch, wincing as the ice cubes smacked into his front teeth.

'How about it then, are you coming with us or not?' Danny's hand was hovering over the phone. 'Because if it's a yes, we can all go in your car.'

The expression on Bruce's face reminded Miranda of a grenade having its pin slowly pulled out. She bit her lip and looked across at Florence, who was in turn gazing lovingly at Danny.

'No we bloody well are not coming with you,' Bruce hissed through clenched teeth. He began to wag his finger at Danny. 'And let me tell you something else—'

'Bruce is tired, he's had a hard day,' Verity broke in at high speed before Bruce managed to instantly disinherit himself. 'Actually, we should be getting back – we did promise the babysitter we wouldn't be late.'

'It's only nine o'clock.' Florence looked dismayed.

'Don't worry, I get the message,' said Danny. 'I'm not stupid. You think I'm only interested in your mother for her money, don't you?' He gazed sadly at Bruce. 'I'm not, though. I'm here because I care about her. I want to make her happy. I'm sorry if I don't earn enough to meet with your approval, but there's nothing I can do about that.'

'My son finds it hard to understand that there are more important things in life than money,' Florence explained.

'You,' Bruce jabbed a finger in her direction, 'are going senile.'

'I'd like it if we could be friends,' Danny sighed, 'but I don't think he wants to be. Oh well, at least I tried. I've done my best.'

'I know you have, darling.' Florence patted his hand. 'Why don't you ring that cab company?'

'And charge it to my mother's account,' snarled Bruce.

Florence shot him a look of reproach.

'I'm sorry you feel this way, Bruce. Now, mustn't keep that babysitter waiting.'

'Oh no, I haven't finished yet—'

'Bruce, you're my son and I love you, but sometimes you have the manners of a hog.'

'But—'

'No, don't interrupt.' Out of the corner of her eye, Florence could see Miranda trying desperately not to laugh. 'If you can't be charming to Orlando, I think you'd better go home.'

Chapter 26

By ten o'clock, Miranda was seven hundred and sixty pounds down and beginning to panic.

'I'm usually lucky. This kind of thing doesn't happen to me,' she wailed. 'I'm normally great at this.'

Across the table, Danny smirked. 'Don't forget you still owe me a hundred as well.'

'You're all heart,' Miranda muttered, counting how much she had left.

Surreptitiously, while he wasn't looking, she slid a couple of fifties into the waistband of her skirt, for emergency use only. Sod Danny, if he didn't know she had them, he couldn't demand his money back.

'Right, my go.' Florence rattled the dice and flung them across the board with panache. 'Six. Hah, Community Chest! "It's your birthday,"' she read aloud, '"collect five hundred pounds from each player."'

'I think you mean ten,' Danny told her.

Florence winked at him.

'Worth a try, darling, always worth a try. Wouldn't care to sell me that funny little blue card of yours, by any chance?'

'That funny little blue card,' said Danny, 'is Park Lane.'

'Name your price,' Florence announced grandly.

'A brand-new Porsche.'

'Oh!' Miranda suddenly squealed. 'Did you see Bruce's *face* when you said Florence had offered to buy you one?' Scrambling into a sitting position, she imitated Bruce's get-ready-for-the-suppository expression. 'Poor old Bruce, I almost felt sorry for him, I thought for a second his eyes were going to bounce out on springs . . . you know, doinnnggg . . .'

Chloe stared at Miranda in amazement.

Florence, raising her eyebrows, said, 'Is she on drugs?'

'Either that or she has something to hide.' Danny was calmly counting his own money. 'It could be a desperate attempt to distract us, so we won't notice she's landed on somebody else's property—'

'Yes! Bond Street!' Chloe cried. 'Hooray, that's mine!'

'Bastard.' Miranda glared at Danny, who was trying not to smile.

'Actually,' he said to Chloe, 'would you take seven hundred pounds for Fenchurch Street Station?'

Chloe, who was turning into quite the wheeler-dealer, promptly said, 'Make it eight.'

Florence said, 'He only has seven.'

Danny looked at Miranda.

'Pay-up time, I'm afraid. I need that extra hundred.'

'I don't have it! Chloe's just cleaned me out,' Miranda protested. Danny could take a hike, he wasn't getting his hands on her emergency fund.

'Give me my hundred.'

'I can't.'

'Oh yes you can.'

'Look, how can I give you something I don't have?'

Florence said, 'Where are you going?' as Danny leapt to his feet.

'Don't you know? I'm a debt collector in my spare time.'

Miranda, who was on her knees, began to shuffle rapidly backwards away from the table. Ow, carpet burns, carpet burns—

'No!' She let out a howl of outrage as Danny made a grab for her. 'You can't *do* that!'

A brief and not very dignified grappling contest ensued on the Persian rug. Miranda screamed as warm fingers burrowed expertly under her T-shirt and slid – eek – beneath the waistband of her skirt.

'Sorry,' said Danny, emerging triumphant within seconds and clearly not sorry at all. 'Had to be done.'

Grinning, he waggled the crumpled fifties under Miranda's nose, then whisked them out of reach before she could grab them back.

'I hate you,' Miranda sighed. 'Now I'm really, really skint.'

'Cheer up, I might land on Old Kent Road in a minute.' Danny rolled his eyes. 'Then I'll owe you . . . phew, two whole pounds.'

'That wasn't gel I put in your hair, by the way.' Miranda tugged her T-shirt down over her midriff. 'It was superglue.'

'You two, stop sniping,' Florence instructed as the telephone began to ring. 'At least while I answer the phone.'

'Maybe I should check your bra,' said Danny. 'You could have thousands stashed away.'

Miranda gazed up at him from the floor, flushed and out of breath.

'You wouldn't dare.'

'Want to bet? Oh, sorry, you can't, can you?' Danny flashed her his wickedest grin. 'I forgot you don't have any money left to bet with.'

'Pig,' wailed Miranda.

'Miranda!' said Florence.

'What? Why can't I call him a pig?'

'I think Florence is talking about the phone call,' Chloe put in helpfully.

'Oh.' Lifting her head from the rug, Miranda saw Florence holding the receiver out to her. 'Who is it?'

'Richard Branson, ringing to ask if you want to borrow a couple of grand.' Florence cackled and blew pretend kisses in the direction of the phone. 'Who d'you think?'

Chloe passed the receiver across to Miranda and wriggled out of her way.

At the sound of Greg's voice, Miranda's stomach did an impromptu jump for joy.

'Sounds lively,' he observed. 'What's going on?'

'I'm just losing at Monopoly. Mainly because I'm surrounded by cheats.' Miranda narrowed her eyes at Danny. 'How about you?'

'Lonely. Missing you,' said Greg.

'Oh!' Overcome by this admission, Miranda tried to shield her mouth so that Danny wouldn't be able to overhear. 'I miss you too!'

'This is so romantic.' Danny sighed, clutching Chloe's shoulder and shaking his head. 'Anyone got a tissue?'

'You may need one' – this time Miranda covered the receiver – 'to mop up the blood.' Moving her hand away, she returned her attention to Greg. 'Sorry about that. Some people have the most infantile sense of humour. So where are you now, out somewhere celebrating the end of the conference?'

'Better than that. Newport Pagnell service station, on the M1.'

Miranda let out an ear-splitting shriek.

'You're joking! What are you doing there?'

'Uh oh,' Danny leaned back on one elbow, 'he's met someone else. He's ringing from Gretna Green to tell her he's just got married. Her name's Susie, she's a stripper – *ouch*.'

Miranda stuck out her tongue and kicked him, for good measure. Did he really think he was being amusing?

'I couldn't stand it a minute longer,' said Greg. 'We all went out to a club earlier. You should have seen the rest of the team, chatting up anything in a skirt. All they care about is picking up some tart for the night and getting their leg over. I left them to it,' he went on. 'That might be their idea of fun, but it isn't mine.'

'So you're on your way home now,' Miranda exclaimed. 'Oh, this is brilliant! How long will it take you to get here?'

'I'll pick you up at eleven.' Greg sounded as if he were smiling. 'Only if you want me to, of course.'

'I do want you to. Oh, I definitely want you to.' Miranda was beaming too, she couldn't help herself. She wished she could purr seductive sweet nothings into the phone but it was hard to purr seductively when you had such a blatantly amused audience.

'I love you,' said Greg.

'Mm. Um, me too.'

He laughed.

'Difficult to talk?'

Across the table, Danny was playing an imaginary violin.

'You could say that.'

'Okay, never mind. See you soon.'

'I sincerely hope that wasn't Richard Branson,' said Danny when she had hung up.

'I don't need a loan any more.' Miranda shot him a sweet, couldn't-care-less smile. 'I'm out, bankrupt. You three can carry on without me. And you,' she pointed a finger at him, 'can apologise, if you like, for all that guff you gave me earlier about men saying they're away at sales conferences when they aren't.'

'I'm sorry. He's clearly mad about you.'

'He is,' said Miranda.

'He's a very lucky man.'

'Absolutely correct.'

Danny grinned, watching her uncross her legs and leap excitedly to her feet.

'So what's he got that I haven't? Oh, don't tell me, he's terrific in bed.'

Florence was by this time practically doubled up with laughter.

'Right again,' Miranda told him as she headed for the door. 'That makes three out of three. Excellent. You could be a clairvoyant when you grow up.'

It was five past eleven.

Downstairs, Chloe could dimly hear Florence and Danny still battling it out across the Monopoly board, each of them determined to win.

Yawning, Chloe climbed into her new bed. It had been a long day and she was shattered. Four hours in the shop, then the trip to the antenatal clinic, followed by the move itself, not to mention the strain of keeping a straight face throughout Danny Delancey's bravura performance as Orlando.

The curled-up strip of photographic paper lay on the bedside table between her rackety old alarm clock and her reading lamp. Reaching for it, Chloe lay back against the pillows and gazed at the fuzzy ultrasound image of her baby.

The doctor had assured her that it was a baby, even though, in profile, it looked a lot like an exotic mushroom.

Chloe's eyes filled with tears of joy as she traced the outline of the head and stomach. To have actually watched the tiny heart beating frantically away on the screen, seen the birdlike legs stretch and kick . . .

Biting her lip, she remembered the hospital waiting room packed with hand-holding couples. All those husbands and boyfriends, actually looking forward to seeing their very own exotic mushrooms for the first time.

Oh, Greg, you stupid, selfish bastard, you don't know what you're missing, you really don't.

Chloe was still studying the miraculous black-and-white image when she heard the sound of a car drawing up outside, followed by a brief toot on the horn. Less than a second later, there was a wild flurry of activity in the next-door room. Cupboards and drawers were slammed shut, the radio switched off and the bedroom door closed.

She listened to Miranda, in high heels, clatter rapturously down the stairs, call goodnight to Florence and bang the front door behind her. Suddenly tempted to sneak out of bed and peer out of the window, Chloe threw back the duvet. The next moment, the car door slammed shut and the engine was revved up. Oh well, how much had she expected to see anyway, in pitch darkness?

Chloe hauled the duvet back up again, switched off the bedside lamp and settled down to sleep.

Lucky Miranda, to have a boyfriend so besotted that he had driven all the way back from Birmingham just to be with her tonight.

As she closed her eyes, Chloe wondered briefly if any man would ever feel that way again about her.

Sex, good grief, she could hardly remember what it was like. It was months, Chloe realised, since anyone had approached her nether regions without stopping first to pull on a pair of surgical gloves.

Chapter 27

Greg lay back in bed and watched Miranda, naked, nudge the bedroom door open with her bottom.

'This was definitely worth coming back for.' He grinned and took one of the cups from her. It was a warm night and two hours of stupendous sex had given him a raging thirst. 'Sorry it has to be tea,' he clunked his cup against Miranda's, 'but I'm all out of champagne.'

'It's probably disgusting,' she warned as he took a gulp. 'You're out of milk too.'

It *was* disgusting, chiefly because Miranda had sprinkled in a bit of Coffee Mate as a consolation prize, but Greg didn't care. She was here and that was all that mattered.

'I meant what I said on the phone earlier.' He looked at her, his grey eyes serious. 'The last few days have been awful. I can't believe how much I've missed you.'

Miranda abandoned her own cup of undrinkable tea and slid back under the duvet.

'I missed you too.'

'I've been thinking,' said Greg. 'I know it's a bit soon to be saying this, but it just seems crazy, me living here and you living there . . . both of us paying rent, not to mention all the extra travelling . . .'

Her heart skipped a lorryload of beats. Was Greg really saying what she thought he was trying to say?

Oh, come on, thought Miranda, how dumb am I pretending to be? Of course he was. Even if it wasn't coming out terribly romantically, she acknowledged with a rush of love. That was the trouble with men, they just didn't watch enough slushy girlie films; they had no idea how it was meant to be done.

'What are you suggesting?' Playfully she danced her fingers across his bare chest. 'We set up a tent on the bank of the Grand Union Canal? That's about halfway between your place and mine, wouldn't you say?'

Greg captured her hand and held it still. This was important; he didn't need that kind of distraction right now.

'I'm suggesting you move in with me. I want us to live together.'

Miranda gazed at him, wide-eyed. Mustn't laugh, mustn't laugh.

'You mean, because it would be time-saving and economical?'

'No,' said Greg. 'Because I love you and I want to be with you. All the time.'

'What's up with you?' said Bev, materialising behind Miranda at the sinks and making her jump.

'Me? Nothing, nothing . . . why should anything be up?'

Bev raised an eyebrow at the scarlet jumble of Molton Browners in the sink.

'No reason, just that you've been scrubbing away at those things for the last twenty minutes. You've missed your coffee break. More importantly,' she pointed out, 'you've missed your Mars bar break. And I've never seen that happen before.'

Oh help, have to tell her soon, thought Miranda. She lifted the Molton Browners out of the sink – it was like manhandling a dead octopus – and began to pat them dry with a towel.

'I wasn't hungry,' she said with a shrug.

'Not hungry? Golly, you must be ill. Better get your appetite back before next week.'

Miranda's forehead creased.

'Next week?'

'Your birthday, dipstick! Sunday lunch at Sexy Sam's,' Bev reminded her. 'It's all arranged, the table's booked for one o'clock.'

Miranda had been so preoccupied with thoughts of Greg, her birthday next week had completely slipped her mind. Meeting up for a raucous celebration lunch was an established salon tradition hugely popular with Fenn's overworked but loyal staff, especially since he was the one footing the bill.

'You'll have to bring your chap,' Bev rattled on. 'Everyone's *dying* to meet him.'

I have to tell her, I really have to tell her, Miranda thought. Oh, but I just don't want to be the one who dies.

She felt sick.

Took a deep breath.

'He's . . . um, got a golf tournament lined up for next Sunday. He won't be able to make it.'

Aah, *bliss*, no wonder people fibbed. It was so easy and it made you feel *so* much better, Miranda thought with a rush of relief. That horrid sick feeling had simply melted away in an instant, like magic.

I'll tell her soon, she promised herself.

Definitely.

Just not quite yet.

'He's away on your birthday? That's a real shame.' Bev's eyes widened with indignation. 'Honestly, men are so selfish. He won't be away for the whole weekend, will he? Where's the tournament being held?'

Unable to think, offhand, of the name of a single golf course – was Murrayfield one? Was Greendale? Stenhousemuir? – Miranda was delighted to hear cross-sounding footsteps marching up behind them.

Phew, saved by the boss.

'Bev, stop gossiping and get back to work,' Fenn said sharply. 'There's someone waiting at the desk.'

Bev glanced over her shoulder at the girl who had walked in off the street. She was wearing an off-the-shoulder white sweater, baggy combat trousers and dark glasses, and her hair was piled up under a khaki baseball cap.

'She doesn't have an appointment. And she hasn't been here before.' When it came to bookings, Bev had a memory like an elephant.

'So get rid of her.' Fenn sounded exasperated. 'Tell her we can fit her in some time next year.'

'Ooh,' Miranda squealed without meaning to as the girl removed her glasses and baseball cap. 'It's Daisy Schofield!'

'Oh dear, your rival in luurve.' Bev gave her a mock-sympathetic pat on the shoulder. 'Daisy Schofield is Miles Harper's girlfriend,' she explained to Fenn, who was looking surprised. Meaningfully she added, 'Remember the day Miranda ended up in Try-it-on Tabitha's swimming pool?'

Surprise swiftly gave way to alarm.

'Miranda? You're not seeing Miles Harper, are you?'

'Of course I'm not. It's just Bev's sad idea of a joke.'

'She fancies him, though. Like mad,' teased Bev.

Fenn raised his eyebrows at Miranda, who did her utmost not to blush.

'Look, I promise you, I don't.'

Miranda had turned a dramatic shade of puce, which was always entertaining, but Fenn was busy rejigging this morning's appointments in his head. They might be fully booked, but business was business, and Daisy Schofield – currently one of the most photographed faces in Britain – would be terrific publicity for the salon.

'So if it's a cut and blow-dry she's after,' the look he gave Miranda was severe, 'I can definitely trust you to wash her hair without trying to stuff her head down the sink.'

Miranda had come across some unchatty clients in her time but Daisy Schofield had to be the unchattiest. It was like trying to hold a conversation with a Pot Noodle.

'Did someone recommend Fenn to you?' She tried again as she massaged shampoo into her head. For someone who famously maintained that her long ash-blonde hair was entirely natural, she couldn't help observing that Daisy Schofield had amazingly dark roots.

Yawning, Daisy shook her head.

'Saw him on TV.'

'Oh. I wondered if Tabitha Lester had suggested—'

'No.' Daisy yawned again, revealing an enviable lack of fillings.

Hate her, hate her.

'It's just that we were at Tabitha's house one day, doing her hair, and we bumped into your boyfriend,' Miranda blurted out. Heavens, Fenn would kill her if he could hear this, but it was like a compulsion, she so wanted to hear about Miles. She couldn't help wondering, too, if Miles had happened to mention their impromptu game of watermelon in the pool.

'I've never met Tabitha Lester,' said Daisy, closing her eyes.

She wasn't being bitchy or deliberately unpleasant, Miranda was irritated to realise. She just didn't want to talk.

Ah well, serves me right, she thought. What did I expect, that Daisy would exclaim, 'Don't tell me *you're* the one who ended up in the water with Miles! He hasn't stopped talking about you since!'

Oh yes, highly likely. He probably wouldn't recognise me if he bumped into me in the street.

I met Miles Harper for ten minutes, Miranda told herself, and now I've got an embarrassing, infantile crush on him.

Honestly, it was as bad as Bev's hopeless infatuation with Greg. Worse even, because at least Bev was single. I've already got a boyfriend, thought Miranda, and I'm still doing it.

Then again, it was a harmless enough hobby. Wasn't the world full, after all, of happily married women fantasising harmlessly over George Clooney?

'Could you get my bag?' Daisy's voice broke into her daydream.

Miranda abruptly stopped shampooing.

'Sorry?'

'My phone's ringing.' Calmly Daisy nudged the black Prada bag next to her foot. 'I can't reach it. I'm expecting an important call.'

From Miles!

Miranda launched herself at the bag, almost knocking herself out on the basin as she jerked upright again. Her imagination, working overtime, galloped through the ensuing phone call from Miles:

'You're where? The Fenn Lomax salon? Hey, is there a pretty girl working there . . . gorgeous eyes, spiky blue hair? You're kidding, that's fantastic! Put her on, will you, let me speak to her!'

The trouble with actual phone conversations was, they were always a big let-down compared with imaginary ones.

'Oh, hi, Suze.' Daisy gestured behind her for Miranda to turn the water off and pass her a towel. 'No, nothing much, just getting my hair done, then off to some music awards thing tonight with Ritchie.'

Ritchie?

Miranda, giving the sink a brisk scrub-down in order to look busy, wondered who the hell Ritchie was.

Luckily, so did Suze.

Daisy giggled into the phone.

'Ritchie Capstick, he's a video-jock with MTV. My agent set it up . . . God, you must be joking, he's really ugly and really gay . . . definitely no comparison with Miles!'

Whoever Suze was, she was having a truly miraculous effect on Daisy. Her whole face had lit up and she was laughing and joking like an actual human being. Miranda, energetically polishing the lined-up bottles of shampoo and conditioner, heard the tinny squawks emanating from the phone but was unable – disappointingly – to make out what was being said.

'No, he's still in Montreal, training for the Canadian Grand Prix. Bloody boring.' Daisy pulled a face. 'Still, can't be helped, and it's only for another ten days.'

More tinny squawking from Suze's end of the line.

'Well of course it's dangerous, did you think that hadn't occurred to me?' Daisy rolled her eyes. 'But that's his job, Suze, it's what makes him exciting! D'you think I'd look at him twice if he was a sheep farmer?'

Tinny squawk, tinny squawk.

'Yeah well, if it happens it happens.' Daisy shrugged. 'Still, great publicity, eh? Think how sorry for me everyone would be . . . the whole world loves a tragedy, not to mention a grieving girlfriend!'

'I have to rinse you now,' Miranda said stonily. 'Fenn's waiting.'

Daisy ignored her.

'Yeah, like Thingy Winslet in *Titanic*.' She grinned into the phone. 'And I've always looked bonza in black.'

Chapter 28

Greg met up with Adrian in the bar of the Prince of Wales for an early-evening drink.

'You've asked her to move in with you?' Adrian spluttered into his pint. 'Bloody hell, you're a sucker for punishment, aren't you? Out with one bird, in with the next! What have you got in that new flat of yours, revolving doors?'

Greg had expected nothing less from Adrian, who spent all his time noisily slagging off women but who was secretly miserable and desperate – like most divorced men – to meet the right girl and settle down.

'I never expected it to happen like this. It's not the kind of thing you plan,' he said with a shrug. 'But it's happened and we want to be together. So why shouldn't she move in?'

Adrian tried not to look envious. How could he blame Greg, anyway, when he'd fancied Miranda himself?

'She isn't bothered about the business with Chloe and the baby, then?'

Greg took a careful gulp of his lager.

'That's the great thing about Miranda, she hates kids too. You should have heard her the other day, going on about her landlady's grandson. Complete monster, apparently, kicks like a mule. Miranda can't stand him.'

Adrian raised his eyebrows.

'So you still haven't told her about Chloe and the baby.'

'Oh come on.' Greg sounded irritable. 'How can I?'

'She should know,' said Adrian.

'Why?'

'Why? Because she'll go bloody ballistic if she finds out and you haven't told her.'

Greg gave him a pitying look.

'She won't, though, will she? There's no reason why she should find out. I can trust you to keep your mouth shut, can't I?'

'Well, yes, but—'

'Look,' Greg said brusquely, 'what happened with Chloe wasn't my fault, was it? So why should I suffer now? Why should I be the one to get all the grief?'

'I know that. I'm just saying, why don't you tell Miranda, then she'll know it too?' Adrian took a great slurp of beer, marvelling at the situation he found himself in; the moral high ground was unfamiliar territory to him. Blimey, he'd be taking up counselling next!

But Greg was less amused.

'Oh, that's great. I'm getting a lecture from the bloke whose wife left him because in his spare time he drank for England and screwed half the barmaids in Battersea.'

'Fine,' said Adrian, offended. 'You don't have to take my advice.'

'Thank Christ for that.' Greg relaxed and grinned at him, signalling to the barman for refills. 'Come on, Ade, you don't need to worry about me. The situation's under control. Telling Miranda about Chloe,' he gestured and-the-rest with his free arm, 'isn't going to make her happy, is it?

219

I know what Miranda's like, it's the kind of thing she'd just fret about.'

'I suppose.' Adrian shrugged, losing interest. He preferred talking about football.

'I don't need the hassle, that's all.' Greg pushed his fingers through his hair. 'You know what women are like. What Miranda doesn't know can't hurt her.' He gave Adrian a cheer-up nudge. 'Isn't that right?'

Adrian lit a cigarette.

'Yeah.'

Miranda, singing noisily and spectacularly off-key in the bath the following Sunday, wondered how old you had to be before you stopped getting excited about your birthday. How much longer did she have before the novelty wore off, boredom set in and she began telling people in blasé fashion, 'Oh no, nothing planned, it's just like any other day.'

'Twenty-four today, twenty-four today,' Miranda yodelled, twiddling the hot tap with her toes and sending a gush of scalding water over her ultra-cool, RayBan-wearing yellow plastic duck. 'Oh, I've got the key of the door, never been twenty-four before.'

'Any more of that caterwauling,' Bev's voice filtered through from the other side of the bathroom door, 'and I'll be the one with the key, locking you in there.'

'You're early!' Miranda splashed into a sitting position. 'Is Fenn here as well?'

Fenn had volunteered to drive them to the restaurant in Soho, but not yet, surely? It was still only eleven o'clock.

'He's dropping Leila at Heathrow.' Leila, yet another supermodel, was Fenn's latest girlfriend. 'I came early because I want you to wear your present from me.'

A present you could wear! Miranda brightened at once.

'Is it a pair of false bosoms?'

'Not telling you.' Bev sounded pleased with herself. 'You'll have to come downstairs and find out.'

It might be a bash over the head with something heavy, thought Miranda, when Bev heard what she had to tell her.

Oh, crikey, it was scary but it had to be done. Lying back in the bath, she took deep breaths and began psyching herself up for the ordeal ahead.

But really, there couldn't be a better time, could there?

It's my birthday, Miranda reminded herself, clutching this fact to her like a security blanket. Nobody was allowed to be horrid to you on your birthday, oh no, that would be too mean for words. Bev couldn't – *wouldn't* – spoil her special day.

Ducking down under the surface of the water, Miranda exhaled a stream of bubbles and began counting. If she reached thirty without coming up for air, Bev would forgive her.

Probably.

And if I don't reach thirty, thought Miranda, I'll have drowned.

Which might actually be safer in the long run.

Florence remained discreetly in the kitchen while Miranda took Bev out into the walled back garden.

'I've left your present inside,' Bev protested, teetering

down the wheelchair-friendly slope in her four-inch spike heels.

All the better to hit me over the head with, thought Miranda.

Aloud she said, 'There's something I have to tell you first. It might make you hate me.'

'What?' Bev eyed her with suspicion. 'If your Walkman's chewed up my Celine Dion tape—'

'It didn't,' Miranda put in hurriedly, glad that no one was around to overhear. Borrowing a Celine Dion tape – phew, now that *was* embarrassing.

'Okay, so it isn't that.' Bev visibly relaxed. 'What is it then?'

'Greg.'

'Greg who?'

Oh, for heaven's sake . . .

'Greg Malone.' Agitatedly, Miranda twisted the silver bangle on her wrist. 'Remember? The bloke you met at Elizabeth Turnbull's party and haven't stopped talking about for the last two months?'

'Oh, right.' Bev nodded. 'That Greg.' She frowned. 'I don't get it. What about him?'

Miranda felt herself going red.

'Um . . . he's who I've been seeing.'

She went redder.

And redder still, under Bev's incredulous gaze.

'You mean . . . ?'

'Yes! He's the one,' Miranda blurted out. 'Oh God, I'm so sorry!'

'Well?' said Florence when Miranda finally reappeared in

the kitchen doorway. 'Want me to call the riot police? Did she go for you with the garden spade and call you terrible names?'

'She did, actually.' Miranda eyed with longing the tray of smoked salmon and cream cheese bagels. 'Well, not the spade thing, but she called me a berk.'

'Is that all? Help yourself, by the way.' Florence nodded at the bagels. 'They're for you.'

'A prize berk. A big wally. And a plonker,' said Miranda through a mouthful of smoked salmon. 'She couldn't believe I'd been so scared of telling her.'

'All that fuss for nothing, then.' Florence reached for the tray and balanced it across her lap. 'What did I tell you? That might be him now,' she went on as the doorbell rang out in the hall.

Miranda shook her head.

'It won't be, I'm not seeing him until tonight.' In deference to the Bev situation, this was what they had agreed.

Except, Miranda realised frustratedly, now that everything had been sorted out, Greg could have come along after all . . .

'You're right, it isn't,' said Florence, who had scooted across the kitchen and was peering out of the window. 'It's that good-looking boss of yours. Long hair, though,' she tut-tutted. 'Are you sure he's not gay?'

Miranda almost choked on her bagel.

'Of course he isn't gay. Fenn gets through supermodels like we get through Jaffa Cakes!'

'So why have you never made a play for him?' Florence's eyes glittered with mischief. 'Rich, handsome, successful fellow like that – you could do a lot worse.'

Miranda found this idea comical in the extreme. It had simply never occurred to her to find Fenn attractive, or to have a crush on him. He was her employer and she was the lowly salon junior regarded – quite unfairly – by Fenn as a hopeless case.

Apart from anything else, it was hard to lust over someone who spent his life telling you off.

'Like I said, he goes for supermodels,' she patiently informed Florence. 'If I was six feet tall and weighed less than six stone, I might stand a chance. At the moment,' she added by way of explanation, 'he's going out with Leila Monzani.'

Florence cocked an eyebrow as she wheeled herself through to the hall to answer the door.

'Ah, but what if he wasn't?'

Once a meddler, always a meddler, thought Miranda.

'If he wasn't,' she raised her voice to make sure Florence heard, 'I'd still be going out with Greg.'

Chapter 29

When Chloe arrived back from the shops, she found an impromptu champagne-and-bagels party in full swing in Florence's sitting room. Bev was there, and so was Fenn Lomax, whom of course she recognised but hadn't met before.

'Come on, have a drink, one little glass won't hurt,' Miranda urged, pouring her one and proudly showing off her new top. 'What d'you think, isn't it great? Bev gave it to me!' She did an arms-up shimmy followed by a twirl, spilling a fair amount of Moët on the way round.

Chloe admired the top, which was black, stretchy and semi-transparent, with strategically positioned red satin butterflies appliquéd across the chest.

'It's very you,' she told Miranda, deeply envious of her slim figure.

'Flighty,' Florence crowed, 'and a bit tight.'

Miranda waved her glass happily.

'I prefer sexy,' she declared, 'and exotic.'

The television was on in the corner. Florence was busy zapping through the channels in search of a weather forecast.

'I still say you should take a jacket, they were predicting

thunderstorms for this afternoon. Hang on, I'll get it on Ceefax—'

'Ooh, look, don't turn over!' Miranda let out a yelp of excitement. 'It's Miles!'

The Canadian Grand Prix was due to take place in Montreal in just a few hours, and an informal pre-race interview with Miles Harper, the great British hope, was being shown. Seeing as it was Miranda's birthday, everyone turned to watch.

'He's so gorgeous,' sighed Miranda. Hastily she added, 'Not that I fancy him, of course.'

'Not much,' said Bev with a grin.

'So the very best of luck, Miles, for this afternoon's race,' concluded the jovial motor-racing commentator, 'from your millions of British fans . . .'

'Oh, shame.' Bev patted Miranda's arm. 'And you thought you were the only one.'

'. . . drive safely . . .'

'Try not to get killed,' said Miranda. 'Honestly, can you believe what Daisy Schofield said last week?' She shook her head in disgust. 'I still can't get over that.'

'Total bitch,' Bev agreed as the commentator wound up the interview.

Florence, with the remote control poised, said, 'Okay if I go on to Ceefax now? Only, if it pours with rain and your butterflies shrink, you'll be arrested.'

'The really irritating thing is, I was sure she wouldn't leave me a tip. And she did,' Miranda marvelled.

Bev winked at Chloe.

'What, like, "Don't get too fond of your racing driver boyfriend in case he dies"?'

'Better than that,' said Miranda, 'she gave me a tenner.'

The mention of money reminded Chloe that in her handbag was the card and present she had bought this morning for Miranda. It wasn't much – she couldn't afford a great deal – but she hoped Miranda would like the stained-glass photo frame.

Handbag, handbag – there it was, where she had left it, on the table over by the window.

'Looking for something?' Fenn had intercepted her gaze, but Chloe was already levering herself upright.

One casual glance out of the window was all it took to suck the air from her lungs and send her mind reeling with shock.

Outside, emerging from his car in the street below, was Greg.

Okay, thought Chloe, don't faint, keep calm, sit back down again before you fall down and *think this through*.

Oh, but he was here, he'd come to see her! And when your ex-husband arrived unexpectedly on your doorstep clutching a bunch of flowers the size of a Christmas tree, it could only mean one thing . . .

I need more time, I need more time, thought Chloe, dimly aware that Fenn Lomax was watching her slowly retrace her steps, empty-handed. But could this really be happening? Had Greg somehow tracked her down – well, of course he had, through Bruce and Verity, no doubt – and come to beg for her forgiveness? Did this mean he'd changed his mind about the baby as well?

Oh God, this was all so confusing, she could barely think and walk at the same time. Every step was like trying to wade through a field of her mother's bread sauce.

'Are you all right?' Fenn said quietly, ducking his head as Bev swished past with a brimming glass in one hand and one of Florence's cocktail cigarettes in the other. Bev was known to accidentally set fire to things when she was allowed custody of a cigarette.

Am I all right? wondered Chloe.

'Ha!' Sparks showered from the end of Bev's Sobranie as she brushed it recklessly past Florence's heavy brocade curtains. 'Speaking of boyfriends, guess who's downstairs?'

Miranda, through a mouthful of chewy bagel, said, 'Who?'

'Greg, you dipstick! Just as well you made your big confession earlier – hey, this is brilliant, he can come with us now that he's here! He can, can't he, Fenn? Greg can come along to lunch?'

Chloe's world was turning crazily on its axis. She didn't understand what was going on, but she'd experienced a similar sensation once before, on the Big Dipper at Blackpool.

Florence's attention had been on her curtains, whose health was in danger of being seriously damaged by Bev's dramatic way with a cigarette. Now, her head swivelled round as she realised that Fenn had leapt from his chair and was lifting Chloe on to the sofa.

Amazed, Florence said, 'Chloe? What's happening?'

'Just lie back and breathe slowly,' Fenn instructed Chloe. 'Is it the baby? Shall I phone for an ambulance?'

Oh no, not a miscarriage, Miranda prayed, not on my birthday. And please don't make it all my fault because I forced Chloe to drink that glass of champagne.

Swallowing her bagel at last, she gazed in horror at

the scene being played out before her. All the colour had drained from Chloe's face and she was clutching Fenn's hand. Fenn, down on one knee – for all the world like Hardy at Nelson's deathbed – was taking her pulse and exchanging serious-looking glances with Florence.

The doorbell rang.

Chloe visibly flinched

'I'll call an ambulance,' Florence decided, reaching for the phone.

Chloe blurted out, '*No.*'

'Where does it hurt?' demanded Fenn.

'I'm okay, I'm okay.' She brushed his hand away from her wrist and tried to sit up, her gaze fixing on Miranda. 'Look, I'm really sorry about this, but is that your boyfriend out there?'

As she spoke, the doorbell shrilled again.

Mystified, Miranda said, 'Who, Greg? Of course he's my boyfriend!'

'Ah. Pass me that glass, would you?' Puffing her hair out of her eyes, Chloe nodded at Fenn. 'It's okay, I don't need an ambulance. Just a drink. You could probably do with another one as well.' She returned her attention to Miranda. 'You see, I'm Greg's wife.'

All eyes were now on Miranda, who looked astonished. Fancy making a silly mistake like that, jumping to conclusions and giving everyone a fright.

'Don't be daft. No, no, it's a coincidence, that's all,' she explained to Chloe, her tone reassuring. 'My Greg isn't married.'

Chloe didn't breathe a sigh of relief.

She said steadily, 'Is his name Greg Malone?'

'Oh, *shit*,' Bev gasped.

It was Miranda's turn to sit down, on a plate of bagels, with a bump.

Chapter 30

Florence answered the front door.

Well, somebody had to.

And there he was on the doorstep, smiling that boyish, winning smile of his, clutching a gaudy bunch of flowers in one hand and a Happy Birthday helium balloon in the other.

Florence smiled at Greg in much the same way as she had once smiled at her first husband upon discovering that he had been sleeping with the wife of his commanding officer.

'Hello,' said Greg, 'I—'

'She's not here,' Florence lied smoothly, as she had been instructed to do. Well, more or less. In reality, Miranda had covered her face with her hands and gabbled, 'Don't let him in, just get him out of here, I can't see him now!'

'It's okay.' Greg nodded easily. 'I wasn't expecting to see Miranda. I just wanted to drop these off for her, so she'd see them as soon as she got back from lunch.' He grinned at Florence. 'You know how girls are when it comes to flowers.'

'Quite,' said Florence. Reaching forward in her chair, she took the bobbing balloon from him. 'I'll tell Miranda you called.'

'And I'll be round to pick her up at six.' Greg handed over the flowers. 'Ask her to be ready on time, would you?'

This was accompanied by a charming smile, to make it sound more of a joke and less of a command.

'Fine.'

Greg's smile faded.

'Is everything all right, Florence? Have I done something to upset you?'

Florence longed more than anything to tell him. The words were swelling up inside her like rush-hour commuters on a tube train, jostling to spill out. Oh, what she wouldn't give to be able to speak her mind . . .

But it wasn't her job, it was Miranda's. And Miranda needed time to collect her own tumultuous thoughts. The last thing she had gibbered to Florence was, 'Just get rid of him . . . *don't say anything* . . .'

Mentally, Florence zipped her mouth shut and triple-padlocked it.

'No.' Wheeling herself backwards, she prepared to close the front door. 'Everything's fine.'

'I don't believe this, I just can't *believe* it,' Miranda wailed, reaching for her champagne glass. Glugging the contents like water, she closed her eyes, opened them again and peered around the edge of the damask curtain. But with Chloe leaning over her shoulder, there was no way in the world it could all be a terrible mistake.

That was definitely Greg climbing into his car.

Her Greg.

And Chloe's Greg.

Miranda felt sick. It was like discovering that the man of your dreams was a puppy murderer in his spare time.

Bev, taller than either of them, stood behind Miranda and Chloe and hissed, 'Bastard,' as Greg's car pulled away. She put an arm around each of them and shook her head. 'I don't know which of you to feel more sorry for.'

Chloe swivelled round, gazing at her in astonishment.

'You don't have to feel sorry for me!'

'Nor me,' Miranda squealed, batting Bev's sympathetic hand off her shoulder. She was quivering, her spiky hair practically standing on end.

'But you must be upset,' Bev protested, taken aback.

'Upset? UPSET? I'm not upset,' bellowed Miranda, 'I'm bloody furious! He's a lying, cheating bastard and I'm just glad I found out now, before . . . before . . . Jesus, how could he *do* this?'

She had a terrible urge to kick holes in the wall, demolish a couple of bookcases, wrench Florence's expensive curtains down from their poles. The bit about not being upset wasn't true, of course, but those namby-pamby feelings would just have to wait their turn. Miranda took a deep, shuddery breath. Right now the anger was uppermost in her mind. In fact she was probably so angry she could explode.

'You never told us your husband's name was Greg.' She turned to Chloe in disbelief. 'All this time and you never even mentioned his name.'

'Neither did you! You didn't tell me your boyfriend's name was Greg. Oh, crikey,' Chloe gasped, her hand flying to her mouth. 'Are you the reason he left me?'

This was too much, this was too horrible for words. Miranda's stomach churned like a cement mixer in freefall.

'When did he leave you? Bev, what was the date of that party . . . oh God, when did we meet Adrian and Greg?'

'You met Adrian too . . . ?'

'It was a charity cocktail party,' Miranda jabbered on. 'Florence gave us her tickets. Daisy Schofield was meant to be there, but she didn't turn up.'

Chloe twigged.

'Bruce had tickets as well, but he couldn't make it so he passed them on to me. I wondered where they'd gone.'

Bev had been busy riffling through the diary she carried with her at all times in case she was ever unexpectedly asked out. Finding what she was searching for, she looked up.

'April the twenty-third.'

'Bruce's wedding anniversary,' Florence remembered with a nod.

'We were meant to be going to that party together. Except,' Chloe said resignedly, 'Greg had gone by then.'

'So he went on his own and met Miranda instead.' Florence snorted with disgust. 'That does it. Next time Elizabeth Turnbull tries to bulldoze me into buying tickets for some bloody charity cocktail party, I'll tie a knot in her neck.'

For Chloe, the relief was tremendous. Greg hadn't left her for Miranda.

'Next time I see Greg,' said Miranda, 'I'll tie a knot in more than his neck.'

Chloe suddenly stifled a giggle.

'Oh, excuse me! If we're talking about my ex-husband, are you sure it's long enough to tie a knot in?'

Glancing at each other, Miranda and Bev collapsed with laughter.

'Anyone want another drink?' Fenn sounded resigned.

'I'm sorry, it's a girl thing,' Florence explained. 'They have this way with words. Not for sensitive male ears.'

Thirteen years in the hairdressing business had more or less desensitised Fenn's ears. In that time, he felt, he had probably heard it all. To take offence now would be like a Status Quo freak objecting to the mewing of next door's kitten. But he was touched by Florence's concern.

'Why don't I ring the restaurant, let them know we're going to be late?' He paused. 'Then, if you like, I could cut your hair.'

Miranda, still hopelessly agitated, had taken up smoking in a major way and was even messier at it than Bev. In deference to Chloe's unborn child and – more immediately – Florence's soft furnishings, everyone had moved outside into the sunny back garden.

Florence ran arthritic fingers over her haphazardly piled-up hair. Normally Miranda dealt with it, but this morning she had executed the task herself.

Actually, executed pretty much described the end result.

'It must be bad.' Florence grimaced. 'I'm sure you don't make a habit of accosting strangers in the street, offering to snip them into shape.'

'We aren't in the street,' said Fenn. 'And I gave up smoking six months ago. It's easier if I keep my hands occupied.'

'From what Miranda tells me, you certainly do that.'

'From what Miranda tells me,' Fenn countered mildly, 'you thought I was gay.'

Florence chuckled, unembarrassed.

'I'm an old woman. Male hairdressers always were in my day.'

'Well, I'm not. And you won't be calling yourself old by the time I've finished with you.' He watched her pull an eccentric assortment of combs from her hair and drop them into her lap. 'Ready to go for it?'

'Why not?' Florence had endured months of badgering from Miranda, urging her to have her hair cut. 'If you're sure you've got time.'

Like Bev and her beloved diary, Fenn never went anywhere without his scissors. As he slid them out of their case, he glanced across at the table, around which Miranda, Bev and Chloe were huddled like witches.

'I should think so. Anyway,' he assured Florence, 'I'm a fast worker.'

Her eyes, bright as a bird's, met Fenn's.

'Miranda told me that too. Just do me a favour, would you, before you start?'

'What?'

'Take that champagne away from her.' Florence nodded in the direction of Miranda and the rapidly emptying bottle clutched to her chest. 'At this rate she's going to spend the rest of her birthday flat on her back. Poor lamb,' she added sympathetically, 'and not quite in the way she planned.'

Chapter 31

'Florence, hi. Is Miranda with you? Any chance of a word?'

Immediately recognising the voice at the other end of the line, Florence said cheerfully, 'I'm so sorry, Miranda can't come to the phone right now, she's unconscious in the garden.'

'Blimey.' Danny Delancey sounded impressed. 'All your own work, or did you get Lennox Lewis round to knock her out?'

'Cheaper than that. Two bottles of Moët,' said Florence, 'and one not terribly pleasant surprise.'

'Will she be all right?'

'Oh, fine. Her friend Bev's out there now, covering her with Factor 15. So she's well oiled in every sense, ha! And Fenn's arranged for the restaurant to deliver the food here as soon as she wakes up. You could come over too,' Florence said brightly, 'even up the numbers a bit. I'm sure Miranda will be pleased to see you . . . poor darling, so far it hasn't been the happiest of birthdays!'

Danny hadn't even realised that today was Miranda's birthday. Furthermore, he was struck by the difference between what Florence appeared to be saying and the tone of her voice. She was sounding distinctly jaunty.

'Hang on.' He frowned, mentally pressing Rewind. 'What kind of unpleasant surprise?'

Oh dear, doing it again, thought Florence, and nobody likes a Told-you-so. Before Miranda woke up she really must practice being more sympathetic and less smug.

'Mr Right.' She glanced happily in the mirror at her chic new hairdo. 'Seems he isn't so fantastic after all.'

'Really?'

Danny, she sensed, was being careful to keep his own voice neutral.

'I know, isn't it fabulous?' Sod diplomacy; if there was one thing Florence knew, for sure, it was that Danny was on her side. Gleefully she confided, 'Turns out he was Mr Total Disaster all along.'

Uuurrgh.

Miranda, with enormous difficulty, peeled her eyelids open.

Uh oh, hangover. Now how had that happened?

More to the point, what on earth had been going on while she'd been er . . . resting her eyes?

Oh dear, as if waking up from a drunken stupor wasn't a bewildering enough experience on its own. Miranda, struggling into a half-sitting position, found herself in a far corner of the garden. The next moment she flinched as Danny Delancey appeared beside her, holding out a packet of paracetamol and a pint mug of orange juice.

'Saw you waking up.' He grinned down at her over the top of his sunglasses. 'Thought you might need these. Want me to pop the pills out of the foil for you?'

'I don't understand.' Moaning gently, Miranda shielded

her own eyes from the sun. She had a pounding hammer-drill of a headache and – mysteriously – the most disgusting taste ever in her mouth. 'The last thing I remember, I was sitting at that table over there, you weren't here and Florence had long hair. The next minute,' she frowned and held up her glistening arms, 'I'm waking up on a sun-lounger with gloopy suncream all over me and my tongue stuck to the roof of my mouth.'

'And a knotted handkerchief on your head,' Danny said helpfully. 'Don't forget the knotted hanky.'

'Oh God.' Miranda whipped it off.

'Not to mention the cigarette butt lodged in your cleavage,' he went on. 'Well, I *say* cleavage . . .'

Great. Peering down, Miranda fished it out. How cool must she look?

She peered suspiciously up at Danny.

'Did you put that there?'

'I did not.' He sounded amused. 'According to Florence, you smoked eleven black Sobranies in seventy-five minutes.'

Oh well, that explained the diabolical taste in her mouth. Hmm, thought Miranda, won't be trying that again in a hurry.

'Two at a time, at one stage.'

'Okay, okay.' She flapped a feeble arm at him to give her a break. 'It's my birthday. You're supposed to be nice to me.'

'This *is* nice. This is me being extra-nice on your birthday.'

Miranda swallowed two of the paracetamol, sloshed them down with orange juice and eyed him with suspicion.

'What are you doing here anyway? I didn't tell you it was my birthday.'

'I know. I rang to fix up a date for filming in the salon.' Danny sat down on the grass next to the sun-lounger. 'Florence happened to mention it.' He hesitated, his expression masked by his dark glasses. 'She also told me about the . . . Greg thing.'

Oh God, the Greg thing.

'Why am I not surprised?' Miranda said flatly. She gritted her teeth, making a mental note to tell Florence that, actually, she'd prefer it if details of her private life weren't blurted out to all and sundry the minute she sank into a drunken stupor.

'I'm sorry,' said Danny.

Miranda closed her eyes as the horrible details, like stampeding wildebeest, came thundering back over the horizon to haunt her all over again.

'Well, there you go, another one bites the dust.' Her voice was brittle. 'Wouldn't it be great if it was an Olympic sport?'

'What – getting plastered, smoking a million fags and falling asleep with a hanky on your head?'

Miranda smiled briefly, because he knew that wasn't what she meant. He was just trying to cheer her up, make her laugh.

'Getting it wrong. Getting it completely wrong every bloody time. Honestly, I'm better at it than anyone else I know.'

'Come on, that's not—'

'True? Of course it's true,' Miranda wailed. 'Look at you, I was convinced you were married and you weren't. Then with Greg it didn't occur to me for one second that he might be married, and he is. So how clever does that make me?'

Since there was really no answer to that, Danny rose to his feet.

'Look, come on over and join in the rest of your party.' He held out his hands. 'Hang on to me and I'll pull you up.'

'Ouch,' Miranda grumbled as he hauled her, in turn, efficiently to her feet. Her arms, slippery with Ambre Solaire, had required a firm grip. 'What time is it?'

'Four o'clock.'

'Already? Oh God, and Greg's coming round to collect me at six.' Feeling fragile, she allowed Danny to guide her across the daisy-studded lawn.

He cocked an eyebrow at her.

'Cancel.'

'No way! I want to tell him what I think of him,' Miranda said bitterly. 'Then I have to tear him limb from limb. And when that's all done, I'll finish with him.'

Florence beamed; this was celestial music to her ears.

'Darling, back with us at last.' Reaching up, she patted Miranda's shoulder. 'Feeling better now?'

'Oh yes, tons.' Miranda collapsed on to the wrought-iron chair next to her. 'Two hours to blast-off. If my head wasn't pounding so much, I'd be brushing up on my kung fu.'

Danny, sitting back down next to Chloe, took off his sunglasses.

'We've been working out the best methods of revenge. Chloe thinks you should let her answer the door.'

'Like in one of those creepy movies,' Chloe explained, 'where I say, "Miranda? Miranda who? I'm sorry, there's nobody by that name living here, this is my house."'

241

'*Gaslight.*' Florence clasped her hands with relish. 'Charles Boyer and Ingrid Bergman. Such a good film.'

'Who cut your hair?' said Miranda, momentarily distracted.

'Darling, what a question! You did, of course, just before you passed out.'

'*What?* My God, did I really?'

Florence barked with laughter. 'While you were nineteen sheets to the wind? What do you think I am, completely loopy? Fenn did it.'

Oh yes, Miranda vaguely remembered that happening now. She must have passed out before the end.

'It's great. Suits you.'

Florence preened; she already knew that.

'Anyway, we're not so sure Greg will actually believe he's going round the twist,' Chloe told Miranda, 'but Danny's come up with another brilliant idea—'

'Look, don't you think you're all being a bit mean?'

Every head abruptly swivelled in Bev's direction. There was a brief, astonished silence.

'Don't look at me like that.' Bev's tone was defiant. 'I'm just saying it doesn't seem very fair. You're ganging up on him because he didn't tell Miranda he was married, but she didn't tell me she was seeing Greg, did she?'

Miranda stared at her. Was Bev seriously leaping to Greg's defence?

'That was because I didn't want to hurt your feelings!'

'So?' Bev retaliated. 'Maybe he didn't want to hurt yours.'

'He's asked me to move in with him! Don't you think it's about time he took the risk?'

'Don't squeal at me.' Bev sounded cross. 'I'm just saying, you liked him a lot. Up until this morning you were ready to move in with him!'

'And?' said Miranda.

'I think you should give him one last chance to tell you, that's all. He might be gearing himself up for it. Teetering on the brink, that kind of thing.'

'Shame he couldn't teeter on the edge of a high building,' Chloe heard Danny, next to her, murmur under his breath.

243

Chapter 32

The last time Miranda had done any real acting, she'd been one half of a pushmi-pullyu in the school production of *Dr Dolittle*. Then, she'd tripped over her tail and fallen off the stage.

Now, acting for all she was worth, she was making the discovery that pretending to be normal was far harder than being the rear end of a pushmi-pullyu.

'. . . I just can't get over how easy it was! It's so silly, I should have done it weeks ago. Bev was brilliant, she understood completely—'

'That's great,' said Greg, 'but you've hardly eaten a thing.'

'Sorry.' Miranda gave her Thai crab cake a feeble prod with her fork. 'Still hungover, I suppose, from lunchtime. It goes to show, though, doesn't it? Honesty's the best policy. All that secrecy for no reason at all. Why couldn't I have just come straight out and told her the truth in the first place?'

Gently, Greg leaned across the table and took the fork from her hand.

'If you aren't hungry, leave it. I won't be offended. And I'm really pleased the Bev thing's sorted out, but could we talk about something else now?' His grey eyes crinkled at the corners as he squeezed Miranda's twitching fingers. 'Like us?'

It's like that film *The Stepford Wives*, Miranda thought, where the woman suddenly realises all the other women are really robots. She was here talking to Greg but he was no longer *her* Greg. He was Chloe's husband, father of Chloe's baby, and he had announced he was leaving her the moment Chloe had discovered she was pregnant.

'Us?'

'I want to be with you. I want to know when you're going to move in with me.'

Despite everything, a lump sprang into Miranda's throat. He was still Greg on the outside, that was the trouble. He was handsome and he loved her and men like that didn't come along every day.

Oh God, it wasn't easy, discovering that the man in your life – the one who *had* come along – was a big fake.

'You have to have trust, that's the thing,' Miranda blurted out. 'Absolute trust. No secrets. We don't have any secrets from each other, do we? Because if we do, we should deal with them now. It's the only way.'

Greg smiled. The drinking session earlier had left Miranda pale, but he thought she'd never looked more beautiful. Her dark eyes, huge and luminous, shone with emotion. Her strappy little black dress fitted like a second skin. She smelled gorgeous.

And she was his, all his.

No way was he going to tell her about Chloe.

Not a chance.

'The only secret I have,' Greg said slowly, 'is how much I love you. Because you'll never know.'

He lifted her hand to his mouth and kissed it, touched by the tears glistening in her eyes. With his free hand, he took a small velvet box from his jacket pocket.

Her breathing quickened.

'Is that for me?'

'No, it's for that waitress over there, the one in the orange wig.'

Miranda no longer had fingers, she had bunches of pork sausages. Clumsily she struggled to open the lid. Oh God, this wasn't supposed to be happening . . . please, *please* let it be earrings . . .

The lid sprang open.

It wasn't.

Only one ring, and not the kind you'd wear in your ear. Actually, not even the kind you'd want to wear on your finger, Miranda had to admit.

Five minuscule diamonds and a lone emerald winked feebly up at her, set in a daisy pattern with a horrid gold filigree surround.

Oh dear, there was no getting away from it.

This was a truly tasteless ring.

'Don't worry if it's a bit big,' Greg assured her. 'I can easily have it altered.'

It probably would be too big, of course, seeing as he had bought it for someone else. But Chloe had always claimed it didn't sit well next to her wedding band; she had simply given up wearing it, a couple of months into the marriage. It wasn't until after he'd moved out that he'd discovered it, at the bottom of his cuff link tin, stuffed carelessly out of sight like a spoilt child's unwanted toy.

Perfectly good ring like that, may as well make use of it,

Greg had reasoned. Chloe might not have appreciated his excellent taste, but he was sure Miranda would.

That wasn't such a terrible thing to do, was it?

No, it was not.

It made perfect sense.

Nothing wrong with being thrifty.

'I don't know what to say. It's . . . incredible,' said Miranda.

The kitchen window was wide open and Florence's state-of-the-art CD player teetered precariously on the sloping windowsill. Frank Sinatra serenaded the small but noisy gathering beneath the mulberry trees. The threatened thunderstorms having failed to materialise, the night air was heavy with humidity and heat.

'I can't believe you're all still here,' Miranda declared. 'Don't any of you have homes to go to?'

As she made her way across the dimly lit back garden she almost tripped over a pile of empty wine bottles and Florence's discarded sun hat.

'Darling, it's your birthday!' Florence, definitely squiffy, nudged Fenn and Chloe to move up and make way for Miranda. 'And we're all agog! So tell us, how did it go? Except we've already guessed, of course, because it's ten o'clock at night and you're back here.'

'I gave him a million chances,' Miranda said flatly. 'Not a dickie bird.'

'So that's that.' Bev shrugged. 'He's a bastard after all.'

'I could have told you that weeks ago.' Chloe sounded amused rather than upset.

'Does he know you know?' Danny's glittering dark eyes narrowed against the smoke from the candles flickering in glass bowls on the table.

Honestly, who does he think he is, the head of M15?

Briskly, Miranda saluted.

'No, boss. Carried out your instructions to the letter, boss. Mouth' – she mimicked the action – 'kept zipped.'

'Well,' Fenn murmured, 'there's a first.'

Bev was frowning.

'Didn't he wonder why you wanted to come back here?'

'I said I felt ill. Told him I'd see him tomorrow, when my hangover was gone.' Miranda picked up a half-empty glass and took an experimental sip. Actually, not bad. Maybe she was ready to start again.

'Aah, "Strangers in the Night",' sighed Florence as the familiar opening bars floated down from the kitchen window. 'I used to dance to this at the Café de Paris . . . da da da da daaa . . . Come on then,' she announced abruptly, jabbing her cigarette in Miranda's direction, 'show us what he got you for your birthday.'

Fenn, spotting the faint glimmer of diamond chips before anyone else, said, 'I think I can guess.'

Oh dear. You could know that someone was a bastard but still feel a bit mean, Miranda discovered. Self-consciously she waggled her fingers.

Whooping, Florence and Bev simultaneously made a grab for her left hand.

'Ouch, I'm not a wishbone.'

Bev gazed across the table at Miranda.

'It's an engagement ring.'

'God, it's tiny!' Florence crowed.

Abruptly, the knot returned to Miranda's stomach. Conflicting emotions tangled inside her like yo-yo string. Greg might be a shit and a deceiver, but it was cruel to make fun of an engagement ring. Okay, so it clearly hadn't cost a huge amount, but it was the thought that counted. Greg had gone along to a jeweller's and chosen that particular style because he had thought it would suit *her* . . .

Across the table, someone was clearing their throat. Miranda looked up.

'Actually, it's *my* engagement ring,' said Chloe.

At midnight, Fenn rose to leave.

'Bev? I'll give you a lift home.'

'I need the loo first.' Rocking on her high heels, Bev made a dash for the house.

'I'll show you out,' said Chloe, observing Danny and Miranda still huddled together deep in conversation. 'It's past my bedtime too.'

At the front door, while they waited for Bev, Fenn said, 'Tell Miranda she doesn't have to be in until ten tomorrow.'

Chloe looked envious.

'I wish my boss would say nice things like that to me.'

'I'm not always nice. I can be terrifying sometimes.'

'I know. Miranda's told me.'

Fenn smiled briefly.

'Then again, I'm not a complete ogre. She's had a hell of a day.'

'She certainly has.'

Chloe opened the front door and peered out, the orange glow from the streetlamps turning her hair to apricot.

'So have you.' Fenn hesitated, feeling awkward. Before today, he had never even met Chloe. 'Are you all right?'

Upstairs, a lavatory flushed. Bev would be back at any minute.

'Oh, I'm okay.' Chloe nodded vigorously. 'Better than I expected, to tell you the truth. It helps to know I'm not the only woman he's treated like dirt. Poor Miranda, though . . .'

Fenn marvelled at her attitude. She really did feel sorrier for Miranda than she did for herself. Accustomed as he was to the tedious, self-absorbed ramblings of much of his female clientele, Chloe's lack of self-pity was like a breath of fresh air.

'Ready,' Bev announced, clattering down the stairs. 'Bye,' she told Chloe, giving her a kiss.

Fenn, following her lead, leaned across and kissed Chloe's cheek as well.

'Bye. Take care.'

There were dimples in Chloe's cheeks that deepened when she smiled.

'I really am fine, you know. You don't have to feel sorry for me. Plus, I always did hate that engagement ring.'

Fenn laughed.

'Okay. See you soon.'

'Absolutely,' said Chloe. The mischievous dimples reappeared. 'See you at the wedding.'

Chapter 33

The salon was packed to bursting on Monday morning, but one voice was still clearly audible above the rest. Eleanor Slater, a former Tory front-bencher with a grossly inflated sense of her own irresistibility, was making sure everyone knew she was there. Since losing her seat at the last election, Eleanor had swiftly relaunched herself as a fearless radio interviewer, famed for her ability to flirt and simultaneously stick the knife in. There was nothing she was too bashful to say. She particularly relished embarrassing other people in public, and accusing them of being prudes.

She was grotesque, and Miranda would have loathed her even if she didn't have a hangover the size of Harrods. She waited for Eleanor to stop booming instructions to her PA into her dictaphone.

'. . . and firm up that interview with Terry for tomorrow morning. If he's pushed for time, we'll do it in his car between meetings.' Leaving the tape running, she smirked provocatively at Fenn's reflection in the mirror. 'It wouldn't be the first time, but don't tell his dull little wife that. Now, what can I do for you, dear?' She swivelled briskly round in her chair, eyeing Miranda with unconcealed amusement.

'Are you waiting to ask me something or can you just not remember what you're supposed to be doing next?'

Patronising old cow.

'Tea or coffee?' said Miranda.

'Tea.' Eleanor was renowned for her split-second decisions; she didn't hang about. 'Anything, so long as it's herbal.'

Miranda wondered if deadly nightshade counted as herbal.

'Oh, and I need some contraception for this afternoon,' Eleanor went on. Delving into her briefcase, she produced a ten-pound note. 'Pop along to the chemist, would you, dear? Pick me up a packet of condoms.' Her strident voice, so used to the tricky acoustics of the House of Commons, effortlessly drowned out a dozen hairdryers. 'Actually, better make that two packets.'

Don't try to embarrass me, thought Miranda.

Aloud she said, 'What flavour?'

Oh bum, now she'd probably get the sack.

But when she finally dared to look in the mirror, Fenn was carefully cutting the back of Eleanor's hair and doing his level best not to smile.

By the time Miranda returned from the chemist, Eleanor had recovered her composure. She opened one of the cellophane-wrapped packs, took out two condoms and tucked them into the back pocket of Miranda's parma-violet jeans.

'There you are, dear. Be Safe, Be Happy!'

This was the slogan adopted by the government for its latest For-God's-sake-*use*-something campaign.

Miranda gazed without enthusiasm at the packet in Eleanor's hand.

Happy? What was that?

Since she was planning on being celibate from now on, she would definitely be safe.

But she had no intention of being happy.

The door swung open behind them as Danny and Tony Vale, loaded down with video equipment, arrived in the salon.

Eleanor, a tireless media-whore, perked up at once.

'Everywhere I go, I'm pursued by cameras,' she trilled. Twirling round in her chair, she eyed Danny with greedy approval. 'Now, now, I don't remember fixing this up.' She wagged a naughty-boy finger at him. 'Which company do you work for, and who told you I'd be here?'

Danny surveyed her, his expression impassive.

'Nobody did. We aren't here to film you.'

Just this once – and despite her cracking headache – Miranda could have kissed him.

Witnessing the deflation of the strident ex-MP nobody liked, several other women within earshot sniggered.

'They're making a documentary,' Fenn explained to a disbelieving Eleanor, 'about Miranda.'

The filming took less than an hour. Afterwards, Tony Vale loaded the equipment into the back of a cab and headed back to the studio. Danny bore Miranda off to the coffee bar around the corner and ordered her a hot chocolate.

'So, are you sure you want to do it?'

Miranda's glass of hot chocolate was topped with whipped cream and cocoa powder. If she tried to drink it she'd look as if she'd been got by the Phantom Flan Flinger.

'Oh yes.' Using her finger, which was on the unsteady side, she scooped off the top layer. Halfway to her mouth, the dollop of whipped cream slid free and plopped messily back into her glass.

'Because I can arrange everything,' said Danny. 'But you have to be really sure.'

'Look, I *am*.' Miranda wished everyone would stop treating her like an invalid; she was trembly because she had a hangover, not because she was upset. 'Didn't we spend enough time going over this last night? Fenn's all for it, Chloe's all for it, it's not going to cost anything because you're going to sell it . . .'

She paused, frowning, and trawled her finger speculatively through the cream mountain once more.

'What?'

'The only thing I don't get is, what's in it for you?'

Danny fiddled with the clasp of his wallet, which was lying on the table. Now how was he meant to answer this one?

Or rather, how was he meant to answer this one without giving himself away completely?

'There's nothing in it for me,' he said at last. 'I just think you deserve better than to be treated the way he's treated you. Chloe as well,' he added. 'You both deserve better.'

'Do you like Chloe?' said Miranda abruptly. For some reason the question had been preying on her mind all week. 'I mean, do you . . . fancy her?'

Danny almost laughed aloud.

'No. No, of course I don't fancy Chloe.'

Next question, he silently willed her to ask.

Instead, Miranda let out a yelp as a blob of whipped cream dropped from her finger, landing on the front of her T-shirt.

'Bugger.' Scooping the worst of it off and gazing in dismay at the chocolate-streaked stain, she dragged a crumpled tissue out of the back pocket of her jeans. Something else flew out at the same time, catapulting through the air behind her and landing at the feet of a man engrossed in his copy of *The Times*.

Danny retrieved it while Miranda scrubbed energetically at her front with the tissue.

'It's no good, it won't come out. Lucky we've got spares back at the salon.'

'Um, you dropped this.'

The look on his face was to die for. He was trying so hard to appear nonchalant.

'Oh, thanks.' Miranda took it from him. 'Always make sure I keep one with me at work.' She patted her pocket. 'After all, you never know who might come into the salon.'

Yes, *yes*, there was that look again . . .

'You are joking,' Danny said finally.

'Of course I'm joking. Ha, you're easily shocked, aren't you?' Beaming, Miranda neatly tucked the condom into his wallet, which lay unfastened on the table between them. 'It was a present from Eleanor Slater, if you must know. And now it's yours.'

'Why?' Danny gazed at his wallet in alarm. God, how horrible if using Eleanor Slater's condom meant he had to think of Eleanor Slater. Now there was an effective contraceptive device in a league of its own.

'You may as well have it,' said Miranda. 'The way my life's going, I won't be having sex again before I'm eighty.'

*   *   *

As they were leaving the coffee bar, Miranda's attention was caught by a photograph of Miles Harper in *The Times* sports section.

Next to her, Danny was saying, 'Everything that happens in life, it's for the best.'

This was evidently meant to reassure her.

Flick, went the newspaper and Miles briefly disappeared from view.

'Okay, come on, that's complete cobblers for a start,' Miranda retaliated. 'If I ran out into the road now and got knocked down by a bus, what would be so great about that?'

'Okay, stupid remark, forget I said it.' Danny smiled. 'I was just trying to cheer you up.'

'Well, don't. You're useless at it.'

The man holding his *Times* turned a page and Miles magically reappeared.

'What are you peering at?'

'Nothing,' Miranda said shiftily. But it was too late; he had already followed the line of her gaze.

'Miles Harper? He did pretty well yesterday,' said Danny.

Miranda had forgotten all about the Canadian Grand Prix. She'd had other things on her mind.

'Where did he finish?'

'Second.'

'Second? That's brilliant!' Her eyes widened with delight. That would really move Miles up the table . . . heavens, it put him only seven points behind the current leader. Not that she'd been keeping score, of course. Well, not much . . .

'There you go,' Danny observed, his tone dry. 'I knew I could cheer you up.'

Chapter 34

'I've got mumps,' Miranda croaked into the receiver. 'It's awful. I look like a gerbil with bulimia.'

'Mumps!' Greg sounded horrified. 'I've never had mumps!'

I know that, you berk, thought Miranda. Otherwise what would be the point of telling you I've got it?

'Isn't it a nuisance? I won't be able to see you for a whole week—'

'Longer than that,' Greg cut in, concerned for certain parts of his anatomy. Didn't mumps cause them to swell up agonisingly, like footballs?

Miranda rushed to reassure him. 'Oh no, six days is fine. I checked with the doctor. Just as well, too, otherwise I'd have had to miss the wedding of the year.'

In the privacy of his living room, Greg stuck his hand down the front of his Nike jogging pants, making sure his testicles weren't quietly swelling up behind his back . . . so to speak.

'Wedding?' No, thank God, they seemed okay. 'Why, who's getting married?'

'Oh, it's *so* exciting.' Miranda's voice was croaky but otherwise she seemed cheerful enough. 'You'll never guess!'

'Not your friend Bev. Don't tell me she's bulldozed some poor sod into marrying her at last.'

'No.' Miranda sounded hurt. 'Oh Greg, don't say it like that, when we've just got engaged! You sound so anti-weddings.'

He grinned.

'Only when they involve saying "I do" to Bev. So who is it then?'

'Fenn and Leila. Next Sunday at the Salinger Hotel in Kensington. Can you imagine?' sighed Miranda. 'They've only known each other a month, but they just couldn't wait. Isn't it the most romantic thing you ever heard?'

'Your boss is marrying Leila Monzani?' Greg marvelled. 'Where's the actual service being held?'

'Right there in the hotel! Oh, and you should see the guest list,' Miranda exclaimed. 'Celebrities flying in from all over the world . . . I mean, are there any famous people Fenn *doesn't* know?'

'And you've been invited,' said Greg, trying not to sound eaten up with envy. God, what he wouldn't give to go along to a wedding like that, to rub shoulders with rock stars and actors and supermodels . . . well, if he wore sixteen-inch platforms he could rub shoulders with supermodels . . .

In her bedroom, Miranda covered the receiver and mouthed, 'Jealous,' at Chloe.

Chloe mouthed, 'Daisy,' back at her.

'Oh yes, and Daisy Schofield's going to be there.' Enjoying herself immensely, Miranda pictured the expression on his face.

'Daisy Schofield,' Greg echoed, unable to hide his disappointment. This was so unfair.

Miranda paused. Timing, after all, was everything.

'So you'll be able to meet her at long last.'

Greg digested these words.

'What?'

'You're invited too, dopey!'

'Really? Hey, great.'

He was grinning uncontrollably, Miranda could tell. And trying so hard to sound cool. Bless his heart.

Bastard.

'So don't forget, will you? Make a note of it in your diary. Midday, next Sunday. Wear your best suit. Oh,' she added as an afterthought, 'and don't breathe a word about this to anyone. We're talking Top Secret here. Fenn and Leila want total privacy – the last thing they need is for the place to be hijacked by photographers.'

'Oh, well, yes, I can understand that. Of course,' said Greg in a trustworthy voice. 'I won't blab. Um . . . who's going to be the best man?'

Miranda thought for a moment.

'Can't remember. I think Fenn said Mick.'

Mick?

Mick!

Deeply, *deeply* impressed, Greg swallowed and said, 'Hucknall or Jagger?'

'Oh, one of them, I don't know,' Miranda replied carelessly. 'Does it matter?'

Christ, no.

'I could get myself a new suit,' said Greg, determined to sound casual.

'A new suit?' Miranda waggled her eyebrows at Chloe. 'That's an idea. Look, sorry to keep on, but Fenn's drummed it into all of us. You won't accidentally let slip about this to anyone, will you?'

The temptation was too great. Leaning across, Chloe listened to her husband's reassuring reply.

'I won't breathe a word,' she heard Greg say. 'Darling, you know you can trust me.'

When she had hung up the phone, Miranda bounced off her bed. She rummaged amongst the tangle of necklaces in a blue china bowl on her dressing table.

'What?' said Chloe, sitting cross-legged on the carpet.

The copper pot-bellied pig, designed to be hung on a leather thong and worn as a choker, went sailing up into the air.

'He said he wouldn't breathe a word.' Miranda pointed. 'See? A flying pig.'

There was a gentle thud as it landed on the rug next to Chloe. Picking the pig up, she ran her finger over its upturned snout.

'Where did you get this? He's brilliant.'

Actually, he was rather brilliant, Miranda modestly acknowledged. Ugly and cross-eyed and with one leg longer than the rest, but with bags of quirky character. And hey, no one's perfect.

'I made him. Years ago, at school,' she told Chloe. 'I joined the metalwork class because I was in love with this boy called Denzil and he said girls who did metalwork were great.'

'And did you end up going out with him?' Chloe gave up on her boring pelvic floor exercises. Eagerly she said, 'Was he your first boyfriend?'

'Oh yes. And it changed Denzil's life forever.' Miranda rolled her eyes. 'One date with me was all it took for Denzil to realise he was gay. To add insult to injury, he was expelled a year later for seducing the metalwork teacher.' She shrugged and held out her hands. 'What can I tell you? The story of my life. This is how much luck I have with men.'

'Well,' said Chloe, 'I know that feeling.'

Miranda watched her pull open the neck of her lime-green cotton sweatshirt, peer down at her stomach and reach for the round cushion on the chair behind her.

'Um . . . what are you doing?'

'I need to be bigger for next Sunday.'

Chloe shoved the cushion up under her sweatshirt, unfolded her legs and solemnly studied her reflection in the dressing-table mirror.

'I don't know.' Miranda was doubtful.

'Too much?'

'You look about fourteen months pregnant.'

The weird thing was, it actually suited Chloe. When you had blonde hair piled up with combs, and golden skin, and blue eyes that sparkled like the sea, Miranda realised, you could get away with almost anything, even stuffing a cushion the size of a sofa down your front.

Chloe thought she looked a fright, of course, but only because it was the automatic response of females everywhere to putting on weight. Plus, her self-confidence had taken a complete hammering when Greg had left.

Which couldn't help.

'That's better.' Miranda nodded approvingly when the big cushion was swapped for her rolled-up denim shirt. 'Size-wise, anyway. I'm not so sure about those bits of collar showing through. Looks as if you're about to give birth to something with huge pointy ears.'

Chloe pulled out the shirt and tossed it back on to Miranda's waiting-to-be-ironed, hopefully-before-Christmas pile.

'I can't wait for next Sunday. God, I hope Greg buys himself a really expensive new suit.' She looked at Miranda. 'Nothing can go wrong, can it?'

'Nothing.' Miranda broke into a grin; she was looking forward to it too. 'Just so long as he doesn't go down with mumps.'

'Flo? Dancing Queen, is that you?'

Florence, who had been wrestling with the *Telegraph* crossword, lit up at the sound of Tom Barrett's gravelly voice.

'Tom, you wicked old man! Are you ringing to tell me the date of the wedding? Hang on, give me a hand with this stinking crossword first. Attempt to hide donkeys in mountain slope before noon, eleven letters, something c, something e, something something something—'

'Haven't the foggiest, but I've got one for you. Old man abandoned by nubile young lassie—'

'Oh, Tom, *no*,' Florence exclaimed, cottoning on at once. 'Not Maria. Don't tell me she's dumped you.'

Tom chuckled at her dismay.

'Well, it was pretty mutual. Maria's a sweet girl, the sex was great, but the novelty soon wears off. All she wanted to do was watch *Home and Away* and bloody *Neighbours*. She speaks broken English with an Australian accent. Oh, it was fun while it lasted, Flo, but it wasn't love. She moved out last week, and the *relief* . . .'

Florence relaxed. He certainly didn't sound heartbroken.

'Where is she now, gone back to Thailand?'

'God, no! Moved in with the fellow next door.' Tom barked with laughter. 'Handy, really. She pops round every evening with a hot meal for me. Even gives me the odd massage if my back's playing up.'

'Humph,' said Florence. 'Being fond of *Neighbours* is one thing, but isn't that taking it a bit far?'

'No ill feelings,' Tom pronounced cheerfully. 'It didn't work out, that's all. And I'm keeping myself busy, still playing golf . . . just joined a local theatre group, matter of fact. Great fun.'

He and Louisa had always been keen on amateur dramatics, Florence recalled. Acting had been their great passion. It was something else Tom had given up when his wife had died.

'I'll never forget that production you put on in Malta.' As she spoke, the germ of an idea began to unfold. 'You were a fine Professor Higgins.'

'I had a fine Eliza,' Tom replied fondly, remembering Louisa. 'And there's something else I haven't forgotten about that show.' His tone grew stern. 'You fell asleep.'

'Never mind that now,' said Florence. 'What are you doing on Sunday?'

'Not watching endless videos of *Home and Away*, that's for sure.' Tom sounded immeasurably relieved. 'Why?'

'We're putting on a small production of our own.' Feeling like a movie mogul, Florence lit a cigarette and blew a row of smoke rings . . . damn, it really should be a Monte Cristo cigar. 'You'd fit the bill perfectly for the role I have in mind,' she told Tom, puff puff. 'And I promise not to fall asleep.'

Chapter 35

'You've been invited to Leila Monzani's wedding?'

Adrian stared at Greg in disbelief.

'Sshh, keep your voice down,' Greg hissed, though the pub was almost deserted. He tried not to smirk with pride, but it was impossible. Just as it had been impossible to keep the news to himself. Still, it wasn't as if he was blabbing it all around town. Ade was his best friend. He knew he could trust him. That was the whole point of best friends.

Adrian whistled, impressed.

'You're going up in the world, lucky sod. Who else'll be there?'

Triumphantly, Greg reeled off the list of names Miranda had given him. Ade gulped them down like lager after a lamb vindaloo.

'Shit! You'll be in *Hello!* magazine.'

'I told you, no press.'

'What, you mean *nobody* knows it's going to happen? That could be worth something,' Ade exclaimed. 'A tip-off to one of the tabloids . . . they pay good money for that kind of info. Who's Buzz Baxter working for now?' he went on abruptly. 'The *Sun*, the *Mirror* – one of the tabloids – a scoop like that'd be right up his street.'

Buzz Baxter was an old schoolfriend they still bumped into from time to time. Greg's forehead creased with doubt.

'But they don't want any publicity, do they?'

'Come on! One photographer, how terrible would that be? Give Buzz a ring,' Adrian urged. 'Earn yourself a few easy grand.'

Regretfully, Greg tilted his chair back on its hind legs.

'Miranda would go berserk.'

'Sometimes I wonder about you. Buzz wouldn't reveal his sources, would he? And Miranda doesn't know that you know Buzz. Simple,' said Adrian, spreading his hands. 'Home and dry. I'm telling you, mate, you're mad if you don't.'

They had another drink. Slowly, Greg allowed Adrian to overcome his reluctance.

'She'd ask me. I'd have to lie to her.'

'Oh, and that would never do, would it?' Adrian jeered. 'Keeping the truth from Miranda.'

Greg's smile was rueful. He didn't mention that he already had Buzz Baxter's phone number tucked away in his wallet. Tipping Buzz off had, naturally, occurred to him as soon as Miranda had stressed – rather insultingly, he felt – the secrecy of the occasion. But this way, his conscience was clear. It had been Adrian's idea, not his own. He was being conned, pressured, practically *forced* into going along with it.

Anyway, as Ade kept reminding him, nobody would ever know.

Thousands of pounds, in exchange for one simple phone call.

In all honesty, who could resist that?

*   *   *

Miranda, ringing him on Sunday morning, sounded breathless and distracted.

'Darling, I'll have to meet you there. I'm helping with the bridesmaid's hair. You can make your own way to the hotel, can't you?'

The Salinger, in Kensington, was one of London's classiest and most discreet hotels.

'As long as they let me in,' said Greg. It was all right for celebrities, with their instantly recognisable faces, but he would be turning up alone, without so much as a printed invitation. So, for that matter, would Buzz.

'Don't panic. Security will ask for the password,' Miranda explained. 'You have to tell them you're here to see Mr O'Hare.'

'O'Hare.' Greg acknowledged the feeble pun with a grimace.

'Then you have to sing "Here Comes the Bride".'

'What!'

'It's a two-part password,' Miranda told him. 'You don't have to do the whole song, just the first two lines. Then they'll let you through.'

'God.' Greg pulled a face; he wasn't much of a singer at the best of times.

'Have you missed me?'

'Of course I've missed you. Are you sure you're feeling better?'

'Oh, tons. Face all back to normal.' Miranda certainly sounded cheerful enough. 'Don't worry, I won't let you down.'

Greg smiled. He really had missed her.

'What are you wearing?'

'Bra, knickers, grey T-shirt with a picture of Screaming Lord Sutch on the front—'

'I meant to the wedding.'

'Oh, a new dress. You'll love it!'

'So long as it doesn't have Screaming Lord Sutch on the front.'

'Greg, I have to go, we're going to be rushed off our feet for the next couple of hours. See you at the Salinger, okay?'

'Twelve o'clock. I won't be late.'

'Blimey, better not be!'

'I love you,' Greg blurted out.

There was a brief pause.

'I love you too.'

'When security stop you, you tell them you're there to see Mr O'Hare,' Greg explained importantly.

'Right.'

'Then you have to sing the first two lines of "Here Comes the Bride".'

'Is this a wind-up?'

'No.'

'Can't I just hum it?'

'No!'

'Fucking celebrities,' sighed Buzz.

'There he is,' Chloe squealed delightedly, peeping through the curtains down to the street below. 'Buzz Baxter, lovely, lovely chap. Danced with me at our wedding reception, tried to undo my bra on the dance floor and asked if

I'd like to have sex with him in the back of his Austin Montego.'

Miranda peered over Chloe's shoulder at Buzz, glimpsing the camera under his baggy jacket as he fished out his wallet to pay off the cab. Moments later, Buzz smoothed the jacket back into place. The camera, like a concealed weapon, was undetectable. As he turned to mount the white marble steps, another gleaming black cab drew up behind him.

'How did you know Greg would tip him off?'

Chloe, drily, said, 'I know Greg.'

At that moment the door of the cab swung open and Miranda's head began to swim. Oh God, this was actually going to happen, it was really really about to happen. Just for a second, Miranda was choked with sorrow. So much for happy-ever-after. How could she have made such a monumental mistake?

No, no, I *mustn't* feel sorry for myself, there's no time for that now. Be brave, be strong, and smile like a bride . . .

'New suit,' Chloe observed with satisfaction. 'Let's hope it cost a bomb.' She took a deep breath, adjusted the padding beneath her uniform and spun Miranda round so fast she almost fell off her high heels. 'Right, the weasel has landed.' Firmly, she propelled Miranda in the direction of the blue ballroom's double doors. 'Go, go, go!'

The security man stepped forward, blocking Greg's path through the foyer. Greg knew he was security because he was wearing Blues Brothers dark glasses and an ill-fitting black suit.

'May I help you, sir?'

'I'm here to see Mr O'Hare,' said Greg.

The Blues Brother nodded impassively.

And waited.

'Um . . . "Here comes the bride,"' Greg sang in a quavering voice. He felt simultaneously foolish and important. '"All . . . all dressed in whi-ite . . ."'

White came out horribly off-key, which was embarrassing.

The Blues Brother didn't smile. He nodded again, grimly, and stepped to one side.

'Through reception, up the stairs and turn right. The ballroom's straight ahead of you.'

His black suit was too tight for him. Greg, squaring his shoulders and instinctively straightening his own jacket, wondered if the man had any idea how it felt to wear a suit that had cost eight hundred quid.

He checked his cuffs, then his watch. Five to twelve.

Mustn't be late.

When Greg was out of sight, Tony Vale removed his Blues Brothers glasses – Camden Market, £1.50 – before turning and switching off the video camera concealed within the pedestal flower arrangement behind him. Then he headed for the staircase. Wouldn't want to miss out on all the fun.

The double doors were closed. Fenn Lomax was pacing up and down outside like a nervous father-to-be.

'Hi. Greg Malone.' As he held out his perspiring-with-excitement hand, Greg wondered how much Fenn's suit had cost. 'Congratulations.'

'Miranda's fiancé. Nice to meet you at last.' Fenn nodded and smiled, shaking the outstretched hand. 'I have to congratulate you too.'

'Is everyone in there?' Greg jerked his head in the direction of the double doors.

'Oh yes, all ready and waiting. Apart from the bride, of course. Right,' said Fenn, taking a deep breath. 'We'd better go through.'

For the first few moments, as the heavy doors swung shut behind them and he found himself being led up the central aisle by Fenn, Greg thought he must be in the wrong room.

He knew he couldn't be, because he was with Fenn. But where, in that case, were all the celebrities?

No Kylie, no Daisy Schofield, no stars of stage and screen . . . and what was more, not a Mick in sight.

Bewildered, Greg wondered why Fenn hadn't seemed to notice that something was seriously amiss. His confusion increased as he recognised Leila Monzani sitting two rows from the front. She was wearing a shocking-pink tube of a dress, and Doc Marten's.

And over there, in her wheelchair, was that old witch, Florence . . .

Greg's neck muscles had by this time assumed a life of their own; his head swivelled from side to side as he spotted first Bev, in a hat the size of a kitchen table, then Buzz, looking as bemused as himself. Towards the back of the room he recognised Danny Delancey, but the dozen or so other guests were all total strangers.

For Christ's sake, where's *Miranda*?

'Over here, please.' The vicar indicated to Fenn and Greg where he wished them to stand.

'You don't mind, do you?' murmured Fenn.

In a daze, Greg shook his head. The Micks had evidently let Fenn down. He needed a best man. Jesus, what was Leila Monzani thinking of, getting married in Doc Marten's?

Music flooded the room, making Greg jump. From hidden speakers poured the opening bars of the Wedding March. Next to him, a muscle twitched in Fenn's jaw as he turned in response to the sound of the double doors swishing open.

Greg turned too.

Miranda, all in white, stood framed in the doorway.

Behind the veil, her dark eyes shone. Grinning broadly, she moved up the makeshift aisle towards him.

The music stopped.

Flinging out her arms, throwing them around Greg before he could react, Miranda cried, 'Surprise!'

The icy trickle of anti-freeze seeped through Greg's veins. Around him, the room erupted with laughter and applause. He felt his heart thudding like a tom-tom in his chest. It was the nightmare to end all nightmares and he could barely breathe.

'I don't . . . I don't understand.'

Greg stammered the words out at last, understanding only too well but playing desperately for time.

'I love you. You love me.' Miranda's cheeks were flushed with elation. 'It's what we both want, so why wait? I've never seen the point of long engagements. Oh darling, we're getting married . . . today! Right here, right now!'

Greg couldn't bear to look at her. Whichever way he turned, he saw something else he didn't want to see . . .

the vicar's benign, smiling face . . . Danny Delancey with a video camera, capturing every moment on film . . . Fenn Lomax searching in his pocket and pulling out two wedding rings . . .

Could there be an experience more excruciating than this?

Miranda, reaching for his hands, laughed and said, 'Darling, you're shaking like a leaf. Don't worry, I've thought of everything.' Leaning closer, she added triumphantly, 'I smuggled your birth certificate out of your flat last week.'

The ironic thing was, he *would* have married her. Like a shot. But what was the average sentence for bigamy? He might love Miranda, but he couldn't face going to jail.

'Could we have some quiet, please?' The vicar raised his hands to the boisterous congregation and nodded genially at Greg. 'If you're ready, maybe we can proceed.'

Greg's mouth opened and closed like a cod's. No words came out. He wondered about slumping to the ground and feigning unconsciousness.

'You are happy, I take it, for the ceremony to go ahead?' The vicar lifted bushy, enquiring eyebrows at him.

Greg stared back in horror.

'Darling?' Anxiety creased Miranda's forehead. 'Please say something. You're not going to turn me down, are you?'

Oh God, how could this be happening to him? How could he tell her?

Miranda's bottom lip began to tremble.

'Greg? What's wrong? Don't you want to marry me?'

She would never forgive him. Never. Oh, *shit*, why did this have to happen to him?

'Well,' declared Florence, her throaty voice carrying effortlessly across the room, 'this is in danger of becoming embarrassing. Come on, Greg, let's get this show on the road! The sooner we start, the sooner it's over with, then we can all have a drink.'

A drink, God, what he wouldn't give for a drink right now. For that matter, what he wouldn't give for a bolt of lightning to crash through the ceiling and knock Florence – interfering old buzzard – out of her wheelchair.

Better still, Greg thought in desperation, one to flatten me.

Daniel Delancey was still filming. Turning to look at him, Greg forced himself to speak.

'Switch it off,' he croaked. 'Please.'

'I can't do that.' Danny sounded surprised. 'This is the happiest day of Miranda's life.'

Miranda, no longer smiling, said, 'I'm beginning to wonder. Is this the happiest day of my life, Greg?' Her eyes bored into him. 'Is it?'

All heads swivelled in unison towards the double doors as they swung open. Desperately praying for some form – any form – of reprieve, Greg's head swivelled too.

A waitress in a black uniform and a white frilled apron backed through the doors carrying a tray of glasses. She turned, balancing the tray against her heavily pregnant stomach, and surveyed the assembled guests.

'Oh, I'm sorry, I thought you'd have finished by now. I was told—'

Chloe's voice broke off as she saw Greg.

Paralysed, Greg stared back at her. He was having an out-of-body experience. This couldn't be happening to him.

'What's going on here?' Chloe's incredulous gaze flickered from the vicar to Miranda to Greg. 'You can't marry him.'

Greg's legs began to tremble violently. He prayed he wouldn't wet himself.

Miranda's eyes were like saucers. Hotly she demanded, 'Why can't I?'

Chloe put the tray down carefully on the table beside her. She smoothed her apron over her swollen stomach – Jesus, Greg wondered wildly, how had she got that big so soon? – and calmly shrugged.

'Because I'm his wife.'

Chapter 36

'What the fuck is going on here?' marvelled Buzz Baxter as Greg stormed out of the ballroom and the place erupted once more. He nudged the tall girl who was crying with laughter next to him. 'What's going on?'

Bev wiped her streaming eyes with a tissue.

'You're the journalist, can't you work it out?'

Greg's wife Chloe was by this time hugging the girl in the wedding dress. The noisy old biddy in the wheelchair was wearing the vicar's dog-collar. And the vicar, now minus his neck-gear, was busy cracking open a bottle of Veuve Clicquot. When the girl next to him rushed up to join them, Buzz went along too.

Whooping at the sight of Bev, Miranda hurled her bouquet into the air. Automatically Bev caught it, then, horrified, let it drop, as if it were crawling with maggots.

'That's not fair,' she wailed. 'You didn't get married! Now you've probably given me a thousand years' bad luck.'

'I almost got married,' said Miranda. 'For a few seconds there, I thought he was going to go through with it.'

Chloe, her waitress's cap askew, nodded cheerfully at Buzz Baxter.

'Hi, Buzz, sorry you didn't get what you came for. I hope you didn't give Greg any money upfront.'

Buzz grinned; he'd always fancied Chloe. He liked her even more now he knew she had balls.

'You set the whole thing up.'

'Well, it was a joint effort.'

'Quite a lot of effort.'

'Worth it, though,' Chloe said with relish. 'Worth every minute, just to see the look on his face.'

Buzz shook his head in admiration. Greg would never live this kind of public humiliation down.

'And if he'd gone ahead with the ceremony, you'd have—?'

'Made my entrance,' Chloe supplied, 'at the crucial point.'

Tom Barrett, handing out glasses of champagne, said, 'Pity he didn't, I was looking forward to that bit.' He cleared his throat and intoned solemnly, '"If anyone here present knows of any reason why this man and this woman should not be joined together in Holy Matrimony, they should speak now . . ."'

He paused dramatically, and Chloe mimed bursting through the door. Brightly she explained, 'That's where I would have come in.'

'Isn't he marvellous?' Florence patted Tom Barrett's arm with pride. 'What a performance, better than Donald Sinden any day.' Teasingly, she tugged his wide black sleeve. 'This cassock suits you, too. I've always had a thing for men in uniform.'

Buzz wondered how many gaskets his boss was going to blow when he went back to the newspaper offices without a story. Ah well, sod it. He gulped down a brimming glass of champagne; may as well make the most of the free booze.

'So who's footing the bill for all this?' He held out his glass for a swift refill.

Miranda's mouth twitched.

'Greg is,' she joked. 'Well, inadvertently.'

'Blimey.'

Behind her, Danny was packing the video camera back into its case. Miranda gestured towards it.

'We filmed the whole thing. There's a new prime-time TV series going out in the autumn, called *Sweet Revenge*. People send in home videos and they pay five thousand pounds—'

'I know, I've heard about it. This is great.' Buzz started to laugh. Turning to Danny, he said, 'I hope you remembered to take the lens cap off.'

The party spilled out into the walled garden at the rear of the hotel. Almost giving a couple of ancient residents heart attacks, Miranda paused at the top of the steps and peeled off her borrowed bridal gown, stepping out of it to reveal the orange vest and mauve Lycra skirt beneath. The next minute she was splashing around in the ornate Italian fountain with Buzz.

Fenn spotted Chloe sitting on a bench eating a plate of coronation chicken from the restaurant. Joining her, he observed, 'You've changed, too. Did I miss it?'

The black and white waitress's uniform had been replaced by a long, floaty cotton dresss the colour of cinnamon, and her golden hair, no longer tied back, tumbled around her shoulders.

'That would really have finished them off.' Pulling a face, Chloe nodded at the elderly residents, who were still looking stunned. She had limited exposure of her own unlovely body to the confines of the downstairs loo.

'Pretty colour, it suits you,' said Fenn.

The dress was ancient. Flustered by the compliment, Chloe attempted to cover the darns in the worn cotton, then realised that Fenn was watching her with amusement. Giving in, she laughed and held up her plate of coronation chicken.

'At least I'm perfectly co-ordinated.'

'Until you eat it.'

'For about the next three minutes, then.' Ruefully, she gazed down at her stomach. 'I can't stop eating. It's scary, having the appetite of a prop forward and being the shape of a rugby ball.'

Fenn didn't think it was scary. Accustomed to the finicky eating habits of the models he'd spent the last few years knocking around with, it was a real breath of fresh air. He liked the way Chloe ate with such evident enjoyment, forking up the tender chicken and licking mayonnaise from her fingers. This was how eating should be, after all. You were meant to enjoy it.

Last week, Fenn had been cutting the hair of a knock-kneed, chain-smoking sixteen-year-old sent to him by one of the more ruthless agencies. When he had caught her scrutinising the wording on her cigarette packet, he had said, 'They damage your health.'

The girl, blinking nervously up at him, replied, 'I don't care about that, I was just checking they don't have any calories.'

'Here comes Leila,' said Chloe. 'Poor thing, she looks jet-lagged.'

Privately, Fenn thought that Leila, in her fluorescent tube dress, looked like the Pink Panther. And as for jet-lag . . . well, it was impossible to tell. The half-closed eyes and dazed expression were pretty much a permanent feature. All the supermodels were wearing them this season. He'd tried teasing Leila about it, but she hadn't got the joke. Beautiful she might be, Fenn thought with a regretful smile, but a sense of humour wasn't her strong point.

He had persuaded Leila to come along with him today because her frequent trips abroad meant their time together was limited.

And about to become more so, Fenn thought sadly, realising that yet another hollow relationship was ready to bite the dust. Why did he do it? What was the point of ever getting involved with these girls in the first place?

But he already knew the answer to that one.

Basically, depressingly – like Everest, only skinnier – because they were there.

'Hi,' said Leila, coiling her body on to the wooden arm of the bench next to Fenn. 'Can we go now?'

Chloe had finished her chicken. Fenn took the empty plate from her.

'I was just about to fetch Chloe a piece of raspberry gateau. Shall I get you one too?'

Leila's eyelids flickered briefly, acknowledging the so-called humour of this suggestion.

'No thanks. The wedding thing's over, isn't it? Why can't we go?'

'We're celebrating.'

'I don't know anyone here.'

'You know Miranda,' said Fenn. 'Go and dance in the fountain with her.' *Please*, he thought, silently willing her to laugh and kick off her shoes. I'd love it if you did that.

Chloe saw the blank expression on Leila's sculpted face.

'Why?'

'You might enjoy it.'

Leila looked at him as if he'd gone mad.

'I'd get wet.'

The Salinger Hotel was famous for its Sunday-afternoon tea dances. Inside, the orchestra played sedate numbers from the twenties and thirties, and elegantly dressed couples moved decorously around the polished dance floor. Outside, in the garden, Miranda danced – rather less elegantly – with Tom Barrett.

'We're raising a few eyebrows,' he told her, glancing up at the windows. 'Monocles are popping out as we speak.'

'That's because I look like a tart, and you're dressed as a vicar.'

'My dear, I'm the envy of every man in that ballroom.'

Waltzing for all she was worth, Miranda said, 'Oh Tom, aren't you lovely? Why can't I meet someone as nice as you, only forty years younger?'

Tom shouted with laughter.

'God, I'm sorry,' mumbled Miranda. 'I suppose I just answered my own question. A walking disaster, that's me.' Stepping backwards instead of forwards, she pulled a face. 'Not to mention a waltzing one.'

'That's no way to speak,' Tom chided. 'You're not a disaster.'

'I am.'

'Refreshingly honest, maybe.' Amused, Tom glanced over at Florence. 'Can't think where you get it from.'

'Poor Florence. I feel guilty, twirling away while she's stuck in her chair.'

'I wouldn't give much for your chances if she heard you calling her poor Florence.' Tom's smile was fond. 'Good old Flo, she was quite something in her day.'

'She still is,' said Miranda. 'And I wouldn't give much for *your* chances if she heard you calling her old.'

He looked thoughtful.

'Can she stand at all?'

'Oh yes, with support.'

They grinned at each other.

'Dare you,' said Miranda.

'Done.'

Florence looked up in alarm as Tom, his vicar's robes billowing and his manner purposeful, approached her.

'You're not leaving already?'

'I am not. I've come to ask for the pleasure of the next dance.'

Astonished, Florence said, 'With who?'

'You, you daft woman. And it's with *whom*.'

'Pah! You're the daft one, Tom Barrett,' Florence snorted, 'if you think I'd let you fling me round in this chair like a child let loose with a supermarket trolley. Ridiculous, that's how we'd look—'

'Not in the chair.' Tom shook his head. 'You can stand, I checked with Miranda. And if I can haul a set of clubs round eighteen holes,' he held out his arms, 'I'm sure I can manage you.'

281

'Lovely turn of phrase you have there,' grumbled Florence. 'Makes me sound like a sack of turnips.'

Tom smiled.

'Turnips are quieter. Turnips don't argue.'

'Go and dance with a turnip then.'

Evocative music drifted through the open French windows as, inside the ballroom, the orchestra struck up the next tune. Irritatingly, it was one of Florence's all-time favourites.

'I'd rather dance with you,' Tom said calmly. 'Much rather.'

'I don't do the tarantella any more.' Florence's tone was truculent. 'I can't twirl.'

Sensing weakness, Tom raised an enquiring eyebrow.

'Can you shuffle?'

'Oh, I can shuffle.'

He nodded with satisfaction, reaching down and clasping his arms firmly around Florence's waist.

'That'll do.'

'Fancy a bop?' said Buzz.

'Why not?' Chloe shook back her hair and stood up. 'But if you try and undo my bra, I shall have to kill you.'

He grinned. Chloe was all right.

'You're a pregnant lady. I do have some scruples, you know.'

'You amaze me,' said Chloe.

It was the sight of Florence and Tom dancing together that finally did it for Miranda. One minute she was sitting kicking her heels happily in the fountain and the next there was a lump the size of the Rock of Gibraltar battling to burst out of her chest.

Shuffle, shuffle went Tom's feet, in perfect time with Florence's. He was smiling down at her, saying something and making her chuckle. And Florence was enjoying herself; the look on her face said it all. With her new short hairstyle, her jaunty hat and flowing dress of violet silk splashed with crimson orchids, she looked fabulous. And so happy that Miranda wanted to cry.

The next moment, to her horror, she realised that she actually *was* crying. Hot tears were spilling over on to her cheeks like lava out of a volcano and there was nothing she could do to stop them. Oh God, please don't let anyone see me like this . . .

Tom Barrett, his snowy surplice billowing in the breeze, was dancing with Bev. Chloe had been persuaded to take a twirl round the garden with Tony Vale, still in his Blues Brothers suit and glasses but now wearing, as a finishing touch, Florence's flower-bedecked velvet hat.

'She isn't inside,' said Danny. 'I can't find her any-where.'

Fenn frowned.

'She wouldn't have left without telling us. And her bag's still here.'

Leila, busy lighting up yet another cigarette, said vaguely, 'When I went to the loo earlier there was someone crying in one of the cubicles.'

Fenn stared at her.

'Was it Miranda?'

'How would I know? All I could see was her feet. Green

nail polish with purple glitter.' Leila exhaled a stream of smoke and pulled a face. 'I mean, totally passé.'

'Those were Miranda's totally passé toes,' Fenn said furiously. 'Why didn't you tell us earlier?'

Leila looked amazed.

'You didn't ask.'

Chapter 37

It was a good job the lid of the loo seat was down. Otherwise Miranda, sitting cross-legged and hugging an empty bottle to her chest, would have fallen in.

'Come on, Miranda, I know it's you. Open the door this minute.'

It was Danny's voice. And he was sounding bossy.

Bossy bloody Danny Delancey, thought Miranda, tipping her head back and draining the last few lukewarm drops of wine. Well, he could be as bossy as he liked. She wasn't scared.

She wasn't about to open the door, either.

'Miranda.'

'Danny,' she mimicked.

'Still alive, then.' He sounded relieved. 'Unlock the door, Miranda.' Pause. 'We were worried about you.'

'No need to worry about me.' She shook her head with such vigour she almost slid off the wooden loo seat. Tut tut, very highly polished, exceedingly dangerous . . . I could sue the hotel for that. Regaining her balance, she glared at the door. 'Anyway, you aren't allowed in here. This is the ladies' loo. And you're a man.'

'Possibly the nicest thing you've ever said to me.' Danny sounded amused. 'Unlock the door, there's a good girl.'

'God,' grumbled Miranda. 'Nag, nag, nag. Oh, and by the way . . . no, I won't.'

'Fine.'

Moments later, she let out a squeal as he dropped over the partition dividing her cubicle from the one next to it.

'Who do you think you are,' Miranda demanded indignantly, 'Milk Tray man?'

'Who d'you think you are,' Danny countered, 'the latest recruit to the Oliver Reed School of Drinking?'

Miranda tried to leap to her feet, but twenty minutes of sitting cross-legged on a loo seat had seized up her knees and ankles completely. Whimpering with pain, she was forced to hang on clumsily to Danny's arms for support as Florence had clung to Tom earlier.

'Ow, ow, my feet, *ow*—' yelped Miranda, her eyes screwed up in agony. The next second she felt herself being lifted up, swung round and plonked down again. The pain had stopped, though the soles of her feet still buzzed with pins and needles. Cautiously opening her eyes, she realised that her suspicions had been correct. Danny was now sitting on the toilet seat lid and she was sitting on Danny. His arms were around her, keeping her in place. She could smell his aftershave. Close up like this – and she had certainly never been this close before – she couldn't help noticing he had really, *really* nice ears.

Well, ear. From this angle she could only see the left one. But the other one – Mr Right, Miranda thought with a stifled giggle – was probably just as attractive. In its own way.

'What?' said Danny.

Better not tell him. He might think she was weird.

'I feel like a ventriloquist's dummy.'

Danny waggled his fingers.

'Look, no hands.'

He was humouring her, Miranda realised. Being kind. Overall, she thought she preferred him bossy – at least that way she could fight back.

For a terrible second, she thought she was going to burst into tears again. As if her eyes weren't already swollen and piggy enough.

Danny, glimpsing her expression, gave her waist a brief, meant-to-be-sympathetic squeeze.

'Don't,' warned Miranda. Her lower lip trembled.

'It's okay to cry. If that's what you want to do, just go ahead,' Danny reassured her.

'Stop it. Please don't be nice to me.' She felt her eyes start to fill.

He gave her waist another squeeze. Miranda's ribcage began to shudder. Oh, the humiliation, this wasn't fair.

'Can't you just say something horrible?' She blurted the words out in desperation. 'Be sarcastic? Give me a slap and tell me to grow up?'

In reply, Danny reached up and smoothed her ruffled hair. His dark eyes were serious. For the first time ever, he wasn't teasing her.

'Bastard,' muttered Miranda, 'you're no help at all.'

Once she'd started, it was impossible to stop. This time she didn't have to pretend she was crying because of Florence and Tom. These tears, held back for too long, were all for herself.

Danny said nothing, he just held her and stroked her back and let the torrent of sobbing run its necessary course.

It felt like hours to Miranda, but when she finally hiccuped to a halt and glimpsed his watch as he wiped her eyes, she saw that it hadn't been that long at all. Less than ten minutes.

Still, she'd managed to honk and bawl her way through an entire loo roll, which was something. Quite an achievement, actually, in ten minutes.

'Better now?' said Danny at last.

Miranda nodded and blew her reddened nose. Reluctantly she muttered, 'Am I supposed to say thank you now?'

'Don't let it trouble you.' He grinned at her. 'Happy to help.'

Miranda swayed a bit on his lap. She felt light-headed with the relief of getting all that pent-up emotion out of her system. Thanks to the amount of wine she had guzzled in a short space of time, she also needed, quite badly, to pee.

'Um, could you go now?'

Danny heaved a dramatic sigh.

'That's right, use me and toss me aside like an old Kleenex. Blub all over me, soak my shirt—'

'If you carry on much longer, it'll be more than your shirt that gets soaked,' said Miranda.

'Ah. Right.'

'Do I look terrible?' She blinked and rubbed her face, which felt salty and raw.

'Not your best, I have to say.'

'Oh God, and my make-up's in my bag, in the garden.'

Danny tipped her off his lap and unlocked the cubicle door.

'You stay here. I'll fetch your bag.'

'Could you call a cab?' Miranda sensed that her face was beyond repair. 'I think I just want to go home.'

'I'll take you.'

'Make my excuses to everyone. Don't tell them I was crying,' she added hurriedly.

'I'll say you're as pissed as a parrot. Again.'

Miranda nodded; that was far less humiliating.

'Thanks.'

Bruce had to attend a trade fair in Bristol on Monday morning. He parked a short distance from Florence's house on Sunday afternoon, not particularly looking forward to seeing his mother but needing to hand the keys over to Chloe so that tomorrow morning she could open up the shop.

In the event, neither of them was in. The house was empty. Scribbling a note for Chloe, Bruce shovelled the bunch of keys through the letter-box and headed back to his car.

Before he could pull away, a green BMW drew up outside the house, reversing niftily into a space Bruce had considered earlier and rejected as too small. Irritated by the other driver's superior parking skills, he peered across to reassure himself it wasn't a woman.

It wasn't.

It was his mother's toyboy, Orlando.

Bruce's immediate instinct was to shrink down in his seat. If that was Florence in the passenger seat, he didn't want her to spot him. The prospect of being dragged into the house and having to witness his mother making sheep's eyes at that gigolo was more than he could handle.

But it wasn't Florence, he realised moments later as a

tanned elbow – a *young* elbow – appeared, resting on the passenger-side open window.

Bruce sat bolt upright. Now this was promising. Well, well, in all honesty he hadn't thought Chloe had it in her.

Then the elbow shifted and the forearm came out, too thin to belong to Chloe. Bruce, peering harder, glimpsed an assortment of vaguely familiar silver bangles, then a flash of telltale blue-green hair.

Not Chloe, the other one . . . what was her name?

Miranda.

Something odd had begun to happen on the way back from the Salinger Hotel. Every time Danny pulled up at a junction or a set of traffic lights, Miranda discovered, he grew more attractive.

It was no longer confined to his ears. Each stolen glance – when he wasn't looking at her, of course – revealed yet another admirable feature. The straightness of his nose, those totally unfair eyelashes, not to mention the way his hair curled over his collar . . .

It was more than odd, Miranda marvelled, it was astonishing. Like digging a hideous old crimplene cardigan out of the back of your wardrobe and realising that you'd made a mistake, it was actually the cardigan of your dreams, pink and perfect and one hundred per cent cashmere.

Breaking into her thoughts – oh, such delicious thoughts – Danny said abruptly, 'We're here.'

'You've been really kind,' Miranda told him. 'Really really kind.'

'I know. And you're really really drunk. When did you last have something to eat?'

She shrugged, trying to think.

'Tuesday?'

'You should eat.' He paused. 'What?'

'What what?'

'Why are you looking at me like that?'

'I don't know,' said Miranda, distinctly light-headed. Her elbow slid off the window frame with a thud. 'Why are *you* looking like that?'

'Like what?'

She pointed an accusing finger at him.

'All gorgeous and, you know, sexy and stuff.'

His mouth twitched. Sexily.

'See?' Miranda demanded. 'You're doing it again.'

'Now listen to me, you've had—'

'Can I kiss you?'

Ha, that stopped him in his tracks! She saw his eyes flicker. Sexily.

'Miranda.'

Even the way he said her name was sexy.

'Or if you want to be masterful about it,' she offered, 'you could always kiss me.'

'I don't think I should.'

Miranda ignored this. He was looking at her with regret, not revulsion. Regret didn't count.

'I want you to.' Reaching over, she grabbed his arms. Gorgeous, sexy arms. 'If you don't do it, I will.'

Danny didn't speak.

So she kissed him. Sexily, and for all she was worth.

Bruce, who liked a tidy car, had despaired of Verity's sloppy habit of leaving spare coats slung across the back seat. This time, twisting round, he sent up a prayer of thanks for sloppy people everywhere. He would never moan at Verity again.

Miranda missed at first, losing her balance and only managing to make contact with – oof – the stubbled edge of his jaw. Undeterred, she levered herself upright and took fresh aim. This time her mouth landed on Danny's and she closed her eyes with relief. Bingo, this was more like it! Oh yes, this is miles better than being squashed into a toilet cubicle together, with his knees going numb and me bawling my stupid eyes out.

Even if the other contestant didn't appear to be giving it his all.

She peeled herself away for a second, to let him know she knew.

'Seven out of ten. Must try harder, could do better.' Miranda cocked an eyebrow at him. 'I think what we need is for you to put a bit more effort into this.'

Chapter 38

Danny glanced sideways as a man in a turquoise cagoule shuffled past, clutching an envelope and heading for the post-box at the end of the road. It was a hot, sunny Sunday afternoon but the hood of the cagoule was pulled up and tied firmly around his face. One of those care-in-the-community types, Danny thought. With a morbid fear of rain.

But he had other things on his mind right now. Like how much longer he could reasonably be expected to fend off Miranda, when she was launching herself at him with all the subtlety of a Scud missile.

'Or was that your best effort?' she was saying now, wagging her finger infuriatingly and sounding like a sarcastic schoolmistress. 'Maybe it was, and you're just a really hopeless kisser.'

Right. Goaded beyond endurance, Danny took her in his arms and gave her what she wanted. Within seconds she was sighing and writhing helplessly against him like an ecstatic kitten. Equally abruptly, he pulled away.

Hopeless kisser indeed.

'Wow,' gasped Miranda, panting for breath. 'That was more *like* it.'

Danny acknowledged the compliment with a brief nod. Even if it was coming from someone who was howling drunk.

'Thanks.'

'I love you.' The wine was well and truly lodged in her bloodstream now. She could say anything, *anything* . . .

'Miranda, don't.'

'But I do love you!'

'You do not.' Christ, did she think this was easy for him?

'The house is empty.' She trailed her fingers enticingly across the front of his shirt, still damp where she had sobbed all over him. 'Shall we go in?'

'Why?'

Miranda rolled her eyes at his stupidity.

'We could go to bed.'

Don't do this, thought Danny.

'Why?'

'Well, the general idea would be to have sex.' She gave him a playful thump on the arm. 'And then maybe a little sleep, then something to eat, followed – with a bit of luck – by more sex. How does that sound to you?'

For heaven's sake, how did she think it sounded?

'What happened to that pledge of eternal celibacy?'

Miranda looked appalled.

'Oh no, I've changed my mind about that *completely*.'

Give me strength, Danny pleaded silently. Aloud, he said, 'Not a good idea.'

He was shaking his head. Miranda stared at him.

'Come on, it's a brilliant idea! Why can't we? Stop shaking your head like that and tell me why we can't!'

'Because,' Danny said slowly, 'you've had far too much to drink. And you'd only regret it in the morning.'

'I would *not* regret it,' Miranda wailed.

'You would.'

'Why, because you're rubbish in bed? Is that it?' Perking up, she recalled that this was the technique that had worked so brilliantly just a couple of minutes earlier. 'Why would I regret it, Danny? Because you're even more useless at sex than you are at kissing?'

Bugger, he was smiling at her. It wasn't going to work.

'Possibly,' said Danny.

'But I want to have *sex with you*!' Miranda thumped the steering wheel for emphasis.

'Not with me,' said Danny quietly, aware that the chap in the turquoise cagoule had posted his letter and was shuffling back towards them. 'Right now, anyone would do. You're just trying to punish Greg for hurting you. And prove to yourself that you're over him.'

Ouch.

'Well, so what if I am?' Miranda pleaded. 'Isn't that a good enough reason?'

'Sweetheart, it's a terrible reason.'

'You're no fun.' She clung to him, her empty stomach emitting a terrific rumble.

Shuffle, shuffle. The man in the hooded cagoule moved slowly past the car.

'Come on, I'll make you a bacon sandwich.' Patting her arm, Danny opened the door.

'Give me another kiss first. I'm miserable.'

He did, exerting superhuman control.

'We could eat them in bed,' Miranda suggested hopefully.

'I'm only coming in because I don't trust you not to set fire to the kitchen,' Danny told her. 'As soon as you've finished your sandwich, I'll be off.'

Back in his car once more, Bruce watched the two of them disappear together into the empty house. Miranda's head leaned on Orlando's shoulder and his arm was around her waist. It was obvious what they were up to.

Damn, what he wouldn't give for a camera now. Still, he would make Florence believe him when he told her what he'd both seen and heard.

Bruce smiled to himself with satisfaction. Excellent. And thanks to that little tart Miranda doing Chloe's job for her, he'd saved himself five grand.

The party at the Salinger Hotel broke up a couple of hours later. Leila, almost comatose with boredom, drawled, 'Fenn, let's get *out* of here.'

'No chance, I suppose, that you two might give it a go for real?' Buzz, seeing that they were about to leave, had sidled up hopefully.

'No chance at all.' Fenn jangled his car keys. 'Chloe? Want a lift?'

Chloe looked up, startled, from her vanilla cream slice.

'I'm fine, I'll catch a bus.'

'Don't be silly. Come with us.'

Leila's slanting eyes narrowed with exasperation.

'If she's in the car, you won't let me smoke.'

'Correct,' said Fenn. 'Tell you what, I'll give Chloe a lift and you can catch the bus.'

'I've had enough of this,' Leila snapped. 'Just because she's pregnant. You care more about her and her stupid baby than you do about me.'

She picked up a glass of red wine. Buzz, hardly able to believe his luck, fumbled for his camera. Stepping out of the way as Leila flung the contents of the glass at him, Fenn escaped almost entirely unscathed. Happily for Buzz, it still made a terrific picture.

'Cheers,' he said, winking and giving the thumbs-up sign to Fenn.

'Oh God,' whispered Chloe, 'I'm so sorry, I'm *so* embarrassed.'

Like a furious pink pipe-cleaner, Leila stalked off. Fenn grinned at Chloe.

'Don't be. I call this a pretty successful day all round.'

'But you must mind,' Chloe protested, still shuddering at the memory of Leila's abrupt exit.

Fenn threaded the Lotus through the dawdling Sunday traffic, dying to stick his foot down but careful not to do anything that might alarm her.

'Do I look as if I mind?'

'No, but . . . oh God, you've got a splash on your shirt.' Chloe squirmed, feeling horribly responsible. Fenn's shirts probably cost more than the average package holiday to Ibiza.

'Look in there.' He indicated the glove compartment. 'I'm pretty sure Leila left a bottle of Perrier behind.'

She had, and a packet of Kleenex. Fenn pulled up in a bus lane, allowing Chloe to soak the blue-red stain with lukewarm sparkling water and go to work on it with a tissue.

She scrubbed so energetically, a sheaf of papers slithered out of the glove compartment on to her feet.

'The car's rocking,' Fenn observed with amusement. 'People are going to wonder what we're up to in here.'

'Until they see my incredible bulk and realise that getting up to anything would be pretty much impossible. This isn't working, by the way.'

'It's only a shirt.'

Chloe peeked at the label inside the collar.

'A Turnbull and Asser shirt. If we don't let the stain dry out, we can soak it in something biological – oh no, now look what I'm doing, wrecking your papers . . .'

Bending over with difficulty, she gathered up the dozen or so sheets and hurriedly smoothed out the heel-marks. They were property details with eye-boggling prices.

'The lease is up on my flat,' Fenn explained.

'Hampstead, what bliss.' Chloe sighed with pleasure as she leafed through the glossy details. This was clearly the area he was concentrating on. She tried not to drool over a photograph of a white stucco villa overlooking the heath, with a pool in the back garden. It wasn't the kind of house-hunting she was used to.

'I'm seeing that one tomorrow, after work,' said Fenn.

Chloe opened her mouth then quickly shut it again. She'd been about to say that if he wanted a second opinion, she would love to go with him . . . heavens, presumptuous or what? Why on earth would Fenn be interested in her useless opinion? Worse still, the estate agent might mistake them for a couple, and how embarrassing would that be for Fenn?

'What?' He was looking at her oddly.

'Nothing.' Chloe went a deep shade of pink.

There was a pause, then Fenn said carefully, 'Look, if you aren't doing anything else, why don't you come along with me?'

Oh Lord, this was awful! He'd guessed what she was about to say and now he felt obliged to make the offer, simply because he was so kind . . .

'No thanks,' Chloe said abruptly. 'I can't. I'm busy tomorrow night.'

'So you're back at last,' said Bruce when Florence answered the phone at ten o'clock that evening. 'Where on earth have you been?'

'Out dancing,' said Florence.

'Oh, ha ha, very good.' Bruce sounded annoyingly buoyant, she realised – how she hated that mixture of sarcasm and joviality in his tone. 'Though not with the gigolo, one presumes.'

One presumes. Honestly, young people today, where did they pick up this kind of language?

'His name is Orlando,' Florence replied coolly. 'And he isn't a gigolo. Why are you ringing, Bruce? If you want to speak to Chloe, she's in bed.'

'I paid a visit to your house this afternoon—'

'I know. Chloe has the shop keys, they're perfectly safe.'

'Mother, will you stop interrupting? This is important. Your so-called boyfriend Orlando is cheating on you.'

Long pause. *Yesss*, thought Bruce triumphantly.

At last Florence said, 'What do you mean?'

'Orlando. And Miranda. I saw them outside your house, bold as brass. They were all over each other.'

'Orlando and Miranda? *My* Miranda? All over each other, you say? I don't believe it!'

Florence was genuinely stunned.

'And I do mean all over each other,' Bruce went on sanctimoniously. 'We aren't talking about a quick peck on the cheek, oh no, this was serious. And then – I'm sorry to have to tell you this, Mother – they disappeared together. Into the house.'

'And then they disappeared together into this very house?' parroted Florence, her eyebrows practically turning cart-wheels as she kept Tom Barrett abreast of developments. 'You mean, to have *sex*?'

Tom, still wearing his cassock and white surplice, refilled Florence's glass with bourbon and tut-tutted in a vicarish way.

Bruce said, 'I'm afraid so.'

'But that's fantastic!' Florence whooped, unable to con-ceal her delight.

'What?'

'Thank you, darling, I'm so glad you rang! You really have made my day!'

Bruce was still spluttering when Florence unceremoniously hung up, cutting him off in mid-quack.

'Well, well, would you believe it? That wicked, wicked boy! To think I actually fell for all that guff about having to take Miranda home because she was drunk.' Florence's face was a picture. 'And all the time they were . . . ha!' She clapped her gnarled hands with satisfaction. 'About bloody time too!'

Chapter 39

It took a while for Miranda to orientate herself. Her watch said seven o'clock, but was that morning or evening? She had absolutely no idea how long she had been asleep.

Help arrived, moments later, in the form of Chloe. Carrying a tray.

Miranda peered at it, searching for clues.

'Hi. Is that . . . ?'

'Breakfast,' said Chloe.

Ah.

'Only tea and toast. I didn't know if you'd feel up to much.'

Miranda didn't know either. It was far too soon to tell.

'You've been asleep for fifteen hours,' Chloe went on, plonking the tray down.

Good Lord, really? Testing her head, Miranda discovered that it hardly hurt at all. How amazing, she appeared to have slept right through her hangover.

Excellent news!

Feeling more cheerful already, she hauled herself into a sitting position and took a noisy slurp of tea. Gorgeous, made just the way she liked it, two and a half sugars and tongue-numbingly strong . . .

Hang on a sec.

'Why are you looking at me like that?'

'It's Florence.' Chloe's valiant attempts at keeping a straight face weren't going well. 'She'd, um, like a word.'

'Florence is up already?' Miranda was astounded. This was unheard of.

'She made me come and wake you up.'

'Why?' Miranda peered suspiciously over the rim of her Bart Simpson mug. Something was going on here and she couldn't for the life of her imagine what it might be. 'Why?' she persisted. 'Is Florence ill?'

Florence couldn't really be ill, she knew that. Otherwise, why would Chloe be smirking?

'I think she's just dying . . .' said Chloe.

What?

'. . . of curiosity.' Another pause, then the words came tumbling out. 'She wants to know all the gory details about you and Danny.'

'Me and Danny? For heaven's sake, what kind of gory details?'

'Well, who made the first move.' Chloe's shoulders were shaking. 'How many times you . . . er, did it. Oh, and she especially wants to know if he's fantastic in bed.'

Miranda dropped her toast. Up until that moment her brain had been merciful, sparing her the horror of having to remember events she would have so much preferred to forget.

Now it all came flooding back in a hideous, toe-curling, spine-tingling technicolour *whoosh*.

'Oh God, oh God, oh noooo!' The tray on Miranda's

lap toppled sideways as she threw herself back against the pillows and dragged the duvet over her head.

Chloe caught the tray with milliseconds to spare. She tugged the duvet away from Miranda's burning face.

'You don't have to be embarrassed. Danny's great, we all really like him.'

'Ooohhh!'

'Miranda, come on, you and Danny got it together and that's wonderful news. You don't have to be embarrassed, just because you had sex with him!'

Heavens, Chloe marvelled, listen to me. I sound just like Florence.

'I didn't have sex with him,' whispered Miranda. To add insult to injury, her hangover was belatedly kicking in. But the spasms of pain attacking her temples were negligible in comparison with the agony of total humiliation. When you were about to be mauled by a pack of lions, you didn't worry too much about being bitten by an ant.

Chloe was looking disappointed.

'You didn't? Damn, we thought you had.' She frowned. 'So why are you so upset?'

Miranda closed her eyes. She didn't need twenty questions, she needed oblivion. Having sex with Danny Delancey wouldn't have been embarrassing at all – well, maybe a bit, but she could have handled that.

Equally, being offered the opportunity of a night of wild sex with Danny Delancey and graciously turning him down would have been fine. No reason to be embarrassed there.

Except I didn't do either of those things, thought Miranda, did I? Oh no, not me, I had to pick the third card, didn't I?

I threw myself at him and forced him to kiss me and then I begged – actually *begged* – him to have sex with me . . . and he turned me down.

Awfully kind of you to offer, old thing, but no thanks, rather not.

Miranda shuddered. Her skin crawled with humiliation.

Oh God, what have I done?

Total, total nightmare.

Why am I such a prat?

There was nothing else to do but come clean. Florence, true to form, thought it was all uproariously funny.

'Never mind, darling, better luck next time.'

Next time, oh yes, Miranda thought miserably. I can hardly wait.

'At least you got a snog out of it,' Florence continued, her eyes alight with mischief. 'You can tell us how that went, surely! Good, bad, indifferent . . . ?'

'Average,' lied Miranda, wondering what she'd done to deserve such torture.

'Hmm. From the way Bruce described it, that's a bit like describing Torvill and Dean as average ice-skaters.'

'Actually, I've got a bit of a headache.'

Florence went off into peals of laughter.

'Poor darling, is that what Danny said to you last night?'

Chloe, feeling sorry for Miranda, said, 'Shall I bring you a couple of aspirins?'

'Make it a couple of hundred,' Miranda groaned. Oh dear, was it possible to feel worse than this?

* * *

The phone rang just as she was crawling out of the house.

'For you,' crowed Florence, behind her.

'Who is it?'

'No idea. Sounds like Jeremy Paxman.' Florence had recently taken to watching *Newsnight* at every opportunity; she thought Jeremy Paxman was the bee's knees. 'Ask him if he wears pants or boxer shorts.' She wagged the receiver hopefully at Miranda. 'It's so hard to fantasise when you don't know.'

Miranda snatched the phone from her, not in the mood for Florence's surreal ramblings.

'Miranda Carlisle? Glad I managed to catch you,' barked Jeremy Paxman, sounding as brisk and disdainful as he did when he was grilling some hapless politician. 'Short notice, I know, but we'd like you to appear on the show tonight, and not that it's relevant, but for the record perhaps you could tell whoever asked that ludicrous question that the answer is neither. Beneath my desk I am at one with the elements, unhampered, as free as a bird—'

Miranda hung up.

Moments later, the phone rang again.

'You weren't supposed to do that,' a more familiar voice complained good-naturedly. 'I was only trying to brighten your day.'

'I don't want to speak to you, I don't, I really don't . . .'

'Not bad, though, was it?' Danny sounded pleased with himself. 'Did I fool you, just for a few seconds?'

'No.' He had, of course. Right up to the moment when he had begun to describe his below-desk preferences in such vivid detail. Thanks to that deadly accurate machine-gun delivery, she had actually believed that Jeremy Paxman was calling to invite a hopeless trainee hairdresser from Notting Hill on to his show.

That's how stupid I am, thought Miranda.

Spending the rest of her life in a tin shack on the Outer Hebrides was becoming an increasingly attractive idea.

She looked at her watch.

'I have to go. I'm late for work.'

For some reason, this didn't appear to bother Danny.

'Dear me, late for work, that would never do.'

'What do you want?' Miranda gritted her teeth. 'An apology, is that it?'

'Don't be daft.' Danny sounded amused. 'Although you could thank me, if you like. For doing the gentlemanly thing.'

Hot waves of shame swept through her. She stood there, mortified and unable to speak.

Sadist.

'And don't think it was easy,' Danny went on, 'because it wasn't. I was tempted, I admit. Turning down offers like that doesn't come naturally to red-blooded males, let me tell you—'

'Okay, okay,' Miranda blurted out. 'Thank you thank you thank you for not sleeping with me, I'm so *grateful* to you!'

'Calm down, no need to yell.' Now he sounded offended. 'I was being responsible. You were upset about Greg, plus you'd had a fair bit to drink. People do daft things when they're pissed—'

Tell me about it, Miranda thought despairingly. Except – damn – he already was.

'—and I didn't want you waking up this morning, flinching at the sight of me and thinking, Oh God, *no*.' Danny paused. 'That's the worst-case scenario, of course. It could have been quite different. You might have been delighted it happened, not embarrassed at all. You might have thought, That was fabulous, why didn't we do it *months* ago?'

There was an odd note in his voice. Miranda couldn't work it out at all, and she didn't want to try. Her brain kept conjuring up hideous images of her flinging herself at Danny in his car, smothering him with kisses, fumbling with his shirt buttons, yelling, 'I want to have sex with you!'

And the pictures kept appearing, over and over again like a video stuck endlessly on Replay.

'Look, I do have to go to work.' She tried huffing her fringe out of her eyes but perspiration had plastered it to her clammy forehead. 'But you're right, it would have been disastrous, the biggest mistake of my life. God, just the thought makes me shudder. I must have been out of my tree.'

'Okay.' Danny sounded taken aback, as if he hadn't been expecting quite such a brutal put-down. 'Well, that's that out of the way. All forgotten. How about dinner tonight, to celebrate the fact that we didn't sleep together and we're still friends?'

'No thanks.' Miranda couldn't face it, she was too ashamed. It was all right for Danny, he wasn't the one who'd been begging for sex. And she didn't believe for one moment that it would be All Forgotten. From now on, their every conversation would be a minefield, because

307

she just knew Danny wouldn't be able to resist teasing her, making the occasional sly remark here, the odd dig there, reminding her – God, as if she needed reminding – what an all-time prize pillock she'd made of herself.

'Go on,' Danny urged.

'I really don't want to.'

'What about the video? I was going to bring it over. Don't you want to see it?'

'I'm going to work now.' Miranda had had enough. 'And I don't want to see you or your video.' As her patience snapped, her voice rose hysterically. 'I just want to be *left in peace.*'

Feigning cheerfulness for the clients at the salon was something you had to do whether you liked it or not. As far as Miranda was concerned, it was a long and trying day. The only time she cheered up was when she handed the parcel Chloe had given her over to Fenn and watched him open it.

'That's your shirt.' She gazed at it in astonishment. It was definitely the shirt Fenn had been wearing yesterday, now laundered and ironed and folded as neatly as a sweater in a Benetton shop.

'Chloe insisted.' Fenn ran a finger over the front where the wine stain had been. 'After Leila got trigger-happy with the claret.'

Mystified, Miranda stared up at him. Fenn was six foot two and broad-shouldered.

'So if you left your shirt at our house, what did you wear home?'

'The only thing that fitted me.' The corners of Fenn's

mouth twitched as he recalled the reaction of his neighbours when they had seen him in the sweatshirt Chloe had bought from Mothercare.

In that moment, Miranda knew.

'The yellow sweatshirt,' she exclaimed, 'with pink writing on it.'

'Maybe,' said Fenn.

Miranda clapped her hands with delight; she could just picture it. Fenn Lomax, emerging from his black Lotus in a pastel-shaded sweatshirt bearing the slogan *I'm Not Fat, I'm Pregnant*.

The house overlooking Hampstead Heath was a dream. It was perfect in every way, from the matching pair of monkey puzzle trees in the front garden to the Tuscan-style marbled kitchen the size of a tennis court, done out in irresistible shades of copper and blue.

The estate agent kept saying what a fabulous property it was, and Fenn could only nod in agreement. He was unable to fault it.

'There's a great deal of interest, as you'd expect,' the agent told him as they left. 'I'm sure you'd like to put in an offer.'

I could be making the biggest mistake of my life here, thought Fenn. I must be mad.

Aloud he said, 'No thanks.'

Chapter 40

Three weeks later, Fenn moved into his new flat. The next day, he gave his overjoyed salon junior a lift home from work.

'This is so brilliant,' Miranda exclaimed when he informed her in his off-hand fashion that since he practically had to pass her front door, they may as well make it a regular thing. 'No more fighting and getting squashed on the tube! And I'll be saving eight pounds a week on fares . . . golly, I'm going to be rich!'

That was a comfort, then. Every cloud . . . Fenn thought drily. Miranda was getting herself chauffeured to and from work and saving eight pounds a week. He, on the other hand, had leased a diabolically expensive flat in Holland Park with no swimming pool, no garden and truly cringe-making décor of the 1960s groovy-man-about-town variety. Even the neighbours were unfriendly, clearly regarding a long-haired celebrity hairdresser as an undesirable member of their exclusive enclave. Then again, maybe they were simply suspicious of anyone who would want to live in a flat with zebra-print fitted carpets, mirrored ceilings and leather-look walls.

And let's face it, Fenn had to acknowledge, who wouldn't be?

But he had been compelled to rent the property anyway, for reasons so flimsy and embarrassing he couldn't admit them to a living soul.

'I thought you'd set your heart on Hampstead.' Rifling through her bag, Miranda offered him a liquorice allsort. 'What made you go for Holland Park instead?'

There was no way in the world he was going to tell Miranda.

'I thought if I moved to Holland Park, I'd be able to give you a lift every morning. That way, you wouldn't be able to be late for work,' said Fenn. 'And we wouldn't have to listen to any more of your bizarre excuses.'

Not true, of course, but close. Closer than Miranda would ever know. Fenn swung the car into Tredegar Gardens and pulled up outside Florence's house.

'You pretend to be a grumpy old stick,' Miranda told him with a grin, 'but deep down you're all heart.'

She was gathering together her belongings, squashing the packet of liquorice allsorts back into her haversack, juggling sunglasses, Coke can and a set of keys.

'How's Florence?' Fenn kept his tone casual.

'Great! People keep complimenting her on her hair.'

He hesitated.

'I haven't seen her since the wedding.'

'Of course you haven't.' Miranda frowned, concentrating on disentangling the cord on her sunglasses from her key ring. 'Bugger, how did I manage to do this?'

Never mind that, thought Fenn, how do you manage to miss a hint the size of a JCB?

'Well,' he went on slightly desperately, 'I'm glad she's okay.'

311

Yay, done it! Triumphantly, Miranda slung her glasses around her neck and waved her keys at him.

'Thanks for the lift, you're a star. I'd ask you in for a drink – Florence would love to see you – but I know you must be dying to get back to the new flat.'

Fenn exhaled slowly.

Mission accomplished.

About time too.

'Of course I am,' he told Miranda with a careless shrug. 'Still, the flat isn't going anywhere, is it? Twenty minutes won't hurt.'

Chloe was dozing on the sun-lounger in the garden, soaking up the late-afternoon rays. When she felt an insect tickling her nose, she batted it away idly without opening her eyes.

Then it happened again. Chloe looked up and saw Miranda grinning down at her.

'Bzzz bzzz.' Miranda waggled the blade of grass in her hand. 'Wake up, we've got company.'

'Who?'

'My new chauffeur.'

'*Who?*' As she sat up, Chloe felt the straps of her bikini top cut into her shoulders. It was last year's bikini, designed for an altogether less inflated figure. These days, her breasts spilled over the cups like extravagant scoops of ice cream crammed into tiny cones.

As for her poor bikini bottoms, straining valiantly away at the seams . . . well, Chloe was just grateful for the miracle of Lycra, and for the security of knowing that Florence's back garden couldn't be overlooked.

'My new *personal* chauffeur,' Miranda announced smugly. 'Fenn.'

'What? Oh my God—'

'No need to panic, I'm pretty sure he's seen underdressed women before.'

Oh yes, underdressed women who weigh about as much as one of my kidneys, Chloe thought wildly.

'Go and get my sarong,' she yelped. Aaargh, her sarong was see-through. 'No, bring towels, lots of towels!'

'You're being silly, you look fine.' Miranda glanced up at the house. 'Anyway, too late. He's here.'

Fenn was wheeling Florence down the ramp. Chloe cringed and wondered if she could hide under the sun-lounger. Her face burned; how could they all be so insensitive?

'Flap flap,' Miranda teased. 'Anyone would think you had a big crush on Fenn.'

'Towels.' Chloe glared at her as scarily as she knew how. Ridiculous; she didn't have any kind of crush on Fenn. She just didn't want him to see her looking like *this*.

Across the lawn Fenn heard the hissed command and guessed the cause of Chloe's anguish in an instant.

'Won't be a sec,' he told Florence and headed back into the kitchen, returning moments later with the emerald-green sarong he had spotted hanging over the back of one of the chairs.

Grateful for Fenn's tact but still barely able to look at him, Chloe wrapped the sarong around herself. Oh dear, it was better than nothing but she still would have preferred a bath towel. Or a king-size duvet. Or, best of all, a nice sturdy body bag complete with six-foot zip.

'Fenn's moved into a new flat,' Florence explained, distributing bottles of Guinness. 'In Holland Park.'

Chloe's eyebrows went up. 'What was wrong with the house in Hampstead?'

Fenn shrugged. Apart from the fact that it was in Hampstead, there hadn't been a single thing wrong with it.

'I was too late. Someone else got there first.'

'Isn't it a shame? So he had to settle for this other place instead,' Miranda crowed. 'And now I don't have to catch the tube any more,' she did a little dance for joy, 'because Fenn's going to give me a lift into work.'

Florence patted his arm.

'If you ask me, you should have stuck to Hampstead.' Her voice lowered. 'She sings, you know. In the mornings.'

Fenn was beginning to wonder if he'd made a horrible mistake.

'Not in my car, she won't.'

'Still, it'll be nice, we'll see more of you,' Florence went on cheerfully.

Maybe not such a horrible mistake after all.

Just so long as he doesn't see more of me, Chloe thought ruefully, attempting to tug the flimsy cotton of her sarong further up over her breasts.

'What's the flat like, then?' Florence took a swig of Guinness. 'Done out all right?'

'Think Peter Stringfellow, twenty years ago,' said Fenn. 'With knobs on.'

'Hah!' cackled Florence. 'A shag pad.'

Miranda grinned. Chloe, still shockable, spluttered into her drink.

Fenn said gravely, 'More like a shag palace.'

'Not your thing?'

'You could say that. Every time I open a cupboard I half expect a leftover bunny girl to come tumbling out.'

'I can help you pick out new stuff,' Miranda exclaimed. 'Honestly, I'm brilliant at that. I should have been an interior designer.'

'Oh right, have my new wallpaper chosen by someone with green and blue hair. Great idea,' said Fenn. He raised his eyebrows at Chloe. 'Help me out here, will you? Think of a way of saying no without hurting her feelings.'

'But I would be brilliant,' Miranda protested. 'I would I would I *would*!'

'No,' Fenn mimicked her pleading tones. 'No no *no*.'

'He'll hire a professional designer,' Chloe explained soothingly. It was the kind of thing rich people did.

'I will not,' said Fenn with a shudder. 'They always go miles over the top and you're never allowed to want anything normal.'

Miranda, losing interest since she clearly wasn't going to be allowed to help, said, 'I'm starving. Anyone else for a crisp sandwich?'

As soon as she had disappeared into the kitchen, Fenn sat forward and said, 'So how's she been with you?'

'Bright and cheerful on the outside, quiet on the inside.' Florence blew a stream of smoke rings. 'Like a Kunzle cake.'

Fenn nodded. 'Same as at work.'

'She stays in every night,' said Chloe.

'Pretending everything's fine.' Florence stubbed out her cigarette. 'When what she should be doing is getting out there and having fun. That's what Miranda really needs, of course. A new man to take her mind off the old one.'

The way Florence's lip curled at this reference to Greg reminded Fenn of something else that had been puzzling him.

'Why hasn't Danny shown her the wedding video yet? I asked Miranda and she said she hadn't seen it.'

'She didn't want to,' Chloe explained. 'He brought it round here and Miranda went out. We watched it,' she went on cheerfully. 'It was brilliant.'

'The question is, which of them couldn't Miranda face?' Florence's tone was arch. 'The video, or Danny Delancey?'

Fenn had finished his Guinness. He glanced at his watch.

'I'd better be off. The faster I clear the packing crates out of my sitting room, the sooner I can rip up the zebra-print carpet.' He glanced at Chloe. 'How are you at picking out what goes with what? I've spent the weekend up to my ears in colour charts and wallpaper samples. I could use a second opinion,' he said easily. 'So long as it isn't Miranda's.'

Startled, Chloe said, 'I'm not an expert.'

'I told you, I don't want an expert. An expert would insist on magenta ceilings, turquoise marble-effect walls and rag-rolled festoon blinds with bloody bows on. All I want is something normal.' Fenn shrugged. 'That won't give me a headache.'

Reassured, Chloe began to nod.

'Well, I can probably manage normal. If you're—'

'There you go!' With an air of triumph, Miranda clattered two plates of leaking sandwiches on to the table. 'Smoky bacon with barbeque sauce, roast chicken and mayonnaise, cheese and onion with ketchup.' She beamed. 'Eat them before they go soggy.'

'And she wonders why I don't want her to redecorate my flat,' said Fenn. He rose to his feet and eyed Miranda severely. 'Eight o'clock tomorrow morning. On the dot.'

Miranda nodded, her mouth crammed with wonderfully crunchy sandwich. For some reason she was the only one eating. Honestly, some people had no sense of adventure.

'How about you?' Fenn turned to Chloe. 'Six-ish, tomorrow evening?'

'Fine.'

Hey-up, thought Miranda, secret assignations being arranged behind my back – what's this all about?

'That's discrimination,' she protested. 'How come she gets six-*ish* and I get on-the-dot?'

'Because Chloe's doing me a favour, and I'm doing you one.'

In a flash, Miranda knew what the other favour was.

'Oh, that is so mean,' she wailed. 'You've asked Chloe to help you choose new stuff for your flat.'

'Perhaps we could both help,' suggested Chloe, embarrassed.

'No you bloody well could not.' Fenn was firm. 'It's my flat and I'll ask who I want.'

'But—'

'No begging, no emotional blackmail,' he told Miranda.

Rebelliously she muttered, 'Just acres and acres of magnolia vinyl emulsion.'

'Look, I know you're fed up at the moment,' Fenn went on more kindly. 'You're bored and you want some fun. I just don't want you taking it out on my flat.'

Miranda's shoulders sagged in defeat. He was right, of course – deep down, she knew they had wildly differing tastes. It would be like asking Margaret Thatcher to sashay down the catwalk in a Vivienne Westwood basque.

Oh, but how long was she going to feel like this, hollow with misery and so lonely she could cry?

Wearily Miranda reached for another sandwich. Soggy already, like her life. Fun, had Fenn said?

The way things were going, she couldn't imagine ever having fun again.

Chapter 41

It was even more depressing deciding to become an entrepreneur and having your brilliant new idea laughed at.

'Miranda,' said Fenn when she had finished explaining it to him at work the next day, 'you can't *do* that.'

'Why not? It's recycling! Anita Roddick would be proud of me.' Miranda gestured at the floor with her broom. 'You cut hair, I sweep it up, it gets chucked in the bin . . . can't you see how wasteful that is? We're talking famous hair here, Fenn. People would pay good money for hair belonging to their favourite celebrities. What I thought we could do was curl up little strands, set them in perspex and sell them as jewellery . . . say you were a huge Barry Manilow fan and you could wear a necklace containing a little piece of Barry Manilow . . . imagine the thrill!'

Silence. She had run out of breath.

'And Corinne does our pedicures,' said Fenn. 'She can save all the clippings. We could call them Toenails of the Rich and Famous.'

Miranda looked at him.

'You're making fun of me.'

'And then there's the waxing, we could call that Leg-Hair to Treasure.'

319

'This is the best idea I've ever had,' she wailed, 'and you won't even take it seriously. We could be rich!'

Fenn, who was already rich, glanced over Miranda's shoulder as the salon door was pushed open.

'Miranda, trust me, stealing other people's toenails isn't the way—'

'Oh, now you're just twisting things.' Exasperated, Miranda could have kicked him. 'All I said was hair. Stealing the toenails was *your* idea, not mine.'

Another stunned silence. Oh dear, maybe she'd been a bit loud. She really hadn't meant—'

'Don't you just love it,' drawled an amused voice behind her, 'when you overhear part of a conversation and can't imagine for the life of you what it's all about?'

Not only an amused voice, but a familiar one. Miranda felt all the hairs at the back of her neck leap to attention. She swung round, mouth idiotically agape, and came face to face with Miles Harper.

He was standing there laughing at her, wearing a black polo shirt and black jeans and looking so drop-dead gorgeous she had to struggle to breathe normally. Heavens, this was embarrassing, it was her turn to speak and she was terrified of trying to say hi in case it came out as something else altogether.

Something excruciating like, Oh, Miles, what are you doing wasting your time with that awful brain-dead Daisy Schofield when you could have me instead?

The name brought Miranda crashing back to earth with a thud. Damn, this must be why he'd come to the salon.

Her tongue magically untied itself.

'She isn't here.'

'Who?'

'Daisy.' Oh, those wicked green eyes, how unfair was this?

'I know she isn't here.' Miles grinned. 'She's in Sydney.'

Floundering, Miranda said, 'So, um, do you want to make an appointment?'

'To see Daisy in Sydney? No thanks.' Miles was clearly enjoying himself.

'Okay if I borrow her for a moment?' He raised his eyebrows at Fenn.

'Hang on to your fingernails,' said Fenn.

Miles led Miranda away from the crowded central section of the salon. When they could no longer be overheard he said, 'I came to see you.'

Miranda felt her knees begin to buckle. She leaned against the chair behind her, forgetting that it was a revolving one. With his legendary reflexes, Miles grabbed her in the nick of time.

'I had to come.' His tone was soulful. 'You never wrote, you never phoned. We were fantastic together, I thought we had a real future . . . but you were cruel, you tossed me aside like an old watermelon. You broke my heart in two . . .'

'Like an old watermelon?' suggested Miranda. This was better, this kind of banter she could handle.

Smiling slightly, Miles shook his head. 'Why haven't I been able to stop thinking about you?'

'A good watermelon partner is hard to find.'

'The trouble is, you think I'm joking. And I'm not.'

He was, he was, he was.

Oh crikey, wasn't he?

'Everybody's l-looking at us,' Miranda stammered.

'So?'

'They're wondering what's going on.'

'Me too. I asked you out and you turned me down. Nobody's ever done that to me before.'

'You didn't ask me out. You got your friend to do it.'

Miles said sorrowfully, 'Only because I'm so shy.'

Miranda jumped a mile as his arms slid around her waist.

'That isn't a very shy thing to do . . . eek!' She let out an undignified squeal as he pulled her against him. 'Neither's that!'

'I've been working hard to overcome it. My therapist says I'm making pretty good progress.'

'I'd say she's right.'

'But I have to persevere. Practice, that's what I need. Lots of practice.'

His mouth was moving closer. It was hard to struggle, Miranda discovered, when your whole body had turned to custard. She didn't have to look to know the kind of effect they were having on the rest of the salon – she could hear the gasps.

Oh Lord, unless that's *me*.

'You can't do this here!'

'I must. It's the next step of my rehabilitation.' His breath was warm against her cheek. 'You want me to be cured, don't you?'

'But I'm embarrassed!'

'Oh dear,' said Miles. 'You need to meet my therapist.'

The kiss didn't happen. In a daze, Miranda found herself being dragged towards the back of the shop. A collective groan of disappointment went up around the salon as Miles

Harper bundled her through the first available door and kicked it shut behind him.

Quite masterfully, for such a shy man.

Bev, every bit as enthralled – and envious – as the rest of the clientele, rushed over to Fenn.

'Aren't you going to *do* anything?'

Fenn was cutting the hair of a new client, who was swivelled round in her chair gazing avidly at the closed door through which Miranda and Miles had disappeared.

'Like what?'

'Well . . . shouldn't you stop them?'

'Don't you dare!' exclaimed the new client. 'It's the most romantic thing I've ever seen in my life.'

'But . . . but he's making a fool of her!'

'Why don't we leave them to it?' Fenn calmly carried on cutting. 'Miranda's had a miserable few weeks. If five minutes in the laundry room with Miles Harper cheers her up, that's fine by me.'

The client, her eyes still trained on the laundry room door, said happily, 'I'm so glad I came here. Free coffee in fancy cups, that's all you get at Nicky Clarke's.'

'There you go,' Fenn said drily. 'We aim to please.'

'Look,' said Miranda, pulling away and hanging on to the tumble dryer for support, 'I'm really flattered. This kind of thing hardly ever happens to me on a Tuesday morning. But I don't want you to kiss me.'

This was, of course, a big lie. What she really meant was, she didn't want him to think she was a complete pushover.

Miles Harper grinned and checked his watch.

'Okay. I have to go anyway. So, what time do you finish work?'

'Six. Why?'

'I'll pick you up.'

Something weird was happening to Miranda's lips; she could feel them buzzing with excitement, clamouring for the kiss she had so meanly denied them. Heavens, her lips had turned into shameless groupies . . .

'Unless of course you're busy.' Miles raised a challenging eyebrow. 'Again.'

'Well . . .'

'Cooking fish fingers for your boyfriend, maybe.'

'Nothing like that,' said Miranda hurriedly. 'But—'

'Good.' He stepped back, and winked. Almost as if he knew the effect he was having on her squealing adolescent lips. She clamped them together before their frantic squeaks could become audible.

'Thanks,' Miles told Fenn, depositing a dazed-looking Miranda back with him. 'I'm glad we've got that sorted out.'

'Any time,' said Fenn.

By ten past six Miranda's hair was finished.

'I still think you're mad,' Bev said fretfully. 'What's Miles Harper going to think when he sees you looking like this?'

'It's not for him, it's for tomorrow.' Miranda inspected the end result in the mirror, tweaking a couple of stray spiky bits into place. 'Anyway, Miles isn't going to turn up. Look at the time.'

Her stomach was in knots. It was hard to pretend you

didn't care when every thud of your heart reminded you that another half-second had gone by and he still hadn't arrived.

'But if he does turn up, how can he take you anywhere nice, with your hair like that?'

Bev was bothered by Miranda's attitude. When a man invited you out, it was your duty to look as good as you knew how. When Bev had a date she could spend anything up to four hours honing her make-up to perfection . . .

'He isn't going to be taking me anywhere, because he isn't coming.' Miranda wished with all her heart that she hadn't told Bev about the supposed date. Miles Harper – rotten bastard – had either forgotten, or found something more exciting to do. 'And anyway, if he does turn up, he'll be too late. Because I'm going home.'

Bev followed her to the door.

'Maybe it's for the best. The last thing you need is to get involved with someone else who's going to muck you around.'

'Is that meant to make me feel better?'

'Come on, you know what I'm trying to say. Daisy Schofield's away . . . he's at a bit of a loose end . . . all he's looking for is someone to amuse himself with until she gets back.'

'Thanks.'

'But it's true!'

Of course it was true. Miranda knew that, she just wasn't in the mood to hear it. She was a nobody and Miles Harper was practically a national hero. She would be a bit of harmless entertainment for him, nothing more. Her crush on him would deepen – oh yes, she knew that too – and it would all end in tears.

Just for a change.

'Anyway,' Bev said kindly as her bus loomed into view, 'you'll have a brilliant time tomorrow.'

A brilliant time, thought Miranda. Have to look that one up in the thesaurus.

The bus eventually jerked to a halt beside them and Bev swung herself up on to the platform. Behind her, a car tooted its horn in appreciation of this slinky manoeuvre. Bev, smirking and flattered by the attention, couldn't resist a quick glance at the driver . . .

'Where's Miranda?' Miles yelled at her above the roar of the traffic.

Bev's smirk faded. As the bus began to pull away, she pointed to Miranda standing on the pavement.

'Jesus,' exclaimed Miles, grinning as he flung the passenger door open for her. 'I didn't recognise you. What have you done to your hair?'

Chapter 42

It was happening and there was nothing Miranda could do to stop it. Everything that Bev had warned her about was coming true, her crush was hurtling out of control like a runaway tank and she'd never been happier in her life.

Then again, maybe this was because she knew it wouldn't last. Like eating an ice cream really slowly and concentrating on every lick, thought Miranda, because first thing tomorrow you know you have to start that crash diet.

Bev would disapprove mightily, of course, but so what? I'm getting involved with someone I really shouldn't get involved with, Miranda told herself recklessly, and I don't care if I am making a fool of myself, or if I end up hurt. This is brilliant and I don't need a thesaurus any more to remind me what it means.

It was scary to think that another thirty seconds and they would have missed each other. Miles would have pulled up outside the salon just as she was disappearing down into the tube station and none of this would be happening now.

'I have to say,' murmured Miles beside her, 'I never thought I'd get to sleep with you on our first date.'

'I'm not asleep.'

'Are you cold? We could always zip these bags together . . .'

'Then we'd definitely never get to sleep,' Miranda told him. 'And we'd probably end up getting arrested.'

Miles was dismayed. 'For a bit of harmless alfresco fornication? If anyone needs arresting, it's that tone-deaf chap who keeps singing "My Way".'

Miranda stifled laughter.

'He was here last year. And it wouldn't be alfresco, it would be altento.'

'I've never done it in a tent before. Unless you count a wedding marquee.' He paused. 'How many times have you done it altento?'

'Thousands.'

Miles heaved a sigh.

'Doesn't seem fair, somehow. You so experienced, me such a virgin—'

'Tell you what,' said Miranda. 'When Daisy gets back from Australia, I'll lend you my tent.'

Another mournful sigh. Followed by the sound of a zip being stealthily unfastened.

'It's two o'clock in the morning,' said Miranda. 'Do it back up.'

'You're a hard woman,' Miles whispered. 'Actually, that's quite a coincidence because—'

'Ahem. The people in the next tent can hear you.' In the darkness, Miranda smiled to herself. 'Go to sleep.'

When she woke up the next morning, the sleeping bag beside her was empty. There were sounds of laughter and plenty of activity outside. Moments later the tent flap was pulled back and Miles – in red shorts, Legionnaire's cap and wrap-around dark glasses – reappeared.

'Morning, gorgeous. Breakfast.' He thrust a melting Cornetto and a can of Lilt into Miranda's hands, and dropped a hot, foil-wrapped parcel into her lap.

Mystified, she unwrapped the foil.

'Where did you get bacon sandwiches?'

'Chap up the pavement's got a barbeque going, selling them for a fiver each.'

'You paid ten pounds for two bacon sandwiches?' Good *grief*.

'Nope, there was a queue.' Miles took off his glasses and flashed his wicked grin at her. 'I bought them off a kid at the head of the queue for fifty.'

'I'm a vegetarian,' Miranda told him, then lunged forwards squealing, 'No I'm *not*,' as he tossed the sandwiches over his shoulder and out through the tent flap. A volley of joyful barks outside signalled their unhappy fate.

'Fifty pounds!' wailed Miranda.

'Worth it, to see the look on your face.' Miles kissed her. 'And I knew you weren't a vegetarian. Now eat the rest of your breakfast – before it melts.'

The early-morning sun was already beating down on the tent. Miranda's ice cream dripped on to her bare legs and the dog out on the pavement – a boisterous chocolate-brown Labrador – poked his nose through the tent flap to see if they had any more bacon sandwiches they might like to fling his way.

'If you can't stand queuing,' Miranda licked her fingers with relish, 'you must be hating every second of this.'

'If I was hating every second of this, I wouldn't be here.' Miles leaned back on his elbows, watching her with amusement. 'In a tent the size and temperature of your average microwave. On a rock-hard pavement. Outside the All England Lawn Tennis Club, waiting for the gates to open with a girl who dyes her hair purple and green and won't even let me join my sleeping bag to hers in case we accidentally have altento sex in the night, and who snores like a train—'

'Oh God! Did I really snore?' Mortified, Miranda clapped her hands over her eyes.

'Ha, got you worried.' He grinned and shook his head. 'And no, I'm not hating every second. I'm loving it.'

Breakfast over, Miles donned his disguise once more and together they dismantled the tent. Miranda didn't tell him that the only reason she hadn't let him zip their sleeping bags together was because there was such a thing as too much temptation. Not on his side; on hers.

'Can't imagine Daisy doing this,' Miles murmured when their overnight kit had been stuffed into bags.

Miranda, who did it every year, said, 'She doesn't know what she's missing.'

He ran his fingers through her spiky purple and green hair.

'Does this wash out?'

Quivering beneath his touch – heavens, and that was only her hair! – Miranda nodded. 'I don't suppose Daisy would do that either.'

'She would,' Miles's mouth curled up at the corners, 'if it was for the cover of *Vogue*.' Idly, he took her hand, inspecting her short purple and green nails. 'When you come to watch me race, will you do this for me?'

His team colours were orange and yellow ochre. For a dizzy millisecond Miranda pictured herself decked out like a satsuma, leaping up and down and cheering Miles on from the stand as he tore round the track at ten thousand miles an hour. Then she pictured Daisy, in a really short skirt, throwing her arms around him on the winner's rostrum, flicking back her blonde hair and flashing her dazzling smile for the photographers . . .

'We're talking weeks away.' Miranda kept her tone flippant. 'You'll be tired of slumming it by then.'

Miles tilted her face round to his. He lowered his dark glasses for a second.

'I might not be.'

Oh dear, it wasn't easy trying to be realistic when you were on the receiving end of that emerald-green gaze.

'Okay,' Miranda managed finally. 'I might be bored with you.'

'What if you're not?' He paused. 'Is that what you think I'm doing? Slumming it?'

'Look, it doesn't matter, I'm not expecting anything to—'

'Sshh.' Miles pressed a finger to her lips, silencing her. 'I don't want to hear this.' He raised an eyebrow. 'Anyway, don't be such a pessimist. You never know, I could be a much nicer person than you think.'

'In that case, you'll be quite safe,' Miranda told him ruefully. 'I only fall for men who are complete pigs.'

'Come on, I know you're bored,' said Miles several hours later. 'Let's go.'

He reached for Miranda's hand. Without looking at him, she pinched it, hard.

'Six games all,' announced the umpire. 'Tie break. Ladies and gentlemen, quiet please.'

The atmosphere on Centre Court was electrifying. The no-hope young British player was having the game of his life against this year's number one seed and Miranda's nails were bitten down to her knuckles. Now, at two sets to one up, victory was within his grasp.

'I love you, I want to marry you,' whispered Miles, 'I want you to be the mother of my children.'

'Ssshhh!'

A fraught ten minutes later, the number one seed smashed the ball into the net and the Centre Court crowd erupted. A great roar went up and wild applause drowned out the umpire's attempts to relay the final score. Tears of joy were pouring down the young British player's face.

'What a nancy,' Miles complained, his tone scornful. 'Won't catch me doing that when I win the world championship.'

Miranda, leaping up and down and screaming with delight, cannoned into Miles and threw her arms around him.

'Wasn't that fantastic? Wasn't he brilliant! Oh God, that was so . . . so . . .'

'Almost as good as watching you.' Grinning, Miles steadied her. She was still trembling all over, awash with adrenalin. 'I thought you were going to jiggle right off your seat.'

'Don't make fun of me. I get excited.' Miranda wiped her eyes. 'Oh, bless him, look, he's signing autographs for the ball-boys . . .'

'You squeaked,' Miles told her, 'every time he hit the ball.'

'. . . and he's still crying . . .'

'That's because he knows he's going to be knocked out in the next round.'

'Heavens, the next round! Who's he going to be playing?' Feverishly Miranda scrabbled in her bag for her programme. 'Yikes, that massive Russian.'

'Oh well, in that case he's going to need all our support.' Miles gave her a nudge. 'You'll have to sleep with me again.'

She heaved a sigh of regret.

'I can't.'

'You can, I'll get tickets for us.'

'I mean, I'm not able to take another day off work. I've used up all my leave. And you can't just buy tickets for the show courts.' Kindly, Miranda explained the rules. 'You either apply for them by ballot about a hundred years beforehand, or pitch a tent out on Church Road.'

'Or become a racing driver,' said Miles, 'and mention to one of your sponsors that you wouldn't mind a couple of Centre Court tickets for the men's semi-finals.'

Miranda stared at him, realisation slowly dawning.

'You mean . . . what you're telling me is we didn't have to queue up overnight?'

Miles shrugged.

'Of course we didn't *have* to. But you kept insisting it was more fun. You said,' he reminded her, 'that sleeping on the pavement was the only way to do Wimbledon, that it made you appreciate the tennis all the more, that people who didn't pitch a tent didn't know what they were – *ouch*.'

Miranda thumped him again for good measure, because if he was laughing it meant she hadn't hurt him enough.

'I only said that because I've always *had* to sleep on the pavement,' she wailed. 'It's called making the best of a situation. Because I've never' – thump – 'had any other' – thump – 'choice.'

'Oh.' Miles was still laughing and rubbing his arm. 'Should have said.'

Miranda shook her head, marvelling at his lack of intuition. Otherwise known as male-ness.

'Should have *known*.'

'But you were right. It was more fun.'

'Only because you did have the choice.'

Miles nodded, put his arm around her indignant shoulders, and kissed her on the cheek.

'You're right. I'm a thoughtless pig, and I'm sorry. Let me get tickets for the semis.'

Pride welled up.

'I still can't. Work.'

If Fenn could hear her now, Miranda thought, he'd be astounded.

'The final, then.' Miles hesitated. 'I wouldn't be able to make it, but you could bring a friend.'

Of course he wouldn't be able to make it. Daisy would be back by Sunday. Feeling like a small child being placated with sweets so the grown-ups could go off and enjoy themselves, Miranda shook her head.

'Don't worry, I couldn't make it on Sunday either.'

'Tell you what. You cancel your arrangements and I'll cancel mine.'

Oh yes, terrific idea.

'Daisy wouldn't be thrilled.'

'What's Daisy got to do with it?' Miles grinned at her. 'I'm racing at Silverstone.'

* * *

It was eight o'clock by the time they reached Tredegar Gardens. Expecting a goodbye peck on the cheek and a vague see-you-around, Miranda raised her eyebrows when Miles jumped out of the taxi with her and paid off the driver.

'Are you Miles Harper?' The cab driver peered at him suspiciously; with that Legionnaire's hat and those dark wrap-around glasses it was impossible to tell, but on the journey back from Wimbledon he had definitely heard them talking about next Sunday's Grand Prix.

'Don't I wish.' Miles's reply was cheerful. 'I wouldn't say no to his money.'

It wasn't him. Disappointed, the driver said, 'Not to mention the birds.'

'Oh, I don't know. I don't do so badly.' Miles grinned.

Miranda, hot and dusty and desperate for a shower though she was, thought indignantly that there was no need for the driver to look at her with quite such blatant disbelief.

'It was the hair,' Miles told her when the cab had moved off.

'Why aren't you going home?'

'Friendly.' He hauled the backpack containing their tent and sleeping bags on to his shoulder. 'Because I'm not bored with you yet.'

'I might be bored with you.' Miranda's tone was challenging.

His mouth twitched.

'No you're not.'

Chapter 43

Inside, the house was empty. So typical, thought Miranda. Where were Florence and Chloe when you were bursting to show off to them? It was like waking up on Christmas Eve, finding Father Christmas in your room and knowing that in the morning nobody was going to believe you.

'Nice place.' Miles gazed with pleasure around Florence's bohemian sitting room.

Patting the back of the sofa, Miranda said encouragingly, 'Sit down, put the TV on if you want. Give me ten minutes to shower and change, and we'll be off.'

Miles didn't sit down.

'What's your room like?'

Eek!

'Messy. Very messy. This one's much nicer.'

'Don't be so boring. I like messy rooms.' His mouth twitched at the corners. 'You can explore in them.'

There was clearly no stopping him; he was already heading up the stairs. Running after him, Miranda panted, 'Better put on your Indiana Jones hat, then. And no *snooping*.'

Miles raised a teasing eyebrow as she pushed open the door to her room.

'Not even in your knicker drawer?'

'Especially not there!'

He grinned.

'Is that where you keep all your old love letters?'

'Actually it's where I keep my knickers.'

And pretty old some of them were, too. The thought of Miles Harper having a good rummage and dragging out her precious I Love Bros pants with the pictures of Matt and Luke on the front wasn't a relaxing one. If she wanted to enjoy her shower she was going to have to cart the whole drawer into the bathroom with her.

'I won't snoop,' promised Miles. 'How about a look at your CD collection – would that be safe?'

Actually, not very. Matt and Luke featured in there too. Really wishing she had more glamorous taste in music – a bit of Ella Fitzgerald here, a dash of Shostakovich there – Miranda shrugged and said, 'All right.'

At least she couldn't be charged with possession of the dreaded Celine Dion tape; that was safely back with Bev.

But when she re-emerged from the bathroom fifteen minutes later with her hair back to its normal – well, relatively normal – colour and her crocus-yellow Lycra dress clinging to her still-damp skin, she found Miles inspecting the contents of the blue glass bowl on top of her chest of drawers.

Oh well, could be worse; he could have been lying naked in bed . . . no, no, mustn't even think those kind of thoughts—

'I'm in love,' said Miles.

Not with Bros, surely.

Miranda braced herself, then saw what he was holding.

'That's my lucky pig.'

'How do you know he's lucky?'

'I tucked him into my bra before my maths GCSE exam.'

He sounded impressed. 'And you passed?'

'God, no, failed miserably.'

Miles shook his head, mystified.

'So why was that lucky?'

'My maths teacher suggested I gave a career in nuclear physics a miss and went into hairdressing instead.'

He laughed.

'Two hours inside your bra, you say? Can't get much luckier than that. Definitely a pig after my own heart. Can I borrow him for next Sunday's race?'

'For luck?' Miranda hesitated. 'You want to tuck him inside your bra? Won't he ruin the line of your Teflon fireproof suit?'

'You don't want me to have him.' Sensing reluctance, Miles dropped the pig back into the bowl.

Miranda wavered. She loved her copper pig.

'No, no, you take him.' She nodded to show she meant it. 'Just don't blame me if you don't win. It could be his way of telling you to become a Kwik-Fit fitter instead.'

'Where are we going?' said Miranda as their cab bowled through the back streets of Putney.

'To the rescue. I'm the Lone Ranger, you're Tonto.'

'Where's Silver, stuck down a canyon?'

'I promised Johnnie we'd meet him. Tricky first-date scenario,' Miles murmured and lowered his voice. 'If he starts talking about star signs, it means the girl's a disaster and we have to get him out of there.'

338

Miranda frowned.

'If she's a disaster, why did he invite her out in the first place?'

'Tonto, you're on form. Okay,' he admitted, 'it's more of a blind-date scenario. But don't make a big thing of it – Johnnie's never been on a blind date before and he's sensitive about it.'

The restaurant was tucked away at the end of a narrow mews, safe from passing trade and the likelihood of Johnnie bumping into anyone he knew. The look of relief on his face when he saw Miles and Miranda told them all they needed to know, but just to be on the safe side he pumped her arm with enthusiasm and said, 'Miranda, great to see you again! Hmm, good firm handshake. Pisces, am I right?'

'Gemini.' Gingerly Miranda retrieved her mangled hand. 'Intelligent, beautiful and excellent at falling into swimming pools with my clothes on.'

'And this is Alice. She's Sagittarius.' Johnnie rolled his eyes fractionally as he spoke but Alice didn't notice. She was too busy braying with laughter at Miranda's swimming pool remark.

'That's so *funny*! Well, Geminis *are* funny, aren't they? Did you just make that up or did you copy it from someone on TV?'

'Um . . .'

Alice beamed at Miles. 'I heard a really funny joke on *The Generation Game* once. I wrote it down and told the other girls at work.' She leaned forward, her pale-blue eyes bulging. 'And guess what? It was awful, they didn't laugh at all! I felt like writing to Jim Davidson to complain!'

Behind them, a waiter hovered eagerly. Miranda couldn't

decide who she felt sorrier for, Johnnie or poor honking Alice.

With an edge of desperation in his voice, Johnnie said, 'I wonder what Jim Davidson's star sign is?'

'I just can't believe I'm sitting here talking to Miles Harper the racing driver,' Alice squealed. 'This is *such* a thrill . . . wait till I tell the girls in my office, they'll just *die!*'

'Hadn't you better tell Johnnie why we're here?' prompted Miranda, because Miles was clearly starting to enjoy the awfulness of the occasion.

'What? Oh, no hurry, that can wait. So Alice, did you crochet that amazing waistcoat yourself?'

Johnnie looked as if he'd quite like to bring a dinner plate crashing down on Miles's head. If you couldn't trust the Lone Ranger to get you out of trouble, who could you trust?

Tonto rode valiantly to the rescue.

'It can't wait.' Miranda's voice was firm. 'I'm sorry, but your godmother phoned up twenty minutes ago,' she told Johnnie. 'It seems she's had a bit of a mishap with a pair of handcuffs and somehow managed to get her-self manacled to her Nautilus machine. She needs you to sort things out. Apparently you're the only one with a spare key.'

A disappointed – but understanding – Alice was dropped off outside Parson's Green tube station. Miranda winced with sympathy as she heard Johnnie, outside the car, awkwardly mumbling his way through the it's-been-great-and-I'll-ring-you routine.

'Yes, but when?' Eagerly Alice clutched at his arm. 'Tomorrow morning, tomorrow evening?'

'That was a nightmare,' Johnnie groaned, collapsing back into the driver's seat. As they sped away, he lit a cigarette. 'And you were no bloody help, you pillock.'

'She's still waving.' Miranda peered over her shoulder at the sad, droopy-hemmed outline of the figure on the pavement. Since nobody else was going to, she waved back.

'We turned up, didn't we?' Miles grinned. 'I *knew* she'd crocheted that waistcoat. Jesus, you won't be doing that again in a hurry.'

'Isn't this a bit mean, dropping her at the tube?' complained Miranda. 'Couldn't you at least have given her a lift home?'

'My godmother's handcuffed to her Nautilus machine. No time to lose,' said Johnnie, after a moment's hesitation. 'Thanks, by the way,' he told Miranda. 'If it hadn't been for you we'd still be there, discussing crochet stitches and bloody horoscopes.'

'Who set you up?' Miranda marvelled. 'I mean, I don't get it. Which of your friends seriously thought you two lovely young people would get on like a house on fire?'

Another pause, a longer one this time.

'Hang a left,' said Miles. 'We'll go to my place. Miranda wouldn't let me jump into the shower at hers.'

'That's because you wanted to jump in with me.'

'Save water, shower with a friend, that's what I always say.' Miles thought for a second. 'So long as it's a female friend. Wouldn't catch me sharing a shower with Johnnie-boy here. Hairy backs.' He shook his head. 'Always a bit of a turn-off.'

'That's the other reason I wouldn't let you in,' Miranda told him. 'So you wouldn't see mine.'

Miles's flat was on the ground floor of a four-storey Edwardian house just off the King's Road. In the living room the walls were conker-brown and hung with framed prints of Formula One cars old and new. The highly polished wooden floor was strewn with multicoloured rugs. Miranda was relieved to see that Miles didn't go in for putting photographs of himself on display.

The sofa, in burnt-orange soft leather, was Olympic-sized, as were the TV, the hi-fi and the bookcase housing every motor-racing book known to man.

'Very tidy.' She nodded at the stacks of magazines in serried piles beneath the glossy walnut coffee table.

'Only because my cleaner's been in.' Amused by her evident astonishment, Miles pulled his white sweatshirt up over his head. 'My turn for a shower. Johnnie will get you a drink. Unless you'd rather keep me company in the bathroom, stop me getting lonely . . . ?'

'Johnnie can get me a drink.' Miranda bounced on to the sofa, which was impressively squashy. 'Gosh, you could sleep on this thing.'

'You can do all sorts on it.' Miles winked as he headed for the bathroom. 'But don't try anything too exotic before I get back.'

'Can I have a look around while you're gone?'

'Feel free, snoop all you like. Nothing embarrassing in my drawers,' said Miles. 'No ancient knickers with pictures of pretty-boy pop stars on them in this flat.'

Miranda hurled a cushion at him. Laughing, he exited,

singing, 'When, will I, will I be famous?' in a breathless falsetto.

It was no good, some things were just too humiliating to hang on to. Those pants were going to have to go.

In the kitchen Johnnie was wrestling with a bottle of Pinot Noir and a hi-tech corkscrew. Her stomach by this time growling with hunger, Miranda admired the range of nifty appliances on show, then peered into a few cupboards.

'This kitchen is all mouth and no trousers,' she announced. 'There's no food.'

'Plenty to drink though.' Johnnie showed her the fridge, stacked with lager, vodka, champagne and fruit juice. 'We're lads,' he added defensively. 'We eat out. Real men don't cook.'

'I'll tell Marco Pierre White you said that. He'll come round and beat you up.' Miranda held out a glass and watched him pour. 'The last time I saw you, you were practically naked and covered with bits of watermelon.'

'I hope you also noticed that I don't have a hairy back,' said Johnnie.

Following him through to the living room, she threw herself back down on the sofa.

'So who set you up with Alice?'

'Hmm?' Johnnie had his back to her. He was busy with the midi system, pressing buttons and flicking through a pile of CDs.

'Okay, put it this way,' said Miranda. 'Did you answer her ad or did she answer yours?'

Chapter 44

Miranda watched the back of Johnnie's neck flush brick-red. Finally he turned round.

'Bloody Miles, I told him not to say anything.'

'He didn't. I worked it out. Basically, because nobody who knew the two of you would ever try and fix you up. Plus,' said Miranda, feeling quite Sherlock Holmes-ish, 'the reason you didn't give her a lift home was because you don't know where she lives.'

Johnnie sighed and pushed a CD into the machine. He came and sat down next to her.

'Don't laugh at me, right? It isn't easy being Miles Harper's best mate. When we go out on the town, girls don't tend to look at the two of us together and say, "Cor, I fancy the fat ugly one."'

He said it jokily, but the expression in his grey eyes was bleak.

'You're not fat!' protested Miranda. Hurriedly she added, 'Not ugly either.'

'Compared with Miles I am. Oh, what the hell.' Johnnie shook his head, clearly regretting his moment of weakness. 'It's not as if I'm desperate to settle down anyway. Plenty of time for that when I'm old and knackered. I was drunk when

344

I answered the ad.' He looked rueful. 'I suppose everyone cheats like crazy, but Alice did make herself sound terrific on paper. No mention of the fact that she had a laugh like a baboon and all the charisma of a severed foot – good grief, what is *that*?'

He stared at Miranda in astonishment. Her tummy, rumbling like a brick-filled concrete mixer, obligingly did it again.

'It's all right for you.' About to give his protruding stomach a prod, Miranda stopped herself in the nick of time. 'You've eaten already. But it's six hours since my last Magnum and I'm practically on my knees here.'

'There's a really good Chinese round the corner,' said Johnnie. 'Tell me what you want and I'll pick up a take-away.'

Miranda, who liked to scrutinise every item on the menu – otherwise who knew what you might miss? – leapt up.

'I'll come with you. Got a pen?'

When they returned, Miles was lying across the sofa watching the highlights from Wimbledon and frowning over the crossword in the *Evening Standard*. He held up Miranda's note and read aloud: '"Dear Miles, I have left you and run off with your much better-looking friend. Love, Miranda. PS Where do you keep your chopsticks?"'

She plonked a red-hot carrier bag into his lap.

'You can't expect to impress a girl with an empty fridge, you know. We need more than ice cream to keep us going.'

'I was about to take you to Orsini's,' Miles protested. 'A romantic dinner for two, lobster and champagne—'

'Too late, we've got mushroom dim sum and teriyaki chicken instead. And we aren't going anywhere,' said Miranda. 'Johnnie and I are playing Trivial Pursuit.' Leaning over, she pulled a prawn cracker out of the bag and crunched it with relish. 'You can join in if you like.'

Johnnie had finally left at one o'clock.

'What are you doing?' Miles looked perplexed.

Miranda, who was on her knees hunting under the sofa for her shoes, located them at last.

'Going home.'

'Can't you stay?'

'No, it's been a long day.'

'It's been a long date.' Miles pulled her up on to the sofa next to him. 'A thirty-one-hour date. I've known marriages shorter than that.'

'I still have to go home.' Help, now he was tickling the back of her neck. Suppressing a quiver of lust, Miranda willed herself to be strong. 'Could you call me a cab?'

He took her copper pig out of his shirt pocket and turned it over in his hand, his expression doubtful.

'Are you sure this is a lucky pig? He doesn't seem to be doing me any favours.'

'You've only just met him,' said Miranda. 'Give him time to get to know you.'

'I've only just met you.' Miles half smiled. 'Properly, anyway. But I already know how much I like you.'

Oh dear, this was more than she could cope with. Desperate to make him laugh, Miranda held up one hand, her thumb and forefinger three-quarters of an inch apart.

'This much?'

Miles raised an eyebrow.

'You still think I'm joking. And I'm not.'

'I don't think you're joking. I think you're just trying it on.'

'I'm serious.'

'Where does this come from?' parried Miranda. *'The Miles Harper Seduction Manual?* Chapter Six: How to Convince Gullible Girlies that This Time It's For Real?'

Miles sat back and heaved a sigh.

'You have no idea how frustrating this is. When I don't give a toss about a girl, you can guarantee she'll leap into bed faster than you can say Murray Walker. But when I meet someone I really like . . .' He threw up his hands in defeat.

'Chapter Eight,' Miranda recited, pulling on her shoes. 'How to Play the Wounded Soldier: Going For the Sympathy Vote.' She rolled her eyes soulfully. 'Next, you'll be telling me you're impotent.'

He raked back his hair. 'You really won't stay, will you?'

'No.' Feeling proud of herself, Miranda stood up. 'Now, are you going to phone that cab for me or not?'

'Phone that cab?' Miles parodied her brisk tone. 'No, I won't.' He paused, then broke into a broad smile. 'I'm giving you a lift home.'

It was twenty to two in the morning when he turned the corner into Tredegar Gardens and pulled up outside Florence's house.

Nobody up, thought Miranda, to peer out of their windows and see me, in a silver Porsche, getting a goodnight kiss from Miles Harper.

Nobody in the entire *street*, dammit.

Honestly, what was the matter with the people in this neighbourhood?

'Can I see you tomorrow night?' As Miles spoke, his mouth lingered over hers.

Daisy isn't due back until Friday, Miranda reminded herself. He's at a loose end. I'm a stopgap, that's all.

Oh, but when they were together she really didn't *feel* like a stopgap.

And if she said no, what would she do instead? Watch *EastEnders*? Flick through old copies of *Hello!* drawing warts and moustaches on photographs of Daisy Schofield? Clear out her underwear drawer so that the next time she managed to lure a drop-dead-gorgeous racing driver into her bedroom he wouldn't be able to tease her about her less-than-stylish back catalogue of knickers?

Frankly it wasn't much of a contest.

In the semi-darkness Miranda nodded.

'Okay.'

'No Johnnie this time,' Miles promised. 'Just the two of us.'

'No sex either,' she reminded him.

His warm mouth brushed her cheek. 'Why are you being so cruel to me?'

Miranda knew why. It was to make up for the fact that she had offered herself to Danny Delancey – well, pretty much hurled herself at him – and been turned down. This was an attempt at restoring her shattered dignity, proving to herself that she really wasn't some sad, pitiful character so desperate for sex she was reduced to begging for it.

That was the difference between men and women, Miranda

realised. She cringed every time she recalled that excruciating scene in Danny's car, when she had pleaded with him – extremely loudly – to make love to her. Yet men, who spent practically their entire lives trying it on, simply shrugged and laughed when their efforts were rebuffed. Okay, so it hadn't worked, but at least they'd given it their best shot.

Would it even *occur* to them to cringe?

Of course not.

Life is so unfair, thought Miranda.

'I'm not being cruel.' She gave Miles a consoling pat on the leg. 'You're just too ugly for me.'

He laughed, picking up her hand and kissing it.

'Remind me again. Why is it I like you so much?'

'I'm just an all-round lovely person,' said Miranda.

'Don't forget what I told you,' Bev said bossily the next morning when she had expertly dragged every last detail of the date out of Miranda. 'He's only playing around while Daisy's off the scene. It's not serious, you do know that, don't you?'

Bev was starting to sound like a stuck record. It was like being lectured by a teacher – deep down, you knew they were right, but it was still deeply irritating having to sit and hear them out. Particularly when what they were telling you was that, basically, you had about as much chance with Miles Harper as Dot Cotton did with Brad Pitt.

Keen to get off the subject, Miranda said, 'You've got a run in your tights.'

'Oh damn!' Bev, who never went anywhere without a spare pair of Donna Karans, reached for her bag. 'I'll have to go and change.' Hooray! 'Just so long as you don't sleep with him, okay?'

'I'm not going to.' The words came out through gritted teeth.

'Are you seeing him again?'

'No.' Miranda prayed her nose hadn't just grown an inch longer.

Bev nodded, pleased to be proved right. Miles Harper was evidently bored with her already.

'Well, it's for the best. If you don't get involved, you can't get hurt, can you?'

Too late for that, thought Miranda. Aloud, dutifully, she said, 'No.'

Bev hesitated. 'What's his friend like anyway?'

Oh, for heaven's sake, did the girl never stop? Miranda tried hard to imagine Bev and Johnnie – the ultimate lad's lad – together. It would be even more of a disaster than his blind date with poor droopy Alice.

Bev was looking hopeful.

Miranda shook her head.

'Definitely not your type.'

When she arrived at Miles's flat at seven o'clock Miranda spotted a photographer lurking on the pavement outside. Following Miles's instructions, she strolled past his house, turned left into Percival Mews, hopped over his neighbour's wall, made her way across their back garden and jumped over another wall on to Miles's patio.

He opened the French windows, stripped to the waist and laughing, and drew her swiftly inside.

'All this subterfuge and we aren't even sleeping together.'

'I feel so sleazy,' Miranda protested.

'Sounds promising.' Miles surveyed her with amusement. 'Is that an invitation?'

'No, and your phone's ringing.'

She tried not to listen to him on the phone, but it was horribly obvious who was on the other end.

Oh God, what am I doing here? Miranda closed her eyes. Why am I such a masochist?

'That was Daisy,' said Miles.

'I guessed.' She stuffed her hands into the pockets of her jeans in don't-care fashion.

'She's flying back tomorrow night. I have to meet her at Heathrow at eight. And wear something decent,' he added wryly, 'because her agent's arranged for a few photographers to be there, to witness our touching reunion.'

Please, please, thought Miranda, don't ask me to iron one of your shirts.

'You don't mind staying in this evening, do you?' said Miles.

'Why?' Miranda raised her eyebrows. 'Where are you going?'

He smiled and led her through to the kitchen.

'I thought I might stay in too, if that's okay with you. Quality time together, with no interruptions. Besides, my team manager gets twitchy if he sees pictures in the press of me gallivanting round town when I should be taking it easy, preparing for the next race.'

'I don't suppose Daisy would be too thrilled either.'

'Sshh, I don't want to talk about Daisy now. Anyway,' Miles's mouth twitched, 'I've got something to show you that I think you might like.'

351

'And I've already told you, I don't want to see it.'

But when he pulled open the fridge door with a flourish, Miranda had to admit that she was impressed.

'This is good. Very good.'

'Last night you cast aspersions on my kitchen. You said some extremely hurtful things about this fridge.' Miles gave the top a consoling pat. 'When I came in here this morning it was very upset, let me tell you. It cried out, "Use me! Fill me! I can hold food, I know I can!"'

Miranda gazed at the dozens of packs of Marks & Spencer ready meals, the wicked selection of puddings, the exotic fruits and cheeses . . .

'I bought it all myself,' Miles told her. 'Wheeled the trolley up and down the aisles, did the conveyor belt thing at the checkout, stuffed everything into bags, the works.' He looked proud. 'I didn't know what you'd like, so I . . .'

'Bought the lot,' Miranda marvelled, 'by the look of it.'

'I'm just desperate to impress you. I've never filled my fridge for anyone else, you know.' He gave her a soulful look. 'It must be love.'

Luckily, she was starving.

'Oh dear, I just wish you'd told me earlier,' she teased him. 'I'd never have had those two Big Macs.'

Chapter 45

Miles dropped her back at Tredegar Gardens at midnight. Switching off the ignition, he turned in his seat to face her.

'I've decided I'm going to convince you I'm serious.'

'Really?' Miranda looked interested. 'How? More snogging and smutty talk? Chapter Eleven: When All Else Fails, Beg?'

Miles calmly ignored this.

'I know what your problem is.'

'Let me guess,' said Miranda. 'Chapter Twelve: Tell Her She's Frigid.'

Miles took her perspiring hands in his before she had a chance to wipe them on her jeans.

'Your problem is Daisy.' He paused. 'You think I only want you as my bit on the side.'

'I d-don't think that at all,' squeaked Miranda.

I do, I do!

'So if I finish with Daisy, will that convince you that I'm serious?'

Oh, good grief, steady on a minute. Deep breaths, deep breaths.

'You're panting,' Miles observed. 'Wouldn't be with lust, by any chance?'

'You don't mean this.' Miranda was floundering, hopelessly out of her depth. He couldn't mean it, surely. It was just another ploy, like married men promising their mistresses they'd leave their wives.

'I don't mean it?' Miles met the challenge with a teasing smile. 'Just watch me.'

'You should be a poker player. Bluff, bluff and bluff again.'

'Okay, let's get this straight. Would you *like* me better if Daisy was off the scene? Would you relax a bit more and stop being so suspicious of everything I do and everything I say?'

Oh, handy, thought Miranda, that's me, the world's greatest expert when it comes to figuring out men and their motives.

But since she couldn't think of a single sensible reply, she shrugged and said carelessly, 'Yes thanks, that'd be great.'

'I'll do it tomorrow night.' Miles slid his fingers through her feathery fringe, tinged aubergine by the orange glow of the streetlamp above them.

'I'll tell her, and I'll ring you on Saturday morning to let you know it's sorted.'

'Fine,' said Miranda. Since it wasn't going to happen, why not play along for the hell of it? 'So when will I see you, on Saturday afternoon?'

Miles, she noticed, was trying not to smile at this. From the look of things she'd made a bit of a *faux pas*.

'You're not a Grand Prix groupie, are you?' Miles said sympathetically. 'I'd love to see you then, but I'm going to be pretty much tied up for the next three days, what with Silverstone . . . practice sessions . . . qualifying laps on Saturday, the big race on Sunday . . . I'm sorry.' He shook his head. 'I know it's a bore, but it pays the rent.'

'Honestly,' Miranda sighed, 'talk about inconvenient. Couldn't you have a word with them, get them to postpone the Grand Prix?'

'Ah, you see, you can't wait to seduce me now, can you?' Miles broke into a grin. 'Have to, I'm afraid.'

'You're no fun,' said Miranda.

'I am, actually. Lots of fun.' Leaning closer, Miles murmured in her ear, 'As you'll have the chance to find out on Monday night.'

Feeling like a secret agent trapped in enemy territory, Miranda didn't breathe a word to anyone about Miles on Friday, though inwardly it was hard to think of anything *but* him. Her brain buzzed with all the old unanswerable questions . . . does he mean it? . . . is he actually going to finish with Daisy Schofield? . . . will he really phone up tomorrow or is this all some big awful joke?

It was hopeless. There was nothing she could do but wait.

'What are you doing this Sunday?' Bev asked the question in loose-end fashion as they were closing up.

Miranda thought fast, keen to come up with something in which Bev would have no interest whatsoever.

'Digging up Florence's garden,' she said with enthusiasm. 'Replanting shrubs, dismantling the rockery, putting in a lily pond . . . feel like giving me a hand?'

Bev shuddered. Earth, compost, worms and those awful scuttly things that shot out from under stones when you were least expecting it. Not, of course, that she'd ever done any gardening herself, but she'd once accidentally watched a programme on the subject and it had happened to Alan Titchmarsh.

'Ugh, no thanks.'

By seven thirty that evening, Miranda had the house to herself. Like a well-organised bigamist, Fenn had dropped her home from work and promptly ushered Chloe on to the still-warm passenger seat she had just vacated.

'I'll be back before eleven,' Chloe promised. She eyed Miranda's pallor and fidgeting fingers with concern. 'Are you okay?'

Chloe wouldn't lecture, but she might tell Fenn. Miranda said brightly, 'Fine. Brilliant. Just going to have a bath.'

Out of the bath and dressed for comfort in her old pink brushed-cotton nightdress with the spaced-out baby elephant on the front, Miranda found Florence about to leave the house as well.

'We're off to the theatre.' She gave Miranda a saucy wink and patted Tom's hand as he manoeuvred her chair towards the front door. 'Don't wait up.'

Not even a gripping episode of *Coronation Street* could hold Miranda's attention. She hated not being able to do anything but sit there helplessly and wait. And why was she even bothering, for heaven's sake? Nothing was going to happen. She'd probably never hear from Miles Harper again.

Oh God, it still felt like waiting seventy-two hours for a kettle to boil.

Eight o'clock. Daisy's plane would be landing at Heathrow now. Daisy, all glossy and groomed and ready for the photographers – flash – would throw herself into Miles's arms – flash flash flash – and Miles would remember that *this* was his girlfriend, not that funny little blue-haired creature he'd been amusing himself with for the last few days, the one who swept up hair for a living and had the gall to sneer at his fridge.

Her stomach in knots, Miranda picked up her almost-empty bottle of Coke. In mid-swig when the doorbell rang, she spluttered and clunked her teeth painfully against the thick glass.

No.

Not Miles, surely?

It *couldn't* be.

It wasn't, of course. Having stumbled off the sofa, banged her hip on the edge of the bookcase and hurtled through to the hall, Miranda could have wept with disappointment when she yanked open the front door.

Oh great, perfect, this was all she needed. Danny Thanks-but-no-thanks Delancey, what an absolute treat.

'Miranda.' As Danny's gaze travelled swiftly over her nightie she could tell he was dying to make some smart remark about it. 'Time we were friends again, don't you think?'

He was smiling at her. In that okay-you-made-a-prat-of-yourself-but-I-forgive-you kind of way that was so infuriating it made you want to spit. Miranda, who had found herself on the receiving end of this kind of smile quite often over the years, said stiffly, 'I don't know what you mean. I'm fine.'

Unable to resist it – surprise surprise – Danny nodded at the chubby animal slumped across her chest.

'Unlike your elephant. I'd give the RSPCA a ring if I were you.'

Her expression bland, Miranda said, 'I'd forgotten how funny you are.'

'Can I come in?'

She tried to hide one furry slipper behind the other. 'Actually, I was just on my way out.'

'When I phoned earlier, Florence said you weren't doing anything this evening.'

Exasperated, Miranda recalled hearing the phone ring while she had been wallowing upstairs in the bath. When she'd asked Florence who it was – in case by some miracle it had been Miles – Florence had said 'Some poor fellow with a stammer trying to sell me a c-c-c-c-conservatory.'

'Don't be like this.' When she didn't speak, Danny shook his head. 'There's really no need to be embarrassed about what happened the other week. Can't we just forget it and start again?'

Great idea, except some things were harder to forget than others. Particularly when they'd been tattooed on to your brain with what felt like a road-drill.

'Look, I'm not embarrassed about that,' Miranda lied. 'But I'm not actually in the mood for socialising tonight. It's been a long day, I'm tired, I—'

'You're tired because you're depressed. I spoke to Florence last week as well,' Danny announced matter-of-factly. 'And she told me everything. So now I'm here and we're going to get this sorted out.' As he spoke, he prised Miranda's hand from the door frame and took it firmly in his own. 'No more arguments, okay? I'm in charge now. I'm going to take you out,' he shot her a warning look, 'and cheer you up if it kills me.'

Miranda went along with it in the end because basically

there was nothing decent on TV, an evening out might distract her from thinking nonstop about Miles and . . . well, what the hell, it was easier to make up with Danny than spend the rest of her life in an unflattering strop with him.

And really, now that she had the Miles thing to occupy her – even if the sensible part of her brain told her that nothing *would* ever come of it – the embarrassing episode with Danny no longer seemed to matter quite so much.

Upstairs, Miranda changed out of her nightie and slippers into a pale-grey shirt and old black jeans. By making as little effort as possible, she hoped to reassure Danny that he was quite safe, she wasn't planning to leap on him crying, 'Take me, take me now!'

No make-up, no perfume either. With only a few precious drops of Eau d'Issey left in the bottle, she was saving them for a more enthralling occasion than this.

If Danny noticed the lack of effort she had gone to on his behalf, he kept it to himself.

They drove to a pub in Shepherd's Bush and found a free table outside in the garden.

'White wine?' said Danny.

'Orange juice.' Miranda let him know that contrary to recent appearances she wasn't a complete lush.

It was a family-orientated pub. While Danny was inside getting the drinks, she watched a group of children hurtle one after the other down the slide. When one of them skidded off the end, kicking up the dry bark put down to cushion heavy landings, dust flew into Miranda's eyes and she wiped them on the sleeve of her shirt. Just as well she hadn't bothered with mascara.

'Here.' Danny, back from the bar, handed her a clean

handkerchief and gave her arm a brief squeeze. 'You think it's never going to happen to you, don't you?'

Puzzled, Miranda said, 'What?'

'But it will, you know. One day.' He nodded at the children leaping and yelling around them.

Was he reassuring her that one day she would have *children*?

'I just got dust in my eye,' protested Miranda.

Danny nodded, humouring her.

'Okay, but listen to me anyway. The thing with Greg . . . he was a louse. It's bound to hurt. But one day you'll meet someone else, someone you *can* trust. You've got a lot going for you, seriously. You're brave and kind-hearted, beautiful, funny . . .'

'Just not quite beautiful and funny enough for some people.'

Unable to resist the dig, Miranda nevertheless regretted the words as soon as they were out of her mouth.

Danny gave her a pained look.

'Let me explain about that. When you and I were in the car outside your house, you'd had a hell of a day. You were drunk as a skunk and miserable. That's why I didn't take you up on your . . . er, offer, and that's the one and only reason, I promise you.' He leaned closer, his dark eyes serious. 'If the circumstances had been different, if it had been any other time, I'd have been more than happy to go along with it.'

Go along with it?

'Well, thank you, that's really generous of you.' Miranda winced. Once again her attempt at sarcasm had failed miserably. Instead she sounded whiny and self-pitying.

Danny said kindly, 'You leapt to the wrong conclusion.'

Oh right, thought Miranda, that would be the old I-wouldn't-touch-you-with-a-bargepole-but-don't-take-it-personally conclusion, would it? Well that was a comforting thing to know.

'I mean it,' Danny went on. 'Any other time. You'd been hurt by Greg. You're *still* hurt.' He shrugged, to show he understood. 'These things take a while, they're bound to. But, say, in the future, when you're over him . . . well,' this time he smiled, 'if you asked me again then, I wouldn't say no.'

Hey, Mr Romantic! Am I really *hearing* this?

Miranda gazed blankly at him, trying to figure out what it was she felt like. Then it came to her. Like a six-year-old endlessly nagging her parents for a puppy and being fobbed off with 'Not now darling, maybe next year.'

Her whole body tingled with indignation. This was outrageous. What a nerve. Talk about patronising. Did he seriously think this was making her feel better?

A consolation bonk in the year 2003, Miranda marvelled. I must make a note of it in my diary.

Honestly, he was lucky there were innocent children about. Otherwise she'd be tempted to rip his eyebrows off.

Chapter 46

Miranda heaved a sigh and took a swallow of orange juice, wishing it was wine. Danny's infuriating remarks had really got to her, but at the same time she knew that – in his own way – he was actually trying to help. He wanted to make her feel better, to boost her poor battered confidence. It wasn't his fault he'd got hold of completely the wrong end of the stick.

'You don't understand.' She made an effort to be patient. 'I'm not upset about Greg, or about you. I'm perfectly happy, I promise.'

In reply, Danny glanced at the handkerchief screwed up in her fist.

'I had dust in my eye!' She hurled it back at him. 'For pity's sake, Danny, I'm happy! Why can't you believe me?'

'Fine, fine.' He made calm-down movements with his hands.

A woman at an adjoining table whispered excitedly to her husband, 'Ooh, lovers' tiff.'

'He's not my lover.' Miranda swivelled round, keen to put the couple straight on the matter. 'I do have a lover, but he's not with me tonight, and to tell you the truth, he's a damn sight better-looking than this one here.'

The couple looked startled.

'Miranda, stop it.' Danny sounded reproachful rather than offended. 'No need to get carried away.'

'I'm not, I'm just stating a fact.' Miranda's smile was triumphant. 'You don't believe me, do you? You think I'm a sad old spinster with no one in her life, but actually you couldn't be more wrong. I do have a boyfriend, as it happens, and he's crazy about me, so there!'

Oh dear, a bit juvenile, that last bit, the kind of playground riposte that usually accompanied sticking your tongue out and going *naa naa na-na naa*.

Danny clearly thought so too.

'You don't have a boyfriend,' he said slowly, as if breaking this news to a particularly dim psychiatric patient.

'I do.'

'Miranda—'

'I'm seeing Miles Harper.' Having blurted the words out without thinking, Miranda spun round in horror to see if the couple at the next table had overheard. Phew, they'd gone, scuttled out in a hurry by the look of things, without even finishing their drinks.

Oh well, she'd started so she may as well finish. Anything, *anything*, Miranda thought wildly, to wipe that irritating, pseudo-sympathetic look off Danny's face.

It did. He started to laugh instead.

'I *am*.' Heroically suppressing the urge to scream, she lowered her voice. 'I couldn't say anything before because obviously it's a bit of a delicate situation. But it's true, Danny, I swear it is. He came into the salon and kissed me in front of everyone. Then he took me out that night and the next day we went to Wimbledon . . . and every spare moment since then, we've been together . . . He's brilliant, and it isn't just a fling, either. He's serious!'

Oh well, a bit of embroidering the facts never did any harm, did it?

'Funny, I haven't seen any mention of this in the papers,' said Danny.

'I told you.' Miranda spoke with pride. 'It's a delicate situation.'

'Yet you went to Wimbledon together, you say?'

'Nobody recognised him. He was in disguise.'

'Centre Court seats, I hope.' Danny's tone was dry. 'Nothing but the best for Miles Harper.'

'He could have got tickets, just like that.' Miranda couldn't resist bragging. 'But we didn't, we queued up overnight. Slept in a tent on the pavement.' She gave him a knowing smirk. 'It's more fun that way.'

'I see.' Danny nodded thoughtfully. 'And did Daisy Schofield sleep in the tent with you?'

'She's been away in Australia. Coming back tonight, actually. He's finishing with her.' Miranda began to feel light-headed. It was such a relief, being able to tell someone at last. Like magic, all her doubts were swept away on a tide of utter certainty. Now that she'd confided in Danny it had to happen, it just *had* to.

Danny picked up his pint glass, stalling for time. He wanted a drink but knew the lager was lukewarm. Miranda, her eyes bright and a triumphant smile on her face, was watching him, waiting for some form of reaction. How much of this story had she made up, for heaven's sake? Ten per cent fact and ninety per cent fantasy at a rough guess. She couldn't, surely, have fabricated the whole thing.

'You still don't believe me, do you?' Miranda demanded.

Danny wondered uncomfortably if she believed it herself. He looked down, watching the condensation from his glass drip on to the knee of his jeans.

'I'm just surprised Florence didn't mention it on the phone.'

'Florence doesn't know. I haven't told her.' Miranda shrugged. 'I haven't told anyone.'

Highly likely. But something to be grateful for, Danny decided. At least she had the sense to keep her mad delusions to herself.

He sighed, still struggling to figure out which part of this bizarre story might conceivably be true. At a guess, she had had a one-night stand with Miles Harper and conjured up the rest of the fantasy to assuage her guilt.

He looked at Miranda.

'Have you slept with him?'

'What do you think?' There was no hesitation; her smile was smug. 'Be honest, Danny. Given the chance, wouldn't you?'

So that was it, she had slept with Miles Harper. Danny looked away, wishing with all his heart she hadn't.

'And he's telling Daisy Schofield tonight that it's all over between them? He's giving her up for you?' Danny wondered if Miranda actually believed this would happen. When she nodded he said, 'So we can expect a red-hot press release to be put out sometime tomorrow?'

In it up to her neck by now, Miranda shrugged and nodded again.

'Maybe. I don't know much about press releases.'

'You'd better learn,' Danny drawled, 'if you're planning

on being Miles Harper's new girlfriend.' His tone was pitying. 'Are you sure he's going to be faithful to you?'

'Why are you being so horrible?' Miranda accused him.

Humouring her hadn't worked. Danny decided to be blunt.

'I'm not being horrible. I just don't believe it's going to happen.'

If it didn't happen, Miranda thought, she was definitely going to have to leave the country. Oh well, in for a penny, in for an awful lot of pounds.

'You know what? I think you might be a tiny bit jealous.' Leaning forward, she patted the back of Danny's hand, mimicking the patronising concern he had shown earlier. 'Never mind, chin up, I know it isn't easy finding a girlfriend but these things take time. One day it'll happen to you too.'

Three rubbish skips were lined up in the road outside Fenn's new flat, much to the horror of his well-to-do neighbours.

'You know you've thrown out a truly terrible bunch of carpets,' he told Chloe, 'when you dump them in a skip and two days later they're still there.'

'It feels like such a waste.' Chloe joined him at the window. 'Couldn't you donate them to some deserving cause?'

The skip looked as if it was bulging with dead zebras. Fenn winced.

'Where did you have in mind? Regent's Park Zoo?'

Turning back, leaning against the windowsill, Chloe surveyed the stripped room.

'Another week and this place will really come together.

You won't recognise it. The last chap who lived here *definitely* wouldn't recognise it.'

'Good,' said Fenn. 'That's the general idea.'

The decorators, still in the process of stripping the wallpaper and sanding the wooden floors, had left hours earlier. The rolls of new paper, chosen by Fenn and Chloe and delivered that afternoon, were stacked in a corner of the room along with a dozen cans of paint in assorted shades of sage-green, lavender and saxe-blue. Between them, choosing the colour scheme had been an effortless process. They shared the same tastes to an astonishing degree. When Chloe had finished browsing through a foot-thick book of curtain samples she had pointed to the exact swatch of silvery-green material that Fenn had decided on himself.

'It's going to be great,' she told him happily. 'All you have to find now are the rugs.'

'Chinese. I was going to have a look in Harrods on Sunday.' Fenn paused. 'I don't suppose . . . ?'

'I'd love to,' said Chloe. 'Honestly, I'm enjoying every minute of this. I won't know what to do with myself when it's finished.'

Fenn felt much the same way. Soon he was going to run out of legitimate reasons to invite Chloe round to his flat. He sighed inwardly, recalling the telephone call he had received last night from his sister. Tina, three years older than him and so blunt she made Miranda sound diplomatic, lived in New Zealand and hadn't been back to Britain for over five years. For this reason, when she had demanded to know what the bloody hell he was doing renting a flat in snotty Holland Park, Fenn had judged it safe to tell her.

Ten thousand miles, that was far enough.

Besides, if he didn't tell someone, he might actually explode.

'Okay, you want the truth? Because there's this girl I know, and she lives in Notting Hill, in the same house as my salon junior. And giving the junior a lift home from work gives me the chance to see this other girl.'

Tina, predictably, snorted with laughter.

'And if you'd moved to Hampstead you wouldn't have been able to do that? Jesus, Fenn, you're priceless. Spending an absolute fortune moving into a flat you don't even like . . . . that's the maddest thing I ever heard. If you're so keen on this girl, wouldn't it be simpler to just ask her out on a date?'

Great idea, now why didn't I think of that? Smiling to himself, Fenn shook his head.

'Can't do it.'

'Of course you can! Blimey, you've been out with, like, a million girls. You must know the routine by now.'

'It's not that straightforward.'

'Oh, I get it. You mean she's married. Fenn, you plonker. Who needs that kind of grief?'

'She isn't married. Well, okay, technically she still is, but they're separated.' Fenn paused. 'The thing is, she's pregnant.'

There, he'd done it at last. And what a relief to finally say it aloud, after bottling it up for weeks.

'Jesus Christ!' shrieked Tina down the phone. 'You got her pregnant and her husband found out? No wonder he left her!'

'Tina, hang on a second—'

'And you aren't interested in actually marrying her yourself but you want to keep in touch for the sake of the baby. Oh, *now* it all begins to make sense. So you're going to be a dad,' she marvelled. 'Bloody hell, this is a turn-up for the books. You do realise it's going to cost you zillions in child support?'

'It's not my baby,' said Fenn, when he was able to get a word in.

A long and expensive silence ensued. He'd never heard Tina at a loss for words before.

'Fuck a duck, Fenn,' she groaned at last. 'So whose kid is it?'

'Her husband's.'

'You're in love with some girl who's pregnant with somebody else's baby. Now I know you're mad.'

'Thanks.'

'What's her name?'

'Chloe.'

'And how does Chloe feel about this?' Tina's tone was cutting.

'She doesn't know.'

'So what are you going to do?'

What could he do? It was hardly the most normal situation in the world.

Frankly, it was bizarre.

'I don't know.'

'Any more thoughts about the bedroom?'

'What?' Chloe's words brought Fenn back to the present with a thud.

'Curtains or blinds, you haven't decided yet.' She pushed

her fringe out of her eyes. 'Come on, let's take another look.'

Without wanting to, Fenn replayed in his mind the rest of last night's conversation with his sister.

'Drop her,' Tina had commanded. 'Drop her like a hot potato.'

'I can't.'

'A hot potato crawling with maggots.' He had heard the urgency in her voice. 'Fenn, we're talking major disaster here. For God's sake, get out while you still can, before anything *happens*.'

Too late. It already had. Fenn led the way through to the master bedroom. What did Tina know, thousands of miles away in New Zealand? She had no idea.

Chloe was sitting on the end of his king-size bed, shaking back her hair and giving the two windows her undivided attention.

'I think blinds, you know.'

'Your fringe keeps getting in your eyes,' said Fenn.

'Not those awful frilly blinds,' Chloe made frilly movements with her hands, 'like Scarlett O'Hara's knickers.'

'Why don't I cut your hair?'

Chloe was already busy flicking through a sample book. She found what she was looking for and held it up.

'Silver and beige, and keep them really plain . . . oh.' Belatedly, Fenn's words registered and her hand flew guiltily to her fringe. 'My Dulux look, you mean? I meant to have a go at it last week but Miranda borrowed my nail scissors to trim the flex on her hairdryer and—'

'I don't want to hear this.' Fenn felt as he imagined a surgeon might feel, upon being told that a patient had decided to dig out his own appendix with a Stanley knife and a rusty spoon.

Spotting the shudder, Chloe pulled an apologetic face.

'Sorry, I'm not usually such a pleb.' She shrugged, embarrassed. 'Trying to economise, that's all.'

'Will you let me do it for you?' said Fenn.

Chloe was overjoyed.

'I'm hardly likely to refuse an offer like that, am I?'

In all his years of hairdressing, this was a first for Fenn. As a rule, female clients fancied him like mad and flirted with him shamelessly. Less often, deciding that he liked the look of one of these clients, he would flirt back, take her phone number and possibly ask her out.

This, though, was a whole new experience, and it was making it hard to concentrate. For the first time since he had known Chloe, he was actually running his fingers through her hair, touching her neck, resting his hands on her shoulders . . .

He could look and now he could touch but he certainly wasn't allowed to flirt. She was six months pregnant with another man's child, Fenn reminded himself. She would be horrified if she knew how he felt about her.

'Cut loads,' Chloe was saying eagerly, making scissors of her fingers and showing him how much she wanted lopped off. 'Not a crew cut or anything, just to the shoulders.'

'Here, you mean?' Fenn scooped the heavy blonde hair up into his hands and rested them against each side of her neck. God, even that simple action gave him a charge. He paused for a second, feeling the warmth of Chloe's skin and breathing in the familiar light scent she wore. It would be so easy now, *so easy*, to bend and kiss the back of her neck—

'FENN LOMAX, WHERE ARE YOOOUU?'

Chapter 47

Fenn and Chloe looked at each other in the mirror; the spell was well and truly broken. In the street outside, someone was yelling at the top of their voice and they both recognised who that voice belonged to.

Wearily, Fenn went to the window and looked out. Fifty yards further up the road, Miranda spotted him and waved.

'Honestly,' she exclaimed when he let her in, 'grumpy neighbours you've got around here. You should have seen the looks they gave me when I called out your name. I mean, I remembered the name of the road but I didn't know what the number of your flat was.' She shrugged. 'How else was I supposed to find out where you lived?'

Another boost to his popularity, thought Fenn. Zebra-print carpets *and* friends with disturbingly blue hair turning up to breach the peace and more than likely mug the first wealthy resident they came across.

'You were pretty loud,' he pointed out.

'Well, if I'd whispered, you wouldn't have heard me. So this is it, is it?' Miranda darted past him, gazing around with bright-eyed interest. 'I saw the dead animals in the skip outside. Hmm, wouldn't have thought you'd go for a flat like this.'

'It'll be fine when it's finished.' Fenn's tone was curt. 'What are you doing here anyway?'

'Just thought I'd pop in.' She gave him a playful look. 'Are you okay? Not interrupting anything, am I?'

Oh great, this was all he needed, Miranda waggling her eyebrows and doing her arch-psychiatrist bit.

'No.' Better warn her, thought Fenn. 'I was just cutting Chloe's hair.'

In the sitting room, Chloe had hurriedly pushed the chair away from the mirror and shoved Fenn's comb and scissors out of sight as guiltily as if they'd been about to launch into a bondage session complete with rubber masks and whips. In the few moments it took Miranda to barge into the room, she hauled out a wallpaper chart and began leafing industriously through it, an expression of deep concentration on her face.

'I used to look like that when I was supposed to be revising for my GCSEs,' Miranda observed. 'As soon as you hear someone coming, kick the magazines under the bed, switch off the music, grab a textbook and look *riveted*.' She gave Fenn a dazzling smile. 'What I want to know is why Chloe's doing it now.'

'I thought you were staying in tonight,' said Fenn.

'Danny turned up. He said it was time we were friends again.' Miranda's heels clicked on the bare, sanded-down floorboards as she strode up and down investigating the room.

'So?'

'He took me out for a let's-be-friends-again drink.'

'And then what happened?' said Chloe.

'First he was a pompous, patronising git.' Miranda began

374

ticking points off on her fingers. 'Then he was totally insulting and rude, refusing to believe a single word I said.'

'It wasn't by any chance one of your excuses for being late, was it?' said Fenn. 'Didn't happen to involve a stranded puppy about to be mown down by a juggernaut?'

Miranda ignored this. She ticked off the third finger. 'So we ended up having another fight and not being friends again after all.' She shrugged to show she couldn't care less. 'I marched out of the pub, forgetting I didn't actually have any money on me. But then I remembered you'd brought Chloe over here, so I thought I'd hitch a lift back with you.' She gave Fenn a winning smile. 'I won't be any trouble, honestly. You two just carry on as if I wasn't here.'

'The thing is, Danny's great,' Chloe protested. 'We all really like him. What I don't understand is how you manage to get into these arguments with him in the first place.'

'*Me?* Ha! Basically, he just opens his mouth and starts laying into me.' Miranda looked indignant. 'All I do is defend myself.'

'So what was it he refused to believe?'

'Something that was true!'

Fenn, who had found his scissors and was repositioning the chair in front of the mirror, murmured under his breath, 'Now who's being evasive?'

'Go on.' Chloe was intrigued by the fact that Miranda was prevaricating. 'Tell us.'

'Okay. I told him that I was seeing someone.'

Chloe frowned.

'But you aren't.'

'I am, actually.'

Fenn gave Miranda a sharp look. He hoped this didn't

have anything to do with Miles Harper's scene-stealing appearance in the salon the other day. No, no, it couldn't possibly. Even Miranda wasn't that gullible.

It was curious, though, that she evidently hadn't mentioned the Miles Harper incident to Chloe. Never one to hug an item of gossip to her chest, Miranda had for some reason certainly managed it this time. Fenn couldn't help wondering why.

'And that's what you argued about?' Chloe persisted. 'Danny didn't believe you when you told him you had a boyfriend, so you had a fight with him and stormed out of the pub?' She took the towel Fenn had given her and pulled it around her shoulders, struggling to understand.

'He said some horrible things about me,' wailed Miranda. 'I'm telling you, Daniel Delancey is a complete pig.'

It went against the grain to even think it, but Fenn was reluctantly forced to admit that he was grateful to Miranda for showing up. Cutting Chloe's hair without a chaperon could have been a risky business. At least now he was able to concentrate on the task in hand.

It was, Fenn reflected, an unreal situation. Normally when he met a girl he liked the look of, they'd end up in bed together within a few hours. And yet here he was now, having met someone as untouchable as a nun, helplessly in love with her and not even allowed to *kiss* her.

Nothing like this had ever happened to him before. All he had to do now was make sure nobody else found out that it had.

'So who is this chap you've been seeing?' said Chloe.

Miranda shook her head.

'I can't tell you.'

'Why not?'

'I just can't, okay?'

Chloe gazed in horror at Miranda's reflection in the mirror.

'Not Greg!'

'Oh, come on, do I look that stupid? Of course not Greg.'

'Who, then?'

'Wait until Monday.' Miranda had been insulted quite enough for one night; she certainly didn't need another snotty lecture from Fenn. 'I'll tell you then, I promise.'

Either that, or emigrate.

The phone rang at seven thirty the next morning while Miranda was on the loo. Typical. Knickers at half-mast, she almost broke both legs crashing downstairs to catch it on the third ring, because third rings were lucky.

Snatching up the phone in the nick of time, she gasped, 'Yu-yes?'

'Hey, heavy breathing, my favourite kind. Don't stop, do some more.' Miles sounded cheerful. 'You know, you could charge fifty pee a minute for that.'

'Did you finish with Daisy?' It was no good, she simply couldn't be laid-back and casual about it – she had spent the night wide awake and with her heart on springs.

'Still trying. I'm doing my best but she isn't taking it terribly well.'

'What's she doing?' Miranda struggled to haul her knickers up; not easy with only one hand.

'Trashing my flat.' As Miles spoke, there was a crash in the background. 'Jesus, and I'm supposed to be out of here by eight.'

Miranda felt dreadful, as if it were all her fault. He had to be at Silverstone for the all-important qualifying laps and now, thanks to her, he had this to contend with, a madwoman smashing up his home.

Another louder crash made her jump.

'I'd better go,' said Miles.

'Good luck.'

He sounded amused. 'With the practice laps, or getting rid of Cruella de Vil?'

He's doing all this for me, thought Miranda, her heart bounding like a gazelle.

'Both.'

There was a click on the line as someone picked up the extension.

'That's her, isn't it?' screamed a hysterical voice. 'You're bloody talking to her now! How dare you DO THIS TO ME, YOU BAST—'

Abruptly the line went dead. Miranda put down the receiver and pulled up her knickers. There was no point trying to ring back – all she could do was go off to work, say nothing about this to anyone, and wait.

Nine hours later, Chloe let herself into the empty house and read the note Florence had left on the table out in the hall:

Darling Girls,

Have been whisked away by a wicked vicar with a fetish for old women in support tights. Gone to Edinburgh, back in a week. Don't do anything *too* naughty while we're away!

Florence had taken on a whole new lease of life since she

started seeing Tom. And it was all thanks to Greg, thought Chloe, marvelling at the sneaky tricks fate could play.

She made herself a cup of tea, tore the wrapper off a Wagon Wheel and wandered through to the sitting room, dying to examine her reflection in the mirror above the fireplace and admire her new, improved hair.

Hooray, it still looked great. All day in the shop, customers had been complimenting her on the cut. Now, swinging her head this way and that – and watching the hair swing too – Chloe experienced a surge of gratitude towards Fenn. The 1960s Shetland pony look had gone for good; he had improved her beyond recognition and boosted her confidence no end.

And she knew he loved Thai curries. Maybe if he wasn't doing anything tomorrow afternoon she could make one for him as a way of saying thank you.

Still busy swishing her hair from side to side, Chloe picked up the ringing phone.

'Hello?'

'I know you're the one he's been seeing,' hissed a furious female voice, 'but you're not having him, okay? He's not yours, he's mine, all *mine*.'

Click, brrr.

Chapter 48

Chloe had never been on the receiving end of an anonymous threatening phone call before. Shaken, she realised that someone had got completely the wrong idea about her friendship with Fenn. They were warning her off because they were jealous of the amount of time she and Fenn had been spending together . . . Good grief, how could they even think anything was going on between them?

It was worrying and embarrassing at the same time.

Dialling 1471 didn't help. Predictably, all Chloe got was Number Withheld, which was frustrating because if she could have rung back whoever it was she would have been able to reassure them that there was absolutely nothing going on between her and Fenn.

Glancing at her watch, Chloe headed upstairs. She had promised to babysit for Bruce and Verity tonight and they wanted her there by six. Since she would be staying overnight, she needed to shower, pack a change of clothes and leave her own note for Miranda.

Chloe did this hurriedly, fifteen minutes later, without mentioning the phone call from one of Fenn's disgruntled girlfriends. It was too complicated to explain in a note and she didn't want Miranda to start winking and teasing her about the top-secret, red-hot, oh-so-passionate affair she must be having with Fenn.

Anyone with an ounce of sense would know at once that there was nothing like that going on between them, Chloe thought ruefully, but it was an undeniable fact that she had been spending a fair amount of time recently with Fenn. And that, clearly, could be misconstrued.

Maybe it was time to take a step backwards.

Cancel the Harrods trip, for a start.

And give that Thai curry a miss.

Snatching up the red biro and the note she had already scribbled for Miranda, Chloe added:

> PS Visiting my mother tomorrow, straight from Bruce and Verity's. Could you let Fenn know he'll have to choose his own carpets.

Pausing to read through the message and experiencing a strange pang, Chloe discovered that she had been looking forward to the shopping excursion more than she'd realised. She went hot all over at the thought that her hormones could be about to start running amok, that she might be developing some form of sad, pregnant-woman's crush on the first man in months to show her a bit of kindness . . .

Oh dear, all the more reason to put the brakes on, Chloe thought with a shudder of alarm. It simply hadn't occurred to her before now that this had been on the cards. That anonymous caller had been absolutely spot-on after all.

And thank heavens she *did* phone, Chloe breathed a sigh of relief, because at least now I know I have to keep my distance before it gets all out of control and embarrassing.

Basically she had to stop seeing Fenn for her own protection.

Gosh, anonymous caller, whoever you are . . . thanks.

'Coming in for a quick drink?' offered Miranda when Fenn dropped her home after work.

Fenn said casually, 'Okay.'

But the house was empty.

'Gone!' Miranda held up the two messages like an indignant ice-skating judge. 'Gone, both of them, and left me all alone. I ask you, how selfish and uncaring is that?'

Fenn, who had spent the last couple of hours planning how he would invite Chloe out to dinner on the pretext of discussing . . . um, windowboxes, said, 'Actually, don't worry about that drink. I should be getting back.'

Never mind, at least he'd be seeing her tomorrow.

'Hang on.' Miranda was busy scanning the rest of Chloe's note. 'This bit's for you.' She waggled it under his nose with irritating cheerfulness. 'Hey, looks like you've been stood up. Want me to come and help you pick out new carpets? Nothing with glitter in, I promise.'

'Good of you to offer, but actually glitter was what I'd set my heart on. So thanks, but no thanks.' Fenn smiled his cool, detached, boss-like smile because he would rather walk barefoot over burning coals than let Mersey Tunnel-mouth Miranda get an inkling of how disappointed he was about Chloe.

'Ah, good evening, I'm conducting a survey on behalf of a well-known women's magazine—'

'Are you really? How exciting,' said Miranda.

'—and I wonder if you could tell me which men, in your opinion, make the best lovers: (a) zoo-keepers; (b) quantity surveyors; or (c) Formula One racing drivers.'

'Oh dear, I'd love to be able to help you,' Miranda sighed, 'but I'm afraid I'm a lesbian.'

'I'm sorry, that was the wrong answer. The correct answer was (c), racing driver. And I'd be more than happy to prove it to you if—'

'How did everything go?' Miranda broke in hurriedly, before he got carried away.

'Mission accomplished. The practice sessions went brilliantly.' As modest as ever, Miles added, 'Starting from pole position tomorrow. Would you like to hear my lap times?'

'I meant Daisy.' Miranda knew he was teasing her but she had to know.

'Didn't I just tell you that? Mission accomplished. She's gone.'

Oh my God, thought Miranda, her hands suddenly clammy with shock and relief. What have I done?

There was a pause.

'You've gone quiet,' said Miles. 'Changed your mind yet about being a lesbian?'

'Was she upset?'

'I *really* hope you aren't thinking of dumping me and running off into the sunset with Daisy.'

'I wasn't actually expecting this to happen.'

'Too late to back out now. I wish I could see you tonight.' Miles sounded regretful. 'But I'd never get any sleep and you'd play havoc with my reflexes. Are you coming up tomorrow, by the way?'

'To watch you race? I don't know.' Without warning, Miranda's stomach contracted. The idea of cheering Miles on from the stand was all very well in theory, but when it actually came to it, she didn't know if she could bear to watch. This was motor racing, not tiddlywinks.

It was dangerous.

'I'll drive carefully,' said Miles. 'Keep to the speed limit, follow the highway code, all that stuff, I promise.'

'I still don't think I can.' Miranda braced herself, expecting him to call her a wimp. 'Sorry.'

There was another pause, then Miles said, 'Don't be. I'm quite flattered. As far as Daisy was concerned, watching me race was basically a photo-opportunity that was too good to miss.'

His tone was dry. Miranda, who had never told him what Daisy had said to her friend on the phone that day in the salon, wondered if he had known all along. As she spoke, a lump came into her throat. 'Good luck for tomorrow, unless it's unlucky to wish you luck.'

Actors said break a leg, didn't they? Maybe racing drivers said burst a tyre.

Miles sounded as if he was smiling.

'Wish me as much luck as you like. And put the TV on tomorrow morning. I've got a pre-race interview lined up and I want you to see it.'

'Why?'

'Don't argue,' said Miles. 'Just do it, okay?'

Miranda was on her fourth bowl of Cheerios the next morning by the time the racing commentator's interview with Miles took place. Sitting cross-legged on Florence's sofa, she squealed and dribbled milk down her chin when she realised why he had been so keen for her to watch.

Her copper pig was making his TV début, attached to a narrow strip of leather and tied around Miles's tanned neck. As he spoke, Miles idly unfastened the second button of his denim shirt and fiddled with the pig until finally the interviewer was forced to comment on it.

'This?' Miles grinned. 'Oh, he's a good-luck present from a close friend of mine.'

The interviewer, who was as famous for his *faux pas* as for his high-octane commentary style, said eagerly, 'And that's the very lovely lady in your life, Australian actress Daisy Schofield, am I right?'

'Actually, no, but I do have a message for the lovely lady in my life.' His tone light, Miles smiled lazily into the camera. 'And that is, when you meet the right person, you know it. That's what happened to me and I—'

'Well, that's all we've got time for,' bellowed the interviewer, clamping his hand excitedly to the side of his head in final-lap fashion. 'I hear through my earpiece that your team manager is waiting to speak to you down in the pits, so for now, Miles Harper, and on behalf of the rest of the nation, may I wish you the very best of luck for this afternoon's titanic race!'

The cameras swiftly turned their attention to Miles's great rival, an ugly Frenchman with a face like a walnut, and Miranda turned off both the TV and the video. Unable to watch the race, she wished she knew how she was going to get through the next few stomach-churning hours.

She wished the commentator hadn't stopped the interview just as things had been getting interesting.

She really *really* wished he hadn't used that word *titanic.*

Halfway through cleaning the kitchen floor – blimey, that was when you knew you were desperate – the doorbell went.

Wringing out her sponge and peeling the wet knees of her jeans away from her skin, Miranda went to answer it.

'Oh no, not you again.'

'That's what I love about you, your unquenchable enthusiasm,' said Danny. 'Tell me, have you ever considered becoming a Samaritan?'

'Have you ever considered becoming a stand-up comedian?' Miranda parroted back. Heavens, sometimes a wet sponge was an awfully tempting thing to have in your hand.

Danny, reading her mind, said mildly, 'This is my best suit. I'd rather you didn't.' He pulled her cheap sunglasses out of his pocket. 'I only stopped by to drop these off. You left them at the pub on Friday night.'

'Oh. Thanks.' Grudgingly, Miranda took the glasses from him.

'I'm surprised you're here,' he went on. 'Thought you'd be up at Silverstone. Isn't there some kind of race going on today?'

'I was asked. I didn't want to go.' God, that sounded feeble, even to her own ears. Danny clearly thought so too. Irritated by his knowing smirk, Miranda said crossly, 'What's the suit in aid of, anyway? Don't tell me you've been to church.'

She would have died rather than admit that actually Danny was looking good. Only someone with his gypsy-dark colouring – and fat-free physique – could get away with a navy-blue suit teamed with a deep-red shirt and blue and gold tie.

'You like it?' Danny's eyes widened in mock-alarm and he held up his hands. 'Stop, better not answer that. And no, I haven't been to church. We're just on our way out to lunch.'

For a moment Miranda thought he was inviting her out. We as in you and me.

Then she realised he didn't mean it like that at all.

Her gaze jerked automatically in the direction of Danny's car. In the passenger seat a glamorous-looking blonde with swept-up hair and a low-cut top was reading a newspaper and calmly smoking a cigarette.

Chapter 49

'Oh.' Unable to think of anything else to say, Miranda asked in a high voice, 'Where are you going? Somewhere nice?'

'The Mirabelle.' Danny indicated his striped tie. 'Pretty smart, hence the suit.'

'Pretty expensive too.'

'Never mind, she's worth it.' Turning, Danny caught the eye of the blonde waiting in his car. She smiled and wiggled her fingers back at him, sex-kitten-style.

Miranda felt her shoulders stiffen. It wasn't jealousy, it really wasn't. She just knew that Danny hadn't really dropped by to return a pair of sunglasses that had cost all of two pounds fifty.

'Right. I'd better not keep you.'

'I don't know,' Danny mused, 'it just doesn't seem fair, somehow. There's Miles Harper, your secret boyfriend, about to take part in the biggest race of his life . . . and here you are, stuck at home like Cinderella scrubbing the kitchen floor.'

Miranda gritted her teeth. 'I've already told you, he asked me if I wanted to watch him race.'

'Oh, that's right, and you said no, you'd rather give Florence's quarry tiles a good going-over.'

'You still don't believe me, do you? You think I'm making this whole Miles Harper thing up.' Losing her temper – oh dear, *again* – Miranda flung the front door wide open and jabbed a finger in the direction of the sitting room. 'Right, let me prove it to you.'

Danny signalled to the waiting blonde that he would be two minutes and she nodded, evidently unperturbed.

In the sitting room, Miranda grabbed the video remote and pressed Rewind. She was going to show Danny once and for all that it wasn't a fantasy affair. The tape finished rewinding and she pressed Play, fingers trembling in her eagerness to wipe that hateful smug smile off his face.

A close-up of a woman with a lot of amalgam fillings appeared on the screen. Her orange-lipsticked mouth was wide open and her epiglottis quivered as she drew breath.

'". . . All things wise and wonderful,"' sang the woman in a trembling soprano as the camera panned back to reveal the rest of the congregation, '". . . the Lord God made them *alllll*."'

'Morning worship from Norwich Cathedral,' Danny observed. 'Don't tell me I'm about to catch a glimpse of you and Miles Harper sharing a hymn book at the back of the church – hey, don't turn it off, I'm interested!'

He was still laughing when she pushed him out of the front door.

'Sweetheart, all you did was tape the wrong channel. It's a simple mistake, could happen to anyone . . . in fact, it's exactly the kind of thing you'd expect a racing driver's girlfriend to do, because after all, video recorders are tricky things to understand.'

'They're tricky things to fit in people's mouths, too.'

Miranda gazed pointedly at him. 'But I could always give it a try.'

Danny grinned.

'When are you getting them done, anyway?'

'What?'

He nodded at the front of her T-shirt.

'Can't be a Grand Prix groupie with a chest that size. You'll be wanting a couple of beachballs in there at least. The hair could be a problem too. What you really need is a Pamela Anderson wig.'

The front door was still open. Across the road in Danny's dusty green BMW, the blonde was peering into the rear-view mirror, carefully touching up her lipstick.

'You're so funny,' said Miranda. 'Where did you find your girlfriend anyway? Hookers "R" Us?'

The race started at two o'clock. Taping it – and this time checking neurotically at least a dozen times that she had the right channel – Miranda sprawled on the floor with a packet of Jaffa Cakes and forced herself to sit through the most boring Wimbledon men's singles final in the history of tennis. Point by monotonous point the grunting, charisma-free pair slugged it out from their respective baselines. It was sheer torture – worse than being strapped to a chair and forced to watch two hours of morris dancing – but Miranda stuck it out to the bitter end. She had to, having managed to convince herself that if she changed channels, even for a second, this action would send Miles's car spinning off the track.

Finally, finally, one of the tennis players got into a muddle and started trying to hit his opponent's grunt instead of the ball. He promptly lost his serve, went to pieces and flung his racquet to the ground as the winning ball hurtled past him. Game, set, match and . . . yes, championship! Miranda was so relieved it was over she could have kissed them both.

The ball-boys and ball-girls trooped out. The officials formed an orderly line. The audience nudged each other to wake up. The obligatory royals made their entrance on court and attempted to make polite conversation with assorted tongue-tied ball-boys and girls.

'Too slow, too *slow*,' hissed Miranda, on her knees in front of the TV. 'Come on, get a move on, for crying out loud, *hurry up.*'

Only when the loser had received his medal, the winner had kissed his trophy, the photographers had taken fifty million photographs and both players had left the court did Miranda allow herself to turn over to the other channel.

When she saw what was happening at Silverstone, her eyes filled with tears. He'd done it, he'd actually done it. Miles had beaten the Frenchman and won the British Grand Prix. There he was, up on the podium, spraying champagne over an ecstatic crowd. He was laughing, joking with the photographers and drenching his overjoyed support team. Miranda, sitting back on her heels, pressed her hands to her mouth. This had to be the best moment of his life, and it was all, *all* thanks to her. Because if she'd watched the race – or even one tiny bit of the race – she knew with superstitious certainty that Miles would never have won.

He phoned her an hour later, yelling above a background of tumultuous noise.

'It's chaos here! Did you see me do it? Miranda, can you hear me? Did you watch the race?'

'I'm watching it now. You're on lap twenty-three.' She looked down at her nails, bitten to shreds even though it was only a video rerun. 'God, I really hope you win.'

He laughed.

'I can't wait until tomorrow.'

'Me neither,' sighed Miranda, feeling very bold.

'No, listen, I meant I'm not *going* to wait. I'm getting out of here as soon as I can and coming to pick you up. Christ knows when, probably not until around nine . . . can you manage that?'

Anything, anything! Giddy with delight and ridiculously flattered, Miranda said, 'Couldn't make it nine thirty, could you? Only I've got a bit of ironing to get through first.'

She heard the sound of champagne corks being popped in the background, punctuated by screams of laughter. How many stunning blondes was Miles currently surrounded by? Stunning blondes with breasts like giant beachballs, Miranda reminded herself, and teeth so dazzlingly white they glowed in the dark like neon . . .

'You do realise I had to win this race,' Miles told her. 'I thought you wouldn't be interested in me any more if I didn't.'

'You're right, I wouldn't have been. I'm fickle like that.'

'What?' The noise level was diabolical. It was hard to be laid-back and witty, Miranda discovered, when only the occasional word was managing to percolate through the din.

'Never mind. I'll see you later.' A thought suddenly struck her. 'During the race – were you wearing the pig?'

'Who's a pig?' Miles's voice grew faint. 'Hang on, the signal's going, this is a useless phone.'

'See you later,' Miranda yelled again, as he began to crackle and break up. ''Bye!'

No Florence, no Chloe. Damn, not even Danny Delancey, thought Miranda as nine o'clock approached. When he was the last person you wanted to clap eyes on, he could be guaranteed to turn up. But when you wouldn't actually mind seeing him – in order for him to witness the glorious spectacle of you being swept off your feet by one of the most gorgeous, glamorous men *ever* – well, then you had . . . how much chance? Well, exactly. None at all.

Instead, Danny was off out somewhere with Rent-a-Trollop, no doubt regaling her with the rib-tickling tale of the blue-haired girl so pathetic and deluded that she'd actually convinced herself she was involved with Miles Harper . . .

Typical, thought Miranda, frustrated. Just when I'm looking so fantastic too.

Nine o'clock came and went.

Then ten and eleven o'clock.

Miranda could forgive him for being late. He had just won the Grand Prix.

At midnight, she squirted on a bit more scent, brushed her teeth again and carefully redid her lipstick.

At half past midnight she spilled orange juice down the front of her white velvet vest. Doggedly refusing to believe that Miles might not, after all, be on his way, Miranda scrubbed the orange juice stain out of the top with neat Ariel, washed it, blasted it dry with Chloe's hairdryer and put it back on.

At ten past one anxiety turned abruptly to relief. Hearing the tick-tick sound of a black cab pulling up outside the house, Miranda grabbed her bag and raced to the door faster than a greyhound out of a trap. Okay, so he was late, but she didn't care. What did four hours of agonised waiting and serious nail-biting matter? Miles had turned up, hadn't he? So much for the race-track groupies, Miranda thought joyfully, wrenching open the front door. Not all men were enthralled by the sight of beachball breasts. Ha, some actually preferred ping pong—

'Hi,' panted Chloe, dragging her overnight bag into the hall. 'You're up late – just got in from somewhere nice? Oof, I'm shattered, a day with my mother's worse than any triathlon.' Pulling a face, she unzipped her bag. 'Wait until you see how much stuff she's knitted for the baby.'

Miranda couldn't speak. Disappointed wasn't the word for it. Biting her lip, she watched Chloe pull a stream of doll-sized matinée jackets, cardigans and bootees out of the bag like a conjuror.

'Can you believe it? I think she even knits in her sleep,' Chloe marvelled. 'And this is only the stuff I could carry. Seven hats, I ask you, how many heads does she think this baby's going to have? Gosh, my throat's dry, let me put the kettle on.' She squeezed past Miranda, heading for the kitchen. 'Fancy a cup of tea?'

'Um, no thanks.'

'Florence not back yet? Honestly, she's turned into a complete gadabout! I bet they're having the most fantastic time in Edinburgh . . . Isn't it terrible about Miles Harper?'

Miranda, her arms full of the soft, hand-knitted baby

things Chloe had dumped on her, felt the blood slow to a halt in her veins.

'Isn't what terrible? He won the race.'

In the milliseconds before Chloe's reply, Miranda's mind conjured up a satisfactory explanation. There had been a steward's enquiry – or whatever it was they called them in motor-racing circles – and Miles had been stripped of his title, found guilty of dangerous driving . . . or not doing enough laps . . . or failing a drugs test, something like that—

'Oh, haven't you heard? Put the TV on,' said Chloe, 'they're bound to be talking about it. After he left Silverstone this evening he was driving back to London and a lorry smashed into his car on the Ml.' She looked at Miranda, her forehead creasing with concern. 'I forgot, you met him once, didn't you? Bev was teasing you about him the day you painted my room.'

Everything was happening in slow motion. Feeling as if she was having an out-of-body experience, Miranda watched herself bend down and place the bundle of baby clothes carefully on the floor. Okay, Miles had failed to arrive because he'd been involved in an accident, that was fair enough, that was an excellent excuse for not turning up. And the reason he hadn't phoned to let her know he was going to be late was because he was having a couple of X-rays just to be on the safe side. Miranda nodded to herself, reassured by this. Everyone knew you couldn't use mobile phones in X-ray departments because they sent medical machinery haywire.

Otherwise of course he'd phone me, to let me know he's okay.

'He is okay.' She looked up at Chloe, seeking confirmation. 'I mean, maybe a few cuts and bruises, but that's all. He's a brilliant driver, you know, he wouldn't have just *let* a lorry smash into him.'

'I'm sorry.' Chloe hesitated, shaken by the depth of Miranda's reaction. She was as white as a sheet and trembling visibly. 'On the news it said the lorry crashed through the central reservation – there was nothing anyone could have done to avoid it.'

'But Miles is all right. He *is* all right.' Miranda felt like a parrot but she couldn't stop saying it. She wished her teeth would stop chattering and she wished Chloe would stop looking at her in that awful, panicky way. 'Okay, he's in hospital, I realise that, but he's definitely going to be all right.'

The boiling kettle forgotten, Chloe came towards her. She led Miranda into the sitting room and made her sit down.

'Miranda, I'm really sorry. He's dead.'

'Oh no, that's a mistake. He can't be dead.' Firmly, Miranda shook her head.

Clearly, thought Chloe, something was going on here that she didn't know about. She put her arms around Miranda.

'Darling, I'm afraid he is dead. He was killed outright.'

Chapter 50

The next twelve hours were a blur. When she had finished telling Chloe the whole story, Miranda huddled on Florence's sofa and watched every news bulletin on every channel. The nation was gripped by the tragedy – and timing – of Miles Harper's shocking death. TV journalists broadcast live from the bridge over the M1 above the scene of the accident. By midday on Monday, the motorway embankment had disappeared beneath a sea of flowers. Photographs of Miles flapped in the warm breeze. People who had driven for miles to lay cellophane-wrapped bouquets shed tears and hugged each other and told reporters with microphones that it was so sad, so unfair, such a terrible, terrible waste.

The driver of the lorry, it was rapidly established, had suffered a heart attack and died seconds before the crash. No one, not even a driver of Miles Harper's calibre, could have escaped the impact of a twenty-ton artic veering abruptly across three lanes and on to the southbound carriageway. Miles had been killed instantly and his car crushed beyond recognition.

It was like reliving her parents' death all over again. Except that all their accident had merited was a couple of paragraphs in the local paper. Nothing like this media circus.

397

As she gazed at the TV, Miranda marvelled at the great outpouring of clichés. Miles Harper's family and friends, naturally, were devastated. The whole country, intoned the especially cliché-prone newsreader on the lunchtime news, was devastated. Most of all, though, he gravely informed a nation in mourning, Miles's girlfriend was . . . *utterly* devastated.

'We now cross, live, to the scene of yesterday's tragic accident,' the newsreader announced. 'Where Daisy Schofield, actress girlfriend of Miles Harper, has arrived to lay a wreath. Dermot, over to you.'

'Well, Michael, as you can see, Daisy Schofield is having to be helped out of her limousine. She's clearly distraught . . . clutching a magnificent wreath of pale-yellow lilies . . . a fragile figure dressed all in black. I must say, Michael, your heart goes out to her at this dreadful, dreadful time.'

'Shall I turn it off?' Chloe said anxiously.

Miranda shook her head. She wanted to see it all. Everything.

'. . . Barely able to stand, she is supported on either side by professional minders. Daisy, Daisy, we have a live link to the studio, I wonder if you feel up to saying a few words.' The on-the-spot reporter shoved a microphone under Daisy's nose. 'Maybe you could tell us how you're feeling right now.'

As asinine questions went, this one pretty much took the biscuit.

Miranda wondered how the man would react if Daisy whipped off her sunglasses, flashed him a big smile and said, 'Oh, not too bad, quite chirpy actually – and black does suit me, don't you think?'

Anyhow, that wasn't going to happen. The state of Daisy's eyes behind the opaque dark glasses was anybody's guess, but her mouth trembled with grief. Clutching the yellow lilies to her chest, she turned to the reporter and whispered brokenly, 'I loved him so much, and he loved me. We were going to be married . . . he asked me on Friday night to marry him . . . We were so happy . . . Oh, this is like some terrible nightmare.' Daisy's voice rose to an anguished wail. 'I can't believe he's gone. My life is over, over!' Shaking her head in desperation, she went on, 'I feel so guilty, because he was hurrying back to London to see *me*. Oh God, I can't bear it!' Sinking to her knees, Daisy buried her face in the lilies and broke down completely, heaving great gut-wrenching sobs and pounding the ground with her clenched fists.

Cringing at the spectacle, itching to turn it off, Chloe indignantly said, 'She's lying, it's all an act. Miles was coming back to see *you*.'

'He might not have been.' Miranda kept her gaze fixed on the screen. 'She might not be lying. Maybe Miles was only stringing me along, pretending to have finished with her.'

'But you heard her on the phone,' Chloe protested. 'You told me she was yelling at him on the extension, calling him a bastard.'

'Someone was calling him a bastard. It could have been anyone, screaming at the top of their voice like that.' Miranda didn't know what to believe any more. She watched Daisy Schofield, on the TV, being helped to her feet. One of the burly minders had passed her a lace handkerchief and Daisy was dabbing under her dark glasses, muttering feverishly, 'He was mine, all mine.'

Chloe's head jerked up. She'd definitely heard that line before. What's more, the voice was the same too.

'She rang here! On Saturday afternoon. I thought it was someone warning me to keep away from Fenn!'

'Warn *you*? Why would anyone do that?' Despite everything, Miranda was momentarily diverted. 'You're pregnant.'

'I know.' Chloe felt incredibly stupid. 'It just didn't occur to me that they might have been trying to scare off the wrong person.'

'So for now, we leave Daisy Schofield to grieve in peace at the scene of her fiancé's tragic demise. This is Dermot Hegarty, handing back to you, Michael, in the studio.'

'Dermot, thank you.'

'Yes, Dermot. Thank you,' said Miranda, switching off the TV at last.

'So he did finish with Daisy.' As Chloe consoled her with a hug, the phone began to ring.

'It's me.' Bruce sounded aggrieved. 'I can't run this bloody shop single-handed, you know. Promise me you'll be back tomorrow.'

Chloe hesitated. Miranda, who could hear every boomed-out word, said, 'It's okay, tell him you'll be in.'

'What about you?' Chloe looked worried.

'Oh, I'll manage. I'll be into work myself.'

'God, are you sure?'

Miranda shrugged.

'Sitting here like a zombie isn't doing me any favours. I'd rather be busy. And Fenn's short-staffed this week, with Corinne away.'

*   *   *

On his way back from a meeting at Broadcasting House that afternoon, Danny slipped into a newsagent's to pick up a copy of the *Evening Standard*. The tiny cramped shop smelled of patchouli oil, and the plump, middle-aged Asian woman behind the counter was sitting on a stool watching a portable television. When she saw Danny, she wiped her eyes with the edge of her emerald-green sari.

'Oh dear, look at me, what must you think? It's so sad though, isn't it, such a lovely boy . . . There now, what can I do for you, sir?'

The TV, perched precariously on top of a pile of *People's Friends*, was reshowing Sunday's pre-race interview between Miles Harper and the excitable racing commentator. Miles was leaning back in his chair, smiling and utterly relaxed, answering questions about his preparations for the forth-coming race. When he unfastened the collar of his denim shirt and began to play, apparently absent-mindedly, with the choker around his neck, Danny leaned across to take a closer look. He hadn't seen this interview before, but he recognised the object attached to the leather choker. It was Miranda's – he'd spotted it while they'd been filming in her room.

Listening intently, he heard the interviewer say, '. . . Daisy Schofield, am I right?'

'Actually, no, but I do have a message for the lovely lady in my life.' Pausing and smiling his famous lazy smile, Miles quite deliberately showed off the copper pig to the camera, turning it this way and that to catch the studio lights. 'And that is, when you meet the right person, you know it. That's what happened to me and I—'

The interviewer charged in at that moment to close the

interview. Miles, cut off in crucial mid-sentence, grinned and rolled his eyes with good-natured resignation.

The clip ended equally abruptly and the Indian lady blew her nose noisily into a pink tissue.

'I'm sorry, I'm not usually like this. But can you imagine how his poor girlfriend must feel? I saw her on the TV earlier, oh, in a terrible state. They were going to get married, you know.' She riffled through one of that morning's papers and pushed it across the counter, showing Danny a recent photograph of Miles and Daisy together at some polo match. 'Isn't it just the saddest thing in the world?'

It felt strange being back at work, realising that the rest of the world was carrying on more or less as if nothing had happened. Miranda, having explained everything to Fenn and Bev the night before, was aware that Fenn had warned the rest of the staff to be gentle with her, even though they weren't entirely sure *why* they were being gentle. In the mean time she kept herself as busy as possible, making coffee and running errands, shampooing heads and sweeping up.

Customers were customers, business was business, after all. Life goes on.

'Excuse me, is Miranda here?'

Bev was surreptitiously reading an article in *Cosmo* about liposuctioning fat out of your thighs and injecting it into your lips – heavens, surely not *all* of it – when she realised she was being spoken to. Guilty at being caught out, she shovelled the magazine under the desk and gave the man asking the question her most intimidating stare. Solidly built, in his late twenties, with uncombed light-brown hair and a less than groomed appearance . . . oh yes, he fitted the bill all right.

'Miranda who?'

He shot her a weary look.

'Please. I know she works here. I need to see her, okay?'

Bev bristled at his arrogant manner. Fenn had warned her just this morning to be on her guard against doorstep journalists. If anyone came round asking questions about Miranda, he had instructed, Bev was to say nothing and get rid of them, smartish.

No problem. Getting rid of men smartish was a speciality of Bev's. Sadly, even when she didn't want them to go.

'Miranda isn't here.' As she spoke, Bev moved around slightly to block the man's view of the salon.

To her fury he reached across the counter, gripped her by the elbows and moved her firmly back again.

'Yes she is. Over there. See?' He pointed out Miranda, emerging from the back room with a mountain of towels.

'She doesn't want to see you,' Bev replied firmly. Typical, this had to happen just when Fenn had popped out for ten minutes.

'You think I'm a journalist, don't you? I'm not a journalist.'

This, of course, was exactly the kind of thing a journalist would say.

'Please,' said the journalist.

In return, Bev gave him one of her best frosty glares – the one that went so well with her perfectly applied frosted-beige lipstick.

'Uh . . . no.'

He began to lose patience.

'Jesus, who do you think you are?'

'Me?' said Bev. 'I'm the person telling you that if you know what's good for you, you'll get out of here before I—'

'AAARGHH!'

A shrill scream from the back of the salon made everyone jump and stopped Bev in her tracks. All eyes swivelled in the direction of the screamer – a salon regular, the pampered young wife of a newspaper baron.

'I don't *believe* it! I said a quarter of an inch above my eyebrows and you've taken off at least half an inch! What are you, a complete IMBECILE?'

The woman was one of Corinne's clients. With Corinne away, Lucy was cutting her hair for the first time. As Lucy reddened, the woman drummed her high heels against the black marble floor and shrieked, 'You've wrecked it, you've totally wrecked my hair . . . you do realise I'll have to cancel my holiday now, I can't be seen out with a fringe like this. Jesus, you've ruined my *life* – hey, you!' She jabbed a finger in Miranda's direction. 'Get me my bag, this minute.'

Miranda, who had been cutting up squares of foil, obediently hastened to the desk and located the bag – Hermès, naturally. Returning and handing it over to the woman, who immediately yanked out a bottle of Valium, tipped half a dozen tablets into her hand and downed them in one, she said, 'Your hair's great, it suits you like that. Makes you look younger.'

'Oh, don't give me that! How gullible do you think I am? Look at it, look at it, she's wrecked my fringe!'

'I'm not just saying it to make you feel better. It's the truth,' said Miranda.

'Oh well, if it's the truth you're so keen on, you won't mind me telling you that you're not looking so hot yourself. Face like a wet weekend, that's what you've got,' jeered the blonde. 'Not exactly the cheeriest little soul in Santa's grotto, are you? Christ, I've seen happier-looking bloodhounds. What happened – boyfriend dump you, did he? Can't say I'm surprised.'

The whole salon held its breath. There was the kind of appalled silence that might follow someone accidentally breaking wind in front of the Queen. Everyone waited for Miranda's reaction and wondered what form it would take. Would she scream back at the woman, perhaps? Burst into tears and run out of the shop? Or – hopefully – pin her back in her chair, grab the nearest pair of scissors and reduce her whole head to stubble?

The journalist, granite-jawed with outrage, made a move towards them. It was Bev's turn to put out an arm and hiss, 'Don't you dare.'

Miranda, to everyone's astonishment, simply rested a hand on the woman's shoulder and gave it a sympathetic squeeze. The woman promptly burst into noisy tears and buried her face in Miranda's front.

'What's really the matter?' said Miranda.

'Oh God, everything!' the woman sobbed. 'The children's nanny handed in her notice this morning . . . my teeth need rebleaching and my dentist's gone off to bloody Florida for a month . . . my cellulite's back . . . my whole life's falling to pieces.'

'Come on, it isn't really.' Miranda's tone was gentle.

'You'll get through this, you know you will. Shall we find you a cab?'

The woman nodded like a small child.

'Sorry I shouted.'

'Doesn't matter. But I meant it when I said your fringe was fine.'

Disentangling herself from the woman's arms clamped around her waist, Miranda signalled across the salon at Bev to flag down the first available cab.

'Thanks.' The woman sniffed dolefully. 'And I meant it when I said you looked miserable. You've always been so cheerful before.'

'We do our best.' Miranda helped her into her jacket.

'What happened then? *Did* your boyfriend dump you?'

Behind the desk, Bev flinched.

Miranda hesitated, then nodded.

'Something like that.'

Fenn returned as Miranda was helping her into a waiting cab.

'She's a good girl, this one. You look after her,' the woman told Fenn.

Mystified, he said, 'Are you sure you've got the right person here?'

Back in the salon, Bev gave Miranda a hug.

'That spoilt, selfish bitch – you should have shoved a water nozzle down her throat and drowned her! I don't know how you managed to stay so calm.'

Miranda knew, but it was too hard to try and explain. Bev would only think she was weird if she told her that, basically, she couldn't be bothered to lose her temper, she had enough to be upset about already. A handful of insults flung by a grown woman in the grip of a toddlerish tantrum were nothing in comparison with the misery she was already carrying like a ton weight around her neck.

Besides, in a funny kind of way, it was almost a comfort to know that – for whatever reason – other people were miserable too.

Even if in this case it had less to do with grief and rather more to do with off-white teeth and cellulite.

'What did she say?' Fenn demanded. 'Something about you and Miles?'

'Sshhh.' Bev gave him an are-you-mad? look and rolled her eyes expressively in the direction of the intruder she hadn't yet managed to get rid of. 'He's a *reporter*.'

'I'm not,' the intruder repeated wearily. 'Miranda, will you please tell this stroppy woman that I am not a reporter?'

Miranda looked up, noticing him for the first time. Oh, the relief . . .

'Johnnie.'

Bev's head jerked from one to the other. Johnnie? Who was Johnnie? And how dare he come into a top Knightsbridge hair salon wearing truly horrible corduroy trousers, a sweater with holes in both elbows and muddy brogues?

Glancing at her watch, Miranda said, 'Fenn, okay if I take my lunch break now?'

Fenn had already recognised Johnnie from the swimming pool incident at Tabitha Lester's house. He nodded, then, to maintain some semblance of normality, added, 'Be back by one.'

'Who is he?' demanded Bev as the door swung shut

behind them. As far as she was concerned, the man was rude, scruffy and ignorant, and she couldn't imagine for the life of her how Miranda knew him.

'Miles Harper's best friend.' Fenn's tone was laconic. 'He head-butts watermelons in his spare time.'

With a dismissive sniff, Bev retorted, 'Why am I not surprised?'

Chapter 51

Miranda's composure crumbled the moment they were out of the salon.

'Oh, Johnnie.' She looked up at him, tears sliding down her cheeks, and he put his arms around her, enveloping her in a massive bear hug. 'I'm so glad to see you. I've been feeling so . . . so *on my own*.'

When he nodded, Miranda realised that he had guessed this already; it was why he'd come to see her. So that she could talk about Miles with someone else who had known and loved him and was as miserable as she was.

More, probably, she thought with a pang, because she'd only known Miles for a few days. Johnnie had been his closest friend for years. They had told each other everything, shared—

BEEP-BEEP! tooted a passing transit van, and through the open passenger window a series of ear-splitting wolf-whistles was followed by a roar of, 'Go for it, mate, give her one from me!'

Tears turned to wry laughter and Miranda wiped the back of her hand across her wet face. They were quite the centre of attention, it appeared. Everywhere she looked, people were watching them, possibly waiting for her to be given one, as the men in the transit had so sensitively suggested.

'What's her name?' said Johnnie, nodding in the direction of the salon.

Miranda peered around his arm. Bev, who had been staring at them, hurriedly looked away.

'That's Bev, our receptionist.'

'Is she always that friendly?'

'She was trying to protect me. Come on, let's go somewhere.' They were still being watched. 'Now I know how it feels to be a panda in the zoo.'

Johnnie led her down a narrow side street and into a quiet, dimly lit wine bar. They ordered coffee and sat down opposite each other at a corner table. Johnnie sighed, pushing his fingers through his already dishevelled hair before leaning back in his chair and lighting a cigarette.

'I didn't know where you lived. That's why I had to come to the salon. He did finish with Daisy,' he said quietly. 'In case you saw her weeping and wailing on the telly and were beginning to wonder.'

Miranda nodded, her throat aching.

'Thanks.'

'He really did love you, you know.' Johnnie drew hard on his cigarette. 'The way he talked about you was amazing. I mean it, a real first.'

Miranda's nose was beginning to run with the effort of keeping her eyes dry. Surreptitiously she made use of a napkin.

'Sorry about this. Bev did warn me not to get involved with Miles. She said it would end in tears.'

Johnnie shrugged and shook his head.

'Yeah well, for me too. Look, the other reason I needed to see you was to find out if you want to go to the funeral. Because if you do, you can come with me.'

'I won't, thanks.' Miranda didn't even have to stop and think about it. She knew she didn't want to tag along incognito, and have to witness Daisy Schofield hurling herself across the coffin and generally playing star mourner.

Johnnie nodded, understanding.

'If you change your mind, let me know.' He patted her hand then reached into the back pocket of his decrepit corduroy trousers. 'Oh yes, and I've got something for you.'

She took the copper pig, warm from Johnnie's pocket, and held it in the palm of her hand.

'Some lucky charm this turned out to be.'

'He won the race, didn't he?'

Miranda felt an uneasy squirming sensation in her stomach.

'Was he wearing this when he had the accident?'

'No. The leather snapped after the race while we were all celebrating. Fairly riotously, I have to admit. Miles gave it to me to look after,' Johnnie explained. 'So you see, it did bring him luck.'

His grey eyes were filling up. It was Miranda's turn to squeeze his arm.

'You're going to miss him so much.'

'Bloody hell, you think you're half prepared for it when your best friend's a racing driver.' Johnnie heaved a sigh. 'But this is cheating, getting smashed into by a lorry on the fucking M1. It definitely wasn't meant to happen like this.'

At five to one, he walked Miranda back to the salon.

'Your minder's still got her eye on us,' Johnnie observed, as he held open the smoked-glass door and Bev – like Owl in *Winnie the Pooh* – swung round on her stool behind the desk.

'Thanks for everything.' Miranda hugged him again, her nose finally unblocked enough to be able to breathe in the scent of his Armani aftershave. She liked the contrast of scruffy clothes and sophisticated cologne.

'I'll be in touch,' Johnnie told her. Then, gazing steadily over the top of Miranda's spiky blue head, he said, 'That's a bad habit, you know.' Bev, at whom this comment was directed, bristled instantly.

'What?'

'Biting your nails.'

Indignant wasn't the word for it. As she thrust out her hands, splaying her long fingers to prove beyond doubt that her polished acrylic nails were flawless, there was practically steam gushing out of Bev's ears.

'I never bite my nails,' she informed Johnnie icily.

No rings on the relevant finger. Excellent.

'That's because they aren't real.' He smiled at Bev, having discovered what he'd set out to discover. 'If you tried you'd probably break your teeth.'

'Oh dear, I'm getting that spooky *déjà vu* feeling,' said Miranda. 'It seems like every time the doorbell rings, it's you again, coming back to hurl a few more insults in my direction.' She eyed the bunch of pale-pink roses with suspicion. 'Who are those for, anyway? Florence isn't here, Chloe hasn't had the baby yet and it's nobody's birthday.'

'Can I come in?'

'Why not? You usually do.'

'I came to apologise,' said Danny. 'And the flowers are for you.'

'Pink roses?' Caught off-guard by this, Miranda instinctively went on the attack. 'You saw pale pink roses and thought of *me*?'

'Yes, well, they'd sold right out of cactus plants.' Striding past her, plonking the flowers down on the hall table, Danny said, 'Just humour me for a minute, will you? This is about Miles. I didn't believe you before, but I do now. And I'm sorry.'

'Sorry you didn't believe me, or sorry he's dead?' Miranda shoved her hands into the pockets of her dark-blue fleecy top. The weather had worsened dramatically over the last few days and since watching the funeral on the six o'clock news she hadn't been able to stop shivering.

'Both. I would have come over sooner but I thought you might not want to see me.' He paused. 'I suppose I felt I'd done enough damage.'

Imagine that, Miranda marvelled. Danny Delancey has a conscience.

'How did you find out?'

'I saw the pre-race interview. He was wearing your copper pig . . . talking about you . . . I realised it was all true.'

'Oh well, not to worry,' said Miranda. 'It would never have worked anyway. As you so kindly pointed out. Another couple of weeks and he'd have been off, chasing after the next conquest.'

'Look, where's Chloe?'

'Antenatal class. Learning how to breathe.'

'And Florence?'

'Love's young dream? Still up in Scotland with Tom.' Miranda smiled, recalling the look of shock on the postman's face when he had glanced at Florence's last postcard. 'They're visiting old friends from their army days.'

'Did you go to the funeral this afternoon?'

'No.'

'Why not?'

'Take a wild guess.' Miranda paused. 'She came into the salon this morning, to have her hair done for it.'

'Daisy Schofield,' said Danny

'Who else? And get this, she brought a photographer along with her, from *Hi!* magazine.' Miranda assumed a *Hi!*-type voice. 'To take pictures of the grieving fiancée as she prepares to say goodbye to the one true love of her life.'

'You're not serious.' Danny looked appalled. 'And Fenn did her hair?'

'No. He told her we were fully booked and packed her off to try her luck with Nicky Clarke.'

'Are you hungry?' said Danny. 'Let me take you to dinner.'

It was Friday evening. Exactly this time one week ago, Miranda remembered, they had gone out together for a let's-be-friends-again drink. And hadn't that gone well.

'I don't know.' It seemed a bit pointless. She wasn't even hungry.

'Hey, I'm trying to say sorry here.' Danny held out his hands, palms upwards. 'Humour me, okay? Anywhere you'd like to go.'

'Anywhere? Oh well,' said Miranda, 'if you put it like that . . .'

*　　*　　*

The bridge over the M1 was banked high on both sides with flowers, their cellophane wrappings crackling in the stiff breeze. Candles flickered in glass jars amongst the multicoloured bouquets. Mourning members of the public walked the length of the bridge, peered silently down on to the southbound carriageway of the motorway where the accident had happened, and wept on each other's shoulders.

Miranda didn't weep. She dug her hands deeper into the pockets of her fleecy jacket and gazed without speaking at the moving spectacle stretched out before her. How could the loss of someone she had known for only a few days affect her so much?

Her fingers closed around the copper pig in her pocket. As she stroked its soothingly familiar curves, Danny came up behind her. Having discreetly hung back for a few minutes, he now rested a hand on Miranda's shoulder.

'Okay?'

'Okay.'

'I've got a handkerchief if you want one.'

'No.' She shook her head. 'I'm not going to cry any more. I've done enough of that.'

'Right.'

'I told you a lie last week, by the way.' Miranda twisted round to face him, her dark eyes bright. 'When you asked me if I'd slept with him, I said I had.' She paused. 'Well, that wasn't true. I never did.'

Relieved to hear it, Danny gave her shoulder a squeeze. 'Doesn't matter.'

'It does matter,' said Miranda. 'I wish I had.'

Chapter 52

Summer ended and autumn swept in with a vengeance. By the second week in September, thunderstorms were battering the country, hurricane-force winds were tearing the leaves off the trees and – with the dramatic drop in temperature – everyone was busy digging out their thermals.

The up side of chauffeuring Miranda to work on cold mornings, Fenn discovered, was that he no longer had to endure her sitting cross-legged in one of the salon's swivel chairs, a hairdryer blasting away in each hand, defrosting her feet.

'Ooh, someone's going to get the sack,' Miranda crowed, poring over the day's appointments and giving Bev a nudge. 'Is that your writing? You've only gone and booked Try-it-on Tabitha in for nine thirty and forgotten to put Home Visit. And Fenn's already got a nine o'clock and a ten o'clock lined up, so he won't—'

'Actually,' Fenn intercepted her in mid-gloat, 'I wrote it in. And she isn't a Home Visit.' He shrugged his way out of his brown leather jacket. 'From now on, Tabitha's coming here for her appointments.'

Miranda boggled at him.

'Blimey, how d'you manage that?'

Fenn rolled up his shirt sleeves, ready to start work.

'She tried to grope me once too often. When I told her to cut it out, she offered me five grand to go to bed with her.' His tone was matter-of-fact. 'So I said that was it, I'd had enough. No more home visits. From now on she either came to the salon or found herself another hairdresser.'

'Wow.' Miranda was impressed. 'Masterful or what? Of course you know what this means, don't you?'

Wearily, Fenn said, 'What?'

'This is going to make Tabitha keener than ever. In fact we'd better get a panic button installed in the VIP room, pronto.' Miranda imitated Tabitha's lascivious, sex-kitten leer. 'She's going to be unstoppable now.'

At nine thirty on the dot, Tabitha Lester made her Hollywood entrance in a floor-length fake-fur coat, dark glasses, a silver tracksuit and pink Manolo Blahnik mules. Bev's hackles rose instinctively as she recognised Tabitha's companion.

Spotting Johnnie, Miranda rushed over to give him a massive hug.

'I have the most embarrassing godmother in the world,' he told her. 'Her personal trainer, her manicurist and now her hairdresser all refuse to come to the house. She's a preying mantis in six-inch stilettos.'

'And you're the one paying the price.' Miranda was sympathetic.

'Having to cart her around from one appointment to the next.' Johnnie nodded in mournful agreement. 'How fair is that?'

'Never mind,' Miranda said soothingly, 'we'll take care

of Tabitha now. You just sit down, put your feet up, and Bev will bring you a cup of coffee.'

Johnnie looked over at Bev, who was stonily flicking through the appointments and listening to every word.

'Only if she promises not to spit in it.'

Bev, who usually enjoyed chatting to the people waiting on the parma-violet sofas next to her desk, vowed not to chat to this one. Who the hell did Tabitha Lester's godson think he was?

Spit in his coffee? Ha, he'd be lucky if she didn't wee in it.

Half an hour, Tabitha had promised; it didn't take long for a wash and blow-dry. Johnnie made himself comfortable on the sofa, deliberately closed his ears to his godmother's louder and more outrageous remarks as she carried on her one-sided flirtation with Fenn Lomax, and glanced up at Bev-the-receptionist, who was making a point of acting as if he didn't exist.

Fine. He picked up one of the glossy women's magazines on the coffee table and skimmed through an article entitled 'The Terrible Mistakes Men Make In Bed!'.

Good God, the detail it went into was mind-boggling, women's magazines these days were sheer porn. And as for the stuff they expected a bloke to get up to – well, that was nothing short of outrageous.

His glance flickering up from the page, Johnnie caught Bev looking at him. She immediately turned away, snatched up the phone and said, 'Yes, hello?' in a high-pitched voice, even though it hadn't rung.

Johnnie smiled to himself and turned the page. Ah, that

was better, he liked questionnaires. This one, called 'Do *You* Always Get What You Want?', sounded right up his street.

If you see a bloke you fancy, do you:
(a)   Ask him out?
(b)   Ask your secretary to arrange it?
(c)   Smile a lot and hope he'll take the hint?
(d)   Engage him in a conversation about the weather then suddenly say, 'Oops, I've just remembered I'm not wearing any knickers?'

Any of the above would do nicely, thought Johnnie. Sadly, none of them had ever happened to him. Well, maybe the smiling option had cropped up in the past but more often than not the girl doing the smiling had followed it up with: 'You're Miles Harper's friend, aren't you? If you could introduce me to him, that'd be fab!'

This time Johnnie was the one caught out. Without even realising it, he had been gazing at Bev. When she looked up and their eyes met, a jolt of something he couldn't begin to describe shot down his spine.

Johnnie coughed loudly to cover his confusion, hurriedly turned over another page in the magazine and stared hard at a Tampax ad.

Oh yes, very brave, very macho behaviour for a grown man. Come on, Tabitha, *come on*, how long can it take for one sex-crazed ex-movie star to have her hair blow-dried?

Finally Tabitha was done. Fenn brought her out to the reception area and she struck a pose.

'Darling, how do I look?'

'Like an old drag queen.' As her beloved godson, Johnnie was the only person on the planet allowed to tease her. Grinning, he helped Tabitha back into her fake-fur coat. As he did so, he became aware that, once again, Bev was eyeing him discreetly from behind the desk.

'I do not, I look wonderful,' cried Tabitha. Pouting, she turned to Bev. 'Don't I, darling?'

'Of course you do. Just ignore him,' Bev said sweetly. Under her breath she added, 'Everyone else does.'

The phone rang as Tabitha and Johnnie were leaving, giving Bev the opportunity to sound incredibly busy and pretend she hadn't noticed they were off.

'Shall I tell you a funny thing?' said Miranda afterwards, when Bev had hung up. 'Every time I looked over, either you were secretly looking at Johnnie or Johnnie was secretly looking at you.'

'Oh, don't be so stupid.'

'I'm not! Neither of you said a word, but there was all this . . . this *stuff* going on.'

'Stuff,' Bev echoed in disbelief.

'You know.' Miranda made mystical movements with her hands. 'Stuff you can't describe.' She speeded up her fingers, wiggling them like worms.

'*You* can't describe it, that's for sure. Anyway, you're talking rubbish as usual.' Badly in need of cosmetic reassurance, Bev reached beneath the desk for her lipstick. Always kept within easy reach, it was Chanel, it was glossy and it was pillar-box red. Since she reapplied it at least a dozen times a day – more, in times of stress – it was also her security blanket. A quick glance in the mirror behind her and a swift one-two was all it took to restore Bev's faith in herself and a sense of Zen-like inner calm.

'Rubbish, is it?' said Miranda gleefully. 'Well, don't look now, but he's coming back.'

As the salon door swung purposefully open, Bev's hand jerked and scarlet lipstick slid up in a line from her mouth to the outer corner of her right nostril. Horrified, clamping both hands over her face, she ducked out of sight behind the desk.

No tissues down there.

Nothing to wipe her mouth on, except the carpet.

'Hello?' said Johnnie, above her. 'It's no good, I know you're down there.'

The carpet was looking tempting, but it was pearl grey and Fenn would kill her.

There was nothing else for it. Crouching on her heels, curled up like a snail, Bev bent forward and wiped the lipstick off on the hem of her skirt. The white Nicole Farhi skirt she had saved up for *months* to buy.

'Hello, hello?'

Finally, in slow motion, she rose to her feet. Johnnie was leaning over the desk, watching with interest.

'What?' Bev snapped defiantly, hating him more than ever now that he'd ruined her very best skirt. And although the worst of the lipstick was off, she still had to keep one hand cupped, toothache-style, over the right side of her face.

'Okay, here goes. I think you fancy me.' Johnnie clasped his hands tightly together to stop them shaking. 'And God only knows why, but I know I fancy you. So how about it?'

Bev stared at him. The nerve, the absolute *nerve*!

'How about what?'

'Oh, come on, don't give me a hard time. I know I'm not great at this,' said Johnnie, 'but I'm pretty nervous, okay? You'd be scared too, if you had to do it.'

Deep breath, deep breath.

'Okay. Try it again,' said Bev.

Johnnie nodded and cleared his throat.

'Right. I'd like it very much if you'd come out with me some time. Maybe this Sunday, if you're free. Is that better?'

It was, but Bev hadn't finished being stroppy yet.

'I think I'm busy then.'

Johnnie snapped his fingers.

'Miranda, what does this one here do on Sundays?'

Miranda, eavesdropping frantically behind them and pretending to fold towels that had already been folded, stopped what she was doing and feigned surprise.

'Nothing. Well, unless you count sorting her make-up into alphabetical order.'

Thanks a lot, thought Bev. That was the last time she told Miranda anything, ever. And why did everyone seem to find it so funny anyway? People sorted their collections of CDs and books into alphabetical order, didn't they? So why couldn't she do it with make-up?

'Sunday it is, then,' said Johnnie. Pulling a pen out of his inside pocket, he helped himself to an appointment card from the pile on the desk. 'Better tell me where to pick you up.'

Oh well, what the heck. It wasn't as if she had anything else to do. Still keeping her hand clamped over her face,

Bev grudgingly told him her address through splayed fingers.

'Fine.' Johnnie clicked the pen shut in a businesslike manner. 'Right, well, Tabitha's waiting for me in the car. Sunday it is, then. Six o'clock.'

'Six o'clock.'

He raised his eyebrows.

'Think you can manage that?'

'Oh, I think so,' Bev replied with sarcasm. 'Just about.'

'Okay, 'bye.'

'Wait,' she yelped as he moved towards the door. 'You haven't told me where we're going! I don't know what to wear – smart or casual?'

Johnnie paused, then shrugged.

'Casual-ish.'

'Right.' Tick-tick went Bev's brain, racing through the contents of her wardrobe. Casual was fine, she could do casual . . . click click . . . caramel wool trousers teamed with her cream silk blouse, conker-brown cashmere sweater, single row of pearls, dark-brown ankle boots, Estée Lauder cinnamon silk eye shadow, Lancôme mulberry lipstick—

'Oh, and don't worry about breakfast,' Johnnie added over his shoulder as he left. 'We'll stop for a fry-up on the way.'

Chapter 53

'You make the best mashed potato in the world,' said Miranda. The candles flickered romantically in the centre of the table, lighting up her eyes. 'Will you marry me?'

'Do the washing-up and I might consider it,' Chloe told her. She watched Miranda dig enthusiastically into the tureen of extra-peppery, extra-buttery mashed potato and pile a third helping on to her plate. 'Actually, there's a favour I've been wanting to ask you.'

'Don't tell me.' Miranda held up her free hand. 'Let me guess. Fenn can't cut hair to save his life and you want me to do it for you from now on.'

'Um, no.'

From across the dining table, Florence chimed in with: 'My son is unbearable to work with and you'd like Miranda to march into his shop tomorrow morning and fire a poison dart into his neck.'

'Not that either.'

'Hang on, I've got it,' Miranda squealed triumphantly. 'You want me to ask Danny if he'd make a fly-on-the-wall documentary about you having the baby! You want him to film the birth so we can all watch you with your legs in the air, panting like an animal, yelling your head off and flashing your bare bottom to an audience of millions.'

Florence was laughing so hard she almost choked on a piece of beef. Miranda leaned across and patted her on the back.

Chloe, smiling at them both, said, 'Well, you're getting closer.'

Florence began to choke again.

'Not seriously,' said Miranda, appalled. 'You can't want it to be filmed. Not . . .' she flapped her hands, in revulsion, in the general region of her own groin, '. . . oh, surely not!'

'Of course I don't want to be *filmed*.' Chloe put down her knife and fork. 'But I'd like you to be there with me.'

'Be where?'

'At the hospital. While I'm doing the panting and yelling bit.' She looked hopefully at Miranda. 'I'm supposed to have a designated birth partner, you see. They keep asking me at the hospital if I've chosen anyone yet. And . . . well, if you're happy to be involved, I'd really like it to be you.'

Miranda stared at her, dumbfounded.

All that blood.

And awful *stuff* gushing everywhere.

Agonising screams of pain.

That hideous disinfectanty smell that all hospitals have.

The sight of needles and, oh God, *forceps* . . .

The very real likelihood of fainting during a grisly bit and crashing to the ground, sending all the sterile instrument trolleys flying and probably fracturing her own skull into the bargain.

'Of course I'll do it. I'd love to be your birth partner,' said Miranda.

'Will you? Really?' Reaching over, Chloe clasped her hand and squeezed it with delight. 'Oh, thank you! I'm *so* glad.'

'Me too,' Miranda fibbed. Touched and flattered, maybe. Squeamish, definitely. But glad? Not really.

Oh well.

Florence raised a knowing eyebrow as soon as Chloe had disappeared into the kitchen to fetch the blackberry tart.

'Liar.'

'If she wants me to be there, I'll do it,' Miranda whispered back. 'Maybe it won't be so bad after all.'

With wicked relish, Florence murmured, 'What if it's *worse*?'

Miranda shrugged. She had to be brave, she couldn't give in.

Basically, when someone does you the honour of asking you to be their birth partner, how can you say no?

The next day, after work, Miranda was sitting in the window of a café on Montpelier Street when she saw Danny making his way along the pavement towards her. Without thinking, she tapped on the glass.

When he came in, Miranda admired his dark suit and lavender-blue shirt.

'Look at you, all dressed up.'

'Business meeting. I've been holed up all afternoon in offices over in Rutland Gate. Just finished five minutes ago.' Pulling out a chair, Danny ordered coffee from the pretty waitress, then glanced at his watch. 'What are you doing here anyway? I thought Fenn dropped you home from work these days.'

Miranda shrugged. 'It wasn't worth going home. I'm meeting Chloe at the Chelsea and Westminster in half an hour. We're being given a guided tour of the maternity wing.'

Danny leaned back in his chair.

'Well, I can understand it being helpful to Chloe, but why do you have to go too?'

Bravely, Miranda said, 'I'm her birth partner.'

She might have known she couldn't expect to fool Danny, who wasn't taken in for a minute.

'Oh dear.' He looked amused. 'And you can't think of anything worse.'

Miranda's resolve – to be strong and cheerful and lie valiantly through her teeth – promptly collapsed. Indignantly she demanded, 'Well, can *you*?'

Danny started to laugh.

'There are lots of worse things and you know it.' His espresso arrived and he began heaping sugar into the tiny steel cup. 'Come on, birth is a miraculous thing. It's the most moving experience in the world.'

'That's easy for you to say.' Miranda gave him a wry look. 'You aren't the one Chloe's asked to be there, are you?'

'But if she did ask me, I'd do it,' said Danny, surprisingly. 'Like a shot.' He held up his hand before Miranda could open her mouth. 'And no, don't even think it. Chloe wants *you* to be her birth partner, not me.'

427

Miranda sighed and with her index finger scrawled her initials in the foam on her cappuccino.

'It's not that I don't want to be there for Chloe. I'm just terrified I'll faint or be sick or something. I don't want to ruin her big day.'

Danny smiled and shook his head.

'You won't do that. Once it's all happening, you won't even think about passing out. Seriously,' he reassured her in a trust-me voice. 'You'll be fine.'

To her amazement, Miranda realised that she *was* reassured. Not totally. But a bit. Danny had psyched her up, like a boxing coach. Oh yes, she could do it, she could, she really could—

'You'll be an honorary aunt,' Danny told her with a grin. 'Auntie Miranda.'

She pulled a face. 'Mad Aunt Miranda.'

'Don't worry about that. Mad aunts are the only kind to have. Much more fun than sensible ones.'

'Did you have one?' said Miranda, interested.

'When I was a kid? Oh yes. Mad Aunt Pearl. She'd take me on cat-tracking expeditions.'

'Where you would . . . ?'

'Find a cat and follow it. Wherever it went. Up trees, along walls, through gardens—'

'And cat-flaps,' said Miranda.

'Mad Aunt Pearl was built like a tank. She wouldn't have fitted through a cat-flap.' Danny was smiling, he clearly had fond memories of his eccentric, tank-sized relative. 'Oh, but she was great. She used to dress up as a pirate. The neighbours thought she was mad.'

Eccentric, outrageous, certainly not run-of-the-mill Aunt

Pearl was beginning to remind Miranda of someone she knew. She thought, so *that's* why he gets on so famously with Florence.

'Okay, I'll do it. When Chloe's baby's a bit older, I'll take it on adventures and get my bottom stuck in cat-flaps.' Miranda was beginning to enjoy herself. 'And we'll go to the circus together, and the pantomime, oh, and ice-skating . . . and I'll be able to read to it, all the stories that I used to love when I was little.'

'Which stories did you love when you were little?'

'God, there were loads. *The Enchanted Wood*,' Miranda remembered. 'And all those Laura Ingalls Wilder books. And *Flambards*, when I was a bit older. Oh, *oh*, and my absolute favourite was called *Footprints in the Snow*.'

Danny frowned. 'I've never heard of that one.'

'My grandmother gave it to me when I was six. It was the copy she'd had when *she* was a girl, so it must have been ancient. But I read that book over and over.' Picturing the old-fashioned cover with its sellotaped-together spine, Miranda recited dreamily, '*Footprints in the Snow*, by Racey Helps. It fell to bits in the end, of course. I remember crying when my mum said we had to throw it out.'

Their cups were empty. Danny was smiling at her reminiscences. Miranda smiled back at him; this was fun, she could sit here all evening exchanging childhood—

'Hell's bells, what's the *time*?'

He consulted his watch.

'Twenty to seven.'

'I'm meant to be at the hospital by seven!'

Danny stood up.

'My car's just down the road. I'll give you a lift.'

'Typical,' Miranda said drily as they sped through the dusty streets to the Chelsea and Westminster. 'I'm so busy telling you what a terrific aunt I'll make that I'm late for my first antenatal class.'

'We'll make it.'

'I'm not even going to have time to make our badges.'

Danny shot through a set of traffic lights on amber. 'What badges?'

'According to Chloe, all the other women will be with their husbands,' Miranda explained. 'I was going to make up a couple of badges saying *We Are Not Lesbians*.'

Raising his dark eyebrows, Danny chided, 'If you're going to be Mad Aunt Miranda you mustn't care what other people think of you. It's your mission in life to get them gossiping behind your back.'

Does he think I'm being prudish and narrow-minded? Is he teasing me, Miranda wondered, or having a bit of a dig?

Right.

'That's all very well,' she retorted smartly, 'but a girl has to keep her options open. What if the place is teeming with gorgeous doctors? I wouldn't want to put them off.'

Returning home from work on Saturday evening, Miranda pushed open the front door and sent a small, well-wrapped parcel skidding across the polished parquet floor. Bending to retrieve it, she realised that the parcel bore only her name, not her address.

Both Florence and Chloe were out. In the kitchen Miranda took off her jacket and flicked on the kettle. Then, mystified, she began to unwrap the parcel.

When she tore open the last layer of bubble-wrap, a lump came into her throat.

She was six years old again.

Footprints in the Snow by Racey Helps.

It was the cover she knew so well, with Millicent Littlemouse and Nubby Tope sledging down a snow-covered hill on a basket piled high with sticks.

The *very same* cover, in the same faded green and beige colours. Only this time the spine wasn't held together with yellowing strips of Sellotape.

Opening it with trembling hands, Miranda saw the date inside: 1946. Then she read the brief note Danny had tucked between the first pages. It simply said:

Is this the right one? Hope so. Happy reading. D.

Miranda blinked hard. What a really, *really* nice thing to have done for her. How he had managed to get hold of a copy of a book that had probably been out of print for the last fifty years, she couldn't begin to imagine.

Smiling idiotically to herself, Miranda made a cup of tea and carried the book through to the sitting room. She had been thinking a lot about Danny during the last couple of days. It had been lovely to bump into him again. They hadn't bickered – well, hardly at all. Danny hadn't brought up the subject of Miles and she hadn't so much as mentioned Danny's finger-waggling blonde. They had been relaxed in each other's company, at ease with each other in a way she had never imagined possible before now.

Amazing, thought Miranda.

Amazing, but nice.

She picked up the phone and punched out Danny's number. He answered on the fourth ring.

Miranda smiled again. It was even nice just hearing his voice.

'How?' she said. 'How? How? How?'

'Are you impressed?'

'Hugely impressed. But you have to tell me how you did it.'

'It was nothing.' Danny sounded modest. 'Just a question of trawling through every second-hand bookshop in the country. Found this one, finally, in a little back street in Newcastle—'

'You didn't!' gasped Miranda.

Danny burst out laughing.

'No, of course I didn't.' Fondly he said, 'See? I can still fool you.'

'Oh, ha ha.' Miranda, going pink, was just glad he couldn't see her.

'If you really want to know, there's a shop on the Charing Cross Road that specialises in tracking down out-of-print books.'

'Well, it was still really kind of you,' said Miranda.

'My pleasure. You'll be able to read it to Chloe's baby when it's older. How did the antenatal class go, by the way?'

'Oh, you know. Not so bad. They definitely thought we were lesbians.' Impulsively she added, 'I'd like to thank you properly for the book. Why don't you come over for lunch tomorrow? I'll cook.'

Danny hesitated. Then he said, 'I'd have loved to, but I have to fly to Berlin tomorrow morning.'

Miranda knew her cooking wasn't brilliant, but was it really *that* bad?

'When are you back?'

'Not sure. Maybe a couple of weeks. Well, two or three.'

Oh dear. She heard the change in his voice. If that wasn't back-pedalling, she didn't know what was.

Miranda's blood ran cold as she realised why. Danny was fine as he was. He already had a girlfriend he was perfectly happy with. And now here *she* was, muscling in . . . He was being kind to me, that's all, Miranda hurriedly reminded herself. The last thing he needs is for me to start making a nuisance of myself, latching on to him like some desperate stray puppy.

'Oh, brilliant! Two or three weeks in Berlin? That's *fantastic!*' She forced herself to sound bright and *totally* unclingy. 'You'll have the most amazing time! Well, better go now, I really just rang to say thanks for the book. You have a great trip, okay? Bye-ee!'

Bye-ee came out as a manic, high-pitched, Joyce Grenfell-ish shriek.

Mortified, Miranda hung up the phone and surveyed her reflection in the gilded mirror above the fireplace.

Oh, well *done*, Miranda. Played a blinder there, didn't you?

You know, don't you, that you sounded completely mad.

Heaven only knows what Danny thinks of you now.

Chapter 54

I must be mad, thought Bev three days later. Completely barking mad. Out of my tree.

'Marks out of ten then,' Johnnie said cheerfully. 'How d'you think it's going so far?'

'Oh, fabulous. Sixteen at least. Here we are, speeding down the M4 at seven o'clock on a Sunday morning, and you won't even tell me where we're heading.' Bev spread her manicured hands in despair. 'I mean, why does it have to be such a secret? Are we going to have lunch at a fabulous country house hotel? Are we visiting friends of yours? Am I being taken to meet your parents? Because if I am, I'd like to know.'

As soon as these last words were out, Bev regretted saying them. Laughing to himself, Johnnie flicked the indicator and moved onto the slip-road leading to the Membury services. He parked the filthy white Mercedes right outside the entrance, switched off the ignition and patted Bev's hand.

'It's the first hour of our first date. We might fancy each other rotten, but we don't actually know each other terribly well yet. Before you start angling for an invitation to meet my parents, why don't we see how we get on over breakfast? Because I'm warning you now, if you eat with your mouth open and slurp your tea, I'll go off you straight away. *Or,*' he went on calmly, holding up his hand as Bev let out a squeak of protest, 'when you see the way I mop the tomato ketchup off my plate with my fried bread, you might go off me.'

The restaurant at this ungodly hour was virtually empty. Bev, her mouth sullen and her arms folded, leaned against the counter and listened to Johnnie laugh and joke with the middle-aged woman serving the food. She wondered what she'd done to deserve such a punishment.

'Just black coffee for me.'

'Rubbish.' Johnnie was encouraging the woman to pile his plate higher and higher with chips, bacon, mushrooms, black pudding – ugh – and beans. 'Got to keep your strength up. Busy day ahead.' He grinned down at Bev's miserable face. 'Hey, don't worry! I said I'd buy you breakfast, didn't I? This is on me.'

Bev's stomach, rumbling away like a volcano, was so loud that even the woman serving the food heard it.

'Double of everything for you too, love?'

'Yes please,' said Johnnie.

'But no black pudding!' yelped Bev.

It was lucky that the Mercedes was so filthy already, otherwise it would have been too much to bear. As it was, Bev's heart was in her highly polished ankle boots as they bounced along the muddy woodland track. The motorway was far behind them now. This was Devon as only the cows truly knew it. Except, of course, no self-respecting cow would be seen dead in such a gloomy, godforsaken forest, they had far more sense than that. You only found cows in rolling fields, up to their ankles in grass and daisies and buttercups . . . what were those kind of fields called? Ah yes, meadows, such a pretty word.

Nothing so green and pleasant around here, Bev thought sourly. Not a meadow in sight.

Just millions of trees, dank and dark and dripping with rain, a narrow stony track pitted with puddles the size of paddling pools, and acres and acres of mud.

At last the track reached a clearing in the forest. Practically numb by this stage, Bev gazed ahead at the army-style trucks lined up next to a massive khaki tent. People in camouflage overalls were emerging from the tent carrying guns. Others milled about, smearing their faces with mud, checking their weapons, wrapping camouflage netting around their heads and studying maps.

'Well?' said Johnnie. 'What d'you think?'

He was actually looking *pleased* with himself. Bev, who couldn't possibly tell him what she was really thinking, said, 'You're in the SAS, is that what you're trying to tell me?'

He laughed.

'It's paintballing. Haven't you ever done it before?'

'Amazingly, no.' Bev marvelled at his gall. 'And I'm not going to do it now.'

'Come on, it's fun!'

'No it isn't. How can it possibly be fun?'

'But we've come all this way!'

'Read my lips, Johnnie. Enn oh, spells NO.'

He had friends here. People recognising the car began to wave. Bev ignored them.

'Please,' said Johnnie. 'You'll enjoy it.'

'I will not.'

He shook his head.

'Miranda said you were a good sport.'

'She lied,' said Bev, deeply insulted. 'I am *not*. I've never been a good sport in my life.'

'I'm really disappointed.'

'Ha, you think *you're* disappointed! I got up at four o'clock this morning to have a bath, do my hair and put my make-up on—'

An earsplitting whistle echoed around the clearing, making Bev jump. More people poured out of the tent, ran towards the first truck and leapt – like lemmings on rewind – into the back.

The next moment the man with the whistle materialised beside the passenger door of Johnnie's car. Six foot six of scary-looking sergeant major glared witheringly down at Bev. The door was wrenched open.

'Don't tell me,' he sneered, 'a virgin.'

'It's her first time,' Johnnie agreed.

'It bloody well isn't,' said Bev, 'because I'm not doing it.'

She shrank back, clutching at the sides of the leather seat as the man leaned into the car. Without warning, his hand shot past her, whisking the keys from the ignition with awesome dexterity. As Bev let out a squeak of horror, he pulled out the waistband of his camouflage trousers and dropped the keys – with a cheery clink – out of sight.

She blinked. Crikey, what a six-pack.

'You can't do that!'

'I can do anything I want.' The terrifying sergeant major gave her a grim smile. 'I'm in charge here. Now, seeing as you're not going anywhere else, perhaps you'd like to make your way over to the tent and get changed.'

Bev gave him a mutinous look.

'Or would you prefer me to carry you?'

Her eyes slithered across to Johnnie.

'I'm never going to forgive you for this. You do know that, don't you?'

'I'm sorry.' He shrugged. 'It was Miranda. She said you'd love it.'

'And I'm never going to speak to bloody Miranda again as long as I live.'

I'm having a nightmare, thought Bev, jolting along in the back of the truck as it headed ever deeper into the forest. Changing into army fatigues behind a *Blind Date*-style partition in the communal tent had only been the start. There were no mirrors on the site. The gunk everyone had been so energetically slapping on to their faces wasn't cosmetic mud, it was the real stuff, scooped out of real puddles. What was more, the helmets were unflattering, the lace-up boots diabolical, and when she had tried to clamber into the truck she had slipped and fallen on her backside into a sea of churned-up mud.

Why everyone else seemed to be so damn cheerful, Bev couldn't imagine. It was bizarre – they actually appeared to be having a whale of a time, chattering noisily to each other, catching up on all the gossip and enthusiastically discussing the day ahead.

'New to this, are you?'

Startled, Bev realised that the girl on her left was talking to her.

'Just a bit.'

'You're going to love it.'

'Actually,' said Bev, 'I'm not. All this . . .' she gestured around the lorry, '. . . really isn't me at all.'

The girl, clearly missing the point completely, exclaimed, 'I know, me neither! Isn't it great?'

Worse was to come. When the lorry finally slithered to a halt and everyone leapt out, the organiser handed out instructions to two burly individuals and announced, 'Okay, these are your leaders. Now line up and move to one side as soon as you've been chosen.'

Bev shuddered. Years of suppressed humiliation came flooding back as she remembered the games lessons at school, being picked for teams – or rather, standing there like a total lemon while everyone else was picked ahead of you.

And now, ten years later, it was happening all over again. Oh no, this was too much.

'You!' yelled the leader of the red team, and it wasn't until someone gave her a hefty shove that Bev realised he'd been pointing at her. The reason she hadn't noticed was because her eyes had been swimming with tears, but now she didn't have to cry because – thank you, God, oh *thank you* – she hadn't been picked last of all. She wasn't the booby prize, left till the end. She'd even been chosen before some of the men.

'You!' the yellow team leader shouted at Johnnie. He grinned at Bev and moved to the other side.

Perfect, thought Bev, adrenalin beginning to pump through her chilly veins. Now I can kill you.

'Aaargh! Help me – they're coming over the hill!'

Hearing the voice, Bev darted through the trees towards

it. She threw herself on to her stomach as two members of the enemy team raced past in pursuit of someone else. A frond of wet fern tickled Bev's nose. She waited until the coast was clear, then half slid, half ran down to the river where Stuart – a fellow red – was fishing frantically in the water for his pistol.

'I dropped it,' he hissed, and Bev plunged into the icy water, feeling around with her feet until she hit something metallic.

'You're a star,' gasped Stuart, refilling the gun with paintballs from the ammunition belt slung around his waist.

'Duck!' Bev flung herself on to the muddy bank as a rustling in the undergrowth and a flash of yellow signalled the presence of the enemy. *Splat*, a paintball exploded against a rock, inches from her left ear.

The next moment Stuart had spun round and fired back.

'Bastard!' howled the enemy as his chest was splattered with red paint.

'Quick, there's another one!'

Rolling on to her back, Bev flicked away the slug that had attached itself to her sleeve and reached for fresh ammunition.

'He's heading for the bridge,' gasped Stuart. 'I'll climb over those rocks, you follow the river. We'll corner him by the—'

WHUMMPPP! went the yellow paintball against Stuart's perspex goggles.

'Oh, shit, he's got me!'

'You're dead,' said Bev. 'See you in the next game.'

'Do me a favour. Shoot the fucker, okay?'

Bev watched Stuart trudge off through the trees, a dead

man, temporarily at least. She flicked her sodden hair out of her eyes and levered herself upright, watching and listening out for the enemy. It was hard to move quietly when you had half a river sloshing around in your boots. Hard to stay upright, too, when the mud was slurping around your ankles, doing its level best to suck you into its murky depths.

Suddenly spotting a flicker of movement through the trees ahead, Bev froze and drew up her gun. Keeping it trained steadily in front of her, she held her breath.

Bugger, it was only a squirrel. She exhaled slowly.

'Don't move,' whispered a voice behind her, and she felt the barrel of a gun being pressed into her back.

Oh, shit, thought Bev, furious with herself. Now I'm dead too.

'Close your eyes,' hissed the voice.

Bev closed her eyes and waited for the splat.

'Turn around slowly.'

She turned, her boots squelching inelegantly in the mud, her breathing fast and shallow.

'Keep your eyes shut. Don't speak.'

Bev's heart was racing like a train. She felt warm breath on her face, then a mouth tentatively brushing hers. Her whole body tingled in response – as it had never tingled before – and she found herself leaning forwards, desperate for more.

Heavens, so this was what they meant by war being an aphrodisiac . . .

'You tart,' said Johnnie, breaking away with a grin. 'I could have been anybody.'

Bev smiled.

'I recognised your aftershave.'

'Can I tell you something?'

'What?'

'That's the first time I've seen you smile.'

'Can I ask you something?' countered Bev.

'What?'

'That thing you just did, the thing that vaguely resembled a kiss. Was that it, or is there more?'

'Oh, there's more,' Johnnie promised. He brushed her wet hair away from her cheeks and thought how beautiful she looked. 'If you're sure you don't mind fraternising with the enemy?'

Trembling, Bev put her arms around him and raised her mouth to his.

This time there was nothing tentative about the kiss. Johnnie slid his tongue into her mouth and she responded for all she was worth. Oh God, he was a fabulous kisser, he really was, and the way he was running his hands over her body, well, it was just too good an opportunity to miss—

WHUMMPPP! WHUMMPPP!

'What the—?' Johnnie gasped, jerking away and twisting round to see the explosions of scarlet paint running down his back. He gazed in disbelief at the pistol in Bev's hand.

'Bang bang, you're dead,' said Bev.

Chapter 55

Ahead of them, at the end of the sweeping gravel drive, the Manor House Hotel loomed out of the mist like a mirage in a desert. Only this was the reverse of a desert mirage. Water they had plenty of on such a damp, grey and increasingly chilly evening. But the sight of warm lights glowing welcomingly in windows, combined with the prospect of lounging in front of a crackling log fire sipping brandy and digesting a fabulous meal was too great to resist.

'What do you think?' Johnnie kept the engine ticking over. As if she was likely to say no.

'Yes yes *yes*,' Bev breathed. Warmth, heat, food, drink, all those unimaginable luxuries, in the most gorgeous of surroundings. A horrid thought suddenly struck her. 'Oh *no* . . .'

'What?'

'Look at the state of us.' She pulled despairingly at her hair and gazed at Johnnie's crumpled rugby shirt and jeans. 'They're never going to let us in, not in a million years.'

Johnnie thought for a second; this clearly hadn't occurred to him either. A few moments later he switched off the ignition, leaned across the car and took Bev's face carefully between his hands.

Her muddy face, now free of foundation and blusher and powder and God-knows-what-else. Those bright eyes, minus all the layers of shadow and gunky mascara. That soft, oh-so-kissable mouth. And the hair the colour of ripe corn, no longer sculpted into one of those don't-touch-me chignon things but falling loosely around her shoulders.

God, he loved hair that just *fell* like that.

'You look beautiful. You *are* beautiful,' said Johnnie. 'I knew you would be.'

This was so ridiculous Bev didn't even try to argue. The man was clearly deranged.

'We're still not going to be allowed into the restaurant,' she said sadly.

'Maybe not.' Johnnie swung open the driver's door. 'But they'll let us have a room.'

'Better now?' he said forty minutes later when Bev emerged from the bathroom wrapped in one of the hotel's white velour dressing gowns.

'Heaven.' Pink, scented and still gently steaming, Bev collapsed on to the sofa and took the glass of wine he held out. Gosh, it was amazing how much more you appreciated a hot bath when you'd actually done something to earn it.

'My turn now.' Johnnie dropped the menu into her lap. 'Choose what you want to eat, then ring down and let them know. By the time I'm back out, dinner will be here. Oh – and order another bottle of wine.'

He was lovely. Muddy, but lovely, Bev now realised. How could she ever have thought he was a pig?

By nine thirty, dinner had been cleared away and it was time to start making a move.

'Two hours to get home,' Bev groaned. 'Work tomorrow. I bet I'll ache like anything. Honestly, nobody's going to believe it when I tell them what I did today.'

'You were a star.' Johnnie gave her arm a squeeze.

Uh oh, more physical contact. Bev felt her heart break into a gallop.

'I still can't believe I actually enjoyed it. You don't mind, then, that I killed you?'

'I forgive you.' Johnnie was smiling, surveying her as if something was on his mind.

'What?' said Bev. Thump, thump, thumpety thump.

'Nothing.' He flapped his hand, embarrassed. 'If I told you, it would only sound stupid.'

'We've talked nonstop for the last three hours. Don't clam up on me now!' Bev twisted round, pulling her legs up under her and covering them with her dressing gown.

'Er . . .' Johnnie gestured discreetly in the direction of her cleavage.

'Oh, sorry.' Realising she was now somewhat agape further up, Bev tugged the lapels together. 'Anyway, carry on. You were saying?'

'Well . . . just that sometimes you meet someone and you know that they're the kind of person you could . . . you know . . .'

'No, I don't know,' breathed Bev, beside herself with frustration. 'Could what? Could *what*?'

Johnnie closed his eyes, feeling himself start to chicken out. God, he'd waited *years* for this moment and now he was about to lose his bottle. How bloody typical was that?

'What I mean is, sometimes you meet someone and you can just picture how they'll be in twenty years' time.' This was semi-bottling out. Veering away from what he'd meant to say, without changing the subject altogether. Oh well, that was allowed, wasn't it? Better than starting to talk about the weather.

'And?' Bev gazed at him eagerly, her lips slightly parted. 'Can you picture me?'

Johnnie smiled. 'Oh yes. Bowling along in your Range Rover with a carful of Labradors and strapping, noisy, rugby-playing sons.'

Without warning, Bev burst into tears. How could be possibly have known that? It was her fantasy, four sons had always been her fantasy and she'd never told a living soul.

'How many?' The tears stopped as suddenly as they had appeared.

'Three boys. And a baby daughter,' said Johnnie, his smile broadening as he pictured them. 'They'll spoil her rotten, of course.'

'I don't believe in any of that psychic stuff,' Bev said warily.

'It isn't psychic. It's what I've always wanted. Only men aren't meant to daydream about that kind of thing. Getting married and having kids isn't a very macho thing to want.' Johnnie pulled a face. 'All we're supposed to dream about is going out, getting wrecked and ripping the knickers off as many different birds as possible.' He paused. 'Preferably with our teeth.'

I'm not wearing any knickers, thought Bev, so you couldn't rip mine off me.

Then she smiled a bit unsteadily, because this was possibly one of the happiest moments of her entire life.

'So what are you saying?'

He gave her a long look.

'You know perfectly well what I'm saying.'

Oh! Goodbye, dusty old shelf! Hello, lifetime of bliss!

'It's still early days,' Bev felt obliged to remind him. Only one day, in fact. As if she cared a jot.

'I know that. I'm just letting you know how I feel about you.' Johnnie shrugged. 'If by any chance you think you might feel the same, please, feel free to let me know. If, on the other hand, you still find me utterly loathsome, well, you can tell me that too.'

Slowly, Bev kissed him.

'I don't find you utterly loathsome.'

'Well, good,' said Johnnie. 'Phew,' he mimed relief, 'that's a start.'

Bev glanced about her at the opulent oak-panelled bedroom with its beamed ceiling, antique fireplace and velvet-canopied four-poster.

'Did you say you'd booked this room for the whole night?'

'Had to. They don't rent them out by the hour,' he explained. 'It's not that kind of hotel.'

'Seems a shame not to get our money's worth then.' Bev kissed him again, snuggling closer and allowing her hand to slip between the lapels of his dressing-gown. Shivering with pleasure as the silky dark hairs tangled beneath her fingers, she murmured, 'I'm really glad you've got a hairy chest.'

Johnnie replied gravely, 'I'm glad you've got a smooth one.'

447

Chapter 56

Miranda knew something weird was going on when she pulled on her baggy khaki trousers, stood up and promptly fell over.

'You've got both legs in one trouser leg,' Chloe pointed out. 'You aren't concentrating.'

No, she wasn't. Instead she'd been thinking about Danny, who was due to arrive any minute now, listening out for the doorbell and wondering if she had time to quickly wash the gel out of her hair after all and go for the natural look.

Well, as natural as midnight-blue hair with magenta streaks could ever look.

Dragging her left leg out of her right trouser leg, Miranda realised with a sinking heart that the thing she most didn't want happening was starting to happen all over again. It had been escalating over the last week, creeping inexorably up on her like a mischievous ghost, and there was no longer any getting away from it.

The Crush was back.

Concentrating this time, she put her left leg carefully into her left trouser leg, stood up and fastened the zip.

'Look at you, with a waist.' As Chloe gave her flat

stomach an envious prod, the doorbell rang. 'Ooh, that'll be Danny. Excited?'

Miranda looked at her hectically flushed reflection in the mirror. Dammit, yes she was, but not for the reason Chloe thought. What was more, she really wished she wasn't excited, because a raging crush on someone who doesn't have a crush on you isn't the coolest, most comfortable thing in the world to have.

The Return of the Crush, thought Miranda, biting her lip. Oh dear, and she'd been so sure it had gone for good when Miles had burst into her life. She'd been cured, oh yes, he'd been just what she'd needed to take her mind off Danny Delancey.

So it was irritating to say the least, having it make an unscheduled reappearance in her life now. Like an annoying old schoolfriend you'd rather hoped never to see again, popping up over the garden fence calling, 'Coo-ee, we've just bought the house next door!'

Funny how you can walk into room quite effortlessly all your life, then all of a sudden it becomes a complicated procedure, fraught with difficulties.

Florence and Tom were in the sitting room, chattering to Danny, who had made himself comfortable at one end of the sofa. Miranda, dithering in the doorway, wondered where she should sit in order not to arouse suspicion. On the floor, close to Florence's chair? Or – the double-bluff – on the sofa, right next to Danny?

And shall I glance at him, smile and say hi, or just ignore him? Which would be more casual? Help, I've forgotten what to do, I can't remember how to be normal, oh, this is horrible—

'Quick, sit down, it's starting.' Florence waved the TV flipper at the screen, upping the volume as the continuity announcer began to introduce the next programme. Chloe, squeezing past Tom and Florence, lowered herself into the last empty armchair. Miranda sank cross-legged on to the carpet.

'There's plenty of room next to Danny,' Florence protested.

'I'm fine, I prefer it on the floor.'

The moment the words were out, Miranda regretted them. Florence and Tom sniggered like teenagers. Danny raised an eyebrow. Florence said to him, 'Make a note of that in your diary.'

'Sshh,' Miranda said crossly. 'I thought we were supposed to be watching this.'

'And now,' purred the continuity announcer, 'a new documentary from the award-winning team of Delancey and Vale.'

'I didn't know you'd won awards.' Chloe was impressed.

'Well,' said Danny, 'mainly my Blue Peter badge.'

'Let's settle down now,' the announcer lowered her voice, 'for an absorbing hour of . . . *Streetlife*.'

'That was brilliant,' said Tom an hour later. He rewound the videotape to one of the interviews with Florence. 'And she's not bad either.'

'To think I fantasised about being spotted by a Texan oil billionaire.' Florence sighed. 'What did I end up with instead? Some old pervert who gets his kicks dressing up as a vicar.'

Chloe, sticking up for Tom, said, 'Only once.'

'Ha, that's all you know,' gurgled Florence. 'He hasn't taken that cassock back to the hire shop yet.'

It hadn't escaped Danny's notice that Miranda wasn't at all her old self. She was quieter these days, ill at ease in company and lacking her usual exuberance and wit.

He cornered her in the kitchen after the programme, where she was making coffee.

'Miranda, are you okay?'

Miranda flinched and shot an anguished glance in the direction of the door. Wouldn't someone please like to rescue her? *Please?*

'I'm fine.'

'You've been different recently.'

'Oh? I don't think I have.'

Danny felt for her. She could barely bring herself to look at him.

'Is it Miles?'

Miranda swallowed. So that was what he thought, was it? That she was still torn apart with grief.

She wasn't. It was the end of September, ten weeks since the accident. She was over it now. And if that sounded brutal, she had, after all, only known Miles for a few short days.

Still, Danny didn't need to know any of this, did he?

Miranda's skin prickled with shame. It seemed a terrible thing to do, using Miles as an excuse for her odd behaviour. Still, not nearly as terrible as the way she'd feel if Danny knew the real reason she was being odd. And Miles wouldn't mind, would he? If he was watching me now, thought Miranda, he'd be roaring with laughter at the mess I've gone and got myself into.

Danny was still waiting for a reply. She shrugged and nodded and carefully measured coffee into the jug.

'Yes, it's Miles, but I don't want to talk about it.' Terrified that Danny was about to be sympathetic, she felt herself going hot again; she could sink low, but not that low. Hurriedly she added, 'Just don't be nice to me, okay? Let's change the subject. How's it going with that blonde girl? Still seeing her?'

Danny leaned against the fridge and folded his arms across his chest. He gazed at her thoughtfully for a second, then smiled slightly, his dark eyes softening.

'Oh yes. I had dinner with her last night, as a matter of fact.'

Ah. Bugger. Changing the subject was all very well, but this wasn't the reply she'd been expecting. Subconsciously, Miranda realised, she'd been rather pinning her hopes on something more along the lines of, 'Blonde girl? What blonde girl?' Accompanied, preferably, by a puzzled frown.

'Dinner! Terrific!' She plastered on a bright smile. 'Anywhere nice?'

'Her place, actually.'

Serves me right for asking, thought Miranda. Bravely she said, 'Is she a good cook?'

Danny thought about this.

'Pretty good. Well, she did one of those Cordon Bleu courses a few years ago.'

Oh well, haven't we all?

And is she good in bed? No, no, mustn't ask that, Miranda told herself, breaking into a light sweat. Phew, thank goodness she hadn't actually said the words aloud.

Talk about a dead giveaway – there were some questions you only ever asked a man if you were besotted with him, secretly or otherwise, and this was one of them. The other great no-no being, 'So, I suppose you're going to marry her?'

Uttered, needless to say, through gritted teeth.

Definitely mustn't ask him that.

'Right. Coffee.' Light-headed with relief at having given those two a miss, Miranda leaned on the cafetière's plunger, grabbed a pile of coffee cups and clattered everything on to a tray. She wondered if Danny had inveigled the title of the blonde's favourite childhood book out of her and surprised her with a copy, too. It was probably a standard ploy he used, to win girls over and convince them how wonderful he was.

Footprints in the Snow, thought Miranda, *tuh*.

Muggins Rides Again, more like.

'You just wait until tomorrow,' said Danny.

She looked up at him, startled. 'Why? What happens tomorrow?'

'You'll be recognised. Everywhere you go, people who saw the programme will come up to you and tell you how wonderful you are.' He grinned. 'Trust me, it'll happen.'

Huh, fat lot of use that is, thought Miranda. If everyone else thinks I'm so wonderful, why can't you think it too?

Biting her lip, she rummaged in the cutlery drawer for teaspoons. 'Just as well, then, that I'm not going out much.'

Five teaspoons. Sugar. What else was missing? Ah, cream . . .

'Look.' Danny hesitated and pushed his hair out of his eyes. 'You've been through a lot and I know these things

453

take time to get over, which is why I'm not pressuring you. But if you do ever feel like going out, give me a ring. I mean it. Any time, okay?'

Miranda winced. Oh dear, those three little words that were another dead giveaway. *Everyone* knew that when a man says he means it, he doesn't mean it.

Still, he was being polite, she had to give him that.

Even if he did sound as if he was thanking some dotty great-aunt for the gorgeous crocheted tank-top she'd given him for Christmas.

'Right, definitely.' Plonking the cream jug on top of the saucers and picking up the tray, Miranda said brightly, 'That'd be great.'

Me, you and Ms Cordon Bleu. Oh yes, couldn't get much cosier than that.

Several weeks passed. One Tuesday at the end of October, Chloe was working in the shop when the bell above the door went *ting*.

'Hello,' said Greg.

Even though she'd been expecting him, her stomach squirmed. So did the baby. Probably wondering who the total stranger was, walking through the door, thought Chloe. Don't worry, pet, no one important, only your father.

'Hello, Greg.' Laying down the order slips she'd been filling out, she glanced first at her watch then across at Bruce. 'Okay if I take my lunch break now?'

'Take it, take it.' Bruce nodded vigorously, jowls aquiver. As the owner of a gift shop stacked with china and glass, he was all in favour of members of staff holding their marital disputes off the premises.

'I'll be back by one.' Chloe pulled on her coat, aware of Greg's gaze on her expanded body.

'Don't be late. I've got an important meeting this afternoon,' said Bruce.

'He means an important round of golf,' Chloe told Greg as the door swung shut behind them.

The car was parked on double yellows outside the shop. Greg unlocked the doors.

'How's Miranda?'

'Missing you terribly. Pining for you. Actually, that's a joke,' said Chloe, arranging the seatbelt around her stomach. 'She's fine and not missing you at all.'

'That was a lousy trick the two of you played.'

'Oh, it took more than two of us.'

Greg gave her the kind of long-suffering look he generally reserved for irritating office juniors who forgot how many sugars he took in his tea.

'I didn't deserve any of it, you know.'

He thought being set up like that had been embarrassing, Chloe marvelled, and the programme hadn't even gone out yet. Just wait until all his friends saw him on *Sweet Revenge*.

'Oh well, let's not argue about that,' she said cheerfully. 'Let's argue about something else instead. I know, how about the divorce?'

'You're in a funny mood,' said Greg. Warily, he eyed her stomach. 'How much longer to go?'

'Another three weeks yet. Don't worry, your car seats are quite safe.' Chloe marvelled at how easy it was to be flippant when you genuinely couldn't care less. 'Actually, I'm pretty hungry. Could we go to Sadler's?'

Greg looked irritated. Sadler's was expensive.

'I thought you rang me because you wanted a divorce.'

'I do. Well,' said Chloe, 'I assume we both do. But can't I have lunch too?'

Chapter 57

It was strange, seeing Greg again for the first time in months. Over lunch at Sadler's, Chloe caught up with all the news, learning that he had found himself a new girlfriend – a chiropodist called Antonia – and that yes, this time she knew all about his estranged pregnant wife.

'How about you?' He watched Chloe's white teeth as she bit into a stem of asparagus.

'Me? Just going for the quiet life. Giving the rock-climbing and the paragliding a miss,' said Chloe. 'Playing quite a bit of Scrabble though, drinking loads of cocoa, that kind of thing . . .'

Bravado, thought Greg.

'You'll meet someone else, you know. One day.' For some reason – guilt, probably – he felt compelled to say it.

'Will I? Who knows?' Chloe shrugged and raised a playful eyebrow. 'I'm not such a catch as you.'

She was teasing him, Greg was stunned to realise. What was more, he found he couldn't tear his eyes away from her. It really was the weirdest thing; Chloe had this massive bulge sticking out in front of her but somehow she didn't look pregnant. She waddled when she walked and massaged her back from time to time but she didn't seem pregnant either. Her gold-blonde hair was glossier than ever, her eyes sparkled, she was laughing and making jokes . . . It was uncanny, thought Greg, bemused. Where had all this confidence come from? Because he'd certainly never seen any evidence of it before.

Actually, it was quite erotic.

'Okay, this divorce,' said Chloe, bringing him back to earth with a bump. 'Cheap and cheerful, are we agreed? Oh, yes, please, I'd love another orange juice.' She gave the waiter loitering beside her a dazzling smile and Greg realised with a jolt that the waiter had noticed it too. He wasn't looking at Chloe as if she were pregnant at all – putting it bluntly, he was ogling her.

Jesus, wondered Greg, what was going on here? His ex-wife was exuding sexuality like some fifties starlet and she was managing to do it in white cotton maternity trousers and a man's pink and white striped shirt.

'Greg? Are you having another drink?'

Still baffled, Greg shook his head.

'Shouldn't you do up a couple more buttons?'

'What?' Chloe glanced down. 'My bra isn't showing, is it?'

'Your cleavage is.'

He was frowning at her chest. Chloe suppressed a sudden urge to burst out laughing.

'Greg, don't you worry about my cleavage. It's my problem, not yours.'

But you're still my wife, Greg longed to yell out. He realised how desperately aroused he was. Good grief, he'd never wanted to make love to a pregnant woman in his life

– just the thought of it had always been enough to make him feel sick.

But he badly wanted to make love to Chloe now.

'What's the matter with you?' chided Chloe, leaning across the table and pinching one of his grilled mushrooms. 'You've hardly touched your food.'

In his mind, Greg raced feverishly through the options open to him. It was twelve thirty – there was clearly no time to whisk Chloe back to his flat now. And Antonia was coming round this evening at eight, dammit.

'I'm glad we're still friends,' he blurted out. 'Civilised, like this. Better all round. You're looking fantastic, by the way. Honestly.'

Chloe sat back, eyeing him with amusement. Whatever had possessed Greg to come over so complimentary, all of a sudden?

'Well, thanks. Now let me give you my solicitor's address—'

'I could pick you up after work, if you like. Talk about it then. You haven't even seen my flat yet, have you?'

It was the casual shrug that did it. The innocent, oh-so-casual shrug accompanying the boyish smile. Like a great gong clanging in the pit of her stomach, Chloe remembered when she'd encountered these particular signals before. Oh yes, almost four years ago, just after she and Greg had first met. When he was doing his damnedest to charm her into going to bed with him.

And now, incredibly, here it was again, unchanged in every detail, the mating ritual of the greater crested wally.

Well, well, who'd have thought it? Some men, marvelled Chloe, really were in a class of their own.

Stifling the urge to shriek with laughter, she fixed him with a sultry gaze – well, as sultry as she could manage at short notice – and lowered her voice to a whisper.

'What would we do when you'd finished showing me your flat? Or,' her smile was slow, complicit, 'can I guess?'

Greg grinned. Of course, she hadn't had sex for . . . how long? Seven months? Blimey, talk about a cat on heat, she must be desperate.

'Don't see why we can't have a bit of fun.' He cocked a playful eyebrow at her. 'For old times' sake.'

Picking up another asparagus stem, Chloe snaked it slowly through the puddle of hollandaise sauce on her plate.

'You mean, bed-type fun?'

'Why not?' Mesmerised, Greg watched her eat the asparagus. Jesus, was she doing that on purpose? 'Just because we're getting divorced doesn't mean we can't enjoy each other's company every now and again.'

Actually it was a pretty exciting thought – illicit sex was always so much more of a thrill than the ordinary kind.

'I don't know.' Chloe frowned and laced her fingers together. 'I'm just a bit worried . . .'

'About damaging the baby? Don't be!' Greg, who had heard all about this on a recent radio phone-in, broke in eagerly. 'I promise you, it doesn't hurt the baby, not one bit.'

'I wasn't thinking about the baby,' said Chloe.

'It won't hurt you either – I'll be gentle, I swear I will!'

'Look, I'll tell you what's bothering me,' Chloe said patiently. 'Think back to when you were six or seven years old, okay? Your front teeth are loose and you keep wobbling and wobbling them but they won't come out. Remember that?'

She stopped. Baffled, Greg nodded.

'Well, yes.'

'Good. And there was always some older boy in your street, telling you that what you needed to do was tie one end of a piece of string around your wobbly tooth and the other end to a door handle. Then someone else slams the door shut and your tooth is yanked out and blood gushes *everywhere* . . . remember that story as well?'

'Uh, yes, I suppose so.' Greg shrugged, mystified by all this.

'Right. Well, the thing is, I'm just a tiny bit worried that when I do exactly the same thing to your bits and pieces' – Chloe's gaze flickered sorrowfully in the direction of his groin – 'it might hurt you.'

It took a couple of seconds for this to sink in. Greg's face fell. Finally, to make sure he'd got it right, he said, 'So you're saying you don't fancy a quickie, just for the hell of it?'

'You mean one with no strings attached?' Chloe couldn't resist the pun. 'I don't think so, thanks all the same. In fact, if I'm honest I'd rather stick red-hot pins under my fingernails and jump blindfold into a snake pit than have sex with you.'

'I only offered because I felt sorry for you,' Greg hissed back. 'I mean, Christ, who else would want to?'

Their waiter reappeared with the pudding menu.

'The coffee and walnut tart sounds gorgeous.' Chloe smiled up at him. 'But I have to get back to work. Could you possibly wrap a piece up for me?'

Blushing furiously, the young waiter said, 'I can put it in a patisserie box if you like. Stop it getting squashed.'

The possibility of an entertaining evening having crumbled to dust, Greg scraped back his chair.

'If you can't even be civil, I don't see why I should have to pay for your meal.' He dug into his pocket and hurled a handful of money on to the table. 'There, that should cover my share. I'm off.'

Startled, Chloe said, 'I thought you were going to give me a lift?'

He glared at his ex-wife, then at the waiter who had been making such a prat of himself over her.

'Find your own way back. Or better still,' Greg snapped, 'get your toyboy here to give you a lift.'

'Gosh,' said Chloe when he'd stormed out. 'Sorry about that. Ex-husband,' she added, by way of explanation. 'Bit of a wally. Actually, quite a lot of a wally.'

'I can't give you a lift.' The waiter looked worried. 'I'm only sixteen and a half. All I've got's a pushbike.'

Chloe tried for a moment to picture herself on it, eight and a half months pregnant and riding pillion.

Maybe not.

'Don't worry. Better cancel pudding, though.' She flicked open her purse, praying she had enough to cover the bill. Scattering notes and coins across the table like that had been an undeniably dramatic gesture, but now that she'd counted it up, Chloe discovered that Greg had actually left her with a petrol receipt, a parking ticket and the fabulous sum of three pounds twenty-seven pence.

Hey, small spender.

Then again, it didn't come as any great surprise. He'd

always been a bit that way inclined. Even before he'd taken to recycling engagement rings.

When the young waiter brought the bill, Chloe discovered that thanks to the large Scotch and ginger Greg had secretly knocked back at the bar while she'd been in the loo, she had enough money on her to pay for lunch and twenty-four pence left over for a tip.

On the pavement outside the restaurant, Chloe watched the bus she could no longer afford to catch sail past her. Stamping her cold feet and pulling her army surplus great-coat around her huge stomach – oh yes, glamour no object – she set off down the road in the direction of the shop. Just over a mile to be covered in twenty-five minutes. It was achievable, but it would have been a lot easier if only her back didn't ache so much.

Four hundred yards along the road, Chloe was forced to stop for a rest. She had a raging stitch in her side and the backache was gathering force. Leaning against a phone box, she waited for the stitch to subside. And then something awful happened . . .

Oh, good grief, thought Chloe, I've wet myself!

Warm liquid trickled in an unstoppable stream down her legs. Thank heavens, the phone box was empty. Crushing her knees together, squeezing her pelvic muscles for all she was worth, Chloe shuffled penguin-style into the phone box.

Phew, right, shame about the glass sides – not a lot of privacy to speak of – but at least nobody could see the puddle forming at her feet, which was the main thing. Flushed with embarrassment – especially when she glanced down and saw that in the cold air the puddle was act-ually steaming – Chloe leaned her forehead against the welcoming cool glass for a moment and tried to work out a plan.

No money, that was the first stumbling block, not even ten pee. Oh dear, don't even *think* of that word, at this rate she'd soon be up to her knees in warm water and the glass would start misting up like a sauna.

Chapter 58

Taking a couple of deep breaths – not that it was doing anything to help the stitch in her side – Chloe dialled the operator.

'I'd like to make a reverse-charge call please.'

She told the woman the number of the shop and waited to be put through. It was all right, no need to panic, everything was under control. Bruce would be able to help.

'Chloe, is that you? What the bloody hell d'you think you're doing?' Bruce sounded irritated beyond belief. 'Have you any idea how much it costs to accept a reverse-charge call?'

'I'm sorry. Look, I'm in a phone box on Dempsey Street.' Chloe tried to find a nice way of saying it. 'My . . . um, waters have broken and I'm in a bit of a mess and I haven't got any money on me—'

'Good grief, girl! If you're in labour, tell that husband of yours to get you to the hospital.'

'Greg's gone.' Chloe felt the prickle of perspiration at the back of her neck. 'But the thing is, I don't think I'm actually in labour. I mean, I haven't had any real contractions—'

'So you want the afternoon off? For crying out *loud*,

Chloe, you certainly pick your moments! I told you I had a vital meeting lined up—'

'Bruce, please, I need some help here.' Don't be a selfish bastard all your life, Chloe longed to yell, but didn't. 'I really hate to ask, but you couldn't come and pick me up, could you?'

'What, miss my meeting *and* wreck my leather car seats? I do hope you're joking, Chloe.'

'I'm not joking.'

'And who's going to look after the shop?' demanded Bruce. 'I'm sorry, but somebody has to stay here. Dial 999, get yourself an ambulance.' He paused and tut-tutted indignantly. 'You have *no* idea how inconvenient this is.'

'But I can't call an ambulance if I'm not even in labour!' Chloe was desperate to make him understand.

'So? Just pretend you are,' Bruce snapped back. 'Clutch your stomach and scream for pethidine, that's all Verity did the whole time she was in bloody labour with Jason. Then when you get to the hospital, tell them the contractions have stopped. They'll clean you up and give you the bus fare home.'

'But—'

'Have to go, customer wants serving, 'bye.'

Brrrrr went the dialling tone in Chloe's ear. She shifted her balance from one foot to the other and felt another warm trickle of amniotic fluid slide down the inside of her leg.

A cramping pain in the depths of her stomach increased in intensity, making her gasp. Was that one? Was that an actual contraction or just another of those Braxton Hicks practice ones she'd been experiencing for weeks?

It was all very well draping yourself across the sofa

reading the books, thought Chloe, perplexed, but when it came to the real thing, how were you supposed to tell?

She waited. The cramping pain receded.

And waited.

Nothing happened.

If I stay in here for just a few more hours, Chloe thought, my trousers might dry out.

It all depended how much water had already leaked out and how much was left.

Oh, hang on . . .

Another cramp was on its way, building up in strength like a giant fist being squeezed gradually tighter and tighter . . .

Yes, yes, this must be labour. Hooray, that meant she could now phone for an ambulance and they wouldn't sue her for calling them out under false pretences.

Weak with relief, and panting a bit as the fist tightened its grip still further, Chloe snatched up the phone. She stood, index finger poised over the 9 button, and pictured the scene. An ambulance, blue lights flashing and siren blaring, screeching to a halt outside the phone box. Paramedics leaping out, ready for anything and clutching those cases they use to jump-start dead bodies back to life—

Oh crikey, not really an emergency, thought Chloe, chickening out. Two contractions and a puddle, that's all I am.

Hardly the same as a multiple pile-up on the M25.

Relieved, Chloe thought of something else she could do. Phone Miranda.

Yes, that was definitely a sensible idea. Miranda, as her designated birth partner, needed to be warned that things could be about to happen. She may have to finish work at six and make her way straight to the hospital. Chloe felt better instantly. She was glad she'd have Miranda there. Not for the technical advice, admittedly – 'Lawdie, Miss Scarlett, I don' know nothin' 'bout birthin' babies!' – but for sheer moral support. Because let's face it, if the going got rough and you wanted someone around to take your mind off things and make you laugh, well, Miranda was definitely your man.

When you worked in the Fenn Lomax salon you became accustomed to seeing celebrities, but even by Fenn's standards, cutting and styling the hair of Magdalena Rosetti was something of a coup.

Currently one of the world's most prized actresses, garlanded with Oscars at this year's ceremony and fêted as much for her beauty as for her stupendous talent, she was over in London to appear at a televised awards bash being broadcast live that evening from the Grosvenor Hotel.

'My hairdresser was scheduled to fly over with me,' Magdalena explained to Fenn. 'But he fell off his pogo stick in Central Park and while he was lying on the ground a six-year-old rollerbladed over his hand. Three broken fingers,' she went on, 'and he's suing for two hundred million dollars.'

'Suing the six-year-old?' said Fenn.

'No, the manufacturers of the pogo stick, for not warning him that if he pogoed, he might fall off.'

'She's amazing in the flesh,' Bev confided to Johnnie when he phoned half an hour after Magdalena's arrival. 'So glamorous, even with her head tipped over a sink, and the smoothest neck I've ever *seen* – damn, there's another call waiting, so what time are you coming round tonight?'

'Seven thirty. Six hours to go.' Johnnie grinned, he couldn't help it; these days he was so happy, he'd taken to counting the hours like a teenager. 'Shouldn't you be taking that call?'

'Let them wait. I'd much rather talk to you.'

'Don't let your boss find out.'

Since there was no chance of that happening, Bev wasn't scared.

'Fenn's locked away in the VIP room with Magdalena Rosetti. Getting up to goodness knows what.'

'Lucky Fenn.' Johnnie laughed, then added, 'But I'd rather be locked in the VIP room getting up to goodness knows what with you.'

Finally, after a couple more minutes of playful banter, Bev whispered, 'Better go now . . . love you . . . 'bye,' and took the call that was, irritatingly, *still* hanging on waiting to be answered.

Honestly, talk about inconsiderate. Was making an appointment to get their fringe trimmed really the high point of some people's lives?

Had they never heard of true love?

'Yesss, the Fenn Lomax salon, how may I help you?' Bev said smoothly in her best don't-mess-with-me-I'm-the-receptionist voice.

'Well, well, at long last,' drawled a woman, employing similar don't-get-uppity-with-me-I'm-the-operator tactics. 'Will you accept a reverse-charge call from a Miss Chloe Malone? She needs to speak to a Miss Miranda Carlisle.'

'Miss Carlisle isn't here, she's on her lunch break.'

Reversing the charges? What was going on? Fenn wasn't going to be thrilled when he heard about this. Bev thought fast, then said graciously, 'But I'll accept the call.'

The operator, sounding bored and not in the least grateful, sighed and said, 'Putting you through.'

'Chloe?'

'Bev?'

'Chloe, what's happening? Miranda's not back from lunch yet, but I can take a message for her.'

'Oh. Right. Okay.' Chloe's voice was high-pitched and she sounded distinctly on edge. 'Can you tell her I think I'm in labour, so if she could make her way to the hospital after work, I'll meet her there?'

'You *think* you're in labour?' Bev was mystified. 'Good grief, don't you *know*?'

'I probably am. It's hard to explain . . . oh God, and there are kids with skateboards banging on the glass . . .'

Fenn, emerging from the VIP room, tapped Bev on the shoulder and said, 'Coffee for my client, please. Black, two sugars.'

Not even hearing him, Bev frowned into the phone – banging on the *glass*? – and said, 'Hang on, where are you?'

'In a phone box on Dempsey Street, in Barnes. Look, I'm really sorry about having to reverse the charges, but—'

'A phone box?' echoed Bev, appalled. 'God, you can't give birth in a phone box – too unhygienic for words!'

Fenn, about to tap Bev on the shoulder again, stopped and stared at her.

'Who are you talking to?'

'And they smell of wee,' Bev went on, wrinkling her nose

in disgust. 'Chloe, if you're in labour, you really should get to a hospital, they have clean sheets there and everything – oh, hang on a sec.' Realising that she was the focus of Fenn's attention, Bev apologetically covered the receiver. 'It's Chloe,' she stage-whispered. 'You know, Miranda's friend. She wanted to let Miranda know – ooh, ouch!'

Fenn snatched the receiver out of her hand before she could finish the sentence. His jaw set, he said tightly, 'Chloe, what the hell is going on?'

Charming, thought Bev, bend my finger right back, why don't you? And don't even *think* of saying sorry, oh no, just gaily inflict a bit of GBH then barge in on some phone conversation that has absolutely nothing to do with you—

'Tell me where you are,' ordered Fenn, making Bev jump. 'Right, yes, I know Dempsey Street. Okay, stay there, don't move, I'm on my way.'

'B-but,' Bev spluttered as he banged the phone down and headed for the door, 'you can't – Fenn, you can't just—'

The door slammed shut behind him.

Too late, he already had.

'Crikey, what's up with Fenn? He just shot past me in the Lotus doing about a hundred miles an hour down the Fulham Road.' Amazed, Miranda unwound her red scarf from around her neck and flung her beret, James Bond-style, at the hatstand. Oh well, James Bond probably practised a lot more than she did.

'Your friend Chloe rang up. Fenn's gone racing off to rescue her from some public phone box.' Bev pulled a fastidious face – much as she wanted babies of her own,

471

she couldn't help wishing that she could pick them up at the supermarket, shrink-wrapped. 'Chloe thinks she's in labour. I must say, it all sounds quite revolting. Talk about disgracing yourself completely – she's surrounded by boys on skateboards, cheering her on.'

'Oh. Cheering her on was supposed to be my job.'

Miranda was disappointed, but not that disappointed. When Chloe had asked her to be her birth partner, she'd naturally assumed the event itself would take place in a hospital, preferably one kitted out with morphine, midwives and all manner of hi-tech medical equipment.

Somehow crouching on the floor of a grubby phone box didn't hold quite the same allure. If Fenn wanted to be the intrepid one, that was fine by her.

'So I missed Magdalena Rosetti, did I?' Miranda looked resigned. 'I suppose she's been and gone.'

'Tuh, that's the other thing.' Bev looked exasperated. 'Fenn was so hell-bent on playing the flying doctor, he forgot all about her. She's still in there.' She jerked her head in the direction of the VIP room. 'Half cut.'

Miranda's mouth dropped open.

'You mean . . . ?'

'Not sozzled. I mean literally half cut.' Bev mimed scissors snapping away. 'I took her a cup of coffee and she asked me where Fenn was. I said he'd be back in a minute.' She shrugged helplessly. 'I mean, what else could I do? Lucy's completely tied up for the next forty minutes, James is at lunch . . . Corinne's just going to have to deal with her as soon as she's free, but that's going to be another half-hour at least.' She shook her head indignantly. 'It's not on, it really isn't. Fenn can't run out on clients and expect to get away with it – think of the ghastly publicity if this got out.'

'You are absolutely right,' said Miranda.

Yes, yes, yes!

Chapter 59

'Oh, well, hi there! I was beginning to wonder if my deodorant wasn't up to scratch.' Magdalena smiled her trademark ear-to-ear smile and put down her empty coffee cup. 'Where's Fenn?'

No point faffing about. Time to come straight to the point.

'Okay, here's the thing,' said Miranda. 'If you were one of those stroppy, scary actresses I'd have made up a really good lie. But since you're so nice, I'm going to tell you the truth.'

Magdalena raised an eyebrow.

'Flattery gets you everywhere. Now I'm far too ashamed to admit that I'm actually incredibly stroppy and the original bitch from hell.'

Miranda pulled up a chair and sat down opposite her.

'Fenn isn't here,' she said simply. 'He had to go out, and I know that sounds terrible but it really was an emergency.'

Carefully, Magdalena crossed one slim, stockinged leg over the other.

'I see. So who's going to cut my hair?'

'That's up to you. If you can wait thirty minutes, Corinne

will be able to do it for you. She's our senior stylist. Otherwise, I can do it now.'

'And you are?'

'I'm more junior than Corinne,' Miranda said truthfully.

'Or there's option three, I could walk out of here and find another salon,' Magdalena pointed out. 'I mean, forgive me, but I do believe you're a trainee.'

'I can cut hair.'

'A chimpanzee can cut hair,' Magdalena said reasonably. 'How do I know you wouldn't leave me looking like a chewed knot?'

Miranda blinked.

'I wouldn't, I promise. But if you aren't happy when I've finished, you can shave all my hair off.'

Magdalena's mouth twitched. She hadn't been a star so long that she couldn't remember those impoverished drama student days, when getting her hair done for nothing by a trainee was all she had ever been able to afford. And she'd never come out with a bad cut, had she?

'There's an offer I can't refuse,' she told Miranda. 'You've appealed to my sense of adventure. Okay, deal.'

'You won't regret it.' Praying fervently that she wouldn't, Miranda stood up and reached for the comb and scissors. 'Anyway, how could you tell I was a trainee?'

'Recognised you from the TV. Last time I was over here I caught you on that programme giving your sandwiches to the homeless guy.' Utterly relaxed, Magdalena sat back and watched in the mirror as Miranda worked diligently away. 'Fenn Lomax salon . . . girl with blue and green hair . . . call it spooky intuition if you like, but I just put two and two together. Okay if I ask you a question now?'

'Go ahead.' Having clipped up the back sections of Magdalena's glossy tortoiseshell-blonde hair, Miranda held her tongue between her teeth and began to cut.

'What was the emergency?'

Miranda glanced up.

'You mean with Fenn?'

'I'm a curious person.' Magdalena apologised. 'It drives me mad not knowing stuff. Back home I'm a member of Nosy Parkers Anonymous.'

'My pregnant flatmate rang up,' said Miranda. 'To tell me that she was in labour in a phone box a few miles away. I wasn't here, so Fenn went off to pick her up and take her to the hospital. Before the baby pops out, fingers crossed.'

'Or legs,' said Magdalena. 'So he's the father?'

'God, no.' Miranda grinned. 'Nothing like that. Fenn's just . . . helping out.'

Magdalena looked dubious.

'Are you sure?'

'Of course I'm sure!'

'I mean, I don't want to sound big-headed here, but to race off without even stopping to let me know . . . abandoning *me* in order to help out some unimportant friend-of-an-employee . . . doesn't that sound the tiniest bit weird to you?'

'Well, now you put it like that.' Miranda frowned, then shook her head. 'But it isn't what you're thinking. Fenn isn't the father and they absolutely *definitely* aren't having an affair.'

Magdalena was by this time truly engrossed.

'So who *is* the father?'

'Ah. Now it starts to get complicated,' said Miranda. 'My ex-fiancé.'

*　　　*　　　*

It was one of those dilemmas, Chloe realised, where you can't make up your mind how you feel.

On the one hand, she had never been so glad to see anyone in her life.

On the other, she couldn't help wishing Fenn didn't have to see her like this, with her wet trousers sticking attractively to her legs and her shoes making squelching noises with every step. Not to mention the fact that she appeared to be walking like John Wayne.

Elegant or what?

'Nearly there,' said Fenn, both arms supporting her as he helped her towards the double-parked black Lotus.

'What can I sit on? I don't want to mess up the seat.'

He shot her a sidelong look of exasperation.

'I don't give a stuff about that. Who do you think I am?'

Puffing a bit but managing a smile, Chloe said, 'I don't know. Maybe Bruce?'

But to reassure herself, she took off her thick coat and arranged it over the passenger seat before climbing into the car.

Oh dear, what with her and her stomach there was barely room for Fenn as well.

'When my sister was desperate to go into labour, she ate a chicken vindaloo,' Fenn said companionably as they pulled out into the stream of traffic. 'According to her, it shocks the body into action.'

'I had lunch with Greg,' Chloe told him. 'Better than a curry any day.' She wiped perspiration from her upper lip and sank back into the seat with a sigh of relief. 'This is so kind of you. You should have let me call an ambulance.

I hope you didn't rush off leaving some poor woman's head in the sink.'

Chloe was joking. Praying that – unlike her New York hairdresser – Magdalena Rosetti wasn't the litigating kind, Fenn said, 'We were pretty quiet.'

'I still can't believe this is happening. I'm actually going to have a baby.' Chloe clutched her stomach as another contraction began to take hold.

'Did it upset you, seeing Greg?'

'Oooh . . . no.'

'What did he want?'

Breathe in, breathe out . . . phew.

'Just to have sex with me,' panted Chloe.

Fenn almost cannoned the Lotus into the lorry in front. Christ, don't say she had!

Chloe laughed at the expression on his face. 'No, I did *not*.'

Relief flooded through Fenn's system like nicotine.

'We're getting a divorce.'

'Well, good.'

She shifted on her seat. 'I'm really sorry, you should have sat me on a bucket. I've leaked through everything.'

Fenn glanced across, taking in the flushed cheeks and damp strands of hair clinging to Chloe's forehead. He couldn't begin to describe how he felt about her.

Aloud he said, 'Oh well, better get out then, and walk.'

By the time they reached the maternity wing of the Chelsea and Westminster, Chloe was puffing away like a bicycle pump. Directed to the waiting area by the receptionist while her hospital notes were located, she leaned on Fenn for support before sinking gratefully on to an uncomfortable orange plastic chair. A television was on in the corner, showing an episode of Oprah. Three other couples were there too, the women panting away just like she was, while the men – looking deeply self-conscious – massaged their partners' backs.

Chloe realised that she was squeezing Fenn's hand. How on earth had that started?

'D'you want me to do that?' Fenn nodded at the men, keeping his voice low.

Embarrassed – because actually she did – Chloe whispered, 'Don't worry, I'm fine.'

The situation grew more surreal over the course of the next few minutes. Chloe watched the nurses flitting back and forth past the door of the waiting room. Apart from the occasional groan, the only sound in the room came from the TV in the corner, where Oprah was hosting a timely debate on the subject: 'My Kids Wrecked My Life'.

Nobody had the nerve to change channels. The women clutched their stomachs and concentrated on their breathing. Two of the men silently watched a teenage boy on the TV jab a finger at his weeping mother and yell: 'Mom, ah wish ah'd nevah bin born!' The other man rubbed feebly at his wife's spine with one hand while surreptitiously turning the pages of *Caravanning Today* with the other.

The next minute, without speaking, the wife slid down from her chair and arranged herself on all fours on the floor. She crouched there, panting like a dog, then glanced over her shoulder, snatched *Caravanning Today* out of her husband's hand and snarled irritably, 'Robert, did I *say* you could stop massaging my back?'

Chloe stifled a terrible urge to giggle. She found a clean tissue in one of her pockets and stuffed it into her mouth.

Over on the TV, Mom yelled back, 'Well, ah hate you too, ya little shit!'

Fenn's chair was shaking. He was trying as hard as she was not to laugh. Leaning across, Chloe whispered, 'You don't have to stay.'

As she said it, one of the other women – not to be outdone – let out a howl like a mountain wolf and moved down from her own chair to lie curled up on the extra-durable – i.e. texture of a Brillo pad – beige carpet. She began to hum, then chant a mantra.

'Omi matani . . . omi matani . . .'

The woman's eyes were closed. She rocked gently from side to side in her floral dungarees. Her husband, more embarrassed than ever, muttered, 'That's it, honey, you're doing great, you're swimming with the dolphins . . . just picture yourself swimming with those dolphins . . .'

Chloe snorted and buried her face in Fenn's shirt. He was shaking so much he couldn't speak.

'You'd better go,' she gasped.

'You're joking. I wouldn't miss this for the world.'

'Mrs Malone? Chloe Malone?'

Her eyes still streaming with suppressed laughter, Chloe looked up at the nurse before her. Hooray, they'd found her notes at last; now she could go and lie down somewhere and get loads of drugs.

'That's me.'

The nurse consulted Chloe's maternity notes, then glanced at Fenn. 'And you're the birth partner?' She frowned, recognising his face from somewhere. 'It says here M. Carlisle.'

Fenn looked at Chloe. Getting her out of that phone box and into hospital had been his prime concern. Once that had been achieved, he supposed his job was over. What he should be doing now was wishing Chloe good luck, driving back to the salon and letting Miranda take his place here.

But that was the last thing he wanted to do.

'Are you M. Carlisle?' The nurse sounded doubtful.

Chloe, no longer laughing, searched Fenn's face. Why wasn't he making a bolt for the door, for freedom? Surely he was desperate to get away from this madhouse?

'Hang on, I've seen you on the telly,' said the nurse. 'You're Fenn Lomax.'

Fenn took Chloe's hand.

'If you want me to stay, I will.'

'But . . .' Oh God, Chloe realised, suddenly overcome, I *do* want you to stay, more than anything. 'But you'd hate it. Look, it's really kind of you, but you don't have to be polite . . . you've done so much already.'

'This isn't being polite and I wouldn't hate it.' Fenn barely trusted himself to speak, he was so terrified of saying the wrong thing. 'I don't want to go, okay? I want to stay. Please.'

They gazed at each other, not daring to move. The nurse, watching them both, clicked and unclicked her pen a few times and glanced ostentatiously at her watch.

'So long as you don't start swimming with the dolphins,' Fenn added as an afterthought.

The woman rocking from side to side on the floor in her straining floral dungarees looked up indignantly.

'I heard that.'

481

Chapter 60

'YUUURRGH!' grunted Chloe, her eyes stinging with sweat and her fingers aching with the effort of gripping Fenn's hand. She blinked and fixed her gaze on her toenails, which Miranda had last week painted a dazzling shade of turquoise. Right, okay, here it came again . . .

'Push, Chloe, *push*,' urged the midwife, crouching like a wicket-keeper at the foot of the bed.

Honestly, what does she think I'm trying to do – suck it back in?

'Nearly there,' Fenn murmured in her ear. 'Come on, you can do it.'

The last midwife had gone off shift twenty minutes ago. This new one, charging in to replace her, was middle-aged, extremely brisk and sported a *Jesus Saves* badge pinned to the front of her uniform. Not having had time to peruse Chloe's notes at leisure, she was also under the impression that Fenn was the proud father-to-be.

Well, Chloe had to admit as Fenn wrung out the cold sponge and pressed it to her forehead, it was the kind of mistake anyone could make.

'Right, all ready now for the final push,' warned the

midwife, flexing her fingers in preparation for that all-important catch.

Breathlessly, Chloe gathered herself. It was like being an Olympic weightlifter, psyching yourself up . . . ooh . . . except they had the option of walking away . . . aargh . . .

'Push right down, dear, as harrrd as you can.'

'I'm puh-pushing.' What does it look like I'm doing, you stupid old witch? Knitting a bobble hat?

'Come on, Chloe, you're doing it,' shouted Fenn as the midwife went into a one-woman scrum at the foot of the bed.

'Ouch.' Chloe winced as her own fingers went numb. 'Fenn . . . I'm supposed to be squeezing *your* hand.'

'God, I'm sorry! Don't talk! Push, Chloe, just PUSH PUSH PUSH!'

Obediently she pushed. The baby slithered out. Chloe gasped, 'Oh!' and burst into tears.

'It's a girl.' Fenn's voice broke as he said it. He still had one arm around Chloe, supporting her shoulders. She turned and gazed up at him, lost for words.

'Let me just clean this wee one up a bit, then you can have her back.' The midwife, expertly snipping the cord, whisked the baby over to a waiting trolley.

Fenn squeezed Chloe's trembling hand. When he spoke at last, he said huskily, 'I love you.'

And Chloe, flushed with a mixture of exhaustion and exhilaration, smiled up at him and said, 'I know.'

To her great surprise, she wasn't at all surprised. It was as if, deep down, she had known it all along.

Fenn bent his head and kissed her, months and months of pent-up emotion compressed into two seconds' worth of kiss.

Chloe tasted salt on his upper lip and whispered, 'I love you too.'

Then the midwife was back, brandishing the wrapped-up baby like a raffle prize.

'Here we are then, a beautiful daughter, seven pounds twelve ounces,' she announced proudly. 'Now, who wants to hold her first?'

Chloe took the baby into her arms and together they examined her.

'She's amazing,' said Fenn. 'The whole thing's amazing. One minute she was a lump in there,' he pointed at Chloe's stomach, 'and the next minute she's a person out here.'

'Ahem.' Chloe glanced up at the clock. 'It took a bit longer than a minute.'

'I want to marry you,' Fenn blurted out suddenly. 'I know it's too soon to be saying this, but I mean it. I'm serious, I want us to be a proper family. And that means marriage.'

Beneath the celebrity-hairdresser-single-man-about-town, Chloe realised with a rush of love, there beat the heart of an old-fashioned traditionalist. Astonishing but true.

And absolutely blissful to discover.

'Just a little prick,' the midwife announced, plunging a hypodermic needle into Chloe's thigh.

'Actually,' said Fenn, 'that's not true.'

'In that case, I'd love to marry you.' Chloe searched his face. 'If you really mean it.'

'I've never been more sure of anything in my life.'

Was it possible to be happier than this? Chloe leaned back against Fenn, her daughter in her arms, her eyes filling up with fresh tears of elation.

Marriage, excellent. The stern midwife, who disapproved

mightily of couples who lived in sin, relented and patted Chloe's just-injected thigh.

'Very sensible, dear. Glad to hear it. Let the Good Lord bless your union, and you'll be so much happier.' She broke into an indulgent smile. 'I must say, it cheers me no end to hear a man repent his former sins.'

'Me too.' Chloe tilted her head back and gazed lovingly up at Fenn. 'And he's not even the father.'

The midwife's untended eyebrows shot up.

'You mean . . . ?'

'I'm not the father,' Fenn said again, helpfully.

'But you've just asked her to marry you!'

Fenn looked down at the baby girl he fully intended bringing up as his own. Already hopelessly besotted, he held out an index finger, and four tiny, almost translucent fingers instantly grasped it. Fenn marvelled at her strength. He didn't understand how he could feel such an instantaneous rush of love for a baby, but he did.

He wasn't paying the midwife the least bit of attention. Perplexed, she turned back to Chloe.

'He just asked you to marry him!'

'I know, isn't it incredible?' Chloe shot her a dazzling smile. 'I don't know what my husband's going to say when he finds out.'

The cutting was finished. The blow-drying was done. As Miranda got busy with the hairspray, a phone began to ring somewhere in the room.

'Not mine,' said Magdalena, patting her silent hand-bag.

'It's Fenn's.' Recognising the tone of the ring and peering

over her shoulder, Miranda located the phone on the marble work surface behind her, half hidden beneath a pile of towels. As she moved towards it, the ringing stopped. 'Oh well, they'll leave a message.'

'It might be Fenn. Calling to find out where he's left his phone,' said Magdalena. 'That's what I do if I forget where I've put mine.'

'There, all done.' Miranda finished spraying and stepped back, pleased with what she had achieved. 'Now be honest, are you happy with this?'

'I am, I love it.' Magdalena sounded distracted. 'But what if it's Fenn, ringing with news about your friend's baby? Aren't you just bursting to know?'

The door swung open and Bev rushed in.

'Fenn just called from the hospital. Chloe's had it!' She looked at Magdalena in surprise. 'Wow, your hair looks *great*.'

Miranda gaped at Bev. 'Really? She's had it already?'

'Mother and baby doing fine,' Bev said importantly.

'Boy or girl?' said Magdalena.

'Girl.'

'Name?' Magdalena and Miranda chorused simultaneously.

'He didn't say. But you can go and see them right away.' Bev waved a tenner at Miranda. 'And Fenn must be in a really good mood,' she went on. 'He told me to take this out of the till to pay for your taxi.'

'Well then, what are you waiting for?' demanded Magdalena, when Miranda dithered. 'We're finished here, aren't we? Get on over to that hospital and tell your friend congratulations from me.'

'She's had the baby.' Miranda realised she was beaming like an idiot. 'Isn't that just *incredible*?'

'Here.' Magdalena picked up Fenn's mobile and lobbed it at her. 'Don't forget to give him his phone.'

Chapter 61

'Stand back, stand back!' Miranda burst into the side ward, almost flattening an auxiliary nurse against the wall. 'It's all right, don't panic, I'm here now, make way for the official birth partner. Oh now, will you look at that? She's only gone and done it without me. For heaven's sake, Chloe, couldn't you have waited?'

'Did my best,' said Chloe as Miranda enveloped her in a massive hug. 'Crossed my legs and everything. Sorry.'

'In that case I forgive you. *So.*' Miranda turned her attention to the baby, lying fast asleep in her perspex cot. 'You managed on your own, then. Look at her, what an angel! Phew, bet you're glad she looks like you and not Greg.'

'Well—'

'And has Fenn seen her yet? I must say, we were all pretty amazed when he rushed out of the salon like that.'

'Actually, he's—'

'Quite the knight in shining armour, in fact. You'll never guess what my client said when she heard what was going on! She thought Fenn must be the *father*—'

'Ahem. Which client was this?'

At the sound of Fenn's voice, Miranda spun round. There

he was, leaning against the door, for all the world as if he *were* the baby's father.

'Um, Magdalena Rosetti.'

Fenn looked startled.

'You mean *you* cut her hair?'

'I had to.' She beamed at him. 'There wasn't anyone else.'

'Jesus, what did you do?'

'Just an asymmetric urchin crop and dyed it olive green.' Miranda shrugged. 'She said she wanted something different.'

'This is a joke, right?' Fenn lowered his voice as the baby stirred in her crib.

'Of course it's a joke. Haven't I been telling you for ages how brilliant I am? Oh, and you left your phone behind.' Miranda tossed it across the room at him. 'There's a message on there somewhere, too. Honestly, you wouldn't believe how nosy Magdalena is – she actually wanted to *listen* to it.' She returned her attention to Chloe while Fenn listened to his message. 'So, tell me *everything*. How did it go?'

As she sat on the edge of the bed and listened to the gory details, Miranda couldn't help feeling relieved that she hadn't, in the end, been called upon to do her birthing-partner bit. Chloe truly didn't seem to mind, and it had all ended well. Phew.

Except . . . except, why did the niggling suspicion persist that something else had happened that she didn't know about?

What in heaven's name could it be? Chloe was looking elated – well, that was understandable, given the circumstances – but wasn't she also looking the tiniest bit apprehensive? And why, Miranda wondered, did she keep glancing across at Fenn, almost as if she was waiting for him to get off the phone before she said whatever else it was she was clearly plucking up the courage to say?

'Is everything all right?' said Miranda, when Fenn had finished listening to his message.

'Yes.' Chloe sounded breathless.

'Are you sure?'

'Um, yes . . .'

There was a long, long pause. Miranda saw Fenn look at Chloe and smile slightly. Chloe went pink, like an actress on stage who has forgotten all her lines.

The silence lengthened.

Mystified, Miranda said, 'Would somebody please tell me what's going *on*?'

Fenn held out his phone.

'Here.' He pressed Replay, turned the volume up to maximum and handed it to Miranda. 'Perhaps it would help if you listened to this.'

She took it.

'Fenn, hi, it's Tina!' sang a female voice with a faint twang to it.

'That's his sister. She lives in New Zealand,' Miranda explained in a kindly aside to Chloe, who was listening as intently as she was.

'Now look, I haven't spoken to you for a fortnight,' Tina carried on, 'and I need to know what's happening over there. It's not fair, Fenn – you can't tell me you've fallen in love with this pregnant Chloe person—'

'*What?*' shrieked Miranda.

'—and then clam up on me like this. Okay, I know I wasn't thrilled when you first told me, but if she's that important—'

'WHAT?' howled Miranda.

'—if she really means that much to you, then go for it. Maybe I overreacted a bit. The thing is, if you've met someone you're completely crazy about and you're sure she's the one—'

THE ONE!!! mouthed Miranda, jabbing an astonished finger at Chloe.

'—then I'm happy for you. And when we fly over to London next month I'd love to meet her. So tell this Chloe how you feel and fix something up, will you? I can't wait to meet the girl who made my little brother finally fall in luuurve . . .'

There was the sound of merry laughter, then a click as the message ended.

Miranda gazed at Chloe in wonderment.

'I don't believe it. This is . . . incredible! And he's done it, hasn't he? He's already told you, and you're both looking so smug and smirky and disgustingly happy, it's obvious you feel the same way about him.'

Imagine, all this *stuff* had been going on and they hadn't even had the decency to so much as *hint* at it before now. Outrageous! Miranda made a brave stab at sounding suitably outraged, but she couldn't pull it off. Her heart wasn't in it. She was happy for them too, dammit.

Fenn and Chloe, who'd have thought it for a moment?

But the weird part was, when you *did* actually think about it, it made absolute sense.

The baby, flailing her feet and fists, opened her long-lashed eyes at last and gazed up at Miranda.

'Blimey, she really does look like you!' Instantly smitten, Miranda picked her out of the crib and held her up to the light for closer inspection. Solemn navy-blue eyes, white-blonde hair like a dandelion clock, strategically positioned dimples designed for flirting, and a fabulous pouty rosebud of a mouth with a streamer of saliva trailing down . . .

'So cute when babies do it,' said Miranda, ducking out of the line of fire, 'so unattractive on grown men.' She kissed each dimpled cheek in turn. 'Oh, look at those eyebrows . . . isn't she just fab? I can still be her mad aunt, can't I? Missing the birth doesn't mean I'm disqualified.' A thought belatedly struck her and she turned to Fenn. 'So where were you when all this was happening? Pacing up and down outside smoking an imaginary cigarette?'

'I was in the delivery room.' Fenn couldn't conceal his pride.

'He stayed all the way through,' said Chloe, reaching for his hand.

'Talk about jumping in at the deep end.' Miranda goggled. 'It *must* be love.'

'It is.' Fenn gave Chloe's fingers a squeeze. 'I've asked Chloe to marry me.'

Good grief.

'And they haven't even had sex yet,' Miranda told the wide-eyed baby in her arms. 'Honestly, some people do things a funny way round, don't they?' Abruptly, she looked up. 'You haven't even told me her name. What are you calling her?'

Chloe shook her head. 'We haven't decided.'

Miranda noted that 'we' with secret delight.

'Something that goes with Lomax,' said Fenn.

Miranda ruffled the baby's dandelion-puff hair and beamed at the pair of them.

'I've got it. You can call her L'Oréal.'

*   *   *

'No sense of adventure, that's what you've got,' Miranda told Fenn, lifting a beaming Mattie out of her car seat and weaving her through the air like Superman. 'I still think you should have called her L'Oréal.'

'That's why I'm marrying Chloe and not you,' said Fenn. 'Now, any more cases to bring out, or is that the lot?'

Florence and Tom were off on the cruise of a lifetime, flying from Heathrow to Miami before boarding ship and spending the next thirty days sailing in indecent luxury around the Caribbean. Fenn and Chloe had come over to Tredegar Gardens to see them off. Mattie, now seven weeks old, flashed her toothless grin at everyone she clapped eyes on, captivating even the taxi driver who was loading the cases into the boot.

Miranda held Mattie, wrapped up in her scarlet snowsuit, against her shoulder. Bending her head and breathing in the smell of just-washed infant, she watched Fenn help Florence out of her chair and into the back of the cab. In less than two months he had acquired a live-in lover and a baby, both of whom he adored beyond measure. It suited him, too; he had never looked happier.

Sometimes, Miranda was beginning to discover, doing things the wrong way round turned out – mysteriously – to be the best way after all.

'How's Bruce getting on in the shop?' Chloe was eager to know. Bruce hadn't been able to disguise his glee when she had rung him straight after the birth.

'So you're telling me you won't be back this afternoon? This is too much, Chloe. It's the final straw. I'm sorry, but you're fired.'

'Okay.' Shrugging happily, Chloe had smiled at Fenn. 'Fine by me.'

'Bruce?' said Miranda. 'Oh, he's got a new assistant, called Petunia. Apparently she's twenty-three stone and looks like a bulldog chewing a wasp.'

'Heavens.' Chloe was alarmed. 'Poor Bruce.'

'Oh no, don't feel sorry for him. She's just what he wanted. Someone so ugly that no man's *ever* going to want to have sex with her,' Miranda explained. 'That way, she's never going to get pregnant.'

Tom came up to them and gave Miranda's shoulder an affectionate pat.

'We're ready to go. You look after yourself, sweetheart.'

'And you look after Florence. If she'll let you.' Miranda rolled her eyes at this – it was a pretty daunting prospect – but if anyone could pull it off, it was Tom. Since getting together, the change in Florence had been heartwarming.

'Behave yourself now,' Florence ordered from the back seat. She cackled with laughter as Mattie, with a ladylike hiccup, gracefully deposited a mouthful of curdled milk on the shoulder of Miranda's black jersey. 'No getting up to mischief.' Florence waggled her eyebrows friskily as she spoke. 'Not unless you know I'd approve.'

'It's been so long, I can't remember what mischief is.' Miranda said it jokily, but it was horribly close to the mark. Everyone, it seemed, had a rip-roaring sex life these days except her. Even Chloe, for heaven's sake, who had last week been given the go-ahead from her unsuspecting GP to 'resume relations with her husband'.

If she wished.

Chloe had certainly wished. And, she had later shyly confided to Miranda, it had all gone Very Well Indeed. Furthermore, having only ever slept with one other man before, she now realised that contrary to what Greg had always told her, he wasn't brilliant in bed at all. In fact, compared with Fenn, he'd been completely *average*—

'Send me postcards,' Miranda blurted out to Florence, banishing the troublesome memory from her mind. It wasn't that she wanted to have sex with Fenn – good grief, no! – but Chloe's verdict had come as a bit of a bombshell, all the same. If Greg was only average, well . . .

I must get out more, thought Miranda. I'm missing out on goodness knows what.

The trouble was, the only person she really wanted to get out more *with* had gone off with someone else and was no longer about.

'Are we ready?' said Tom, as Chloe leaned through the open window to give Florence a kiss goodbye.

'Got my hip-flask.' Florence patted her coat pocket with satisfaction. 'That and a passport's all I need.'

'You should behave yourself too,' Miranda said, when it was her turn at the window.

'Are we allowed to get married?'

'Only to each other.'

'Me, marry some pervy vicar? Hah, you must be joking.' Florence exchanged a look of mock horror with Tom. But beneath the folds of Florence's dashing black cape, Miranda realised, there was some serious hand-holding going on.

Honestly, what were they like?

'If they had acne, they'd pass as a couple of teenagers,' she said when the taxi had disappeared around the corner.

'Except teenagers can't afford to cruise the Caribbean,' Chloe pointed out. 'Oops, Mattie's just thrown up on your shoulder again. D'you want to give her to me?'

495

'Come in for a bit,' Miranda urged, feeling suddenly lonely. A whole month alone in an otherwise empty house loomed ahead. What if she went a bit mad and started talking to herself?

But Chloe was still holding her arms out, ready to take Mattie back.

'We can't. We're driving up to my mother's for the day.' Sensing Miranda's disappointment, she said, 'It's a big family party. Oh, but you could come along too if you like.'

Miranda shuddered and shook her head, recalling the last time she and Chloe's mother had met, outside Adrian's house in Milligan Road.

'It's okay, I'm fine. Loads to do, really.'

Fenn, taking Mattie from her, said, 'Like changing into a clean sweater.'

'Is he always this bossy?' Miranda rolled her eyes. 'Because if you decide you can't stand it a minute longer, you could always run away, you know, come back and live with me.'

Fenn swiftly fastened Mattie into her car seat in the back of the new Volvo. The days of the black Lotus had long gone. Chloe smiled.

'Thanks, but I think I'll stay where I am.'

Envying them for being so happy, Miranda stood and waved until the dark-green Volvo was out of sight. She turned and made her way back into the house, catching a whiff of baby-sick as she went.

Right, now what?

Apart from stripping off her sweater, which appeared to be a bit of a must.

Chapter 62

In Miranda's experience, when heroines in slushy films found themselves depressed and with too much time on their hands, they always seemed to find something deeply worthy and constructive to do in the way of housework. Miranda, who wasn't heroic in any shape or form, had noticed this and decided they must be barking mad. If you were miserable, doing something as awful as scrubbing the kitchen floor was only going to make you feel *much* worse, surely. Any fool could see that.

Anyway, what on earth was the point of cleaning the house when Florence had just jetted off for a month and nobody was going to see it?

Miranda tapped her fingers fretfully against the telephone, then punched out Bev's number. How often had Bev been at a loose end on a Sunday and rung her, to suggest going out somewhere nice – i.e. containing plenty of men – for lunch?

But the phone rang and rang. Bev wasn't there. Of course she isn't, thought Miranda as she hung up, she's over at Johnnie's being all happy and coupley and so lovey-dovey it made you want to be sick.

Honestly, talk about ingratitude. You take the trouble to sort out your friends' hopeless lives for them, you find them their perfect partners . . . and the next thing you know, they've swanned off into happy-ever-after-land without so much as a by-your-leave. Huh, you'd be lucky to get a postcard.

If it wasn't for me, Miranda thought, Bev would never have met Johnnie in the first place. And Fenn wouldn't have met Chloe. Indignantly, she pulled her jersey over her head, bundled it up and flung it in the direction of the stairs.

Typical, as long as they're all right, that's all that jolly well matters.

Never mind *me*.

When the doorbell rang an hour later, Miranda knew that whoever was at the door, she really didn't want to see them.

Sprawling across the sofa in front of the TV, plucking your eyebrows whilst watching *Little House on the Prairie*, was possibly the most effective method going if you were desperate for that white-rabbit-struggling-to-break-in-a-new-pair-of-contact-lenses look.

Oh yes, massively flattering, thought Miranda, survey-ing the result in her eyebrow-plucking mirror and making the unhappy discovery that her eyes exactly matched her Germolene-pink thermal vest. Of *course* I'm going to open the door and frighten whoever's on the doorstep witless.

The doorbell rang again.

She ignored it.

It rang for the third time.

Miranda crawled across the sitting room floor and up on to the window seat, inching her eyes over the window ledge like a sniper in the forest . . .

And came face to face through the glass with Danny Delancey.

Hugely embarrassed, imagining how silly she must look, Miranda instantly ducked down again.

'Too late, Miranda.' Danny, his voice carrying clearly through the closed window, didn't bother to hide his amusement. 'I looked just now and saw you with your big bottom in the air, wiggling across the carpet.'

Yanking the front door open, clutching her coat around her, Miranda said indignantly, 'I do *not* have a big bottom.' As an afterthought she added, 'And even if I did, it wouldn't matter. There's absolutely nothing wrong with having a big bottom.'

Not that she wanted one herself – no thanks very much – but it seemed only sisterly to make the point. After all, Chloe's bottom wasn't what you'd call petite and Fenn seemed pretty smitten with hers.

'Would you like me to say I saw your delectable little bottom wiggling across the carpet?' Danny grinned, unperturbed by this outburst. 'I will if you want. I just thought it might alarm you, seeing as I'm not normally the flowery-compliments type.'

This was true, Miranda couldn't deny it. Still, she was almost sure there was a hint of a compliment lurking in there. Deep down.

Somewhere.

'I didn't want to answer the door in case you were a Jehovah's Witness.' She stepped back reluctantly, and wished with all her heart she hadn't been quite so vigorous with the tweezers. 'And I haven't been crying, okay? I've just plucked my eyebrows.'

'I'll believe you, thousands wouldn't.' His dark eyes flickered over her clothes. 'Why are you wearing a thermal vest and a coat?'

'I had to take my jumper off, there was sick on it. Not my sick,' Miranda added defensively. 'Mattie's.'

'Glad to hear it. Florence and Tom get away on time?'

'How did—?' Miranda stared at him, wondering how he could have known they were leaving today. Then she wondered why she was bothering to wonder, since pretty obviously Florence had rung and told him herself.

'She was just keeping me in touch. Thought I might be interested.' Danny's tone was neutral.

'If she told you I was lonely and needed cheering up—' Miranda began furiously, but he stopped her in her tracks.

'She didn't. Actually, I'm the one in need of help.'

Oh well, that stood to reason, he looked so *utterly* helpless standing there in his dark-blue sweatshirt and faded Levis, with his battered leather jacket slung over one broad shoulder and his humorous dark eyes glittering down at her in that completely unfair way.

'Go on,' muttered Miranda, wondering if she was ever going to be able to look at him without experiencing that swooping sensation – like leaping dolphins – in the depths of her stomach.

'I've got a new kite in the car,' Danny told her. 'I need to get some serious practice in, so that I can dazzle that nephew of mine with my skills. And I need someone to untangle me when it all goes horribly wrong.' He paused. 'Fancy a trip to Parliament Hill?'

'Dazzle him with your skills?' echoed Miranda. 'Better take a tent with us, then. This could take years.'

Danny's mouth began to twitch at the corners.

'Is that your charming way of saying yes?'

Determined not to let him see how overjoyed she was,

Miranda replied, 'Actually, it's my charming way of saying: what the hell, I could do with a good laugh.'

When had she last come up here, that time with Florence? It must have been back in April, Miranda finally worked out. And now it was November, but the kites were still out in force.

The sun was out too, brightening a cloudless hyacinth-blue sky, but it was colder than before, an icy north-easterly wind zinging through Miranda's hair and numbing the exposed tips of her ears.

All over the hill, children wrapped up against the cold raced around, battling to seize control of frantically flapping kites and miles of unravelled nylon cord. The adults, expertly coaxing their kites into performing gymnastic displays of Olympic brilliance, stood their ground and scarcely moved at all.

Racing around like a lunatic and getting garrotted by your own kite string was clearly a very immature thing to do.

To impress his nephew, Danny had bought a monster of a kite, crimson and double-winged and as uncontrollable as a charging rhino. Every time Miranda threw it up into the air, it leapt skywards for a few seconds, lulling them both into a false sense of security, before plummeting back to earth with a vengeance. Twice, it had missed her head by inches and she'd had to learn to dodge out of the way. When she took her turn at trying to fly it, it promptly hurled itself into the nearest tree.

Danny inched his way along the high branch around which the cord was tangled.

Fit body. Very fit, Miranda couldn't help noticing. For about the hundredth time in the last hour.

'I don't know why you're bothering,' she shouted up

at him. 'That kite is a psychopath. It doesn't deserve to be rescued. You should teach it a lesson and leave it up there to rot.'

The kite was released at last, amid a flurry of falling leaves. Danny swung himself down from the branch and landed next to Miranda. Having glanced briefly at her, he busied himself brushing bits of bark from his jeans.

'The thing is, some kites are easy, you get on with them from the word go. Others need a bit more work. You can either give up, or you can persevere. But if you get there in the end . . . well, that makes it all worthwhile.'

Miranda's nose and cheeks were pink with cold. She had tugged the sleeves of her warmest sweater over her knuckles and her arms were wrapped around her waist, but she was still prone to fits of uncontrollable shivers. She watched the kite slither off across the grass then begin to leap upwards, straining against its leash like a slavering Rottweiler.

'Take it to the vet. Have it put down. If you really want to impress your nephew, take up rollerblading instead.'

'You're freezing. Here, put my jacket on.' Danny shrugged it off and placed it around her shoulders.

'I didn't know it was going to be this c-cold.' Surreptitiously, Miranda sniffed the collar of the jacket, breathing in a lungful of that oh-so-familiar aftershave. 'I suppose you tried to persuade your girlfriend to come up here with you, but she had more sense.'

There, managed it at last! She'd slipped the subject into the conversation but in such a deft and casual manner that he wouldn't guess how long she'd been dying to bring it up.

'Girlfriend,' Danny said thoughtfully, winding the kite back towards him.

'You remember. Blonde. Posh-looking. Waves at you like this.' Miranda waggled her fingers in pseudo-friendly fashion, accurately mimicking the girl she'd seen sitting in his car.

She was careful not to sound bitchy. That wouldn't do at all.

'I think you must be talking about my sister,' Danny said. 'Caroline. Eddie's mother.' Helpfully he held out his hand, palm downwards, indicating the height of his nephew. 'You remember Eddie.'

'Your sister.' Miranda breathed out slowly. 'You made me think she was your girlfriend.'

'Did I?' Danny frowned, not altogether convincingly. 'Oh no, she's definitely my sister. Although she certainly wishes I *had* a girlfriend. In fact she's so desperate to see me settled down, she spends her life trying to fix me up with her single friends.'

He wasn't exactly looking thrilled. Exercising caution – and a degree of jealousy – Miranda said, 'And you haven't found one yet that you like?'

The kite, fully rewound now, had arrived back at Danny's feet. It flapped rebelliously amongst the fallen leaves like a truculent teenager.

'It can't escape if we sit on it.' Danny held one wing down with his Timberland-booted foot until Miranda was settled on the kite, then he joined her. 'Oh yes, I've definitely found one I like.'

His faded denim knee was inches away from her own, his tone amazingly casual. Almost as if he was telling her about a car he had seen and was thinking of buying.

Miranda swallowed and tried to concentrate on the panoramic view stretched out before them. This was London, home to millions and millions of people. But at this moment in time, could any of them possibly be more confused than she was?

At last, lamely, she said, 'Well, good. What's this girl like?'

'Difficult.' Danny shook his head and tapped the crimson material beneath them. 'Like this kite. Never does what you want her to do. Veers off in all the wrong directions . . . keeps getting tangled up with other kites . . .'

Miranda's heart began to thud like a marching band. In her stomach, the dolphins leapt.

'Is she seeing anyone now?'

'No. I've kept away for the last couple of months, to give her time to get over something that happened.' He paused. 'It hasn't been easy, but it was something I knew I had to do.'

Crash bang, crash bang, *thud thud thud*.

'What does she look like?' said Miranda, her gaze fixed helplessly on the distant horizon.

'Oh, ugly. No, that's a joke,' said Danny as her shoulders stiffened. 'Not ugly at all. Incredible dark-brown eyes. Very kissable mouth. Dark-green hair with gold bits at the end.'

'Tendrils,' Miranda murmured. 'Not *bits*.'

'And, of course, she has a delectable little bottom. Not that there's anything wrong with having a big one,' said Danny. 'Big ones are fine too.'

The view, Miranda discovered, was becoming a bit blurred. She wiped the back of her hand hurriedly across her eyes.

'Why now, Danny? After all this time, what made you change your mind?'

'I haven't.' He shrugged. 'My mind was made up months ago.'

'But—'

'Other kites,' Danny said simply. 'Like I said, she kept getting tangled up with other kites.' He paused, his dark eyes serious. 'Are you over Miles?'

Miranda nodded, unable to speak. Directly above them, a large yellow and brown kite hovered like an eagle. Twenty yards away a young girl jumped up and down yelling, 'Don't crash it, Daddy, don't let it crash on those people's heads!'

'Concussion,' Danny sighed. 'Just what we need. Have you any idea how long I've spent rehearsing this moment? It was supposed to be so romantic.'

'It still is.' Miranda spread her arms wide. 'Sitting here with me, risking brain damage to be with me . . . I call that madly romantic.'

Danny smiled and touched her icy cheek.

'Mad, certainly.'

'Go on,' Miranda whispered, 'kiss me, I dare you. And the first person to look up at the kite is a sissy.'

'Daddy, Dad, what are those people doing?'

'Making a spectacle of themselves, Rachel.'

'Daddy, why has one of them got green hair?'

'Because he's an exhibitionist, darling. Just ignore them both.'

Miranda began to giggle helplessly and the kiss disintegrated. She rolled over on to her back and watched the yellow and brown kite disappear as it was towed down the hill.

'I think perhaps it's time I grew my hair.'

'I think it's time we went home,' said Danny. 'Before I really do turn into an exhibitionist.' He gave her a long look. 'I love you. More than anything. You do know that, don't you?'

505

'Well, I do now,' said Miranda. 'But next time, could you not wait quite so long to mention it?'

'Right from the start, the first time I saw you.' Danny shook his head, remembering.

'Love at first sandwich,' murmured Miranda, feeling ridiculously happy.

He stood up and hauled her to her feet. The next second, a gust of wind carried away the kite they'd been sitting on. Miranda let out a cry of alarm and made a helpless grab for it as, with a defiant flick of its tail, the kite whisked joyfully skywards.

'Leave it.' Danny reached for her frozen hand. 'One difficult kite at a time is as much as I can cope with.'

They made their way downhill towards the car.

'Florence is going to be so mad she missed this,' said Miranda.

'She'll know soon enough.'

'They're away for a whole month.'

'When she rang me yesterday, she gave me the phone number, the fax number *and* the e-mail address of their hotel in Miami,' Danny explained. 'She wants to be told the millisecond anything remotely romantic happens.'

'Honestly!' Miranda tried hard to look indignant.

'And there's something else she wants you to know.' Danny sounded pleased with himself.

'What?'

'She definitely approves.'